THE POWER

Paula Grey comes within minutes of death when a lunch party at a remote mansion in Cornwall is brutally massacred.

Tweed was due to be among the guests. Within hours his London headquarters is blown to pieces by a huge bomb. Is Tweed the target? As a vast apparatus closes in on him, he is abandoned by the British Prime Minister.

What role is played by attractive Jennie Blade, girl friend of arrogant 'Squire' Gaunt? By equally attractive Eve Amberg, English wife of Swiss banker, Julius Amberg?

The shadow of Washington, DC, seems to hover over them like an immense vulture. Tweed's struggle for survival becomes trans-Atlantic. Losing the support of Downing Street, he flies with his team to Zurich. Switzerland proves no longer a safe haven as attempts to exterminate Tweed and his team continue. The action sweeps from Zurich to Basle to the snowbound Vosges mountains in France.

What is the great secret which must remain concealed no matter how many are murdered? Is there a link with six unsolved serial killings in America's Deep South?

Tweed fights on, slowly fitting together the pieces of the jigsaw. The mystery's solution is almost too frightening to contemplate. In the last few pages – returning to Cornwall – the novel climaxes with a diabolical twist more shocking than anything previously narrated.

THE POWER

Colin Forbes

PAN BOOKS
London, Sydney and Auckland

AUTHOR'S NOTE

All the characters portrayed are creatures of the author's imagination and bear no relationship to any living person. Also residences and companies are non-existent.

First published 1994 by Pan Books Limited
a division of Pan Macmillan Publishers Limited
Cavaye Place London SW10 9PG
and Basingstoke

Associated companies throughout the world

ISBN 0 330 33118 3

1 3 5 7 9 8 6 4 2

A CIP catalogue record for this book is available from the British Library

Photoset by Parker Typesetting Service, Leicester
Printed and bound in Great Britain by
Mackays of Chatham plc, Kent

FOR JANE

CONTENTS

Prologue

Carmel, California, February. The man, windbreaker open at the top, exposing his thick neck, forced the screaming girl inside the one-storey log cabin. One large hand gripped her long blonde hair, the other shoved at the small of her back.

Joel Dyson, one-time society journalist, now a successful member of the notorious international paparazzi, crouched in the undergrowth at the edge of the clearing in the wood. His film camera was aimed at the struggling man and woman as they disappeared through the open door. He had their faces perfectly recorded on film.

The cabin door slammed shut from the inside. The crude edifice was perched in the centre of the clearing, shut off from the outside world by the dense screen of encircling trees. The shutters were closed across the windows but Dyson could still hear the girl's screams of terror.

He glanced down at the ground where his tape recorder was in motion, the revolving tape registering the horrific screaming which suddenly stopped. Had the man struck her in the face to shut her up? There was a loaded pause which Dyson found more disturbing than what he had seen and heard earlier. The stillness of the wintry forest had a menacing atmosphere. Something warned Dyson the silence was ominous.

He had his film camera ready for another close-up when the cabin door opened. He expected two people to emerge, but only the man appeared. He came out, closed the door, rammed a key into the lock, turned it, tossed the key on to the roof. Why had he done that?

The answer surfaced a moment later as smoke drifted out from behind one of the shutters, then the window burst into flames. God! He was leaving her there to burn to ashes. Dyson caught the expression on the man's face, a look of vicious satisfaction, his skin streaming with sweat despite the cold of the early morning. Instinct made Dyson switch off the recorder, haul the tape free, ram it into the pocket of his duffle coat. The man was staring towards Dyson's hiding place. Grabbing a gun from inside his belt, he walked slowly towards where Dyson was crouching.

Had he detected some movement? Dyson had the man's face in his film lens again and the expression was grim, determined. A full-length shot now, showing the gun. Dyson saw the cabin suddenly flare into a raging inferno. Roof ablaze, about to collapse on the girl inside who must be unconscious, maybe dead? The quiet crackle of the flames erupted into a roar.

The man paused, glanced back. Dyson's camera had recorded his initial advance, the pause, the cabin flaring into a funeral pyre. The man turned towards the undergrowth, began that familiar slow deliberate tread. Time to get the hell out of it. Alive if possible. Dyson was thoroughly scared.

Still crouching, he backed away from the undergrowth screen. Camera looped over his shoulder, the tape nestling safely in his pocket. He reached a copse of trees, stood up, resisted the temptation to run. The ground was littered with dry leaves. For the moment his flight was covered by the powerful roar of the dying cabin. He had to get as far away as possible before his flight made too much noise. It was a long way to his Chevy parked inside the woods out of sight of the nearby road.

He paused, heard the deliberate tramp of heavy feet on the leaves behind him coming closer. And there would be others the man could call on – if he dared risk that. On the edge of panic Dyson reached the foot of a tall pine tree. *No one ever thinks of looking up.*

'It's my last chance to survive . . .'

Dyson said the words to himself as he shinned agilely from branch to branch. Higher and higher. He had to reach the cover of the foliage. Clawing at branches he heaved himself inside the prickly cover, straddled a stout branch with both legs, waited, terrified.

Through a small hole in the dense screen he could see down to the base of the giant pine. The man appeared, wiped sweat off his left hand on his denims, his right hand gripping the .38 Police Special. Dyson froze when the man paused at the base of the pine, head cocked to one side, listening. In the next minute Joel Dyson knew he could be dead, his body toppling down through the network of branches until it landed at the killer's feet. With the film camera looped over his arm, the tape in his pocket. It would be all over.

The cold was penetrating Dyson's duffle coat, his hands were frozen. The man below seemed impervious to the temperature made worse by trails of a mist off the Pacific Ocean which were now drifting amid the trees. Dyson forced himself to remain motionless. He'd begun to wonder whether his actions had been worth it – even for so great a potential prize, a vast fortune.

For a few seconds his thoughts filled his mind paralysed with fear. He looked down, blinked. The man had gone. He heard the heavy footsteps withdrawing, crunching dried leaves, retreating towards the cabin which must now be a pile of smoking embers.

Dyson checked his watch. 8 a.m. He compelled himself to stay motionless in his hiding place for half an hour. The man could have set a trap, moving away a short distance and then waiting. But in the deathly silence of the mist-bound forest Dyson had heard the sinister footsteps fading away and no sound of anyone returning.

3

'Move now,' he told himself, 'before he seals off the whole area . . .'

Despite the veils of grey mist Dyson had no trouble making his way back to the parked Chevy. He walked rapidly, treading on soft moss wherever he could. At intervals he paused, listening for any signs of pursuit. Nothing. He hurried towards the parked car.

As he threaded his way between the tree-trunks Dyson came alive again, thinking furiously. The nearest airport was San Francisco International. But they'd be watching and waiting there, he felt sure. Far safer to drive the much longer route south through California to Los Angeles Airport. The all-powerful forces the man controlled wouldn't expect him to take that route.

From LA he could catch a flight to London. There he could transfer to another flight direct to Zurich in Switzerland. Julius Amberg, president of the Zurcher Kredit Bank, owed him. Dyson's mind went back several years.

Bob Newman, the famous international foreign correspondent, had done him a bigger favour than he'd realized at the time. Dyson had taken some embarrassing photos of Amberg with his mistress in Geneva. He'd been going to sell them to *Der Spiegel*. Amberg was hitting the headlines at that time, acting as go-between in a big financial take-over.

'Give those pics to Amberg,' Newman had urged. 'He is a powerful man and you might need his help one day. Forget the money just for once, Joel – important allies are worth their weight in gold . . .'

Reluctantly, Dyson had agreed. Now Amberg could repay the 'debt' by holding the film and the tape in his vault. What safer place in the world to hide a fortune?

As he came closer to his Chevy Dyson checked in his mind any loopholes in his plan. He voiced his thoughts aloud in a bare whisper.

'The Chevy was hired in Salinas. They'll take time

4

tracing the car, the description and registration number. I'll dump it in LA. By the time they track it I'll be long gone . . .'

He approached the concealed vehicle cautiously. *They* might just have found it. God knew there were enough of them – and professionals to their fingertips . . .

An hour later he was driving south along the coastal highway, crossing the bridge at Big Sur. Hardly any traffic. To his right the wind off the ocean blew against the side of the car. Huge waves created a curtain of white surf rising thirty feet high. Dyson had reached Santa Barbara when the shock hit him.

The tape recorder! In his haste to escape the man he had left the machine on the ground. It wouldn't take *them* long to visit his insurance company – to check the serial number of the machine with his insurance policy. Jesus! They'd then have a positive identification of who had crouched in the undergrowth near the cabin. Up to that moment Dyson had half-cherished the illusion it would take them time to finger him.

It was a very worried Joel Dyson who reached Los Angeles, crawled with the traffic, handed in his Chevy and took a cab to the airport. Here he walked into another piece of bad luck.

He entered the vast concourse, carrying the bag containing a set of clothes he'd been careful to purchase at several shops after handing back the Chevy. He bought a United Airlines return ticket to London – the return was to throw off his track anyone who traced the reservation.

The flight left in three-quarters of an hour. Dyson was congratulating himself on his speedy departure as he checked in his bag. That was when he heard the crafty voice as he left the counter.

'Found a chick in London who's dropping her panties for the wrong man?'

'What?'

5

Dyson swung round and stared at a small man with a face closely resembling a monkey's. Which was why he was known as the Monkey. Nick Rossi was a small-time operator who watched the airports in the hope of picking up useful information he could peddle to the press for a small sum.

'I'm taking a well-earned holiday,' he snapped. 'And if I'm lucky I'll find an available chick. Sorry, Nick, no sale.'

'Which is why you're taking your camera with you?'

The Monkey grinned knowingly. A dead half-smoked cigarette was glued to the right-hand corner of his thin lips.

'You should know opportunities hit you in the kisser when you least expect it. Keep out of the rain . . .'

Dyson hurried away, swearing foully under his breath. He had thought of offering the Monkey a fistful of bills to keep him quiet – but that would have whetted his greedy appetite. Dyson only relaxed when the jumbo jet had taken off, swung out over Catalina Island and the Pacific Ocean, then turned east back over the mainland on its non-stop eleven-hour polar route flight to London. A double whiskey provided by the stewardess also helped.

His mood of relaxation didn't last long. As the machine flew on through the night, still climbing, he furtively glanced round, checking the other passengers. His chance encounter with Nick Rossi could prove fatal. Had *they* had time to rush a man aboard at the last moment? He doubted it. A second glass of whiskey relaxed him again.

Dyson dared not go to sleep even though most of the passengers of the half-filled jumbo were now comatose. The film camera nestled on his lap, concealed under a newspaper. Frequently he put his hand inside the pocket of his coat folded on the empty seat beside him. He felt relieved when he found the tape was still there . . .

Bob Newman. The name kept repeating itself in Dyson's mind as he disembarked at Heathrow. He changed his plan of action on impulse. Instead of immediately buying a

6

Swissair ticket to Zurich he hurried outside the concourse, climbed into a taxi and gave the driver the address of Newman's flat in Beresforde Road, South Kensington. In his haste, he failed to notice the small stocky man in a dark belted raincoat who watched him, followed him, signalled with his hand, stroking the left side of his face as a grey Volvo appeared. Then the man ran to a phone box.

'Ed, here. London Airport. The subject came in off the LA flight, walked out, took a taxi somewhere.'

'Did he now?' The gravelly voice of Norton was abrasive. 'With a tail, I trust?'

'The grey Volvo was passing. We had three cars cruising round . . .'

'I know that. Nick Rossi came across good. Wait there. Don't go to sleep. The subject may come back. Report to me any developments.'

'I'll stay tuned . . .'

The stocky man realized the phone had cut out, the connection broken. Typical. He had never seen Norton, had only heard his gravelly American voice on phones. He had commented on this to another member of the unit.

'That's your good luck,' his colleague had warned. 'No one knows what he looks like. You ever meet Norton, know who he is, you're dead . . .'

Arriving at Newman's flat, which faced the church of St Mark's, Dyson told the cab driver to wait. An elegant slim blonde girl answered the door, but made no attempt to invite him inside. Dyson produced an old press card carrying his photo.

'Sorry to disturb you. I'm Joel Dyson, an old friend of Bob Newman's, I need to see him urgently. He's expecting me,' he lied.

7

'He didn't say anything . . .'

'He wouldn't. Our business is confidential. And urgent,' he repeated. 'Matter of life and death.'

My death, he thought. The blonde examined the press card, looked at him, seemed uncertain how to respond as she handed back the card. Dyson forced himself to smile, to relax. She didn't smile back at him, but nodded.

'Have you something to write down an address? He's with the General & Cumbria Assurance Company in Park Crescent. Twenty minutes from here by cab . . .'

Thanking her after he'd scribbled in his notebook, Dyson, camera looped over his shoulder, hurried back to the cab, gave the driver an address in Soho. Earlier, on his way from the airport, he had glanced back a couple of times through the rear window. He didn't notice the grey Volvo driving one vehicle behind the cab. He really had little anxiety that he could have been followed.

Joel Dyson had badly underestimated the energy and power of the force reaching out towards him. During the eleven-hour flight from LA his San Francisco apartment had been turned over, examined for clues under a microscope. All main Californian airports had been checked – hence the swift contact with Nick Rossi. Wires had hummed between the States and Europe. Arrangements for the target's 'reception' had been made. Identity had been established by the tape recorder.

En route to the Soho address, Dyson was contemplating the value of the film and the tape. *Five million dollars?* No. *Ten million dollars* at least. The man would find ways of raising the money when faced with total destruction. Joel was on a big high when he left the cab in a street in Soho. He never even noticed the grey Volvo which slowed, then parked.

*   *   *

8

'Need to use your copying room for a film and a tape, Sammy. And I'm in a pissing great hurry,' Dyson told the cockney owner of the shop.

Outside it appeared to be an outlet for soft-porn films. But Dyson knew London well and had used the cockney's facilities in the past.

'Cost you, mate,' Sammy told him quickly. 'I don't let just anyone muck about with my equipment. Extra charge in case it's illegal, which it probably is.'

'Just watch the door. I don't want interruptions,' Dyson snapped. 'And here's your outrageous fee.'

Before disappearing into the back room he dropped two one-hundred dollar bills on the counter. Sammy, a ginger-haired hunchback, suppressed a whistle of surprise. He held the bills up to the light. They looked OK.

When Dyson came out of the room he had four canisters inside his bag. Two originals – film and tape – and one copy of each. Nodding to Sammy, he walked into the street, hailed a passing cab, told the driver to take him to Park Crescent.

Dyson had taken another impulsive decision the moment the cab had moved off from Beresforde Road – changing his next destination to Sammy's in Soho. Much safer to have twin sets of the film and the tape – one hidden in London, the other in Zurich. He prayed Newman would be at Park Crescent.

Inside a first-floor office at the Park Crescent HQ of the SIS, Bob Newman sat drinking coffee with Monica, Deputy Director Tweed's faithful and long-time assistant. Of uncertain age, Monica wore her grey hair tied back in a bun. Seated behind her desk, she was enjoying a chat with the foreign correspondent. In his early forties, of medium build, and clean-shaven, his hair brown, with a capable manner, Newman had been fully vetted and had often worked with her chief.

9

'I said Tweed was away,' she remarked. 'Actually he's in Paris. Expected back any time now.'

'He's like a dragonfly,' Newman commented. 'Zigzagging all over the place. I think he likes travel.'

'You're one to talk,' she chaffed him. 'As a foreign correspondent you've been everywhere—'

She broke off as the phone rang. It was George, the ex-Army man who acted as door-keeper and guard downstairs. Monica frowned, looked at Newman, said 'Who?' for the second time. 'Tell him to wait – and keep a close eye on him.'

'Someone for you,' she said as she put down the phone. 'A man called Joel Dyson. Says it's desperately urgent he sees you at once.'

'Joel Dyson? How the devil did he know I was here? He used to be one of my journalist informants. Nowadays he has sunk to the level of one of the paparazzi. Takes pics of so-called celebrities – married – enjoying a tumble with the wrong woman. Sells them to the press for huge sums. I suppose I'd better see him, but not up here.'

'The waiting-room,' Monica decided. She phoned George to give him instructions. Newman said he'd like her to come with him as a witness. 'I'll bring my notebook, then,' she replied.

Facing George's desk, the waiting-room was a bleak bare room with scrubbed floorboards, a wooden table and several hard-backed chairs. It was not designed to encourage visitors to linger.

Monica was surprised at how smartly Joel Dyson was dressed. While driving down through California he had stopped at a motel, hired a room, stripped off his duffle coat, denims and open-necked shirt. Substituting from his bag an American business suit, a Brooks Brothers shirt and tie, a vicuña coat, he had then slipped away from the motel unseen by the proprietor, his room already paid for the night.

A small slim man, in his thirties, he had a plump face with pouched lips, a receding chin and an ingratiating smile. Monica instantly mistrusted him. Her second surprise was his voice. He spoke with an upper-crust English accent. Joel could switch from convincing American to equally acceptable English with ease. He had, in fact, British nationality.

'How the devil did you find me here?' Newman demanded.

'No need to get stroppy. Called at your apartment. You do have a nice taste in blonde companions. She said you'd be here.'

Molly! Newman groaned inwardly. He was on the verge of gently ending the friendship – she was quickly showing signs that she expected him to take her seriously. Now he'd have to speed up the process of disengagement.

'Didn't know you were mixed up with insurance,' Joel went on cheerfully. 'Come to think of it, what an ideal set-up to learn people's dark secrets.'

He had been fooled by the brass plate outside which was engraved with *General & Cumbria Assurance* – the cover name for the SIS. Not asked to sit down, he was still standing.

'What is it you want?' Newman snapped. 'I happen to be very busy.'

'Insurance companies have top-security safes.' Dyson smirked at Monica who had sat down at the table and was making notes. She stared at him blankly, then dropped her eyes to the notebook. Which fazed Dyson not at all.

'I have a tape and a film,' he went on, addressing Newman, 'and they're a bombshell. I'll keep the originals and you store the copies. In case anything happens to me.'

'And what might happen to you?'

Dyson waited until he'd slapped his case on the table, unlocked it, produced two canisters, which he slid across to Monica.

'I may end up dead,' he said quietly.

The seriousness of his tone, the abrupt change from his previous breezy manner intrigued Newman. He was half-inclined to believe Dyson, but still not fully convinced.

'And who would want to kill the world's most popular paparazzo?' he enquired ironically.

'Don't like that word. I'm a highly professional photographer, one of the best – if not *the* best. And I can't answer your question.'

'Can't – or won't?' Newman snapped again.

'Pass.'

'Then get to hell out of here and take your junk with you.'

'The contents of those two canisters could shake the world, shatter Europe to its foundations, destroy any influence Britain has internationally. I'm running scared, Bob – scared as a rabbit with the ferrets inches from its tail.'

Dyson took a cigarette from a gold case and Newman tried an experiment: he used his own lighter to ignite the cigarette. Dyson couldn't hold the tip still, his hand trembling like a leaf in the wind. Reluctantly, Newman decided he was not putting on another of his chameleon-like acts.

'If we agree to keep this stuff we have to know where to get in touch with you,' he said. 'Otherwise, forget it.'

Newman had noticed something when Dyson had extracted the two canisters inside his case. Rammed in on top of some clothes which looked new – and American in style – was a film camera with a coiled hanging strap.

'I've got to rush now,' Dyson protested, lifting his case off the table.

'I said, how do we get in touch with you? Where will you be staying?'

'Contact that Swiss banker you introduced me to. Julius Amberg in Zurich. Look, I'm going to miss my plane . . .'

'Then shove off.'

Monica escorted him to the door, nodded to George to unlock the front door. Dyson disappeared like the wind.

'I'm taking these canisters straight down to the explosives boffins in the Engine Room for testing,' Monica said the moment she came back.

'Wise precaution,' Newman agreed. 'Then what?'

'Put them in Tweed's safe until he gets back . . .'

The driver behind the wheel of the grey Volvo, still parked within sight of the building where Dyson emerged, signalled to the driver of another car, a silver Renault, parked behind him, by stroking a hand over his head. 'Volvo' picked up his mobile phone as Dyson stepped inside a taxi he'd hailed, dialled.

'Jerry here again.'

'Developments?' Norton's gravelly voice demanded.

'Subject called at a soft-porn shop in Soho. Came out, took another taxi to a Park Crescent building. Went . . .'

'Park Crescent? God Almighty, not there! Number of the building?'

'General & Cumbria Assurance.' The driver gave him the number. He had strolled round the crescent and back to his car while Dyson was inside. 'When Dyson left the Renault took over—'

'General & Cumbria.' Norton had interrupted him, sounded to be thinking aloud. 'I know what that place is. What was Dyson carrying – when he left?'

'Just his bag . . .'

'He must have left them there for safe keeping.' The voice became even grimmer. 'We'll have to take out the whole building. You'll be needed to prepare the vehicle – and the explosives. The job must be done in the next forty-eight hours. Get back to headquarters . . .'

PART ONE

The Massacre

1

Two days later Paula Grey was following the other guests into the large dining-room of Tresillian Manor for lunch. The Elizabethan gem was located on an isolated stretch of Bodmin Moor in Cornwall. She had been staying with friends in Sherborne when the call from Tweed came through early in the morning.

'Paula, a strange emergency has arisen. I'm just back from Paris and I had a call from Julius Amberg, the Swiss banker. He sounded frightened. He's flown over here from Zurich to a friend's house on Bodmin Moor . . .'

He had given her careful directions where to turn off the A30, which spanned the moor. She had said she would drive there at once.

'I'll be there in time for lunch,' Tweed had continued. 'I am bringing a heavy bodyguard – Butler, Nield and Cardon. Armed. Which is what Amberg begged me to do.'

'What on earth for?' she had asked.

'He wouldn't say on the phone. He was calling from Tresillian Manor. Apparently he flew from Zurich to London Airport this morning, called me here at Park Crescent before I'd arrived. He then caught a Brymon Airways flight to Newquay Airport and called me again from Bodmin Moor. He has his own team of guards with him but doesn't have that much confidence in them. He spoke as though in fear of his life. That isn't like Amberg. We'll all meet up at the manor . . .'

It had been a pleasant drive from Sherborne for Paula – a cold February morning with the sun shining brilliantly out of a duck-egg blue sky. Pleasant until she had turned down the side road across Bodmin Moor. The sense of isolation had descended on her immediately, the bleak deserted moor closing in on her.

She had stopped the car, switched off the engine for a moment, listened. Not a sign of human life anywhere among the barren reaches of gorse-covered heathland. In the distance she saw a dominant cone-like hill rising up – Brown Willy. It was the silence which seemed menacing.

Despite the sunlight, a sense of doom gripped her. Of impending tragedy. She shook off the dark mood as she started up the car and drove on.

'You're just being silly,' she told herself.

Tresillian Manor was hidden from the outside world because it was located in a bowl. Wrought-iron gates were wide open with a curving drive beyond.

Lousy security, Paula thought as she drove in past the stone pillar carrying the name of the house on a brass plate. Tall firs surrounded the estate, isolating it further from the outside world. Paula gasped as she turned a corner, slowed on the tarred drive.

Built of grey stone, it was a smaller manor than she had expected but a beauty. Stately gables reared up at either end. A massive stone porch guarded the entrance. Six cars, including a Rolls, were parked below the terrace which ran the full width of the house. Mullion windows completed the architectural masterpiece.

'Welcome to Tresillian Manor,' a small portly man greeted her. 'I am Julius Amberg. We met briefly in Zurich.' He peered over her shoulder. 'Where is Tweed?'

'He's coming down with his people from London. I'm sure he'll be here shortly.'

Behind Amberg stood a blank-faced heavily built man. Paula was shown a cupboard where she divested herself of her trench-coat. She kept her shoulder-bag, inside which nestled her Browning .32 automatic.

Drinks were served in a room Amberg called the Great Hall. Spacious, lofty, with a sculpted plasterwork ceiling, it seemed as old as time. A few minutes later Paula followed the other guests across the large entrance hall into a long narrow dining-room. The table was laid for lunch. Paula counted twelve places. Plenty of room for Tweed and his contingent.

She glanced at her watch. Unusual for him to be late. Her stomach felt queasy again: she must have eaten something the previous evening which had disagreed with her. She'd be relieved when Tweed *did* arrive. The sensation of imminent catastrophe had returned. She studied Amberg, who sat at the head of the table.

The Swiss banker, in his fifties, wore his black hair without a parting, slicked back from his high forehead. Under thick brows his blue eyes were shrewd, his face clean-shaven and plump. He smiled at Paula, who sat on his left.

'Tweed is usually so prompt.'

'He'll be here any minute,' she assured him.

She looked down the table at the other six men, none of whom had spoken a word. All were in their thirties and wearing black suits. She suspected they were hired from a private security firm in Switzerland. They didn't inspire her with confidence – there had been no one at the entrance gate, and Amberg had opened the door himself with only one guard behind him.

'It's very good of Squire Gaunt to rent the manor to me at such short notice,' Amberg continued. 'Even though I have spent longer periods here before. And the butler and kitchen staff.'

'Squire Gaunt?'

'He owns the manor. The locals call him Squire. He finds it rather amusing in this day and age.'

'Where is he?'

'Oh, probably riding across the moor. While I'm here

19

he stays in a cottage he owns at Five Lanes.'

He looked up as someone knocked on the door. The butler who had served the drinks earlier appeared, his manner apologetic.

'Excuse me, sir, Cook says she is ready with the luncheon whenever it suits you.'

Mounce, a Cornishman, wore a black jacket, grey-striped trousers, a white shirt and black tie. A tall, heavily built man, he had the perfect manners for a butler, Paula thought.

'I'll let you know in a minute, Mounce,' Amberg replied.

'Very good, sir.'

'Gaunt has an excellent cook,' Amberg chattered on as Mounce closed the door. 'I hope you will like the lunch. Asparagus mousse for a starter, followed by venison with wine. She is so good I'd like to steal her off him.'

'Sounds wonderful,' Paula said automatically.

The mention of food had brought back the queasiness. She was about to speak when Amberg checked his watch.

'Perhaps we ought to start. I'm sure Tweed will understand. In any case, that will probably bring him post-haste!'

'Mr Amberg . . .' Paula lowered her voice. 'Will you please excuse me for a moment? You showed me where the toilet is. Do start the meal – I'll only be a moment.'

'Of course . . .'

As she stood up she looked out of the windows overlooking the curving drive. A postman had appeared, riding slowly on a cycle. She recognized who was arriving from the blue uniform, the peaked cap pulled well down over the forehead, and for a second sunlight flashed off the red and gold badge. Perched on the front carrier was a large canvas bag.

'The postman's on his way here,' she said to Amberg.

'Mounce will attend to him.'

Amberg was slowly drumming his clenched knuckles on the table. Intuitively she guessed it was not with

20

impatience but with nervousness at the non-arrival of Tweed and his men.

As she left the dining-room and crossed the wood-block floor the front doorbell rang. Mounce appeared, used both hands to pull down the edges of his jacket, walked erectly to the door. Paula, carrying her shoulder bag, entered the toilet, walked down two stone steps, closed and locked the door. It was heavy wood, insulating all sound from the rest of the manor.

Mounce opened the door and stared at the postman. Wrong time of the day. Also it was not the usual postman who stood with a heavy bag looped over the left shoulder. The postman held a parcel in the right hand which was extended to the butler.

As Mounce glanced down, noticed it was addressed to Julius Amberg, the postman's right hand slid swiftly inside the uniform jacket, emerged holding a long stiletto knife. It was rammed upwards into Mounce's body, carefully aimed to penetrate with great force between two ribs. Mounce grunted, an expression of amazement creased his face, then he slumped to the floor, still clutching the parcel.

The killer stepped inside, hauled the body clear of the threshold, quietly closed the front door. Stooping, the figure checked the neck pulse. Nothing. Straightening up, it whipped off the cap, shoved it into the bag, grabbed a Balaclava helmet from inside, pulled it over its head, adjusted the eye slits.

It next extracted a pistol with a wide short barrel from the bag, walked over to the closed kitchen door, opened it wide. The 'postman' was inside, door closed again, before the four occupants – Cook and three local girl helpers – had time to react. Grasping its nose with its left hand, the intruder fired the pistol, the tear-gas shell aimed at the

21

flagstone floor. The gas filled the sealed room – all the windows were closed against the cold.

The four women were choking and reeling as Balaclava produced a leather sap like a small truncheon. Methodically Balaclava ran round the kitchen, coshing each one on the head. Up to this moment the 'postman' had worn leather gloves. For the next weapon sensitive finger control would be needed. Stripping off the leather gloves carefully, hands encased in surgical gloves were exposed.

The 'postman' checked the time. Two minutes since the butler had been dealt with. On the central table lay a silver tray with mousse in individual glass bowls. Venison and other items were cooking in a modern oven against a wall. A hand switched off the cooker – no point in risking a fire. Glancing round at the unconscious forms slumped on the floor, Balaclava extracted an Uzi machine-pistol from his bag. A firing rate of six hundred rounds a minute. Balaclava left the kitchen, closed the door.

Able to hold a breath for a minute, the 'postman' sucked in air. Rubber-soled shoes made no sound as Balaclava approached the dining-room door. A hand hovered, grasped the handle, threw the door open.

Seven men stared at the Balaclava-clad figure holding the Uzi. For a brief second in time they froze. They had been expecting the butler whom Amberg had summoned by pressing a wall bell. That brief second was fatal. Balaclava pressed the trigger, aiming first at the guards, spraying them as Amberg jumped to his feet. The last six bullets stitched a neat row of red buttons down his shirt front, buttons which rapidly enlarged. The banker fell backwards, sagged into the seat, hit the rear of the chair with such force the top half broke. He was grotesquely sprawled at a reclining angle, supported by the intact lower half. His face stared sightlessly at the ceiling.

The assassin extracted the empty magazine, which had

22

held forty rounds, and shoved it in a pocket, then inserted a fresh mag. Walking round the table, he emptied it into already inert corpses. Best to be sure.

Cradling the Uzi, Balaclava brought out a glass spray bottle two-thirds full of sulphuric acid. The spray was aimed at Amberg's face, the plunger pressed. A jet of acid enveloped the face from the bridge of the banker's nose to the chin. Replacing the cap, the assassin thrust it into a pocket, shoved Uzi and empty mag into the bag still looped from the shoulder. After leaving the dining-room, the door was closed.

In the hall the Balaclava helmet was removed, dropped inside the bag, replaced by the 'postman's' official cap. The front door was opened with gloved hands, closed from the outside, the bag was placed on the front rack of the cycle propped against the wall. The 'postman' rode off down the drive.

'Well, I delivered the parcel,' the assassin commented aloud with cold-blooded indifference.

2

Paula checked her appearance in the toilet mirror. She was feeling better, stomach settled, but rather weak. 'Not bad,' she said to her reflection. 'A bit white round the gills.'

Her image stared back. An attractive girl in her early thirties, long raven-black hair, good bone structure, calm eyes which missed nothing, a firm shapely chin. She wore a cream blouse with a mandarin collar, a navy blue suit, pleated skirt, flesh-coloured tights and soft-soled loafers.

Paula had been sick. Which left her with a washed-out

feeling. She had cleaned up the basin. She suddenly felt empty, hungry.

'Maybe I could tackle a little venison,' she said to herself as she mounted the steps, unlocked the door.

She took two paces into the hall, stopped. Mounce lay flat on his back near the closed front door, the handle of a knife protruding from his midriff. A red stain discoloured his white shirt. The Browning .32 automatic was already in Paula's right hand. She edged against the wall, listened, looked.

All doors closed, including the dining-room and the kitchen. She forgot her weakness, glanced up the staircase. Was the killer still in the house? Her loafers made no sound as she crossed the floor, bent over the butler, whose hand was still clutching the package. The 'postman' . . .

Her mind was racing as she quickly checked his carotid pulse. Dead. What the hell was going on? She straightened up, approached the dining-room door. She listened before her left hand reached out for the handle. Another solid door which shut out all sound. She revolved the handle slowly, using her handkerchief to avoid leaving finger-prints, opened the door suddenly, stepped one pace inside, her gun ready to swivel on any target.

'Oh, my God!'

She had the presence of mind to whisper the words. Her mind struggled to take in the macabre horror. It was a massacre. Two guards were still seated, sprawled across the table in lakes of dark red blood. Some security, she thought bitterly. Four other guards had toppled out of their chairs, lay on the floor in pools of blood. She closed the door quietly, still wary that the killer might be inside the manor. Facing the door, she bent down again and checked the pulses of the two men on her side of the table. Nothing. Corpses ready for the morgue.

Sucking in her breath, she moved to the top of the table where Amberg's body was bent over the broken-backed chair. Paula was about to check his neck pulse when she suddenly saw his head. She gasped, trembled with shock. Julius Amberg was faceless. Large parts of the flesh had been eaten away. Even as she watched, the original face was rapidly being converted into a skull.

Forcing herself to stoop closer, her acute sense of smell caught a sharp whiff. Some kind of acid? Why? Why this extra barbarity? She stood up, looked round the walls of the panelled dining-room – panelled from floor to ceiling. A beautiful room – which seemed to emphasize the horror of what she was witnessing.

Her eyes whipped up to the ceiling, then gazed at it. Like the Great Hall, where they'd had drinks, the plasterwork was sculpted in an artistic design of scrolls and ripples. But what caught her attention was a disfigurement. A vivid splash of blood spread immediately above the banker. One of the bullets must have hit an artery, sending up a spurt of blood. As she watched, a drop fell, landed on the relics of Amberg's skull-like head.

She looked at the table. In front of where she had been seated she had thrown her napkin over her place setting – which was probably why the killer hadn't noticed the absence of a guest. In any case it was clear he had moved with great speed to complete his devilish work.

'Get a grip on yourself,' she said under her breath.

She felt terribly alone but she went back into the hall. *The staff!* Inside the kitchen. She paused before opening the door, fearful of what she would find.

'Not them, too,' she prayed.

Another faint whiff met her sensitive nostrils when she eased the door open. Tear-gas. Four bodies sprawled on the stone-flagged floor. Swiftly she checked their pulses. She was startled to find they were all alive. Unconscious, but *alive*. She assumed the plump older woman, clad in white overalls and a white cap slumped near the venison, was Cook. Paula took a cushion off a chair, eased it gently under her head. The younger girls, also clad in white overalls, were less likely to have suffered serious damage.

It was then she noticed the cooker had been switched off, which puzzled her. She was careful not to touch the dials. Fingerprints. She opened a window to let in fresh air to clear the remnants of tear-gas and, warily, explored the rest of the ground floor.

One door led to a study furnished with expensive antiques. Another opened on to a large living-room with french windows at the back facing a gap in the firs framing a view of the bleak moor beyond. The sight emphasized her solitariness. Paula ploughed on, entering the Great Hall. Empty, like the other rooms. The long stretch of windows looked out on to the drive. Two cars were approaching.

Tweed climbed out from behind the wheel of the Ford Escort followed by the sturdy Harry Butler dressed in a windcheater and corduroy trousers. Behind them Pete Nield and Philip Cardon left the Sierra.

'Sorry we're so late,' Tweed began and smiled. 'We were held up by running into a convoy of those travellers – gypsies, whatever. I hope Julius will excuse . . .'

He had spoken rapidly and stopped as he saw Paula's expression, the gun she was still holding in her right hand. His manner changed instantly.

'What's wrong, Paula? Trouble? What kind?'

'The worst kind. And I'd expected Bob Newman to come.'

It was the type of pointless remark made by someone suffering from delayed shock – by someone who had held herself together by sheer will-power and character. No longer alone, she was giving way. She made a great effort: they had to be told.

'Newman had gone off somewhere,' Tweed replied. 'Monica left a message on his answerphone to come and see her. She'll tell him where we've gone.'

Tweed had deliberately answered her question to introduce a whiff of normality back into her life. Middle-aged, of medium height and build, he wore horn-rimmed glasses. He was outwardly the man you pass in the street and never notice – a characteristic which had served him well as Deputy Director of the SIS. He walked quickly up the steps, put his arm round Paula, squeezed her.

'What's happened here?'

'It's ghastly. No, that isn't data, which is what you always want.' She took a deep breath. 'They're all dead.'

'Who exactly?' Tweed asked calmly.

'Julius Amberg, his guards and the butler, Mounce. Eight corpses waiting for you inside that lovely house. The postman did it . . .'

'Tell me more later. I'd better go and see for myself. This postman you mentioned has gone?'

'I haven't had time to search the upper floor. Downstairs is clear.'

'Harry,' Tweed said, taking command immediately, 'go upstairs and search for a killer, who will be armed. Take Philip Cardon with you.'

'On my way . . .'

Butler, a 7.65-mm Walther automatic in his hand, entered the manor followed by Cardon also gripping a Walther. As Paula and Tweed followed them they saw Butler, holding the gun in both hands, creeping up the wide staircase. Cardon was a few paces behind, sliding up close to the wall, starting at the upper landing.

'They're in here,' Paula said. 'Prepare yourself for something pretty awful. Especially Amberg's face.'

Tweed, wearing a trench coat over his navy blue business suit, paused. Hands deep inside his trench coat pockets, a stance he used to adopt when interrogating suspects in the old days when he had been the youngest

Scotland Yard superintendent in the Murder Squad, he stared at the dead body of Mounce.

'I'd like to know what is inside that package the postman delivered. But we mustn't disturb anything until the police get here. We'll call them in a minute,' he said, glancing at the phone on a table against the hall wall. He listened as Paula thought of something else.

'The kitchen staff behind that door were attacked with tear-gas, then I think the killer knocked them unconscious with something. One of the three girls has an ugly bruise on her head. They're all alive, thank heavens.'

'Pete.' Tweed addressed Butler's partner, a very different character. Slim, dressed in a smart blue suit under his open raincoat, he had neat dark hair and a small moustache. 'The staff are unconscious in the kitchen . . .'

'I heard what Paula said, Chief.'

'Go and see what you can do for them. Get a statement if any of them recover and are up to it.'

'I'll get it all down on my pocket tape recorder,' Nield assured him.

He produced the miniaturized recorder the boffins in the basement of Park Crescent had designed. Giving Paula a smile and a little salute, he headed for the kitchen.

'Now for it,' Paula warned.

She opened the door to the dining-room. Tweed walked in ahead of her, stood still after taking two paces. His eyes scanned the carnage, stared briefly at the red lake on the ceiling, walked slowly past each body until he arrived at the head of the table.

'It's a blood bath,' Paula commented. 'You won't like Julius Amberg's face. It's been sprayed with acid.'

'Ruthless,' Tweed said, looking down at his old friend. 'Also intriguing. Julius has – had – an identical twin brother. Julius was Chief Executive of the Zurcher Kredit Bank in Zurich, the driving force. Walter, the brother, is Chairman, does very little except draw a fat salary.'

He looked up as Butler appeared at the door, the Walther still in his hand. He nodded to Tweed.

'All clear upstairs. No one else is here.' His gaze swept round the room. 'Bloody hell.'

'A perfect description,' Tweed responded. 'Lucky we were late. Paula, how did you avoid this massacre . . .?'

His expression changed. His hands jumped out of his pockets and he was alert as a prowling tiger.

'My God!'

'What is it?' Paula asked.

Tweed had grasped something everyone else had overlooked. His own remark about being lucky to be late triggered off the alarm bells inside his head.

'*We* were supposed to be the targets. I must phone Park Crescent instantly. This is a major emergency.'

'I'll call them immediately,' Butler said, ran into the hall and picked up the phone. He was dialling as Tweed hurried into the hall. 'Shouldn't be long now . . .'

'Hurry!' Tweed urged him. 'Park Crescent could be in terrible danger . . .'

It took Butler several minutes – he had to dial again and Tweed stood close to him. Butler listened, nodded and handed the phone over.

'Pray God I'm in time,' Tweed said as he took the instrument.

3

'Tweed and the others have driven down to a Tresillian Manor on Bodmin Moor,' Monica told Newman as she closed a file on her desk at Park Crescent.

Newman had just arrived in response to the urgent call from Monica waiting for him on his answerphone at his flat. He took off his favourite Gannex raincoat, hung it on the stand, settled in a chair facing her desk.

'Bodmin Moor? That's Cornwall. Who are the others and why has he gone down to that remote spot?'

'He took Butler, Nield and Cardon with him as guards . . .'

'A heavy delegation. As guards? That's unlike Tweed. Were they armed? What's going on?'

'Yes, they were armed.' Monica sounded disturbed. 'He was going to meet a Swiss banker, Julius Amberg, who flew in from Zurich.'

'Amberg. That nasty little berk, Joel Dyson, knows Amberg. A very odd coincidence. Has Tweed seen that film or listened to the tape?'

'No, they're still in the safe. He hadn't time. It was action stations from the moment he arrived and took the call from Amberg – begging him to hurry to Cornwall.'

'More and more mysterious. And why did you call me?'

'Tweed wanted you to drive down there if you contacted me in time. I think it would be pointless your going now. The meeting at the manor was for lunch. It will all be over—'

She broke off as the phone began ringing. Picking up the receiver she started to announce 'General & Cumbria Assur—'

'Monica, this is Tweed. You recognize my voice? Quick.'

'Yes, is something . . .'

'Exit One! Exit One! *Exit One!* For Christ's sake . . .'

'Understood.'

Monica rammed down the receiver, took a key from a drawer, knocked over her chair in her haste. Inserting the key in a metal box attached to the wall, she pulled down a red lever, slammed the door shut. The moment the lever was operated screaming alarm bells alerted every office in the building – including Tweed's.

'Emergency evacuation!' Newman shouted to make himself heard as he jumped up, grabbed his Gannex. Monica stuffed her Filofax in her handbag and Newman held the door open. Men and women were already moving down the staircase. There had been rehearsals: no one panicked. They kept moving.

In the entrance hall George, the guard, was slamming down a phone. He had a clipboard in front of him and ticked off people as they filed out through the front door. The bell in the hall was more subdued.

As Newman reached the entrance hall with Monica he glanced at Lisa, the fair-haired girl who operated the switchboard. He saw row upon row of red lights. Every phone was – had been – in use. Lisa snatched up her coat and handbag, as Newman asked the question.

'So many calls all at once?'

'Switchboard jammed,' Lisa replied quickly. 'Except for Tweed's line, which is separate.'

'I had a crazy call,' George commented, ticking off more names. 'Some nutcase said he was phoning from Berlin, had an urgent message. Been jabbering away for five minutes . . .'

Howard, the Director, appeared at the foot of the stairs. Immaculately dressed in a Chester Barrie business suit from Harrods, tall, plump-faced, he had thrown off his usual lordly manner. He stood by the desk next to George.

'Better leave,' said Newman as Monica vanished through the open doorway. 'It was Tweed himself who sounded the alarm from long distance.'

'I'm staying here until the last man and woman has left the building,' Howard said quietly.

Newman was surprised and his previous opinion of Howard as a pompous woodentop changed. He nodded, slipped outside ahead of a fresh file of staff coming down

31

the staircase. On the doorstep, standing to one side, he froze.

A maroon-coloured Espace station wagon was parked alongside the building. Newman went down the steps, stood close and ran back inside the hall as the fresh batch of people walked rapidly off round the Crescent. They were assembling out of sight round the corner in Marylebone Road as planned.

'George,' Newman said as the guard showed the list to Howard. 'There's one of those large Espaces parked just outside.'

'Ruddy 'ell,' George blazed, 'I'd have seen the blighter if I hadn't had that loony from Berlin on the blower.'

'Which is precisely why he was on the phone.'

'Time to leave,' Howard announced, gesturing towards the list. 'All present and correct. Present out of danger, that is. Fancy a quick stroll, Bob?'

'That will do me . . .'

They followed George out of the building, down the steps, turning left along the curve. All three men gave the Espace a quick glance then strode briskly towards where the staff were waiting. It was very quiet in the Crescent and no one else was about. Thank God, Newman thought.

'There was no one inside that vehicle,' he informed Howard.

'Let's hope we don't make fools of ourselves.'

'You've overlooked one point,' Newman commented. 'All the lines were jammed up with calls – phoney calls is my guess. If this is what I think it is we're up against a genius of a planner.'

'I'll call the Bomb Squad from one of the offices along Marylebone Road,' Howard decided. 'It's probably all a false alarm.'

'That doesn't link up with the avalanche of calls – including the crazy one to George,' Newman reminded him. 'I'll stay here.'

They had rounded the corner and Newman stayed behind a wall in a position where he could watch the building. He saw a silver Renault parked just beyond the far side of the Crescent. That was the moment when the world blew up.

Newman had put on sun-glasses he used for driving when the sun was low in the sky. There was a blinding flash. An ear-splitting roar. A cloud of dust dense as a fog. A brief nerve-wracking silence, succeeded by a sound like a major avalanche crashing down a mountain. No shock wave, which puzzled Newman.

The dust cloud thinned. He stared, hypnotized. The Espace had vanished. The section of Park Crescent which had been SIS headquarters was a black hole. Masonry rumbled as it slid down on to the pavement, out across the street. What staggered Newman was the clean-cut destruction of the target. On either side of where the building had stood as a section of the Crescent the walls stood scarred but erect. It was as though a vertical rectangular wedge of a giant cake had been sliced away. The sinister rumble of more debris slithering down over rubble continued, grew quieter, ceased. RIP, SIS headquarters.

Newman glanced across the Crescent. The silver Renault had disappeared. Howard came running up to him.

'What the hell was that? I called the Bomb Squad . . .'

'Hope they brought their sandwiches. No work left for them.'

'Oh, dear God!'

Howard stood like a man transfixed as he gazed at the ruin.

Automatically, he used both hands to adjust the knot of his tie, a mannerism Newman had noticed before when Howard was under pressure. With an effort he pulled

33

himself together, looked back at the small groups of people standing on the pavement.

'It's cold,' Newman said. 'Some of them are shivering. Send them home. Tell them to stay there pending fresh orders.'

'Best thing to do.'

Like a zombie Howard walked back slowly and began talking to his staff. Newman stood very still, thinking about the silver Renault. Odd – the way it had been parked at that observation point and had then disappeared. By his side Monica was recovering from her shocked state.

'Tweed should know about this urgently.'

'How can I reach him?'

'I have the phone number of Tresillian Manor. He might still be there.' She extracted her Filofax and a notebook. On a sheet of paper she wrote a number, handed it to Newman. 'Tresillian Manor.'

'Howard will be back in a minute. He may want a word with Tweed. More likely the other way round . . .'

The driver of the silver Renault was stopped temporarily in a traffic jam in the Euston Road. He picked up his mobile phone, dialled a number.

'Ed here. The property has been liquidated. The contract closed . . .'

'What about dispossessed occupants?'

Norton meant dispossession of their lives.

'A general evacuation took place a few minutes before we closed the contract.'

'It did?' Norton's American twang was a rasp. 'Could anyone have carried out the film and the tape?'

'I'm sure they didn't. No one carried anything which might have contained the canisters.'

'Any sign of Tweed? You have his description. No?

34

That I don't like. We'll have to trace him. He's due for a long holiday, a permanent one . . .'

'I'll report back in.'

Ed was talking into air. Norton had slammed down the phone.

'The Bomb Squad sent the top brass,' Howard observed while they stood in Marylebone Road near the corner of Park Crescent.

'Is it any wonder?' Newman remarked.

The door of a cream Rover opened and Commander Crombie, chief of the Anti-Terrorist Branch, stepped out. Several trucks had arrived, Bomb Squad operatives in protective gear were cordoning off the crescent, evacuating buildings. Other men stood in front of the pile of rubble.

'You're not here for a story, Newman, I trust?' were Crombie's opening words.

A powerfully built man with broad shoulders, in his forties, clean-shaven with a large head, he wore an overcoat with the collar turned up. As he spoke his eyes scanned the area of devastation.

'No, of course not,' Newman snapped.

'Just checking. You saw this thing happen? Any casualties?'

'None,' Howard assured him. 'We evacuated the building in the nick of time. I'll explain why later. The IRA?'

'I don't think so,' said Newman.

'How would you know?' Crombie demanded aggressively.

'No shock wave. Look, I'll show you where I was standing when the Espace blew itself to pieces . . .' He was walking fast and Crombie, a fit man, was hurrying to keep up. 'It was a maroon-coloured Renault Espace parked outside,' Newman continued tersely. 'Don't ask me for the

35

registration number – I didn't get it – we were intent on saving our lives. Here is where I stood.'

'And no shock wave, you said?'

'Exactly. Look at the garden railings opposite. Not a scratch on them. *All* the blast went *one* way – into the building. From what I've seen of photos of IRA bomb damage the blast flies in all directions.'

'That is true. Excuse me. I'll want to see you later.'

'When you're ready . . .'

Newman walked rapidly back to where Howard was escorting the last three staff members into a taxi. Monica was still standing on the pavement.

'I'm going to call Tweed from a phone box in Baker Street Station,' Newman said, hardly pausing.

'I'll come with you,' Howard decided.

'Me too,' Monica said. 'There's something Tweed should know. We might just have a link.'

'Tweed here, Bob,' the familiar voice responded when Newman had dialled Tresillian Manor.

Tweed listened in silence as Newman reported concisely the events leading up to the catastrophe. Monica was squeezed into the box with him. Howard stood outside, erect, hands clasped behind his back, looking none too pleased at being excluded.

'Any casualties?' Tweed asked at one stage, expressed relief at the news. He listened as Newman told him about the visit of Joel Dyson two days earlier. Newman then handed the phone to Monica who explained that no one had seen the film or listened to the tape and that both had been still in the safe when the building was wrecked. Tweed asked to speak to Newman again.

'Bob, I'm speaking from Cornwall, as you know, so I'm phrasing this carefully. The phone doesn't appear to be bugged, but still. Now! Do you remember – no names – a

36

place down here we once stayed at overnight?'

'Yes.'

'Drive down to the same place as soon as you can. Make sure you're not followed.'

'For Pete's sake, I'd know . . .'

'*Make sure!* Now put Howard on the line. Tell him I am short of time.'

'Wherever you are I want you back in London quickly . . .' Howard began.

'No! Now listen to me and don't argue. You'll need a fresh base . . .'

'There's that concrete horror down at Waterloo . . .'

Howard was referring to what the public thought was the new HQ of the SIS. Pictures had appeared of it in the press but it was purely for low-level admin.

'I said listen to me!' Tweed snapped. 'I suspect we're up against the most powerful network in the world – and don't ask me to identify them yet. That network is out to exterminate all of us. I'm not sure why yet. You've got to go underground. Move the whole of our staff – and yourself – to the training mansion at Send in Surrey. It's surrounded with large grounds and is well guarded. That is if you value your life. And I'll only phone you at Send.'

'I don't like running . . .'

'We're all running from now on, Howard. Running to survive. Think of the lives of your staff.'

'All right. Send it is. A bit of peace and quiet might be quite a change. What are you going to do?'

'Go underground.'

4

'Lord, it's marvellous to be outside in this fresh air,' Paula said as she walked with Tweed, climbing up the moor.

Below them Tresillian Manor was a miniature house huddled in its bowl. Butler walked a few paces behind. He had insisted on accompanying them for their protection.

Tweed had earlier phoned the police after talking to Cook, who had recovered quickly. She had not been optimistic about an early arrival.

'No good phoning Padstow. The police station's just a cabin and most of the time no one is there. In the phone book they advise phoning Launceston but I think your best bet is Exeter. That's a real headquarters.'

Tweed had phoned Exeter. He had sensed the inspector's shock at the other end when he'd given details of the massacre waiting for him.

'Never 'ad anything like that. Might be best if I called Lunnon.'

'Just so long as someone gets here fast,' Tweed had snapped and put down the phone.

The ground was hard, ribbed with rocks, covered here and there with gorse. As they climbed higher Paula pointed to a rocky eminence rearing up in the distance from the shallow bleak moor surrounding its base.

'That's High Tor. I once climbed—' She broke off. 'I wonder who that is? There's a man on a horse at the summit of the tor.'

Tweed looked up. Too far away even to guess at what he

38

looked like, the horseman remained stationary for a brief interval and Tweed had the impression he was studying them through field-glasses. Then he was gone.

'Saw you, mate,' Butler said with unconcealed satisfaction.

Tweed and Paula swung round. Butler was holding a small slim monocular glass, another sophisticated device created in the basement at Park Crescent. It operated like a high-powered telescope.

'A big chap,' Butler continued. 'Wearing a deerstalker hat. That's all I observed before he vanished.'

'You really are a wizard,' Paula commented. 'The equipment concealed among your clothes.'

She turned round, started walking, stopped and grabbed Tweed by the arm.

'Up there, midway down High Tor. I saw the sunlight flash off something. More binoculars.'

'That horseman again,' Tweed suggested.

'No, it's someone else. Look at the bottom of the tor.'

On the level, a long way below the summit, a horseman was riding off at a furious gallop. Tweed frowned as Butler came alongside them, Walther in his right hand.

'This is sinister,' Tweed said. 'We have the massacre at the manor, which I'm convinced was supposed to include us. The killer was probably instructed to wipe out the whole lunch party without knowing his targets – with the exception of Julius Amberg. And now we are under surveillance. Then there was the Park Crescent bomb.'

'I can't see any one outfit – however large and well organized – synchronizing both atrocities so close together. Not one in London and the other in Cornwall. Amberg only phoned you this morning,' Paula reminded him.

'Except that is what appears to have happened,' Tweed rejoined.

'A motorcade is approaching the manor,' Butler warned.

They all turned round and looked down on the distant road snaking over the moor towards the entrance. Three police cars and one private car leading the procession.

'Better get back,' Tweed said. He looked at Paula. 'How are you feeling now?'

'Tons better.' She patted her stomach. 'All's well. That dried toast Cook made me was just what I needed.

'That's a terrible thing which happened at Park Crescent,' she went on as they hurried back down the sandy track. 'At least no one was injured or killed. I don't understand what's going on.'

'A wholesale and frighteningly professional attempt to wipe us all out. And I have only two clues as to who is behind this extermination campaign.'

'Which are?' Paula asked, not expecting Tweed to tell her.

'The fact that so few people know the location of our HQ, that so few knew we were due to arrive at Tresillian Manor. Those go together. The other clue is Joel Dyson . . .'

He stopped speaking as they neared the entrance and out of the front of the private car, a Volvo station wagon, a tall, lean and lanky figure stepped. The last man on earth Tweed wanted to meet at this juncture.

'No one mentions the Park Crescent outrage,' he warned. 'Not unless someone else mentions it first. We don't know about it.'

'What's the matter?' Paula enquired.

'Don't you recognize him? That's our old friend and my sparring partner, Chief Inspector Roy Buchanan of the Yard.'

*   *   *

40

'Tweed. Miss Grey.' Buchanan was formal in his greeting. As though we were mere acquaintances, Paula thought. 'And who, may I ask, is this?' Buchanan demanded.

'You just did,' Tweed told him in a neutral tone. 'Harry Butler, one of my staff. There are two more inside. Pete Nield and Philip Cardon – guarding the place and looking after the staff of four, who are in a state of shock. It's a blood bath,' he warned.

'Which is why I flew down here in a helicopter. At the request of the Commissioner.'

What's going on? Tweed wondered. The Commissioner of Police. As high up as you could go. Why? Buchanan was a calm and highly efficient detective. Detached in manner, his thick brown hair was neatly trimmed, as was his moustache. His grey eyes were alert and shrewd. He took charge immediately.

'Let's walk up the drive, give me a chance to get an idea of the surroundings. What were you doing out on the moor?' He asked suddenly as they neared the manor, followed by the cars. A typical thrusting question aimed at catching off guard Buchanan's target.

'We went for a walk to get the atmosphere of what's inside there out of our minds,' Paula replied.

'I was addressing Tweed.'

'Same answer,' Tweed said.

'I gather from what you told Exeter,' Buchanan continued, 'this Swiss banker, Julius Amberg, invited you down to lunch and you arrived late. I spoke to Exeter myself before boarding the helicopter at Battersea.'

'You gathered correctly,' Tweed replied.

'Look, Tweed, I understand there are eight bodies inside the mansion, shot to death . . .'

'Seven. The butler was stabbed.'

'A detail. You're answering questions like a suspect . . .'

'A detail!' Paula burst out. 'It wasn't a detail to Mounce the butler. It was his life. In his forties, I'd guess.'

41

Tweed smiled to himself. Paula had vented her indignation to give him time to cope with Buchanan.

'Possibly not the best way of phrasing it,' Buchanan agreed. 'But this is a murder investigation.'

'Why has the Commissioner intervened?' Tweed snapped, using Buchanan's surprise question tactic against him.

'Well . . .' Buchanan was thrown off balance. 'First there is the scale of the crime. Then an important foreigner is involved. Amberg was a member of the BIS which meets in Basle. The Bank for International Settlements.'

'We *are* aware of what the initials stand for,' Paula told him drily.

'Is that your only explanation for this unprecedented intervention of the Commissioner?' Tweed pressed.

'It's the only one you're going to get,' Buchanan snapped.

He paused. Paula guessed he was annoyed at losing his cool. He stood staring at the manor, with its curved Dutch-style gables surmounting the towers at either end. He studied the large window behind which was located the Great Hall. The grey, mellow stone and the mullion windows showed up at their best in the sunlight.

'It's beautiful,' Buchanan remarked and Tweed recalled that one of his interests was architecture. 'To think such a tragedy should take place in such an ideal setting. Who owns it?' he asked suddenly. 'Amberg?'

'No. A man called Gaunt. The locals call him Squire Gaunt. He's rented it to Amberg before,' Paula replied.

'How do you know that?' Buchanan demanded.

They were walking again. As they approached the mansion Philip Cardon came out of the front door, waited for them on the terrace.

A small well-built man of thirty, Cardon was the most recent recruit to join the SIS. Clean-shaven, he had an amiable expression. An expert linguist, he had penetrated

42

the inner fastnesses of China, speaking Cantonese and passing for a native.

'That's Philip Cardon,' Tweed remarked.

'I asked you how you knew this Squire Gaunt owns this little jewel,' Buchanan persisted.

'Because Julius Amberg told me,' Paula replied. 'That was just before lunch was served, the lunch the poor devils never got a chance to sample.'

'Wait a minute.' Buchanan paused at the foot of the steps leading up to the terrace. '*You* were here before this massacre took place? I understood you all turned up later.'

'You understood wrong,' she rapped back. 'And can we go inside before I explain? It's cold out here.'

'Yes. And you've got a lot of explaining to do,' Buchanan informed her grimly.

An hour later Buchanan had taken separate statements from Paula and then Tweed. Scene of the Crime teams were still swarming over the manor, mainly in the dining-room. A doctor who had arrived with them had officially pronounced that all eight corpses *were* corpses. Photographers and fingerprint men were still busy with their different tasks.

Cook had supplied umpteen cups of tea, secretly grumbling to Tweed at the amount of sugar they put in a cup.

'It's bad for them. Don't they know anything?'

'Only their own jobs,' Tweed had replied wearily.

Buchanan's interrogations had been intensive. At the end he felt sure Tweed and Paula were concealing information but he realized he'd never break them. On each he sprang his bad news near the end of the interrogation.

'Miss Grey, something strange is going on.'

'It most certainly is.'

'I have grim tidings from London. Your headquarters at

43

Park Crescent has been totally destroyed by the most massive bomb. Not a stone left standing.'

He waited. She saw the trap and nodded her head. Crossing her shapely legs she responded.

'Isn't it dreadful?'

'I'd have expected you to ask whether there were serious casualties.'

'Oh, we know all about it – and no one was even injured, thank heavens. Bob Newman happened to be talking to Monica in Tweed's office. They noticed the Espace parked outside and evacuated the building just in time.'

'And how do you come to know that?' Buchanan asked in his most persuasive tone.

'Because Bob – Newman – phoned the news to us.'

'He knew you were down here, then?'

'Only because Monica told him. She had the phone number of Tresillian Manor and Bob phoned in the hope we were still here.'

'You do realize,' Buchanan said, bearing down on her, 'that the only explanation of the two outrages – the massacre here which might have included you as victims and the bomb outrage at Park Crescent – suggests someone is trying to exterminate the SIS? Now who would want to do that?'

'I wish to God we knew,' she said fervently. 'No idea.'

'I see.' He sounded as though he didn't believe her. 'And you were the only one who saw the mass murderer. The fake postman. If only you'd seen his face.'

'He was too far away. I knew – I thought – it was a postman because of his blue uniform ribbed with red. And the sun flashed off his badge, as I told you. Plus the satchel perched on his front carrier.'

'Which undoubtedly hid the machine-pistol he used. I find it difficult to believe that when you were inside the toilet you didn't hear the shots.'

'It's a heavy door. The door into the dining-room is also heavy, assuming he closed it.'

'Can we try an experiment . . .?'

Buchanan escorted her out of the study, gave instructions to one of his detectives armed with an automatic, warned everyone what was going to happen. He then accompanied Paula to the large toilet and closed the door. Mischievously, Paula sat on the closed oak lid of the toilet.

'Let's do it properly.'

She had omitted to tell him she had been sick and had the satisfaction of seeing Buchanan look embarrassed for the first time. They waited. After a short interval someone tapped on the outside of the door which Buchanan opened.

'What is it, Selsdon?'

'I've just done it, sir. Fired six shots out of the dining-room window – with the door into the hall open.'

'Thank you. Go and do something useful.'

'I never heard a thing,' Paula said as they re-entered the hall.

'I must admit neither did I . . .'

Buchanan's interview – even longer – with Tweed produced no fresh information, which Buchanan found frustrating. He said as much to Tweed.

'I find this unconvincing and unsatisfactory.'

'The first is your suspicious mind, the second I agree with completely. I've answered all your questions.'

Which was true. But Tweed had omitted certain data.

No reference to Joel Dyson's visit to Park Crescent.

No reference to a film.

No reference to a tape, stored in the safe with the film, a safe now buried under tons of rubble. In the study, alone with Tweed, Buchanan stood leaning against a table, jangling loose change in his trouser pocket.

'I may want to talk to you again.' His manner was casual

45

and Tweed, knowing Buchanan's ploy of throwing a witness off balance at the end of an interview, braced himself for the unexpected. 'Incidentally,' Buchanan continued, 'the whole country knows you're down here.'

'How could they possibly know that?' Tweed asked quietly.

'Your presence here has been linked with the massacre. In a stop-press item in a London evening paper. Reported also on the radio and in a TV newsflash. You were named – Deputy Director Tweed of the SIS, et cetera.'

'I still don't understand,' Tweed persisted.

'Neither did I, so just before flying down here I phoned the paper, the BBC and ITV news editors. They all told me the same thing. An anonymous caller contacted all three, told them to check with the Exeter police. Reporting the massacre all the media were careful to use the phrase "it is strongly rumoured that eight people have been shot to death at Tresillian Manor", et cetera. Then your rumoured presence was reported.'

'I find this extremely sinister. Only the killer could have had that information. But why broadcast the crime?'

'You tell me,' Buchanan said, again sounding frustrated. 'You're going back to London?' he went on. 'Where will you operate from now?'

'You can try my flat in Walpole Street. It's up to Howard to answer the second question.'

'That's it, then. A fleet of ambulances has arrived to take away the bodies. The dead guests' cars have been driven away for examination. Any idea where I can contact this chap Gaunt?'

'None at all,' Tweed replied as they went into the hall.

Two white-coated men were carrying out a covered body on a stretcher towards the front door. The man at the rear called out over his shoulder.

'This is the last one from the abattoir back there.'

'The forensic team seems to have finished the job,'

Buchanan remarked. 'I understand they've gone, so I think I'll be gone too. I'll be up half the night when I get back. What about you?'

'We'll try and persuade that nice cook to make us some tea. Sustenance to fuel us for our trip away from here.'

'As you wish.'

Paula came out of the Great Hall at that moment. Buchanan looked at both of them, didn't make any effort to shake hands and walked out.

'I don't think he likes us much,' Paula observed.

They went to the door and watched Buchanan driving off followed by the last patrol car. Tweed put an arm round her shoulders and briefly told her what Buchanan had just told him. Paula was stunned.

'On the radio, TV and in the paper! I feel frightened. Is this place a death-trap?'

'We'll be out of here soon.'

They had wandered out on to the terrace and as the cars' engines faded the silence of the moor descended on them. It was late afternoon and would be dark within the hour. Paula was taking in deep breaths of fresh air to cope with what Tweed had told her. After a few minutes they were going inside when she grasped Tweed's arm.

'Listen . . . Horses' hooves.'

They waited as the clip-clop came closer. Two riders appeared, approaching the manor along the drive – a man and a woman. Tweed went back out on to the terrace as the newcomers halted at the foot of the steps. The man, large and with a hawklike face beneath a deerstalker, barked out his question.

'Who the blazes are you?'

'I might ask you the same question,' Tweed snapped back.

'I'm Gregory Gaunt. And I just happen to own this damned place.'

5

'Welcome to Tresillian Manor,' Gaunt said breezily. He had accompanied the girl to leave the horses in a stable on the left side of the house. 'I thought Amberg and all his guests would have pushed off by now. It was a flying visit from Zurich.'

'Stop here a moment, please,' Tweed said as they reached the terrace. 'There's something you should know before you go inside. You're in for a ghastly shock.'

'Shock? What kind of shock?' boomed Gaunt. 'A burglary? Is that it? Spit it out, man.'

Gaunt was six feet tall, heavily built, muscular and about forty, Tweed estimated. His complexion was weather-beaten under thick sandy hair and he seemed to be a man of the great outdoors. Under prominent brows his eyes were swift-moving and intelligent. His manner was dominant without being domineering. Tweed sensed he was in the presence of a strong personality and he could see why the locals called him 'Squire'.

'I'm forgetting someone,' Gaunt went on. 'This is my girl friend, Jennie Blade. Say hello, Jennie.'

'Greg, I don't need a prompter,' Jennie drawled. 'Hello, everyone. Who is that peach of a man who just came out?'

It was Philip Cardon, joining Butler and Nield, who had heard voices. Cardon smiled at her as Tweed made introductions. Paula and Jennie eyed each other up and down like two cats warily summing up the opposition. Jennie switched her gaze back to Cardon.

'Life is looking up, Greg – becoming interesting again.'

In her late twenties, Jennie was attractive. Five feet six tall, her riding outfit emphasized her superb figure. Her slim legs were encased in jodhpurs. Golden hair fell in smooth locks to her shoulders. Her face was triangular – a wide forehead, thick gold brows and a good bone structure tapering to a pointed chin below full red lips. Strong competition, Paula admitted to herself.

Bearing in mind the girl's presence, Tweed gave a terse account of the tragedy. He explained that Amberg had invited them down to lunch because he had been a friend of Tweed's. He omitted mentioning that Paula had witnessed the aftermath.

'I don't believe this,' Gaunt rumbled. 'Police trampling all over my property. And why should anyone want to harm Julius, a Swiss banker? I'm going to see for myself.'

'I'll come with you,' said Jennie.

Cardon stopped her. He took her arm as Gaunt marched inside. She looked at him through half-closed eyes.

'Better not,' Cardon advised her.

'I'll be all right if you'll come with me,' she replied, openly flirting with him.

'Glad to be of service,' Cardon agreed, who seemed not averse to accompanying her anywhere.

Tweed slipped in ahead of them. He found Gaunt standing very erect and still in the dining-room. The tablecloth, stained with pools of blood, was still there, to say nothing of the dark brown lakes on the ceiling and carpet.

'My God! Looks as though you were right.'

'I'd hardly make it up,' Tweed responded. 'And Amberg's face had been splashed with acid after being shot dead. He looked like a skull.'

He watched Gaunt's reaction but no emotion showed on the Squire's face. He walked slowly to the head of the table and stood looking down where Amberg had lain over the broken chair.

'Cost me a bloody fortune to clean up this place,' Gaunt rasped. 'And there are holes in the panelling. That will have to be attended to. Damned expensive.'

'Greg is money-conscious,' Jennie said as though she felt it diplomatic to explain Gaunt's apparent mercenary attitude. 'It's understandable. Keeping up a place like this these days is a drain on his purse.'

'Do you mind not discussing my personal affairs with a stranger,' Gaunt rapped at her. He looked at Tweed. 'I return from a day away which I enjoyed and find this. I still can't take it in.'

'How did you spend the day?' Tweed enquired.

'None of your business. You sound like a policeman.'

'*Greg!*' Jennie spoke sharply. 'It was a polite question.' She turned to Tweed. 'He has a small cottage at Five Lanes on the edge of the moor. The arrangement was we'd stay away from here from eight in the morning until now. Amberg holds – held – business meetings here.'

'Do belt up, Jennie,' Gaunt said with less force. 'You know something, Tweed? I don't feel like staying in here. Let's repair to the living-room. Thank God the staff survived. It's hell getting fresh servants.'

'He won't admit it,' Jennie whispered to Tweed as Gaunt marched out, 'but he's in a state of shock. Would you please join us for some tea? If Cook is up to it. I'll go and have a word, maybe give her a hand.'

'I'll come too,' Paula said.

She glanced at Tweed who was gazing out of the window into the distance. The light was fading and night fell over the drive like a menacing shadow. Knowing they were hemmed in by the desolate moor, Paula shivered.

'Where are you people off to when you leave?' enquired Gaunt.

They had just devoured a huge tea of sandwiches and

home-made fruit cake. They sat in the living-room on couches and armchairs. Gaunt faced Tweed and Paula while Cardon sat on a couch next to Jennie. Butler and Nield had chosen chairs facing the windows which they watched constantly – no one had closed the curtains.

'London,' Tweed lied smoothly. 'There shouldn't be a lot of traffic on the roads at this hour.'

'I'd have expected you to stay somewhere down here until the morning,' Gaunt persisted.

No one had mentioned the bomb outrage at Park Crescent to their host. He reached for a box of cigars and, when everyone refused, lit one for himself. It was quite a ritual: trimming the tip off, after rolling it close to his ear, then using a match to ignite it. He took a deep puff and sighed with enjoyment.

'That's better. After today. Tweed, I have been wondering what happened to all the cars Amberg and his guests must have arrived in. Amberg always had a Roller.'

'The police drove them away for further examination.'

'Fat lot of use that will do them.'

'It's surprising what forensic specialists can detect.'

'You really do sound like a policeman.' Gaunt's eyes gleamed as though scoring a bull. 'What do you do for a living?'

'I'm an insurance negotiator.'

'Insurance!' Gaunt jumped up. 'Oh my God! I'll bet my insurance doesn't cover damage caused by mass murder.'

'Depends on how the policy is worded,' Tweed said in a soothing tone.

'Blast it, Greg!' Jennie raged. 'Stop being so obsessed with money. You should be worried about how this terrible experience has affected the staff.'

'It hasn't,' Tweed assured her. 'The police brought a doctor with their team. He examined your staff, said all they'd suffer from were temporary headaches. Celia, the new girl, was tapped only lightly on the head.' He saw

Paula watching him, startled by his recent slip of the tongue. He covered it, looking at Gaunt. 'The reason I know about the forensic business is the chief inspector – a man called Buchanan – explained to me why they needed the cars. Incidentally, he said he would need to talk to you.'

'He won't be welcome, I can tell you that.'

'You said,' Jennie began, to ease the tension, addressing Tweed, 'that this fake postman delivered a parcel which poor Mounce was still clutching when the police examined him. I wonder what it contained?'

'A technician opened the package outside in the garden,' Tweed told her. 'You'll never guess what it contained. A box of Sprüngli truffle chocolates.'

'I find that rather beastly,' Jennie commented.

'Sprüngli?' repeated Gaunt, who had sat down again. 'A firm in Zurich – where Amberg came from.'

'I don't think Buchanan overlooked that,' Tweed remarked drily. Checking his watch, he stood up. 'I think we really ought to be going. Thank you for your hospitality.'

'It was nothing,' Gaunt said gruffly.

Jennie looked at Cardon. 'I live in Padstow in a rented flat. Here is a card with my phone number. It's a strange port – located on the estuary of the River Camel. Greg and I go there quite often. At this time of the year it's so gloriously quiet and hidden away. If you're down that way do come and see me, won't you?'

Tweed kept a blank expression. Padstow was their real destination.

The door to the hall had been left ajar as though Gaunt was expecting a phone call. The bell began ringing at that moment. Gaunt walked briskly out of the room. He was back again, almost at once, looking rather annoyed.

'It's someone for you, Tweed. Wouldn't give a name. People are so rude these days. No manners at all . . .'

Tweed closed the door behind him, crossed the hall, picked up the phone. All the staff had gone home – Jennie had explained they arrived early in the morning and cycled home again in the evening.

'Tweed here.'

'Hoped I might catch you,' the familiar voice said, deadpan. 'I'm back at the Yard – flew to London from St Mawgan Airport. Exeter has been on the line. I wondered how someone got hold of a postman's outfit. Now we know.' Buchanan paused, waited.

'All right, you want me to ask how. So – how?'

'They stole the uniform of the genuine postman from his cottage at Five Lanes.' He paused. 'They've just found his body, throat slashed open from ear to ear.'

6

Tweed drove the Ford Escort with headlights undipped as he followed the lonely road in pitch darkness across the moor, heading back to the A30. Paula, acting as navigator, sat beside him while Cardon was alone in the back. Behind them Nield, driving the Sierra, had Butler sitting alongside him. He used the red lights of the Escort to warn him of oncoming bends. His own headlights were dipped to avoid a blinding glare in Tweed's rear-view mirror.

'Why are we going to Padstow?' Paula asked.

'To go underground until I've identified the enemy.'

'Not like you to run,' she probed.

'A tactical retreat. We may be up against the most

53

powerful and dangerous enemy we've ever confronted.'

'What makes you think that?'

'First, Amberg begs me to join him at Tresillian Manor. With a lot of protection. Maybe we were the targets for the killer as much as he was.'

'And second?'

'Within a short time of the massacre a massive bomb destroys Park Crescent. Diabolical synchronization?'

'Not plausible,' she argued. 'I still maintain that no one could have timed the two events so close together.'

'I suspect the whole plot was triggered off by the arrival of Joel Dyson two days ago from the States. That conjures up a very powerful network with a long reach. Also, how many people knew the location of SIS HQ? The top-flight security services in Europe – and America.'

'You make it frightening,' Paula commented.

'You should be frightened. It must take a vast network to organize all that. Which is why we're spending a day or two in Padstow. Right off the beaten track.'

'So it could be unfortunate,' Cardon suggested, 'that by chance Jennie Blade lives in Padstow.'

'It doesn't help,' Tweed agreed, 'but I've booked rooms at the Metropole – which is in a strategic location. I stopped there overnight with Newman a few years ago.'

'And Philip,' Paula teased Cardon, 'you seem to have fallen for the golden lovely.'

'Fooled you, didn't I?' Cardon chuckled. 'She was pretending to take a fancy to me, that she thinks I'm the best thing since sliced bread. I wondered immediately: "What's this girl really after?"'

'Didn't know you were a cynic about women.'

'Not a cynic,' Cardon told her cheerfully. 'Just a realist. Are you offended?'

'Not in the least. Now I think you've got your feet on the ground. And what on earth is this ahead of us?'

Tweed had slowed. In his headlights red and white cones

barred the way with a large notice. It carried the word DIVERSION and an arrow pointing to the right up a narrow lane. It was raining now and between the wipers he had set in motion Tweed saw men in yellow oilskins and peaked caps. A burly individual waved a red lamp and walked towards the driver's side of the car as Tweed stopped, keeping the engine running. In the back Cardon had his Walther in his right hand, inside his windcheater.

'Sorry, buddy,' the burly man with the lamp shouted as he came closer. 'There's been a multiple pile-up on the A30. Go this route and you're back on the highway a short way to the west . . .'

Accent and language were muffled American, Tweed noted.

'Tweed,' Paula whispered, 'I've checked the map and the only turn-off to the right is a dead end. That is, before we reach the A30. The lane he's diverting us to leads close to another tor with a stone quarry close by.'

'Could I see some identification?' Tweed asked through his open window.

'What the bloody hell for?' The man's face turned ugly. He was reaching inside his slicker as he went on. 'You can't get through . . .

'Don't do it!' Paula warned.

Her Browning automatic was pointed past Tweed at the man outside. He withdrew his hand as though he'd burnt it. He was looking uncertain and then turned to signal to the other men when Tweed reacted.

Ramming his foot down, he shot forward, scattering cones like ninepins. Men jumped out of the way and a missile of some sort landed on the bonnet, burst, spread a light grey-coloured vapour.

'Tear-gas!' Tweed snapped.

He closed his window, driving with one hand, maintaining his speed. A glance in his rear-view mirror showed him the Sierra roaring after him. He heard two reports.

Shots had been fired. Nothing hit his vehicle. A quick second glance in the mirror showed him the Sierra rocketing up behind him: no apparent damage.

'Thank you, Paula,' Tweed said. 'I was suspicious but you confirmed it. A multiple pile-up? On the A30 in February and at this time of night? And a road crew with an American foreman? The whole set-up was phoney, stank to high heaven.'

'So what had they waiting for us up at that dead end?' Paula mused.

'A *dead* end – for all of us,' Cardon suggested.

'You have a macabre sense of humour. It doesn't bear contemplating – out in the middle of that moor . . .'

She started checking her map again. Tweed was driving at speed, lights undipped, swerving round corners. He was anxious to reach the main road.

'What worries me,' he said, 'is how did that gang of thugs know we would be travelling along that road at this hour? Again it suggests a powerful, well-organized network. I get the feeling our every move is being monitored.'

'We're close to the A30,' Paula warned. 'As to how they could know where we were – Buchanan told us your presence down here was reported by all the media. They could have flown down from London to St Mawgan Airport – arranging in advance for hire cars to be waiting. And this is where they stole the equipment from . . .'

Tweed had slowed down, paused at the T-junction on to the A30 to look both ways. Yards to the left, road repair equipment was stacked on a verge, flashing lights illuminating cones and other material. Tweed drove out, turned right to the west, his headlights showing a great belt of the road descending a long hill. No other traffic in sight. The rain had stopped but the road surface gleamed in the moonlight.

'You could be right, Paula,' he remarked. 'There would be time for the opposition to fly down from London. But these are people who can move like lightning. I still find it puzzling why the anonymous call was made to the media. I'm going to pull in here, have a word with Pete Nield, make sure they're both all right.'

Paula saw a lay-by was coming up. Tweed signalled, pulled off the main road into it. He stopped, still keeping his engine running as the Sierra drew in behind him. It was Butler who got out of the car, used a torch to check the side of his vehicle, then walked up to Tweed who had lowered his window.

'You handled that well, Chief,' he commented. 'Nothing like a reception committee to welcome us to Cornwall.'

'I heard shots,' Tweed replied.

'You did. One bullet went wide. The other ricocheted off the side of the Sierra. I just found the point where it dented the metal. Maybe time we moved on . . .'

They were driving again through the night along the deserted A30 when Paula made her suggestion.

'There are only three people who could have co-operated with the killer who committed the massacre,' she said.

'Gaunt or Jennie Blade,' Tweed anticipated her. 'And we saw two people on High Tor. But who is the third?'

'Celia Yeo, the young red-headed girl who was helping in the kitchen.'

'Why pick on her?'

'Because I ask questions. After the police doctor had examined the staff he remarked that the one who had got off lightest from being coshed was Celia. Said he was surprised she had become unconscious – so slight was the bruise on her head.'

'Not very conclusive,' Tweed objected.

'There's more. I talked to Cook when Celia was outside in the scullery. Apparently the girl she recently replaced was knocked down by a hit-and-run driver, had both legs broken. Celia turned up at the manor offering her services

57

the following day, which Cook thought was rather odd.'

'Still not sufficient to convince our jovial Chief Inspector, Roy Buchanan,' Tweed persisted.

'There's more still. I had a little chat with Celia on the quiet. She's a mulish type, hard as nails, and has avaricious eyes. That girl would do almost anything for money. And she lives in Five Lanes – where the real postman came from. I think I'll drive over there and talk to her again. Her day off is tomorrow. And I saw her sneak back across the grounds with a scarlet tea towel in her hands. She said she'd hung it out to dry – it was still dripping water. She could have hung it from the branch of a tree at the edge of the estate to signal to the killer – signal to him that Amberg had arrived. I don't think she'd known what was going to happen.'

'Bit of a far-fetched theory,' Tweed commented.

'Hold on, Chief,' Cardon called out. 'Paula has made a pretty solid case for your so-called far-fetched theory.'

'If you say so,' Tweed responded impatiently, concentrating on his driving. 'One thing I insist on, Paula. You're not going back to Bodmin Moor on your own.'

'Maybe Bob Newman will come with me – if he's reached Padstow . . .'

Paula saw why Tweed had referred to the Hotel Metropole's strategic position as soon as they arrived. Perched high up, it looked down on and across the estuary of the River Camel. Gleaming like a sheet of quicksilver by the light of the moon, it appeared to be about a quarter of a mile wide from Padstow to the opposite shore.

Parked outside, in the forecourt in front of the large Victorian building, was Newman's Mercedes 280E. Its owner appeared from inside as Tweed was registering for his party. Newman frowned at Paula, slipped her a sheet of folded paper as he passed her, which she palmed. He walked outside as though he'd never seen them before in his life.

She showed Tweed the note as they travelled up in the lift to their rooms. Tweed had a suite, No. 11, on the first floor, while Paula's double room was on the second.

'Come down and see me within five minutes,' Tweed told Paula after he'd read the note.

Butler and Nield, acting as guards, had rooms close to Paula's. Tweed had requested this at the desk.

'Miss Grey is recovering from a serious illness,' he had informed the receptionist. 'Pneumonia. She might need assistance walking when she leaves her room . . .'

Paula closed her room door. The lights were on, the curtains drawn. She moved swiftly, sensing the urgency in Tweed's order. Opening her case, she threw the lid back, lifted out her favourite navy blue suit, hung it in the wardrobe, hurried back to the lift.

Tweed had a much larger room with a sitting area. He stood in the middle, still wearing his trench coat in spite of the heated atmosphere. Handing her the note, he began pacing like a caged tiger. The note was terse.

Meet me in my car – parked halfway up Station Road. Have phoned H. Very big trouble. H. wants you to call him. Have found safe phone. Bob.

'You said you were ravenous just before we reached here,' Paula reminded him.

'Food will have to wait. I phoned the dining-room. They will serve us later.' His brusque tone softened. 'But you can go straight down to dinner – you've had a pretty rough day.'

'Nothing doing. I'm coming with you.'

'So is Butler . . .'

Outside the hotel an icy breeze blew from the north. As they climbed the hill Paula asked her question.

'Why do they call this Station Road?'

59

'Because at the bottom of the hill behind us is a building which is the old station. Now it's Customs & Excise. The trains don't run here any more. Haven't for years. The line was eliminated long ago. Here we are. You sit next to Bob. Maybe he'll be better company than I am tonight. While I remember, Bob, I'd like to borrow your field glasses.'

Newman drove to the top of the road, turned right down New Street. Lined with two-storey grey stone terrace houses, it made Paula feel they had arrived in old Cornwall. Newman paused, pointed to a wooden cabin set back from the road. No light in the windows.

'Believe it or not, that's the police station. Unmanned. So, if we hit trouble, don't expect any help from the police.'

'Comforting,' Paula commented.

Newman swung right again down St Edmund's Lane, an even narrower and bleaker street at night. It descended steeply and it too was hemmed in on either side with old grey stone terrace houses. No one about, not a soul, and the lighting was dim. Newman paused for a moment, pointed to a gap in the wall to their right with a shadowed pathway leading uphill.

'That's a short cut on foot back to the Metropole.'

'I wouldn't advise going up there after dark,' said Butler, seated next to Tweed.

It was the first thing he'd said since they had entered the car. Paula, feeling edgy, took the remark personally.

'I suppose that was for my benefit. Harry, I'll have you know I *can* take care of myself.'

'I wouldn't go that way at night myself,' Butler told her equably.

Newman drove to the bottom of the lane and Paula leaned forward, anxious to get some idea of Padstow's layout. Turning to the left along a level road, Newman gestured to his right.

'That's a dock beyond the car park with the estuary on

the far side. I'm now driving along a one-way street. If I'd turned right at the bottom of St Edmund's Lane it's two-way traffic. Ahead is the harbour, a complex system. I can show you better in the morning. Tweed, I decided it might be better if I stayed elsewhere as an unknown reserve. I have a room overlooking the harbour in the Old Custom House, the building on your left. It's a very good hotel. And there is your phone box. I have to park a bit further on. See you in the morning?'

'Yes. We'll be walking past your hotel at ten o'clock on the dot. Good night. Take care . . .'

Newman had paused, while Tweed and Paula got out of the car. Butler followed them, crossed to the carpark where he had a clear view of the old-fashioned red phone box. The raw wind hit them as Tweed struggled to haul the door open and Paula dived inside with him. It was with some trepidation that Tweed dialled Howard's number at the Surrey mansion.

'Who is this?' Howard's voice enquired after Tweed had been passed through an operator.

'Tweed. I gather you wanted to talk to—'

'Is that a safe phone?' Howard interrupted, his voice tense.

'It should be. It's a public call box. If you don't mind I won't say where I'm speaking from.'

'Oh, damn that, I don't care. As long as you're well away from London . . .'

'I am . . .'

'Tweed, the situation is desperate, unprecedented. You'll hardly believe what's happening.'

'Try me,' Tweed suggested quietly.

'As you know, our HQ has been totally destroyed by the bomb. But I can't get through to the PM. He seems to have cut himself off from me. Every time I try to reach him some fool of a private secretary feeds me a load of codswallop as to why I can't contact him. But I know the PM is in

Downing Street. The secretary let that slip.'

'I see. Any theory as to why this is happening?'

'Well, the PM is having trouble with Washington. He needs America's support, as you know, over Europe and the Middle East. Washington is being very distant with London.'

'Precisely who in Washington?' Tweed enquired.

'I gather it's the Oval Office. President March himself.'

'Rather a rough diamond, I've heard.'

'Should never have been elected,' Howard stormed. 'Just because he's a powerful orator, talks the language of the people.' He sighed with disgust. 'The people – and some of them he mixes with are hardly out of the top drawer.'

'What you're saying is we've lost the PM's support? Even with this bomb outrage?'

'It would seem so. I can't believe it.' Howard sounded to be in despair. 'I really can't believe it,' he repeated, 'but it's happening.'

'I want you to call Commander Crombie . . .'

'I spoke to him a few minutes ago. At least *he* is talking to me. He said it was too early to be positive, but his experts have found relics of the device which detonated the bomb. It's definitely not IRA, Crombie says. A very sophisticated and advanced mechanism was used – something they've never encountered before. The press will continue to say it was the IRA, and Crombie won't contradict them.'

'He sounds to be moving fast.'

'Something else difficult to believe. Crombie has teams working round the clock on clearing the debris – three shifts every twenty-four hours. I think it's discovery of this new device which has electrified him.'

'Howard, phone Crombie on my behalf. Tell him it is very important to find amid that mountain of rubble my office safe. It contains a film and a tape recording. They could be the key to all that's happening. I'm guessing.'

'You usually guess correctly,' Howard admitted. 'I will make that call to Crombie – mentioning you. What do the film and the tape contain?'

'If I knew that I might know who is masterminding these attacks on us.'

'Could take weeks to find,' Howard warned. 'And then it may be crushed to nothing – or its contents will be.'

'That's what I like about you, Howard – your eternal optimism. Just call Crombie.'

'I've said I will. Have *you* any solid ideas?' Howard pleaded.

'One or two. Give me a little time . . .'

Tweed's expression was grave as he left the box with Paula. Butler strolled across the road to meet them. The alert bodyguard was smiling.

'Cheer up! We'll break this thing sooner or later. Oh, while you were on the phone Newman came back for a moment on foot. Full of apologies. He forgot to mention that Monica took a call from Cord Dillon earlier in the afternoon before the fireworks display. Dillon is some-where in London.'

Tweed stared. Cord Dillon was Deputy Director of the CIA. A very tough, able man – what was he doing in London at a time like this?

'Dillon wants to talk to you urgently.' He handed Tweed a folded piece of paper. 'Newman gave me that to hand on to you. The number of some London phone box. You can reach Dillon between 9.30 a.m. and 10 a.m. at that number tomorrow morning. Monica said it sounded as though he was keeping under cover. Wouldn't say where he was staying.'

'Let's get back to the Metropole . . .'

Tweed walked beside Paula, told her the gist of his talk with Howard. They turned up St Edmund's Lane. Butler was following several paces behind them, reeling as though he was drunk. His right hand gripped the Walther inside his windcheater as they plodded uphill and took the long way back, ignoring the short cut to the hotel. Paula was relieved: the path which turned off the lane was a tunnel of eerie darkness.

'What on earth is going on?' she asked. 'That business about not being able to reach the PM. I'm scared.'

'With good reason. Interesting that Washington business – and now Dillon turns up out of the blue. My thoughts are turning towards America.'

'Why America? Because of Dillon's arrival?'

'Not entirely. Something rather more sinister.'

'Sorry. Perhaps I'm being rather thick. Probably fatigue. And I do want to drive with Bob Newman back to Bodmin Moor tomorrow to talk again to Celia Yeo. What is it about the States which has suddenly grabbed your attention?'

'America,' Tweed repeated, half to himself, 'where there is so much money and *power*.'

'Power?' Paula queried.

'Work it out for yourself.'

7

Feeling dopey when she woke the following morning in her double bedroom, Paula bathed, dressed for the moor, fixed her face in two minutes and only then pulled back the curtains. She stared at the view in disbelief. Something very weird had happened overnight. The River Camel had disappeared!

She stared at the vast bed of sand, rippled in places, stretching from shore to shore. When she phoned Tweed he said he was just ready for breakfast, so why didn't she come down to the suite?

She was closing her door when another door opened and Pete Nield appeared. He fingered his moustache and grinned.

'Good morning. Just checking to make sure you're not wandering off on your own.'

'Makes me feel like a ruddy prisoner,' she mocked him. She liked Pete. 'I'm on my way to Tweed's suite. Come and join us.'

'What on earth has happened?' she asked as Tweed unlocked his door and ushered her inside. She went over to his extensive bay window which gave a better view. 'The river has vanished.'

'Leaving behind a vast sandbank,' he explained as he joined her. 'There's a very high tidal rise and fall here. The tide is out now.' He pointed to his left through a side window. 'That rocky cliff protruding at the edge of the town blots out a view of the open sea. Straight across from us is Porthilly Cove. No water there at all at the moment. There is a narrow channel which remains along the shore of that weird village over there.'

'Where is that?'

'Place called Rock. A small ferry shuttles back and forth between Padstow and Rock. At low tide – now – the ferry departs from a small cove at the base of the rocky cliff. When the tide rises it departs from the harbour.'

'What a strange place. This is my idea of Cornwall.'

She gazed to her left, beyond Rock towards the invisible Atlantic. The far shore was forbidding. Climbing up steeply was a wilderness of boulders, scrub and heathland. A sterile, inhospitable area. Yet further in past Rock there were green hill slopes undulating against the horizon as the sun shone out of a clear blue sky.

'You haven't heard that tape on the recorder I had hidden in my pocket when I talked to Cook,' Nield pointed out. 'It doesn't add much to what Buchanan later told us.'

'Let's hear it quickly, then get down to breakfast,' Tweed urged.

He stood with Paula staring out at the endless sandbank. Nield placed his small machine on a table, ran through the first part, then pressed the 'play' button.

'I spent time putting her at her ease,' Nield explained. 'Now, listen . . .'

'Cook, can you tell me what you saw when the kitchen door was opened and closed again?' Nield's voice.

'It was an 'orrible shock, I can tell you . . .' Cook's voice quavered, then became firm. 'He was standin' there with this awful gun. A short wide barrel – bit like a piece of drainpipe. He aimed at the floor, something shot out and the place was full of a greyish sort of vapour.'

'The tear-gas,' Nield's voice broke in gently. 'But you probably had a good look at him?'

'Like a nightmare. That woollen hood over 'is 'ead with slits for the eyes. He moved gracefully, like a ballet dancer. But those eyes – without feeling, without any soul. A chill ran down my spine. Those eyes were blank – like a ghoul's eyes.'

'What happened next?' Nield pressed, still gently.

'We're all choking. Tears running down our faces. Then this beast walks straight up to me and 'its me on the 'ead with something. I just dropped to the floor and didn't know what was 'appenin' till I came round . . .'

'That's the relevant part,' Nield said. He switched off the recorder. 'There's more but nothing informative.'

'Interesting that reference to moving with the grace of a ballet dancer,' said Tweed. 'Time for breakfast.' He picked up a copy of the *Daily Telegraph* which had been slipped under his door. 'The late edition. They must fly them down.' He showed them the headline.

HUGE IRA BOMB DESTROYS LONDON BUILDING

'That's not the significant item. I'll show you in the dining-room.' Butler joined them outside and they took the lift to the ground floor. Tweed held on to Paula's arm, keeping up the fiction that she was an invalid.

In the dining-room Tweed sat with Paula at a table with a panoramic view of the harbour over the grey slate rooftops of the small port. After ordering a substantial breakfast of bacon and eggs he folded the paper, handed it to Paula.

'That's the intriguing bit,' he told her, keeping his voice down.

'GHOST' ROADBLOCKS IN WEST COUNTRY LAST NIGHT

Paula read the text below the headline. The gist was that a series of roadblocks had been established on all the main routes out of Cornwall. Motorists had been stopped and told it was a census to check the amount of traffic passing through. The strange twist was that no police force or council office had any knowledge of them.

'What is this weird business?' she asked Tweed.

'Not reassuring,' Tweed replied quietly. 'They – whoever they are – were looking for *us*. Again it confirms my fear about the extent of the vast network we're up against. To be able to organize something like that so rapidly.' He smiled. 'Enough to put me off my breakfast – but it won't.'

'It's like a noose closing round us,' Paula commented.

'Oh, we'll find a way of eluding them.' Tweed checked his watch. 'I must be at that phone box to call Cord Dillon just after nine thirty.' He glanced across at a distant table where Butler sat with Nield. 'Luckily you'll have some

67

reliable company while I'm away.'

'But I'm coming with you to the phone box,' she insisted.

'Certainly, Paula, I fancy a drive to Bodmin Moor myself,' Newman told her. 'I'd like to get the atmosphere of where this ghastly massacre took place. Odd there's nothing about it in the paper. Meat and drink for the tabloids.'

They were standing outside the phone box while Tweed held the door half open in case someone else tried to use it. Tweed swung round.

'That's something else I find sinister – the absence of any report about the massacre at Tresillian Manor. It looks as though someone has silenced Roy Buchanan – and he's a man not easily silenced.' He looked back the way they had come as Cardon loped towards them, smiling.

'Morning, everyone. What a beautiful day. Sorry to be late but I slept in. I usually do if nothing's happening.'

'Too much *is* happening,' Tweed snapped.

'Bob is taking me for a drive to Bodmin Moor,' Paula reminded Cardon.

'Can I come too?' Cardon asked. 'Butler and Nield are ample guard for Tweed.' He grinned at Newman. 'Carry your bag, sir?'

'As I told you, we're going to interview one of the servant girls who works at Tresillian Manor,' Paula said. 'I think she might not say a word if too many people arrived. But thank you, anyway, Philip.'

'I could stay with the car if you're keeping it out of sight,' Cardon persisted.

'We'll be doing just that,' Paula agreed.

'Take Philip with you,' Tweed ordered. 'I don't like this idea of yours, but as you're being obstinate I'll only let you go if you have two men with you. Now, I must make that phone call . . .'

*　　*　　*

At the London end the receiver was lifted swiftly when Tweed had dialled the number. He instantly recognized the distinctive American voice that answered.

'Who is this calling?' Dillon demanded.

'Tweed. Monica said you wanted to talk to me urgently.'

'Monica was dead right. Are you OK? I walked to Park Crescent . . . Say, where are you calling from?'

'Public phone box . . .'

'Like me. I said I walked to Park Crescent – saw your building. A hole in the wall. Are you sure you're OK?'

'I wasn't inside when it happened,' Tweed assured him. 'Neither was anyone else. They were warned in the nick of time. Why are you in London?'

'Tweed, I'm on the run. In Washington I'd have ended up on a slab. This is a tough one. Certain people – a small army of professionals – are out to liquidate all of us. They're controlled from the very top. We haven't a hope.'

'Cord, I need to know what it's all about. Up to now I'm in the dark. Shadow-boxing. Give me a lead, for God's sake. Where are you staying?'

'At a crummy little London hotel which I've just left. I can see the entrance from this box. Keep moving is the name of the game. Survival. I called to warn you to do just that – if you want to go on living.'

'Cord, I need data,' Tweed said grimly.

'It's about a guy called Joel Dyson – some film he took, a tape recording he made. That's all I can tell you till we meet some day. If we're both still standing up. Get out of the country, Tweed. One thing I'll give you – the only other American you can trust is a Barton Ives, Special Agent, FBI. He knows it all. I'm on my way. Jesus! I don't even know where I might be safe.'

'Cord.' Tweed spoke with great emphasis. 'Head for Switzerland. For Zurich. Stay at the Hotel Gotthard – same name as the pass south into Italy. It's a three-minute walk from the main railway station.'

'I'll think about it . . .'

'Don't. Just do it. I'll meet you there when I'm able to make the trip.'

'You could be right. Jesus!' Dillon repeated. 'They are arriving at my hotel. I've left my bag inside a locker at one of the main terminals. Got to go now.'

'Cord . . .'

'One more thing, Tweed, then I'm moving. You ever meet a man called Norton, shoot him before he kills you . . . *Norton*. Got it . . .?'

The connection was broken.

8

Ed, a small pock-marked American, dialled the new number for Norton as he stood inside a phone hood in Piccadilly Underground Station. Norton kept constantly on the move, never stayed at the same place for more than one night.

'Who is it?' Norton's abrasive voice demanded.

'It's Ed. I've been staring at wallpaper since we tracked Joel to London Airport.'

'*We?* Bill tracked him to the Swissair flight he boarded for Zurich . . .'

'Well, we're a team . . .'

'You're a schmuck who takes orders from me. And we have more schmucks in Zurich. Guess what happens.'

'No idea,' Ed replied cautiously.

'You always were short of ideas. The people waiting at Zurich Airport lost Joel. Can you believe it?'

'Yes, you just told me . . .'

'Don't get smart-ass with me. I had another team grouped by the entrance to Amberg's Zurcher Kredit Bank in Talstrasse. Guess again.'

'No . . . You really had Zurich sewn up.'

'Wrong again. I *thought* I had Zurich sewn up. So, Joel walks into the Zurcher. Never comes out again. The staff leave, the doors are locked. Still no Joel. You have one guess.'

'Beats me . . .'

'Seems most things do. Joel must have been let out the back entrance – which the schmucks who call themselves operatives didn't know about. You know Zurich. You know Joel. Get out there to Zurich pretty damned fast. Find him. Got it now?'

'Sure. And when I do find him?'

'Goddamnit!' There was a pause and Ed would not have been surprised to hear a snarl. 'I'll tell you what you do . . .' Norton's voice had gone deceptively soft. 'You break his fingers one by one. You break his arms, his legs, until he tells you where he's hidden what we must find fast. And then you snuff him out.'

'Got it . . .'

'I do hope so, Ed,' the soft voice went on. 'For your sake.'

'What about Tweed?' Ed ventured.

'He's still around. Not for long. He's a walking corpse. And when you get to London Airport don't forget to buy Swiss currency.'

'I had thought of that.'

'You amaze me . . .'

The phone went silent.

Tweed was stunned when he left the Padstow phone box and was joined by Butler. Nield waited on the far side of the road. Tweed had never known Dillon be frightened of anyone. So what group could have scared the tough American, made him start running?

'Where is Paula?' he asked.

'She went off with Newman and Cardon towards the harbour. They're collecting the car ready for their drive to Bodmin Moor.'

'I don't like it,' Tweed commented. 'Lord knows what they will run into on that blood-soaked moor . . .'

Newman had led Paula and Cardon to the harbour to show them the complex layout. Paula saw there was an inner harbour full of water, which puzzled her since the tide was out. She stopped to look at a large luxurious cabin cruiser with an array of radar equipment. *Mayflower III*.

'That's cost somebody a bomb,' she remarked.

A gnarled old fisherman sorting out his orange-coloured fishing net near by looked up. Paula smiled at him and he walked over to her.

'Admirin' the Squire's boat? It could sail to Europe in bad weather.'

'The Squire?' Paula queried.

'Yes. Squire Gaunt. Lives on the moor. Comes down 'ere quite often and takes her out for days.'

'To somewhere in Europe?' she asked casually.

'Ah! No one knows. Keeps a tight mouth on his doin's, does the Squire. You'll excuse me, lady. This won't earn a crust of bread. Enjoy yourselves.'

Newman led them back into the car park. He pointed to a single-storey building.

'Harbour Master's office. I enquired there about the tidal rise and fall. Seven point six metres, they told me.'

'That's fantastic.' She did a quick calculation. 'Over twenty feet.'

'I'd say you need to be skilled sailing round here,' Newman commented, leading them along a quay.

They reached a narrow footbridge linking one side of the harbour with the other. As they strolled over the white metal bridge Paula stopped, looked down. She realized they were walking over a large lock gate. To her left was the inner harbour full of water, to her right a drop like an abyss to a mudbank. Water trickled through the gate. Only then did she see an outer harbour, exposed to the sea.

It lay to her right and was a basin of mud. Small craft moored to the walls were canted over at a drunken angle. Beyond the closed lock gate on the seaward side a thin channel of water led out of sight towards the ocean. Newman pointed across to the outer jetty enclosing the waterless harbour.

'That's what they call the Pier. When the tide starts coming in you catch the ferry to Rock from some steps on the far side. Now you have to take that coastal path to the cove further out where there is still water.'

Paula saw a flight of steps leading up to a steep path which disappeared behind a new development of flats, directly overlooking the river.

'Wouldn't like to live there,' she remarked. 'No wonder they're all for sale. It must be as lonely as hell.'

'Padstow is pretty much hidden away,' Newman agreed. 'Which is why Tweed has chosen this place to give himself a little time to think. Turn round and you'll see the whole of the little town.'

Paula swung round. Beyond the harbour and the quays a densely packed series of old buildings was stepped up like a giant staircase. Newman checked his watch, looked at Cardon.

'Now I think it's time we headed for Bodmin Moor and bearded this Celia Yeo – if you can do that with a girl. Philip, you sit in the back and keep your eyes open . . .'

*　　*　　*

73

There was a little more traffic on the A30 as Newman swooped down a huge slope and then whipped up the other side. The sun shone down on the moor out of a clear blue sky but Paula found it no less hostile. A strong wind beat against the side of the Mercedes 280E as Newman made his suggestion. He perched dark glasses on the bridge of his strong nose, then rammed a black beret on his head.

'Paula, I think you ought to disguise yourself. We've no idea what may face us at Five Lanes. It's possible we won't want to be recognized.'

'A smart idea,' she agreed.

She took a pair of dark glasses from her shoulder-bag. After putting them on she took out a scarf, wrapped it over her raven-black hair and framed her face. Both actions completely altered her normal appearance. Newman grinned.

'You look like a madonna.'

'Just so long as I don't look like the contemporary Madonna. I suppose not – I'm wearing too many clothes.'

'While I'm waiting with the car,' Cardon called out, 'I'll sit hunched up like a midget.'

'You look like a midget normally,' Newman retorted, which was unfair. Cardon stood five feet ten tall and was very muscular.

Paula called out a warning to Newman. 'We're approaching the turn-off to Five Lanes. Celia lives in a cottage called Grey Tears on the outskirts.'

'Let's hope that peculiar name isn't prophetic,' Newman remarked.

Grey Tears was a small single-storey stone dwelling set in a hollow outside the village of Five Lanes. It was almost on the moor and Paul noticed that High Tor reared up as a clear-cut cone against the blue near by. Newman parked the car in another hollow off the road and followed Paula

74

who was lifting a brightly polished knocker carved in the form of a sheep's head and hammering it down.

'That polishing job doesn't look like Celia to me,' she whispered.

The ancient wooden door swung inward to reveal a stooped crone wearing an overall over her flowered dress. Her lively eyes studied the new arrivals.

'We have come by arrangement to see Celia Yeo,' Paula began. 'She told me this was her day off from her job at Tresillian Manor.'

'Not one of we locals will ever work there again. Not after what 'appened yesterday. 'Orrible.' She clamped a worn hand to her lips, the hand of a worker. 'Dearie me, we're not supposed to talk about that to anyone.' She brightened up. 'Still, I 'aven't told you anything, come to think. Celia's gettin' ready to go out.'

'Well, perhaps you wouldn't mind telling her a lady has arrived who'd like a word with her.'

'See what she says . . .'

The door was closed slowly, not rudely, in their faces. Newman, keeping his voice down, stared at Paula.

'Why didn't you mention your name? Just your first name? There are other Paulas in the world, so it wouldn't have positively identified us.'

'Intuition. I have a feeling Celia may be reluctant to talk to me.'

They waited several minutes. Newman paced backward and forward and Paula bit her lip to stop telling him to for God's sake keep still. Then the door opened slowly again. Newman studied Celia. She had an odd-shaped head, almost misshapen. Not a lot of intelligence and her eyes reminded him of a cow's. Celia pulled the door to without closing it and stood outside with them.

'What was it you were wanting, miss?' Sullenly.

'We agreed to meet today, Celia. There are a few questions I'd like to ask you.'

The servant girl's eyes opened wider. She stared at Paula like a startled fawn.

'It's you, miss. I never recognize you till you spoke.'

Newman glanced at Paula. Wearing ski pants tucked inside the tops of leather boots and a windcheater, she looked very different from when she had arrived at the Metropole. Celia's eyes swivelled to Newman, gazed at the eyes she couldn't see behind the glasses.

'Who is he?'

'My brother,' Paula said quickly. 'Now, about yesterday. That tea towel – the bright red one I saw you bringing back from so-called drying. It was a signal, wasn't it?'

'Information costs money.' Her manner was suddenly truculent. 'I've no boy friends. No man ever looks twice at *me*. I have to get something out of life, don't I? Like money.'

Newman took out his wallet. He extracted a twenty-pound note, saw her expression, added another one to it. He held the banknotes folded between his fingers.

'First, answer my sister's question, please.'

'You guessed right,' Celia said after a brief hesitation. 'It were a signal. I was paid a hundred pounds just for doin' that after the guests arrived for lunch. Then another . . .'

She stopped in mid-sentence. Celia was dressed for going somewhere. Above her shabby raincoat she wore a bright yellow woollen scarf. Her frizzy hair did nothing to improve her appearance.

'Who paid you to do that?' Paula asked quietly.

'I 'ad nothing to do with those awful murders at the manor!' she burst out. 'So don't you go thinkin' I did.'

'I'm sure you didn't. Who paid you, Celia?' Paula asked again.

'A man . . .' She hesitated. 'Never seen 'im before,' she went on quickly. 'And I've left a pot on cooker for Mrs Pethick. Talkin' about payment, before I says any more I want me money.'

Newman handed over the forty pounds to her. She grasped the notes eagerly, shoved them deep into a pocket of her raincoat. Glancing back inside the house, she retreated, opening the heavy door wider.

'Before I tells you more I must attend to pot. It will boil over and then Mrs Pethick will throw me out. I need these lodgings . . .'

The door closed in their faces with a heavy thud. Paula looked at Newman.

'Tweed was right. The massacre was diabolically well organized. And I think she does know who paid her.'

'So do I . . .'

They waited. There were no sounds from inside the small primitive dwelling. Five minutes later – Newman had timed her disappearance by his watch – he voiced the same worry that had entered Paula's head.

'I think she's run off. There's probably a back way – let's check.'

At the rear of the cottage the 'garden' was a miserable vegetable patch. There was also a back door. Closed. Paula took off her glasses, looked towards High Tor, pointed.

'There she is. That flash of yellow. She's headed out across the moor.'

'And,' Newman replied grimly, 'she was on the verge of saying her paymaster was going to pay her another hundred pounds today. God knows what she's walking into. We have to catch her up. Before it's too late . . .'

Newman began running along a track which led towards the base of High Tor. He could still see the flash of yellow scarf in the sunlight. He was surprised at the speed Celia Yeo could keep up as she ran. Behind him Paula followed. When they were out of sight of the cottage Newman grabbed his .38 Smith & Wesson out of the hip holster.

Paula lost sight of Newman as he kept up a marathon pace, descended into a deep gulley. She came to a fork in the path. Which way? She chose the left-hand path, kept on running, her eyes watching the ground which was uneven, making it easy to stumble.

She was nearing High Tor when she realized she had chosen the wrong fork. Newman was racing up the east side of the tor. No sign of Celia. 'Might as well go on, see where this leads to,' she said to herself.

She paused for breath and the ominous silence of the moor descended. A silence she could *hear*. Not even a hint of birdsong. The undulating moor stretched away on all sides, in a series of gorse-covered hillocks, cutting her off from any distant view. Paula shivered and then looked up. The view upwards was even less reassuring.

She was close to the west side of High Tor. Unlike the shallow slopes she had associated with it, at this point from the peak it fell sheer into an abyss. At the base she saw a tumble of huge boulders. She was about to resume running when she caught sight of movement at the summit.

'Oh, God, no!'

She spoke the words aloud. Even at that height Celia was easily identified by the yellow of her scarf. She stood perched on the edge of the fearsome drop. Why? Seeing her – and what happened next – took a matter of seconds.

Celia seemed to push out her stomach and Paula realized there was someone – out of sight – immediately behind her. One moment she was poised there. The next moment she plunged into space, her body cartwheeling in mid-air as she fell and fell and fell. Her scream of terror echoed over the moor as Paula watched in horror. The scream was cut off suddenly. It might have been her imagination, but Paula thought she heard the dreadful thud as her body hit the boulders. The silence of the moor returned like a threat.

Paula ran like mad, heading for the point where Celia had landed. Once, she glanced up briefly, but saw no one.

Whoever had shoved Celia into eternity had kept well hidden. Paula slowed down as she saw what remained of the servant girl.

She was sprawled, face up, over a boulder of massive size. Paula shuddered as she thought of the impact. She kept running until she stood by the boulder. Celia's spine was arched over the rock, her neck twisted at an angle. Blood and brains which had oozed from her skull were already drying in the sun. Without hope, Paula bent down, checked the carotid artery. Nothing.

She was about to close the eyes, staring sightless up at the summit where Celia had started her death plunge, when Paula decided not to touch anything. She wasn't sure at that moment why she took this decision.

She was breathing heavily when she glanced up again at the summit. Newman stood on the edge, staring down. She beckoned to him. Cupping her hands round her mouth, she called up to him.

'Come down, Bob.'

Her words echoed round the moor, recalling that terrible scream.

Newman's legs had never stopped moving since he started to climb High Tor. Boulders and smaller rocks were scattered across the surface above him. He couldn't see the summit and he had long since lost sight of Celia as he followed the twisting path.

As so often happens with climbing heights, he reached the summit suddenly. Flat-topped, it had more rocks – some perilously close to the edge, he saw in time. With the gun still in his hand, he walked slowly to the brink, gazed down. He sucked in his breath at what lay below.

He could see the bright yellow scarf *now*. A small flash of colour on the tiny crumpled form lying across a huge boulder. He was startled to see Paula looking up, her right hand raised as she beckoned, then cupped both hands against her mouth.

'Come down, Bob.'

Her cry was faint but he heard the words clearly. He waved to acknowledge he had heard her. Had Celia thrown herself over? Seemed most unlikely. Newman stood where he was for a moment, looked round. Just behind him was a patch of grey sand. Clearly imprinted in it was the outline of a large fresh footprint. Much larger than Celia's small feet. And, he recalled, she had worn flat-heeled walking shoes. The imprint showed small indentations inside the outline. Studded climbing boots. Celia had been brutally murdered – shoved over the precipice.

The view from the summit of High Tor was panoramic and he could see over the moor for miles in every direction. Newman took a small pair of field-glasses out of his coat pocket, removed his dark glasses, began to scan the moor. He must have missed the murderer by minutes.

Through the lenses he saw how rough the country below was. Deep gullies where a horseman could ride unseen. Stretches of dense gorse which could mask sunken paths. Avoiding the footprint, he walked to the four points of the compass to look down the slopes. No sign of anyone, but there were boulders the size of houses. He decided he must hurry back to join Paula.

9

'I really hated leaving her like that,' Paula said. 'And I wish I'd closed her eyes.'

'Don't worry about it,' Newman said. 'You did the right thing.'

They had hurried back to the car from High Tor and were now driving back towards Padstow along the A30. Cardon stirred in the back.

'I make the body count ten now,' he observed. 'Eight wiped out in the massacre at Tresillian Manor. The postman at Five Lanes. Now this Celia Yeo is number ten.'

'All right,' Paula said edgily. 'Now we know you can add up.' She returned to the previous subject, which was gnawing at her nerves. 'We can't just leave Celia lying out there. Supposing it rains tonight? I know that must sound silly . . .'

'Not at all.' For a moment Newman drove with one hand and put an arm round her, gave her an affectionate squeeze. 'I had two reasons for not touching her. They have an advanced fingerprint technique these days which can sometimes take a print off flesh. You'd have had to touch her eyes to close them. But my main reason is we should leave everything for the police without disturbing anything.'

'When they eventually find her,' she snapped.

'Oh, they're going to find her today. When we get back to Padstow my first job is to call Buchanan from that phone box outside the Old Custom House. I'll disguise my voice. That's another reason for handling it this way – if Buchanan knows we were there when it happened Lord knows how much more time would be wasted while he questions us. Maybe several days. And I suspect time is something Tweed is short of.'

'You've made me feel better,' she said. 'But why are we visiting Tresillian Manor?'

'Can't you guess? I think it might be significant to find out whether Gaunt and Jennie Blade are at the manor. Bearing in mind what happened at High Tor.'

* * *

81

Spiky hedges lined the section of the side road leading to the manor. At one point where the fake diversion had been set up Paula pointed to an open gate leading on to the moor.

'We told you last night about the ambush, Bob. I think they hid their vehicles inside that gateway.'

'Tweed took a chance crashing through,' Newman commented.

'What would you have done, then?' Paula challenged him.

'Exactly what Tweed did . . .'

No one was about as they entered the drive to the manor. As it came into view and they drove closer Paula noticed the curtains were closed over the dining-room windows. Again they left Cardon to mind the car while Newman and Paula climbed the steps to the terrace, walked into the large square porch. Paula pressed the bell and quickly the door was opened on a heavy chain. Cook peered out. Behind her loomed a shadowy figure.

'Well, what do you want?'

'It's me.' Paula swiftly took off her glasses, whipped off her scarf. 'We talked yesterday.'

'Lordy me, never recognized you.' She released the chain, opened the door wide. 'Cousin Jem is here with his shotgun. Come in and have a good strong cup of tea.'

'That's kind of you. This is my friend, Robert,' she introduced Newman. 'I was hoping Squire Gaunt was here.'

'Been gawn 'ours. Both of 'em. One took the Land-Rover, the other a horse. Not sure which took which. I was out back in kitchen. There's a proper upset 'ere. Two girls never came for work – don't expect as we'll ever see them again, considerin' what 'appened yesterday. I 'as to serve meals in the Great Hall for the master and Miss Blade. The police said they 'ad to seal the dinin' room . . .' It was all pouring out in a torrent as though Cook was glad to talk to

82

someone she could trust. 'But Wendy's turned up – worth the other two of 'em, she is. Police said they'd be comin' back later.'

'Thank you, Cook. I wonder if you'd mind not mentioning our visit? It's a surprise for the Squire. And I don't think we have time for that cup of tea, but thank you.'

'We've been told not to say a word to a soul. I hope Celia's keepin' her mouth shut. She'll be back tomorrow. Don't worry, dear. I won't say a word to anyone about your visit.' Her ruddy face creased into a grin. 'Me, I likes secrets . . .'

Newman said nothing until they were heading back along the drive. The reference to the police returning had alarmed him. He made his remark when they were driving back to the A30.

'That was interesting. Both Gaunt and his girl friend could have been on the moor near High Tor.'

'But not the one in the Land-Rover,' Paula pointed out. 'We'd have heard it. Pity we don't know which one was on horseback . . .'

Newman swung out on to the A30. He was just about to drop out of sight down a steep slope when he saw a car a long way off in his rear-view mirror. A patrol car turning off down the road to Tresillian Manor.

'That was a damn near run thing,' he commented, 'which Wellington remarked after Waterloo. Now, Padstow, here we come, so I can make my phone call to Buchanan. And Cook little knows that poor Celia is keeping her mouth shut,' he said grimly. 'For ever . . .'

Paula waited with Cardon in the Mercedes in the car park opposite the Old Custom House. It was the most impressive building in Padstow, a solid block of an edifice, three storeys high. From the roof projecting up was a large dormer with two closed wooden doors. Paula pointed to it.

'At one time, ages ago, they must have hauled cargo up there from the street.'

'It's ancient history,' Cardon agreed. 'I wonder how Bob is getting on . . .'

Inside the phone box Newman had dialled New Scotland Yard. When the operator answered he spoke quickly through a silk handkerchief stuffed into the mouthpiece.

'Get me Chief Inspector Buchanan and 'urry it up. I'm callin' about a new murder on Bodmin Moor. Don't interrupt me. Just get 'im. I'll call back in five minutes and expect to be put straight through or I'll ring off again.'

He replaced the receiver. It was the only way to ensure Buchanan had no time to do what Newman was certain he'd try to do – trace the call. He looked at his watch and dialled the number again in exactly five minutes.

'I called a few minutes back. Put me on to Buchanan. Now! Or forget it.'

'Chief Inspector Buchanan speaking,' the detached voice answered after a moment. 'Who is this?'

'No names, no sorrow. Just listen and take this down. There's a fresh corpse at the western base of 'Igh Tor outside Five Lanes. Servant girl who worked at the manor. Thrown down from the top. And you'll find a big footprint on summit. I s'pose you likes clues.'

'Thank you. Now if you'll just give me your name . . .'

'You're the detective . . .'

Newman put down the receiver. No time to trace that call – even with the sophisticated equipment they had now which could often pinpoint a location in three minutes. Stuffing the silk handkerchief into his pocket he stared across the car park at his Mercedes. Paula and Cardon had company. Drawn up alongside was a Land-Rover: the occupants Jennie Blade and Gaunt.

* * *

84

'A hearty welcome to Ye Olde Port of Padstow,' Gaunt had called out jovially as he stopped the vehicle.

'Hello again, Philip,' Jennie greeted Cardon with a fetching smile. 'We must have a drink together sometime. Oh, Paula, I'm ignoring you,' she went on saucily.

'But then I'm not a man,' Paula shot back.

As they climbed out she noted they were both dressed in sheepskins and jodhpurs. So who had been riding the horse? She got out of the car, stretched, glanced in at the back of the Land-Rover. It was crammed with cool bags, coils of rope and a ship's compass. She was wondering whether there was a pair of studded climbing boots hidden under the heap.

Both new arrivals wore gleaming leather riding boots. Gaunt leaned over into the back, grasped hold of a whip. He straightened up, saw Newman coming.

'I'll take the crop. And who have we here? The famous foreign correspondent. Read your book, Newman. Can even remember the title. *Kruger: The Computer Which Failed*. Rattling good stuff. And an international best-seller. Must have made you a mint.'

'It did reasonably well,' Newman said.

He didn't mention that he'd made a fortune out of the book – enough to make him financially independent for life. Jennie grabbed Gaunt by the arm.

'Don't forget the parking ticket. They check the cars here regularly.'

'What are you waiting for, then?' Gaunt asked in his most imperious manner. 'You know where the machine is.'

'I'll come with you,' Paula said.

She hadn't taken to Jennie up to that moment, but Gaunt's treatment of his girl friend aroused her ire. She asked the question as Jennie fed the machine with coins.

'Why do you put up with him?'

'Oh, he's utterly impossible,' Jennie replied. 'Then he turns on the charm and is utterly irresistible. You must

85

have found out,' she continued as they walked back to the Land-Rover, 'that men are not perfect, to say the least.'

'He's pretty damned imperfect, I'd have said.' Paula looked at Jennie as she went on: 'Incidentally, have you two been taking the fresh air this morning – roving round on the moor?'

Was it her imagination or had Jennie's expression frozen for several seconds? Were these two putting on a big act? Jennie lifted her hand to push back a wave of golden hair from her face and glanced sideways at Paula. She made a throwaway gesture with both hands.

'Floating round the back streets of Padstow. His lordship is trying to kid me he'll buy me a flat here. I don't believe a word of it. What's he on about now?'

'Come on!' Gaunt barked. 'I've just invited our friends to a drink. The Old Custom House. Best bar in town.'

'I can't wait,' Jennie said savagely as she attached the ticket. 'Now you can drink all day.'

'Makes me sound like a real boozer,' Gaunt roared. 'One of the great leg-pullers, my Jennie.'

'Your Jennie,' she said sweetly, 'would like to pull a leg off you. And this time you can buy the drinks for a change.'

'She's a joker, a real joker.' Gaunt slapped her on the rump. 'Likes to make out I'm mean and God knows what else. I like a woman I can cross swords with.'

'If I had a sword I'd stick it in you . . .'

Gaunt had gone, waving his arm in a dramatic gesture for everyone to follow him. Cardon joined him inside the entrance on the South Quay side. Newman paused until Paula and Jennie had entered. Beyond the doorway Jennie waited for Newman, looped her arm round his.

'Let's get to know each other better.' She gave him a wicked smile. 'I think you and I would make a wonderful team.'

86

'If you say so,' Newman replied neutrally.

She doesn't waste any bloody time, Paula thought, reverting to her original opinion of Jennie. Paula examined the bar with interest. An inviting place, it had an oak-beamed ceiling, a long bar to her right, and the main area in front of the counter had plenty of tables with comfortable chairs. To her left there was an elevated split-level section behind a wooden railing. Two steps led up to the entrance to the upper level.

The walls were cream-washed stone and the spacious room was illuminated by wall sconces with milky glass shades shaped like bells. A number of customers were already drinking and the atmosphere was warm and welcoming.

'What are you drinking, Paula?' boomed Gaunt. 'And you, Philip,' he said, turning to Cardon. 'And our distinguished foreign correspondent,' he went on booming. 'I suppose you'd like something too, Jennie,' he added as an afterthought. 'This is my round.'

'A gin and tonic,' Jennie snapped. 'If it won't break the bank.'

Her expression suggested she was amazed – that this was the first time Gaunt had stood a round of drinks. Newman frowned at the fair-haired girl behind the counter. He knew she was about to say, 'Your usual, sir?' He did not want Gaunt to know he was staying at the Old Custom House. Quick-witted, the girl kept silent.

'I'll have a Scotch. No water,' Newman decided.

'Make that a double!' Gaunt ordered.

'Very good, Squire . . .'

That was the first hint Paula had that Gaunt was a well-known customer. She had to admit he cut an impressive figure. Doffing his deerstalker, he turned, spun it across the rail where it landed in a green button-backed armchair in front of a blazing log fire.

He swept off the sheepskin coat he had been wearing

and underneath was clad in a check hacking jacket. Very much the country gentleman, Paula thought. He handed her the gin and tonic she had ordered and Paula passed it to Jennie. He frowned, shrugged his broad shoulders, collected another one, handed the second glass to Paula.

'Thanks,' Jennie whispered to Paula. 'He's in one of his roguish moods. I'd have been left to the last. Cheers!'

'Now, this way, ladies,' Gaunt commanded when they all had their drinks. He grinned impishly at Newman. 'You chaps come too – if you must. But I assure you I can cope with two exceedingly attractive females by myself . . .'

Before Newman could reply Gaunt had marched up the steps, bellowed out cheerful greetings to people at several tables, stood by the armchair where his hat rested and pointed.

'Jennie, you take that chair. Paula, my dear, come and sit by me . . .'

The instructions continued but Jennie outmanoeuvred him. Grabbing Newman by the arm again she led him to one of the green leather couches for two. Gaunt clapped his hand to his high forehead in mock frustration.

'Can't get people organized. I had it all planned so you'd enjoy yourselves. I'm pretty good at assessing who will get on with who.'

'The cool bags are still in the Land-Rover,' Jennie reminded him. 'Shouldn't they be put aboard? And I'm not carting them.'

Gaunt's expression changed. He looked furious. 'Haven't you realized it's like the Arctic out there? They'll be all right for the moment.'

'Aboard?' Paula chipped in. 'You mean aboard your super cabin cruiser, *Mayflower III*? Going somewhere in her?'

Gaunt looked ready to explode. 'Who told you that?' he barked at her. 'About my vessel?'

88

'One of the locals.' Paula gazed steadily back at him. 'I couldn't even identify him now.'

'That's the trouble with a place like Padstow.' Gaunt had lowered his voice. 'So parochial, so incestuous – they know all your business. I couldn't afford to own a vessel like that,' he went on more breezily. 'I just lease her for short trips. Down to Plymouth or up to Watchet.'

Paula nodded, not believing him. She stared at a shelf above the front of the bar. It was crammed with old suitcases, attaché cases and several ancient trunks. All pre-Second World War. She glanced towards the door.

Tweed was standing there. He gestured for her to join him.

'Excuse me,' said Paula. 'Back in a minute . . .'

'I'm going to phone Howard again,' Tweed told Paula as she joined him outside in the bitter cold. 'I'd like you to hear how he reacts. And there's someone else I want to try and contact afterwards . . . Later, tell me how you got on at Five Lanes. Too much happening at the moment . . .'

Squeezed up against Tweed inside the phone box Paula waited while he dialled the Surrey mansion. She had one ear close to the receiver. The operator put Tweed straight through to Howard. His first words were not reassuring.

'Tweed, I've never known a situation like this. I just don't know what the hell is going on.'

'Tell me why you say that,' Tweed suggested quietly.

'I've been trying to get through to the PM ever since we last talked. No dice. Always before he's taken my calls immediately – even in the middle of a Cabinet meeting.'

'Exactly what happens when you call Downing Street?'

'I get that bloody private secretary. Excuse my swearing, but this is crazy. The secretary always says he's busy, in the House or away. Anywhere except at

Downing Street. He said I should cease all operations until I do hear from the PM. Ruddy sauce!'

'And have you – ceased all operations with our people abroad?'

'I damned well have done nothing of the sort. Tweed, I feel like a prisoner, shut up here in this mansion.'

'You are a prisoner – but a safe one so long as you do not venture out,' Tweed warned.

'Have you any leads?' Howard asked desperately. 'You and your team are the only ones on the outside.'

'I might have. Just leave everything to me. Soon I'll be very active. Stay calm . . .'

Tweed stared at Paula after he'd put down the receiver. 'What do you think?'

'Scared. Who has the power to manipulate the PM to this extent?'

'I'm going to make that other call. To Jim Corcoran, our friendly Chief of Security at London Airport. That is, if he is still friendly. I have his private number at the airport.'

He dialled a number and it rang and rang. When it was answered the speaker sounded irritable.

'Corcoran. Who is it?'

'Hello, Jim, this is Tweed. I need your help.'

'That could be difficult. Under the circumstances.' He sounded cautious. 'What is it?'

'What circumstances? Come on, you owe me more than a few.'

'True, Tweed, true.' Corcoran sounded warmer. He paused. 'What can I do for you?'

'Three days ago someone called Joel Dyson – I'll spell out that name . . . may have flown to Zurich. I need confirmation if he did. You could find out by checking the passenger manifests. I can be—'

'Check the passenger manifests! Have you any idea just how long that would take?'

'I was going on to say I can be precise. Three days ago, I

said. Sometime in the evening. By Swissair.'

'That's better. I'm not promising anything. I have to use another phone . . .'

'I'll hold on,' Tweed repeated. 'I'm a long way off and it would be difficult to call you back.'

'Hang on, then . . .'

Paula, who had listened in, looked at Tweed, puzzled. He shook his head so she wouldn't speak. He put more coins in the slot. Corcoran was back within minutes.

'I've got it. A Joel Dyson travelled first class to Zurich three days ago. Aboard Flight SR 805. Departed Heathrow 2350 hours, ETA Zurich 0225 hours, local time.'

'I'm grateful. One more favour. This call was never made. You haven't heard from me – whoever puts pressure on you.'

'You know, I have a terrible memory sometimes. Tweed, are you OK?'

'No bones broken, not a scratch on me. I was born lucky.'

'Just make sure you *stay* lucky,' Corcoran said in a grave voice.

10

'I don't understand,' Paula said after they had left the phone box. 'Why these enquiries about Joel Dyson?'

'Let's walk about for a few minutes. There are things I should have told you.'

'Bob and Philip will start wondering what's happened to me . . .'

The words were hardly out of her mouth when Newman

came out of the bar, staring round. Paula waved to him, gave a thumbs-up signal. Newman grinned, relieved to find she was with Tweed. He waved to them and went back into the bar.

Paula led Tweed to the brink of the inner harbour. She pointed to the *Mayflower III*.

'Believe it or not, that belongs to Gaunt. When I mentioned the fact to him in the bar he looked annoyed that I knew, then said he only leased it. I didn't believe him.'

'Interesting. That's a millionaire's vessel.'

'Could Gaunt be a millionaire? He's always talking as though he's at the end of his tether financially.'

'Millionaires often do that. Talk as though they can't afford to spend a penny or a cent. Which gives me an idea I should have thought of. I'll call Monica down at the Surrey mansion and get her to run a check on our Squire Gaunt. Now, Joel Dyson . . .'

Paula led him across the car park as Tweed told her what Newman had reported over the phone from Baker Street Station after the explosion. He gave her all the details of Dyson's rushed visit to Park Crescent, about the film and the tape he had left.

As they walked over the white metal bridge above the barrier holding back the level of the water inside the inner harbour, she realized it wasn't really a lock gate. More like a mobile dam which could be opened and closed.

'I once met Joel Dyson,' she said when Tweed had completed his explanation. 'Bob took me into a pub in London for a drink and Dyson was there. A small man with pouched lips and shifty eyes which didn't miss a thing. He speaks with a well-educated English accent – Bob said afterwards he is British. But then he can suddenly mimic being an American and you'd really think he was a Yank.'

'Nasty piece of work, from what I hear,' Tweed remarked.

'Why did you think Dyson might have flown to Zurich?'

'Because Newman told me about Dyson taking compromising photos of Julius Amberg with another woman – Julius was married – and the fact that he persuaded Dyson Amberg could one day be a powerful friend. Dyson then handed the pics to Amberg. I imagine Dyson sacrificed a big fee from *Der Spiegel* or an American tabloid.'

'So?'

'Dyson made a big song-and-dance to Newman and Monica that he was handing them copies of the film and the tape, keeping the originals for himself. What safer place to hide those originals than in a Swiss bank vault? Specially, at Amberg's Zurcher Kredit Bank.'

'Why narrow his flight to Swissair? Other airlines fly to Zurich.'

'Dyson is an experienced globe-trotter. He'd feel safer aboard a Swiss plane. Especially travelling first class. And their security is first rate.'

'You're right. Incidentally, I was studying Jennie Blade. At the manor when we first saw her I guessed her age at twenty-eight. Now I think she's in her mid-thirties – and very experienced. She intrigues me, does our Jennie. Maybe I'd better get back to the bar or they'll think me rude.'

Paula pointed to the coastal path to the cove where the ferry left for Rock at low tide, then they turned back. Just in time to see Gaunt trooping out of the bar, leading the procession with Newman and Cardon behind him and Jennie bringing up the rear.

'Typical,' Paula said. 'Gaunt treats her like a lapdog. Thank Heaven she can bite back.'

Even as she spoke Jennie, taking long strides, caught up with Gaunt, chattered away to him and then pointed towards Tweed and Paula. She waved and Paula returned the wave as the party approached them.

'You know what you ought to do now, Tweed,' Gaunt boomed out across the car park. 'Take the ferry to Rock.

93

From over there you get the most terrific view of Padstow – and if you enjoy climbing that's the place for you.'

'We'll consider it,' Tweed replied.

'What do you think of the rowboat?' Jennie asked gleefully, pointing to the *Mayflower III*.

'Rowboat?' Gaunt roared. 'That's one of the most powerful cabin cruisers in the world.

'He's sensitive about his toy,' Jennie told Paula.

'All aboard that's comin' aboard,' Gaunt bellowed.

He shinned down a short ladder attached to the harbour wall, jumped on to the deck, spread both arms wide.

'Isn't she a beauty? I keep her in perfect trim.'

'Like hell you do!' Jennie burst out. She gestured to the brass rails gleaming in the sun like gold. 'I've spent days cleaning up this old tub.'

'I think the ferry is a good idea,' Tweed said.

Anything to avoid getting trapped aboard the *Mayflower*. Lord knew where Gaunt would decide to sail them to once the tide returned – maybe down the estuary and way out into the Atlantic.

'Have to take the coastal path to the cove, then,' Gaunt shouted. 'Now it's low tide. Have a good trip . . .'

As Tweed approached the steps leading to the path with Newman and Paula he saw Butler and Nield appear out of nowhere. They had accompanied Tweed from the Metropole and had then melted away when he was joined by Paula.

The group of six was climbing the steep path beyond the steps when Paula noticed Cardon was still holding the canvas bag looped over his shoulder from a strap. He had held it close to his side all the time they had spent in the bar at the Old Custom House.

'Philip, what goodies have you got inside that bag?' she asked, walking alongside him.

'This and that. Might come in handy. You never know. Remembering what's already happened in peaceful Cornwall. The body count is now ten. Eight at the manor. Celia Yeo. And last night Tweed told me about Buchanan's call to him yesterday. So the real postman was found with his throat cut near Five Lanes. A very hospitable part of the world, Cornwall.'

Ten, Paula thought grimly. *Ten* bodies now – including poor Celia Yeo lying at the foot of High Tor. She must tell Tweed about their 'outing' as soon as she had him on his own.

In the brilliant sunshine they went on climbing out of sight of the town at the bottom of a green slope to their left. The sea to their right was masked by a thick hedge lower down. Paula kept thinking of the estuary as 'the sea' – it didn't seem like a river.

A signpost bearing the legend TO FERRY pointed to a side path descending the side of the hill. The path led to a flight of wide stone steps dropping steeply to a small cove surrounded with abyss-like rock walls. Not realizing it was the clear air, Tweed estimated it was only a two-minute crossing to Rock.

At the bottom of the steps they found themselves inside a tiny cove, hemmed in from the world by sheer granite walls. Paula glanced back as she picked her way to the water's edge over a scatter of ankle-breaking rocks. Under the cliffs at their base were dark deep caves disappearing into black gloom inside their granite alcoves. She didn't like this cove. She found the atmosphere eerie and they were the only people waiting for the approaching ferry.

Tweed raised his binoculars to his eyes, focusing on a tall thin old house halfway up the slope on the Rock shore. There was a series of flashes originating from an upper window.

'Someone across there is sending a signal,' he said grimly.

'It's just the sunlight reflecting off some glass,' Newman said.

'It was a brief Morse code signal with a lamp,' Tweed insisted. 'A series of long and short flashes. I'll tell you why I know later . . .'

The ferry had arrived. Paula wondered how on earth they were expected to board it. The ferry was a small craft capable of carrying only a dozen passengers. The wheel-house was a box-like structure close to the prow – hardly more than twice the size of the phone box Tweed had used outside the Old Custom House. There were only two elderly passengers coming over from Rock.

The boat aimed for the shore prow-first. One of the two tough-looking crew jumped ashore, hauled a plank out of the ferry, balanced it to provide a dry crossing platform to the shore. As the two passengers walked separately and gingerly along the plank the man ashore held one of their hands.

Tweed was the first to board the small vessel. Ignoring the extended helping hand, he climbed the plank nimbly, stepped into the craft. Passengers sat in the open on wooden plank seats with their backs to the gunwales.

Paula sat next to Tweed and studied him. He looked very tense. She knew he hated boats and water and he hadn't taken one of his Dramamines which neutralized sea-sickness.

'Are you all right?' she asked as the boat backed off from the shore.

'We could be in great danger,' Tweed warned Cardon and Newman who sat close to him.

'It's being on the water,' Paula soothed him. 'But it's only a short crossing. A couple of minutes.'

'At least five or more,' Cardon told her.

He unfastened the capacious canvas bag looped over his shoulder. As they proceeded down the narrow channel between sandbank and cliffs he slipped a hand inside and kept it there. Paula wondered what he was holding. A gun?

The two crew were squeezed inside the wheel-house and the skipper stared straight ahead, gripping the wheel. They reached the end of the sandbank and shortly afterwards the skipper swung his wheel. Paula realized there was open water now between them and the beach near Rock. Where do we land? she wondered.

'Quite a view,' Newman commented a minute later.

They had moved out towards Rock into the middle of the estuary. To the north they could see the open Atlantic, beyond two capes. In the exact centre of the oceanic expanse out at sea a huge brutal rock reared up shaped like a volcano. In places the sea glittered dazzlingly where the sun reflected off it. A sharp cold breeze rippled the blue surface.

'Soon be there,' Paula reassured Tweed.

'I hope so,' said Newman, his tone serious.

He leaned back to see past the wheel-house. Coming in from the ocean a large powerboat had suddenly appeared. It was rocketing towards them, its prow high above the water, curving in a wide arc towards them, leaving behind a great white wake stretching out towards the Atlantic. Newman stiffened, slid his hand inside his windcheater, then withdrew his hand empty. He'd never hit a target moving at that speed. They all heard the skipper's words, a mix of anger and anxiety, as he spoke to his mate.

'Bloody maniac. Never seen that boat before . . .'

Paula stiffened, then felt Tweed's hand on her wrist, squeezing it. She looked at him. He sat perfectly still, all signs of tension gone. She thought she detected an expression of satisfaction, but that was impossible. Tweed glanced across at Butler opposite him as the huge projectile thundered down closer on them.

Butler nodded to Cardon. She glanced at Philip. He was nodding back to Butler, the briefest of motions. Newman was staring inside the wheel-house at the skipper. His

97

hands gripped the wheel tightly. He swung it a little to the left – to port – which appeared to be the wrong manoeuvre. It seemed he had panicked, was making a futile attempt to head back for the shore they had left from – taking them straight into the path of the advancing powerboat, which Paula now saw was huge.

Tweed took out Newman's binoculars, which he had put in his own pocket. Cardon, who had been switching his gaze swiftly from the wheel-house to the powerboat, reached across, took the glasses from Tweed's hands. Like Newman, he had summed up the skipper as a man who did not easily lose his nerve.

Cardon focused the field-glasses on the powerboat, which had changed course, was now slantwise to them. Through the lenses he saw the sole occupant, a figure at the wheel. A bizarre figure wearing a skin-diver's helmet and goggles. No chance of ever identifying who was guiding the powerboat. Cardon shoved the glasses back in Tweed's lap with his left hand. Both of his hands dived inside the canvas satchel as Paula watched him.

The roar of the powerboat was deafening as it swept even closer. Paula clenched her fingers tight inside her gloves. They were going to be smashed to matchwood, capsized into water which would be icy in February. Nield calmly inserted a cigarette between his lips without lighting it.

'The skipper knows what he's doing,' Tweed told Paula, his mouth close to her ear.

'You could have fooled me,' she snapped back.

In the brief time before a shattering collision took place the skipper suddenly swung his wheel hard over to starboard – away from the powerboat's course. It was tricky timing. The huge prow of the monster seemed to Paula to loom over them like something out of the film *Jaws*. One of her hands was now clamped round the plank beneath her, waiting for the frightful impact.

There were inches between the two vessels as the power-boat skimmed past them on the port side. And as it did so Cardon lobbed the grenade he had withdrawn the pin from. It landed in the well behind the hooded figure. Cardon immediately began counting silently, mouthing the numbers clearly as he stared at Paula.

'One . . .

'Two . . .

'Three . . .

'Four . . .'

On 'Four' something made Paula swivel round to the stern of the ferry which was now rocking madly under the impact of the wash from the powerboat. Tweed was already staring with the others in the same direction.

The explosion was thunderous. One second the power-boat was swinging round in a half-circle, ready to come back towards its target. The next second, as the detonation rang out, it split in two – the prow shooting skywards. Paula stared as a gigantic column of water like the geyser in Yellowstone Park soared up, taking with it dark objects which were debris from the shattered wreck.

The water boiled briefly where the powerboat had died, then it became calm with the surface ruffled only by ripples. Tweed was confident neither of the crew had seen Cardon lob the grenade, so intent had they been on steering the ferry clear of disaster at the last moment. The skipper handed over the wheel to his mate and his first words as he came out of the wheel-house confirmed Tweed's assumption.

'Sorry for that, folks. We've 'ad similar fools in the past. Think it's fun to scare the 'ell out of my passengers. But I don't know what that was. And then 'is petrol blew. That's 'appened before, too. Young idiots buys these expensive fast boats – must be fast for 'em – and then 'asn't the money to keep up any maintenance. I'm givin' you all your money back . . .'

'You most certainly are doing nothing of the sort,' Tweed said forcefully. 'Only one pound each for the return trip to Rock – and you saved our lives by your expert seamanship.'

'Anything that keeps you 'appy.' The skipper frowned. 'Never seen quite so big an explosion when petrol tank goes. Still, was a big boat. Now, we're landin' in a moment . . .'

11

They landed from the ferry by the same method – walking down the plank while the mate stood alongside, ready to give anyone who needed it a hand. Paula had no hesitation in reaching out for her hand to be grasped – her legs felt like jelly after their recent experience.

'See that stick with the flag stuck in beach?' called out the skipper. 'When you want to come back wait wherever it's been moved to. Tide will start to come in in the next hour . . .'

Tweed had walked down the plank, again ignoring the hand offered. His feet immediately sank into the sand which had recently been covered with water. Ploughing his way up to a ramp leading off the beach was like walking on a giant sponge. Paula and Newman caught him up as the other three men followed at a distance, spreading out, their eyes everywhere.

'You look smug,' Paula accused Tweed.

'Sorry. Just satisfied that my instinct was right.'

'What instinct?' Newman demanded.

'That the enemy had now tracked us to Padstow.'

'Anything to back that up?' Newman continued. 'You're always so keen on data to back up a theory.'

'Last night I couldn't sleep. As you know, my bedroom window gives a panoramic view of the estuary and this shore. You remember, Bob, you lent me your binoculars.'

'You saw something, then?'

'Oh, yes, I saw something.' Tweed chuckled, outwardly unaffected that they had just escaped sudden death. 'I saw something. Switching off the lights, I pulled back the curtains. Soon I saw a lamp flashing on and off over here. Red, then green, then red. Morse code – but the message was in cipher, if you understand me. A stream of meaningless letters, so I couldn't read what they were sending. But I could guess.'

'And you guessed what?' Paula pressed.

'That the sender in Rock was informing someone in Padstow that we have arrived at the Metropole. That was the first stage of targeting us.'

'And the second stage?'

'That was the lamp flashing which I noticed from the cove while we waited for the ferry. It was probably signalling to that powerboat cruising out at sea just beyond the estuary – that we'd be aboard the ferry.'

'Sounds thin,' Newman objected. 'It presupposes someone was watching the ferry for hours. We might never have come here.'

'So maybe they were watching the inner harbour through binoculars from Rock. These people leave nothing to chance. After we left perhaps a certain pennant was hoisted up the mast of that cabin cruiser, *Mayflower III*. Remember who suggested we take that ferry?'

'Gaunt!' Newman grated out the name. 'He waits until he's persuaded us to cross to Rock and then hoists the signal which tells whoever is waiting over here, wherever that might be.'

'Oh, last night through your binoculars I pinpointed the source where the lamp was flashing from.'

The shore of Rock was deserted and there was an atmosphere of being cut off from the world which Paula found disturbing. Tweed led the way off the soggy beach up a ramp which started out as concrete and then became wooden ribbed. He turned left, away from the few buildings which were Rock. They entered a desolate quarry which was apparently used as a car park during the season. Not a single vehicle was parked in the grim amphitheatre enclosed by granite walls.

'Don't point or look at it obviously,' Tweed warned. 'I saw the lamp flashing last night from that strange house perched on its own above us. From the first-floor window on the right.'

Paula glanced round as though taking in the view. Strange was hardly the word for the house. Weird, she said to herself. Isolated well up the steep slope it had a Victorian appearance but gave the impression half of it had been sliced off and taken away at some distant time.

Tall and thin, built of the universal grey stone, it had a single high gable with a turret below it at one corner. The building had a derelict appearance and Paula thought she'd never seen a more sinister house. Like something out of Hitchcock's *Psycho*.

'We'll climb up and have a look at it,' Tweed said as Butler joined them under the lee of the granite wall.

'What's the objective?' he asked tersely.

'That tall house above us. We're going to have a look at it.'

'I'll tell Cardon and Nield. We'll spread out. I'm going to approach it from the rear, which means a little alpine climbing . . .'

Tweed headed for a small flight of crude steps leading up out of the quarry to a winding footpath. He climbed so quickly that Paula and Newman had to move to keep up with him. Newman tucked his Smith & Wesson inside his belt.

'What an awful area,' Paula commented when they reached a point halfway to the house.

The steep slope had an air of desolation and to her right was a dense wood of miserable firs hanging over Rock. The trunks were stunted, bent at an angle away from the sea, their branches twisted into ugly shapes like deformed arms. Now they were higher up a wind, blowing in off the ocean, whipped against them. No wonder the trees were so crippled. Beyond the path was scrubby grass and the undergrowth had a shaggy look, hammered over the years by ferocious winds.

'What a glorious view,' Newman said, pausing.

The wind was stronger, the Atlantic had come into sight. As they stood together the wind was battering like a thousand flails. Surf-tipped rollers were roaring in to the outer reaches of the estuary, breaking against the base of the eastern cape, hurling skywards great clouds of white spray. More rollers advanced up the estuary.

Tweed averted his eyes, looked across the estuary to the far side. The grey mass of Padstow sheered up like a gigantic fortress wall. The Metropole was well elevated and he realized why he had seen so clearly the lamp flashing from the house above them.

'Let's keep moving,' he urged.

The narrow path snaked from side to side in its gully, which made walking difficult. They were near the tall thin house which, close up, had an even more derelict appearance. Three steps led up to the front door inside a porch. No garden, no fence – the property was open to the wilderness. Then Tweed saw how it could be reached by car. A wide sandy track led downhill, went round a bend, vanished.

Butler suddenly appeared from the rear of the building. He was pocketing the compact tool-kit which he always carried.

'No one here,' he reported. 'No furniture inside, no carpets on the floor.'

'I'd like to have seen inside the place,' Tweed remarked.

'Follow me, then. Someone left a window unfastened at the back,' he said with a straight face.

Cardon appeared on a hillock in a commanding position above the house, gave a brief wave. Nield stood up from behind a dense patch of undergrowth closer to the house.

'They've established outposts to watch over us,' Newman commented as they followed Butler round the back.

Paula stared at the sash window which was open at the bottom. There were jemmy marks close to the catch on the inside which was turned to the open position. She spoke to Butler in a tone of mock severity.

'Breaking and entering? That's against the law, Harry.'

'So someone got here before us,' Butler retorted, grinning.

Tweed crouched to step over the ledge and ease himself inside. Butler, followed by Paula, was by his side in seconds. He put a finger to his lips, whispered.

'It *appears* to be unoccupied,' he warned.

Paula, with Newman by *her* side, studied the ancient floorboards, the window ledges and the mantelpieces with a housewife's practised eye. Undisturbed dust everywhere. She paused before entering the narrow hall while Tweed, followed by Newman and Butler, ran lightly up the bare wooden staircase.

In the hall the floorboards were perfectly clean, dust-free. Paula frowned as she mounted the staircase slowly. Every tread was equally clean and a familiar smell was assailing her nostrils. Pleasant, distinctive.

Tweed had entered the front bedroom at the left-hand side of the house. He took out of his coat pocket Newman's binoculars, stood in front of the clear glass of the window, focused them. His own windows in the suite at the Metropole seemed amazingly close.

'This,' he said, 'is where someone used a lamp to send a signal last night.'

'And have you noticed the floorboards?' Paula enquired from behind him.

'No, I . . .'

'Men are so unobservant,' she teased him. 'The room we came in by at the back had a musty smell and was covered in dust. Look at these floorboards – they've been scrubbed, probably during the past twenty-four hours. Was the door closed here?'

'Yes, it was.'

'Which is why the smell of the cleaner used – liquid Flash – is so strong in here. But you can smell it on the stairs and in the hall.'

'What's the idea of cleaning up the place so well?' asked Butler.

'Maybe to eliminate footprints,' Newman said, looking at Paula. 'Footprints with studded soles. Climbing boots.'

'If you say so,' replied Butler, mystified. He turned to Tweed. 'Want some evidence that you're still a good detective? Follow me.'

'In a minute.' Tweed was stooping over a corner of the window ledge. 'I'm doing a Sherlock Holmes. There's an intact roll of cigar ash here, a slight burn where the cigar rested while the smoker operated the lamp. Paula, give me one of those sample bags.'

Paula unzipped a section inside her shoulder-bag where she always carried several self-sealing polythene wallets. Tweed had taken out a penknife, used his other hand to take the wallet from Paula, used the knife to coax the ash off the edge and inside the bag, which he sealed and handed to her.

'There are experts who can identify ash. Now who have we seen recently who smokes cigars?'

'You want to see my evidence?' Butler broke in. 'Then follow me . . .'

105

He led them down the stairs, returned into the back room where they had entered, climbed out of the window and walked to a lean-to shed next to the rear wall of the house. A large new padlock hung loose and dangling from an iron ring.

'I suppose you found it just like that?' Paula asked.

Butler grinned again, took a ring of skeleton keys from his pocket, jangled them. He edged the heavy wooden door open with his foot, stood back and gestured for them to enter, handing a small torch to Tweed. Paula wondered what else Butler might have in the capacious pockets of his made-to-order coat.

'Satisfying to find you were right,' Tweed commented as Paula joined him.

He was aiming his torch beam at a large brass signalling lamp perched on top of a heavy wooden box. Bending down, he examined the lamp without touching it, stood upright again.

'It has a red filter which can be slid across the lamp. And a green one. Hence the signal flashes I saw from my suite.'

'So all we need to find out is who owns this dump,' Paula replied.

Tweed and Paula had had enough of the gully path. With Newman, they started down the sandy track which showed the ruts of a vehicle's recent passage.

'A four-wheel drive job, like a Land-Rover,' Newman said.

Before leaving the house with no name, Butler had donned surgical gloves, had fastened the padlock on the lean-to shed, then closed the entry window. He vanished from the trio's view along with Cardon and Nield.

'They're enjoying practising the fieldcraft they've been trained in,' Tweed commented.

He knew the three men were close by but didn't hear one

sound of their progress down the bleak heathland. He pointed to the channel of water which remained. Waves were tossing up and down.

'One thing I'm not going to enjoy is the ferry trip back to Padstow.'

'It may have calmed down by the time we return,' Paula suggested, not believing a word she said. 'And in summer-time this place must be where the boaty types come.'

In the narrow channel of water a number of craft moored to buoys were wrapped in blue plastic to protect them against the elements. More were beached on the vast sandbank stretching clear across the estuary. Several boats were slowly circling the area where the powerboat had exploded. Paula still found the disappearance of the river extraordinary.

'It's as though there's a huge plug further out which they pull out and water just vanishes down it,' she remarked. She looked at Tweed. 'Was our journey here of any use?'

'Definitely. It's providing me with more pieces of the vague jigsaw I'm building up in my mind.'

The track fell more steeply and they saw the road leading to the quarry car park over to their right. Outside a bungalow a smartly dressed woman was shaking a blanket. Tweed stopped.

'Excuse me, have you any idea who owns that house at the top of this track?'

'A man called Gaunt. He lives somewhere way out on Bodmin Moor.'

'I might be interested in the property,' Tweed lied amiably. 'It appeared to be empty. I suppose he never comes near the place, this Mr Gaunt?'

'Someone does. Just occasionally. They did only last night. I had the TV on but I heard some kind of vehicle driving up there after dark.'

'Thank you for the information.'

'Wouldn't consider buying that old ruin,' the woman

warned. 'We bought this place in summer. Never do that. We did – and we'd sell up and get out tomorrow if we could. It's spooky. Rock is only an old hotel further along the road and a few terrace houses. Nowhere to buy everyday necessities. I have to cross in that beastly old ferry to Padstow. Keep away from here.'

'You said spooky,' Paula reminded her.

'Every now and then lights appear in that house up there you've just been to see. I don't mean the room lights. More like someone prowling round with a torch. Gives me the creeps.'

'Well, thank you for your advice. It has not fallen on deaf ears,' Tweed assured her.

He waited until they had reached the bottom of the track. Paula looked along the lonely road which led to the rest of Rock.

'A waste of time,' Tweed said. 'She described it perfectly. Bob and I explored it when we were once at the Metropole for a day and a night. What are you looking for?'

Paula was delving deep inside her bag. With a triumphal air she brought out a small press-pack of white tablets.

'Look. Dramamine! And just down the road there's a shop which sells soft drinks, according to that madly flapping flag . . .'

They sat inside a glassed-in enclosure overlooking the estuary. Tweed swallowed a tablet washed down with orange juice and Paula checked her watch, timing thirty minutes. The water was churning now like a cauldron. Since the woman who had served them was cleaning the counter close behind they sat in silence for some time. Then Newman heard the engine of the approaching machine.

'Let me have my glasses,' he told Tweed.

The grey chopper, flying low, came in from the direction of the Atlantic. In the lenses Newman saw two men at the controls – both with their heads covered in helmets and wearing goggles. Very similar to the figure which had been behind the wheel of the powerboat. The woman behind the counter disappeared through a doorway, slammed it shut. They were alone, so could talk.

'You'll say I'm paranoid,' Newman commented, 'but I think that chopper is searching for us.'

'Which would be alarming,' Tweed said quietly. 'Because it would mean someone has an excellent communication system. The crew of the chopper are either checking to see the wreckage of the ferry . . .'

'Or,' Paula interjected, stiffening to quell a shiver, 'they know we survived and, as Bob suggested, they are searching for us.'

'Looks like the latter,' Newman agreed. 'The ferry is just going back to Padstow, it's in mid-river.'

They sat in silence again as the chopper swept low over the outgoing ferry, circled it, then flew inland over Rock. Paula found herself sitting very still, although it would be impossible for the helicopter crew to see inside the café.

'The copilot was also using binoculars,' Newman told them.

He had hardly spoken when they heard the machine above their heads, a reverberating roar. Newman stood up, peered out of the window to his right. They could now hear it hovering. Newman sat down again and a minute later the machine reappeared, flying over the estuary, heading out towards the Atlantic, its engine sound fading. Paula let out her breath.

'It checked that old house we explored,' Newman reported.

'Then it *was* looking for us,' Paula said grimly. 'How the hell do they know so much? I feel like a bug under a microscope, our every move foreseen, monitored. It's uncanny, nerve-wracking.'

'They've also committed a major tactical error by

coming out into the open,' Tweed responded. 'I can see the ferry starting to come back so we'd better make our way to the landing point on the beach – wherever that may be now. The tide is starting to come in.'

They had barely stepped down on to the road when Butler, Cardon and Nield materialized from the rough ground behind the café. They were brushing themselves down when they reached the road.

'Did that chopper see you?' rapped out Newman.

'Silly question,' Butler rapped back, then changed his tune. 'Sorry. No, it didn't. We were flat on our backs under dead bracken and undergrowth. We saw it, heard it coming, but they didn't spot us.'

'Messy up there,' the normally immaculate Nield grumbled. He was wearing a smart business suit. 'Incidentally the joker next to the pilot had field-glasses. He particularly scanned the old house up the slope you went into.'

'We know that already,' Tweed told him.

There was a bounce in his walk as he headed for the gap in the hedge and made his way down the ramp on to the beach. The stick with the flag showing the landing point was closer to the ramp than when they had disembarked. Was that a day ago? Paula wondered. It seemed so. And why was Tweed so pleased with their diabolical trip to Rock?

12

'How dramatic!' Paula exclaimed.

As the ferry pitched and tossed and dusk began to fall the sea was surging in like a small tidal wave. The Atlantic was inundating the sandbanks which were shrinking in size even as she watched them. She was surprised – relieved – when the ferry arrived close to the Padstow shore and moved on past the bleak cove where they had boarded it.

'We're going to land at the harbour now the water has risen high enough,' Newman told her.

The narrow channel they had left behind on the outward trip was far wider. They arrived at the foot of a flight of steps leading up the outer side of the pier. Tweed stepped ashore on the bottom stone step, where he stayed to help Paula.

'Careful,' he warned. 'The first flight only has a rail on the inner side against the wall . . .'

She clung to it as she followed him up. Glancing to her left, she looked away quickly. With no rail on that side there was a sheer drop into the river. Higher up there was a rail on both sides which made her feel more comfortable. She stepped on to the pier, took two paces forward, stopped, stared.

'They've opened the lock gate to the inner harbour.'

'That's because the river level is now the same as the water inside the harbour,' Tweed explained as he cleaned his glasses with his handkerchief.

'But it's gone!'

'What has?' Tweed asked, putting on his glasses again.

'The *Mayflower*.'

'She sailed soon as the gate was opened,' a seaman leaning against the wall told Paula. 'Don't expect we'll see her awhile.'

'Why do you say that?' she asked.

'Amount of provisions they took aboard her. So many cool bags. Fridge an' freezer must be stacked to gunwales.'

'Who was aboard when she moved out?'

'Squire Gaunt was at the helm . . .'

'Anyone else aboard?'

'Couldn't say . . .'

The seaman moved away as though he felt he'd already

111

said too much. The others had joined Tweed and Paula. Because the gate was open and no bridge spanned the gap they had to walk round all the quays encircling the harbour.

'That does surprise me,' Paula said. 'Gaunt leaving at such short notice and never mentioning it in the bar.'

'Doesn't surprise me at all,' Tweed replied. 'But I have no doubt we shall see Squire Gaunt again.'

Tweed said he wanted to make a strictly private call to Howard and went into the phone box. Paula walked into the bar with Newman and Cardon. Butler and Nield remained outside, taking up positions where they had the box under close observation.

Tweed dialled the Surrey mansion first. Howard came to the phone quickly.

'Have you made any progress? Any solid news?' he pressed anxiously.

'I can tell you that where we are – out in the wilds – we're being watched night and day. And I expect you are too . . .'

'*Who* is behind all this?' Howard asked vehemently. 'I tried the PM again. No luck. He's abandoned us.'

'What about Crombie? Are you still in touch with him?'

'Yes, bless him. He phones me with regular reports. There's still a mountain of rubble to remove. No sign of that safe you mentioned yet.'

'They've overlooked Crombie,' Tweed said with grim satisfaction. 'Try and throw an iron cordon round someone and a loophole is always left. Now, listen to me, Howard. I want you to phone Crombie, tell him when he uncovers that safe to let you know at once and keep it hidden. The moment you hear he has found it send that armoured car disguised as a security truck to collect it and take it down to you. Understood?'

'I'll call him as soon as we've finished talking. We are all feeling marooned here, Tweed. I tried to reach the PM three times today. Blocked off every time. He's abandoned us,' he repeated.

'Face up to it, Howard. He's done just that . . .'

Tweed's next call was to Jim Corcoran at London Airport. Again he had to coax the Chief Security Officer to do what he asked him. Eventually, he agreed. Tweed thanked him, told him in due course he'd realize he had done the right thing.

His third call, the briefest, was to Newquay Airport. He made certain arrangements on the basis of the data the girl receptionist gave him, then mopped his forehead, walked out of the box and into the bar. But he felt better. Very shortly they would be on the move.

Inside the bar, which was quiet, Tweed joined Newman, Paula and Cardon who were occupying the secluded corner on the upper level in front of the fire. When Newman asked him what he was drinking he said mineral water.

'Did you phone Howard?' Paula asked. 'I thought so. What sort of a mood is he in?'

'Feeling trapped. He's had no contact with the PM. He can't get through to him.'

'That's how I feel,' Paula said. 'Trapped.'

'Cheer up. And have your bag packed for an early departure tomorrow morning. You'll have to ditch the Browning before we leave. I must warn the others. No weapons.'

'I'll dump mine in the sea. But where are we going? Is anywhere safe any more?'

'One place is. Which is where we're going. It's time to smoke out whoever is after us. I'm leading them into a trap. Thank you,' he said as Newman put a glass before him. He drank greedily. All the recent activity had dehydrated him.

113

'We've been trying to work out who is behind all these attempts to wipe us out,' Newman began. 'The answer could be summed up in the name of one individual: Gaunt.'

'An assumption so far,' Tweed pointed out. 'Evidence?'

'Gaunt leased his manor for varying periods to Julius Amberg. Whoever unleashed that massacre knew the banker would be there. Who could have told them? Gaunt. We were nearly killed by that powerboat. Who knew we were taking that particular ferry to Rock? Gaunt. Who was absent from Tresillian Manor when Celia Yeo was hurled from the summit of High Tor? Gaunt – and Jennie.'

'Possibly.' Tweed drank more water. 'Are you suggesting he has the organization to arrange for that massive car bomb to be parked outside our building? He doesn't even know where SIS headquarters are – were.'

'That is a difficult one to answer,' Newman admitted. 'Incidentally, Butler and Nield followed you in here at separate intervals. Butler is sitting in a corner behind you where he can survey the whole bar. Nield is chatting up the barmaid . . .'

Leaning against the counter, Pete Nield was joking with the fair-haired girl. He asked her a question when he felt he had established an easy relationship.

'I hear that Squire Gaunt is off on his travels again in that floating palace of his. He could cross the Atlantic in that huge cabin cruiser.'

'Oh, I don't think he's done that. He flies to America. You see, he likes to go off in her by himself to Europe.'

'A trip to jolly old Paris?' Nield suggested.

'Maybe. But he's been cruising up the Rhine. I heard that when he was in here one night and he'd had rather a lot to drink.'

'A nice chap, though,' Nield probed.

114

The girl paused polishing a glass. 'That depends on his mood, between you and me. Sometimes he is and then again he can cut you dead.'

'I hear he lives in a lovely manor on Bodmin Moor. Must be peaceful out there.'

'Too lonely for me. I'd get the creeps . . .'

The very courteous and able manager of the Metropole met them in the hall as they returned. He spoke in a low voice to Tweed.

'I thought you might like to know two Americans have been enquiring about you, sir. Wanted to know how long you were staying. I said I'd no idea.'

'Are they staying here?' Newman asked quickly.

'No. But they're in the bar at the moment.'

'Think I'll pop in and take a look at them . . .'

Newman headed for the bar as the others waited for the lift. Two tall heavily built men were standing by the bar counter with drinks in front of them. Both wore loud check sports jackets and denims and had American style trench coats folded over their arms. Newman ordered a Scotch. The larger of the two men was standing next to Newman, had dense black hair, thick brows which almost met across the bridge of his broken nose.

'Your Scotch, Mr Newman,' said the barman, recognizing his customer. 'Thank you, sir,' he said as Newman paid.

'Newman? Robert Newman, the nosy foreign correspondent?' the big American enquired in a bullying tone.

'I'm retired,' Newman replied, refusing to be provoked. 'So no longer nosy, as you put it.'

'Old habits die hard,' the American said aggressively.

His elbow toppled his own drink. Liquid spilt over the counter and the barman hastily mopped up.

'Buddy,' the American went on, 'that was my whisky

you just knocked over. So what are you going to do about it?'

'Buy you another,' Newman continued amiably. 'Give this gentleman a fresh drink, please,' he said to the barman and put more money on the counter.

'They said you were something else again at one time,' the American sneered. 'Good thing you retired – seems like you lost your guts.'

'Your friend has just collapsed.'

As the American jerked his head to his left where his companion stood looking puzzled, Newman grabbed his drink, walked out of the bar and up the stairs. The enemy was moving in at very close quarters.

'I'm calling a council of war, Paula. In my suite. If you have just stepped out of the bath, five minutes from now will do.'

Paula put down the phone in her room on the second floor. Tweed had sounded imperative, calm, determined. She had not just stepped out of the bath. She went back to the window, her lights off, watching in the dark the final incoming surge of the tide. In the moonlight the edges of the remaining sandbanks looked like filleted fish. Even as she watched they were submerged. The water now stretched from shore to shore and Porthilly Cove, which had been a huge sand beach, was filled with water.

It was frightening, she thought, as she descended the stairs – the unstoppable force of the sea. She made a similar remark to Tweed as she entered his suite while Newman closed and locked the door.

'And that's what we're up against,' Tweed said, 'an unstoppable force. Power in its most extreme and ruthless form.'

His audience remained silent. They were all there – Cardon, Butler and Nield, seated while Tweed stood in the

116

middle of the large room, the curtains closed behind him. He looked at Newman.

'Tell them about your encounter in the bar downstairs.'

They listened while Newman related tersely what had happened in the bar. He was inclined to play down the confrontation. Paula was surprised he had kept his temper and said so.

'His reaction was perfect,' Tweed told her. 'They were trying to start a fight, probably challenge him to come outside with them. Supposing they had knives?'

'Why would two Americans pick on Bob?' she persisted.

'The enemy is closing in on us. It's the moment I have been waiting for. We are going to break out. My crazy idea as to who was behind all this murder and destruction could be right.'

'And the enemy's identity?' Paula pressed on.

'Work it out for yourself. You have the same data I have. List what has happened. From the beginning.'

'There was that horrible massacre at Tresillian Manor – when I was nearly a victim,' she reminded him.

'Chief target – besides ourselves?' Tweed rapped out.

'Julius Amberg, Swiss banker from Zurich.'

'Now, go back a few days to my office in Park Crescent. When Bob and Monica had an unexpected visitor.'

'Well, he left them a film and a tape recording. Copies, he said. He took the originals with him.'

'You've missed something,' Tweed snapped. 'Newman gave us a detailed description of that visit by Joel Dyson. What was inside his case?'

'Oh, I remember. Several lots of American clothes . . .'

'Which strongly suggests he had just flown in from the States. Dyson spent most of his time operating over there although he's British. Found there were much more profitable pickings on the other side of the Atlantic. Go on. Next event.'

'That massive bomb parked outside Park Crescent which destroyed the whole building.'

'Just another bomb?' Tweed enquired.

'No. You told us Commander Crombie had said they'd found relics of the trigger device – that it wasn't the IRA. A more sophisticated device than he'd ever seen.'

'And,' Tweed reminded her, 'how many people know where SIS headquarters were located? What sort of profession? What sort of organization could arrange for the massacre at the manor which almost coincided with the bomb outrage in London?'

'A pretty big one.'

'An international one,' Tweed added.

'I still don't think the massacre and the London bomb are linked,' Paula said obstinately. 'There wasn't time.'

'What happened next?' Tweed continued.

'Celia Yeo, the servant girl I feel sure had signalled the arrival of Amberg's guests, was thrown off High Tor.'

'And then?'

'We arrived here. Gaunt turns up with Jennie Blade. While we're crossing to Rock – at Gaunt's suggestion – that powerboat tries to run us down. We check the house with no name and find the signalling lamp used to send coded messages you spotted from the cove. Then we find out the house with no name belongs to Gaunt. Finally, that helicopter appears to search for us.'

'Not finally yet,' Tweed observed. 'What happens when we get back to the hotel this evening?'

'Oh, those two Americans who've been asking for you try to incite Bob into a free-for-all.'

'Now go back a year or two. To Zurich.'

'I'm not with you . . .'

'Tweed,' Newman intervened, 'is referring to when I persuaded Joel Dyson to hand to Julius Amberg the compromising photos he'd taken of the banker – instead of selling them to the press.'

'I'd forgotten that for the moment,' Paula admitted. 'I do remember that Jim Corcoran at London Airport found out that Dyson flew to Zurich after he'd left the film and tape copies at Park Crescent. And he'd just been in America.'

'It begins to link up, doesn't it? Tweed summarized.

'Does it?' Paula frowned. 'I must be thick.'

'Not at all,' Tweed reassured her. 'It's simply that if I'm right the truth is so awesome, *of such magnitude*, it is difficult to grasp. We are in real peril here – so we are leaving tonight. Before dinner. We tell reception we've been called away on urgent business. Philip, Pete, Harry – pay your bills separately, including your rooms for tonight.'

'I'd better go pack. Won't take me long,' Paula said. 'But where are we going?'

'There's a small pub hotel at a place called St Mawgan out in the country near Newquay, further west. Newman and I stayed there overnight once when we were down here. I'll phone them from that infernal phone box. I'm beginning to feel I live inside that box.'

Newman jumped up, a newspaper tucked under his arm. 'I am off to pack my things and check out of the Old Custom House. I'll wait for you by the phone box.' He waved the paper. 'Still nothing in the press about the massacre on Bodmin Moor, which I find sinister. News is all about the States and President March not yet agreeing to back the PM over the crises in Europe and the Middle East. Without American co-operation we can't take strong measures, can't take any measures . . .'

'Hurry, everyone,' Tweed urged. 'We want to get out of Padstow alive.'

119

13

President Bradford March sat sprawled in his swivel chair behind the antique desk in the Oval Office. His stance was, to say the least, inelegant. The chair was pushed well back from the desk and his stockinged feet rested on the surface, crossed at the ankles. He was looking out of the tall Georgian windows at Washington's Pennsylvania Avenue. The view was fuzzy due to the grey drizzle still falling. He turned back to face the only other occupant of the room, a woman.

'Shit, Sara, I'm goin' to have to kick ass to get those jerks in Europe movin' – Norton hasn't reported for two days.'

'He does have a difficult assignment, Brad,' she reminded him.

'Which is why I appointed him head of Unit One. Time he wrapped up the whole job in my book.'

Unlike most presidents – who were often six feet tall or over – Bradford March was a stocky man of medium height with a lot of black hair and thick black brows. Fifty-five years old, his aggressive chin was running to jowls, black as his hair. He shaved twice a day, when he felt like it. Above his short thick nose his ice-cold eyes moved restlessly.

He wore crumpled blue denims and a creased check shirt, open two buttons below the neck, exposing the dense hair on his barrel chest. He belched loudly, slapped his hard rounded stomach.

'That's good beer. Fix me another. Then call Norton. I'm going to kick ass.'

'Is that wise, Brad?'

Sara, March's personal assistant, the only person privy to his secrets, was a hard-faced woman of forty with long dark hair, a prominent nose and a wide thin-lipped mouth. She had been with him since the early days of his career – all the way from when he had sneaked in to become senator of a Southern state by a handful of votes. A handful delivered by a power broker after Sara had handed over to him one hundred thousand dollars in used currency.

Tall and slim, always dressed in black, she was the only person – apart from his wife – permitted to call him Brad. March's wife, Betty, had drifted away from him although she still lived in the White House. Sara was the one who kept a watchful eye on her.

'Time for Betty to have a lollipop, Brad,' she would say.

'Jesus Christ! Do I have to? Again.'

'We don't want her walking, do we? A sable stole will settle her for a while.'

'OK. If you can find the cash.'

'Brad, I can always find the cash. I just twist someone's arm, somebody who owes us a favour. Plenty of them around . . .'

March sat facing the north wall occupied by an elaborate marble fireplace. Sara came back with a bottle of beer from the fridge, uncapped. Knowing what he wanted she wiped the top and neck of the bottle with a crisp white napkin. March took the bottle from her, upended it and drank.

'That's better,' he said, placing the bottle on the desk and wiping his mouth with the back of his hairy hand. 'You know what? Some faggot on the staff here – I posted him to the Aleutians – wanted me to see a speech therapist.' He opened his mouth and bellowed with laughter. 'A speech therapist! You know how I barnstormed my way into the White House? Because I talk like the folks down in the street. It's called empathy – whatever the hell that is. Get Norton on the private phone.'

Sara was used to these sudden switches in subject. She

stood with her arms folded, frowning at him. He looked up, spat out the question.

'You got something on your mind?'

'Brad, what is it Norton's looking for? Besides certain people?'

'Certain people being Cord Dillon and Barton Ives. Is my ass covered with Dillon runnin' out? Deputy Director of the CIA. Questions will be asked when the press wakes up, finds he's gone missing.'

'Your ass is covered. I've spread the rumour he's been ill, has gone abroad for a long vacation.'

'Long vacation?' March grinned to himself. When Norton found Dillon his vacation would be permanent. No point in letting Sara know how rough he could play. 'What's getting to you?' he snapped.

'This Unit One. I think Senator Wingfield has caught a whiff of its existence.'

'That aristocratic old creep? Just because he happens to be Chairman of the Senate Foreign Relations Committee. Maybe his ancestors were one of the Pilgrim Fathers. He looks like one.'

'He carries a lot of clout, Brad. And Unit One is strictly an illegal organization. Trouble is, some members of Unit One are still here, not in Europe.'

'You're smart.' March grinned again. 'Real smart. So we may send the rest to Europe to Norton as reinforcements. Nothing left here then for old Wingfield to get a whiff of. I'll think about that.'

'That would be best. As you say, nothing left for him to get a hold on.'

'It's like tapes and documents,' March went on, folding his hands behind his thick neck. 'Never record anything on tape – reading about Nixon taught me that. Nothing goes down on paper. That way, no evidence. We go on keeping everything verbal.' He winked.

'Best way,' Sara agreed. 'It's worked like a dream so far.

Is the British Prime Minister co-operating?'

'The Brits do what I tell them to do. Norton is operating in London like he was in Louisiana. No interference. Their Prime Minister has no balls. He has two volcanoes smoking on his stoop – Russia and the Mid-East. He daren't move without my backing, which I'm withholding.'

'Sitting in his shoes I wouldn't either,' Sara commented. 'How do you handle the guy?'

'Oh, I borrow a tactic our wily Secretary of State uses if he wants to stall . . .' March was referring to the American equivalent of the British Foreign Secretary. 'I tell him I have the problem under consideration.'

'This FBI agent, Barton Ives, who has also disappeared – how does he fit into the picture? Operated in the South, didn't he – when you were a senator?'

'He could get in my way.' A crafty expression appeared on March's face, his eyes half-closed like a hyena poised to strike. 'You can leave him to Norton.'

'Pardon me for treading in the wrong territory.' Sara smiled. She knew she'd made a mistake. 'Brad, I don't tread on sensitive ground – could be a minefield.'

'Sara Maranoff,' the President said slowly, 'you could get blown to small pieces doin' just that – walking into a minefield.' His expression changed, became amiable as a family man. 'That was a clever idea of yours – suggesting I tell the Prime Minister we have people over there tracking a gang of terrorists planning to assassinate me. He shut his trap fast when I fed him that one. You're a real smart lady.'

Sara, arms still folded, bobbed her head in acknowledgement of the compliment, but she wasn't fooled. March had used that trick on her before – first hammering her for an indiscretion, then following that up with a tribute to her loyalty. Bradford March might have come from the sticks but he had a native cunning when it came to manipulating people. Wisely, she changed the subject.

'Can I ask you something else? Has Norton found the

123

two pieces of equipment he's endeavouring to locate? I don't know what they are but I do know they worry you.'

March's expression became brooding. 'No, he hasn't. But he will. His job's on the line and he knows it. Sara, maybe we should put a tail on Senator Wingfield? Don't trust him as far as I can spit.'

'Don't do it,' Sara warned. 'He'll know. Then he'll guess there's something to conceal. He could start digging up dirt about Unit One. Let him rest in peace.'

'Which is where I wish he was. In the cemetery. Now, try and get me Norton on the private line. Then go take a shower or something . . .'

Which was another precaution March had learned from reading up the history of previous occupants of the White House. Never completely trust the one closest to you – man or woman. In a crisis it was the loyal friend who stabbed you in the back. Today's friends – tomorrow's enemies.

Bradford March was not psychic, but on that cold drizzly February morning a meeting of three men was being held not a world away from the Oval Office. The meeting took place in one of the luxurious mansions in Chevy Chase, the most sought after – and exclusive – residential district near Washington.

The small group was seated round a Chippendale table in the study of Senator Charles Wingfield. Even though it was daytime the curtains were drawn closed in the large room at the rear of the house. Illumination came from the glass chandelier suspended above the table.

The Senator, a white-haired vigorous man of sixty and Chairman of the Foreign Relations Committee, looked at his guests as they began sipping the excellent coffee he served.

The short plum-faced guest, in his fifties, was the most

powerful banker in the States. Alongside him sat a man known as an elder statesman. The latter was of medium height, bulky build, clad in an immaculate suit and he wore horn-rimmed glasses. Behind the lenses strange penetrating and shrewd eyes watched the other two men. The Senator opened the meeting, going straight to the point.

'I'm getting more and more worried about the President's behaviour. There are two crises brewing up in Europe and both could damage our vital interests.'

'And March is doing nothing to support Europe,' the statesman snapped. 'All he can think of is his "America First, Last and All the Time".'

'Which was the slogan which won him the election,' the banker pointed out.

'You can interpret "America First" as the best reason for our intervening in Europe, for supporting the British in this situation,' the statesman replied waspishly. 'God knows enough history has proved our front line is on the European continent. The Veep has more grasp of foreign affairs in his little finger than March has in his ugly ape-like head.'

By Veep he was referring to the Vice-President, Jeb Calloway. March had chosen Calloway as his running mate because he was from Philadelphia and was popular in the north-east and the so-called 'rust' states of Michigan, etc.

'Calloway is a very different man,' Wingfield agreed. 'He's a cultured man with a global view. But he's still the Veep.'

'Nothing more than a decoration with no say in policy,' the banker reminded them. 'So what can be done?'

'Politics is the art of the possible,' the Senator said in a soothing tone. 'March has done nothing yet we can openly criticize him for. He's quick on his feet and a

125

master of the Washington ball-game. Gentlemen, all we can do is wait.'

'You did say you'd heard rumours that March has secretly organized his own private paramilitary force,' recalled the statesman.

'Rumours. Nothing I can get my teeth into. Washington abounds in rumours. The private army thing may be a trap March has set. We go public about what is nothing but a rumour, he proves we're off the wall, and any influence we possess is destroyed.'

'I may make a statement criticizing his inaction over foreign policy,' the statesman insisted. 'The position is we *have* no foreign policy. It might stir Calloway into urging immediate action.'

'I still advocate silence,' Senator Wingfield replied.

In certain circles, limited to a very few old Washington hands, they were known as the Three Wise Men. Wingfield was very strong on the strategy of their remaining in the shadows.

They talked for a little while longer. The banker could hold himself in check no longer. He burst out with unusual vehemence.

'The President has done nothing to reduce our soaring deficit. America is going bankrupt. The way he's increasing our debt, we're heading for a crisis right here.'

'He's very popular still,' the Senator warned. 'I would advise both of you to make no public statements pending our next meeting.' He looked at his watch. 'And I am due at the Senate in thirty minutes . . .'

Courteously he ushered them into the hall, shook them by the hand, but was careful not to be present when the front door was opened. The statesman and the banker left the mansion separately – with five minutes between their departures. Outside a chauffeured limousine waited in the drive when each man hurried out of the front entrance.

Back in his study Wingfield decided he would make a

126

few very discreet enquiries. The problem was always to find an ear where the mouth would stay shut afterwards. Calm and dignified during the meeting, inwardly the Senator was a very disturbed man.

14

It was dark as they waited close to Padstow harbour. Newman sat with Paula alongside him in his Mercedes. Cardon had taken over the wheel of the Escort. Butler and Nield had taken the Sierra – but at that moment they were both outside, watching the phone box with Tweed inside it.

A storm had blown up, the sea was in a rage. Paula got out of the Merc., leaned in to speak to Newman.

'I'm going to get a closer look. It's really wild tonight.'

'I'll come with you,' Newman said, jumping out of his seat.

They walked near the edge of South Quay, but not too close. The gale nearly blew them off their feet. Fascinated, Paula watched the boats in the outer harbour swaying and tossing. Huge waves rolled in, crashed against the rear wall, exploded in a burst of surf and spume rising way up above the wall. One smaller craft looked as though it was going to be upended at any moment.

Newman grasped her arm to prevent her getting any nearer to the brink. She glanced over her shoulder where the interior light shone down on the occupant of the telephone box.

Tweed had dialled the Surrey mansion, was put through very quickly to Monica. He spoke rapidly.

'Short of time. Monica, I want you to prepare a profile

on a man called Gaunt. Lives at Tresillian Manor on Bodmin Moor. You won't hear from me for some time, but don't worry.'

'What the hell is going on?'

It was the first time he'd ever heard her swear. Even on the phone he could sense her tension – a tension which probably pervaded the whole mansion.

'No idea yet,' he answered. 'Now, put me on to Howard . . .'

'Tweed, are you all right?' were Howard's first words.

'Yes. We're moving on. Had a word with the PM yet?'

'No, we're completely cut off from the outside world – which is an eerie feeling. I did get one thing out of that fool of a private secretary when I threatened to go up to Downing Street. He said I wouldn't be admitted, that there's a major terrorist hunt in progress. I can't imagine what he's talking about.'

Then you haven't got much imagination, Tweed thought. He had a pad and a pen at the ready.

'Can you give me Commander Crombie's private number? I may need to contact him.' He scribbled down figures of a phone number in London. 'Thanks. Now listen, Howard, you may not hear from me again for a while. Don't worry about it. I'll be in a safe place with my team.'

'Well, I hope you know what you're doing. Where is this safe place?'

'Sorry, I'm leaving no forwarding address. Must go . . .'

'Wait! I've just remembered. Had a call from Cord Dillon. Take down this number . . . Got it? He must be in Switzerland. He wants you to call him urgently. Gave me different times. Half a sec. Just checked my watch. You could get him now, allowing for the time difference. There are only fifteen-minute periods during the times he gave me.'

'I'd better get off this line, then . . .'

'But I need to know where I can get in touch with you.'

'No forwarding address . . .'

Tweed put down the phone, fished in his pocket. He needed more coins. The wind nearly hurled him back inside the box as he emerged. Battling against the gale he beckoned to Butler and Nield as Paula and Newman came back to the Merc. Tweed climbed into the back, called out brusquely.

'I need all the change you've got to make a long-distance call. Hurry it up . . .'

'Not another call?' Paula exclaimed. 'Maybe we'd better set up a coffee and sandwich bar for you inside that box,' she teased.

'It's not funny. Just give me the change. Cord Dillon is waiting for me to ring. Sounds like a fugitive, from the way Howard reported it. The Deputy Director of the CIA – something is terribly wrong . . .'

Armed with a large collection of coins Tweed returned to the box. The first number Howard had passed to him was 010.41. Switzerland. Followed by 1. Zurich. Followed by the rest of the numbers. The operator put him through quickly and he began listening to the ringing sound. He checked his watch. He was damned close to the end of the fifteen-minute period.

'Who is this calling?'

Dillon's abrasive American voice. No doubt about it.

'Tweed here. I got your message from Howard . . .'

'Where are you calling from? I can't hang about here much longer . . .'

'Public phone box . . .'

'Like me. In Shopville. Just listen. Joel Dyson is here. Still alive. Least he was when I spotted him, then lost the guy. So is Special Agent Barton Ives, FBI. Again I go and lose him. At least he's here.'

'You're staying at . . .'

'The place you suggested. No names. Don't see how

they can tap every goddamn phone in this country, but you just never know.'

'Cord . . .'

'I said just listen. I'm filling you in on the situation. Too many Americans here who don't look like tourists. I guess they're after Dyson. Ives, too.'

'Tell me about this Barton Ives . . .'

'Not over the phone. Maybe we can meet some place some day. If I'm still walking around . . .'

'Cord. You may see me sooner than you think. Keep under good cover . . .'

'What is good cover in this situation? Got to go. Hang in there, Tweed . . .'

There was a click. Tweed sighed, pushed open the door as another gale-force gust tried to slam it shut on him. He walked back to the Merc. with his head bowed, followed by Butler and Nield, and dived inside the back. The wind closed the door for him. Paula twisted round in the front passenger seat.

'It's quite a night. You should see what's happening in the harbour.'

'Which is exactly what I shouldn't see. Bob, get moving. You've found St Mawgan, Paula?'

'I can take us straight there.'

'That will be a miracle.'

Paula didn't reply. Tweed was tauter than a guitar string.

Newman drove along the A389 once he was clear of Padstow. Cardon followed in the Escort and the Sierra, with Butler at the wheel and Nield beside him, brought up the rear. The wind beat against the side of the Merc., bent over hedges as though intent on tearing them up by the roots.

'We're heading for Wadebridge,' Tweed called out.

'We could have taken a side road and come out on the A39 much further west.'

'Who is the bloody navigator?' Paula snapped. She'd had enough of Tweed's brusqueness. 'I'm keeping us on A-roads. On a night like this we don't want to be driving on windy B-roads. Not until we have to later.'

'She's right,' Newman said. 'I'm driving and this is a big car to take down narrow country roads on a night like this.'

'Sorry, Paula,' said Tweed, who realized he'd been sharp with her. 'I'll leave the two of you to get us there.'

Tweed was enduring a mixture of emotions – impatience to reach their ultimate destination and anxiety about the safety of Cord Dillon.

'What about accommodation for the night?' Paula queried after a while. 'Did you manage to fix up rooms for the night at St Mawgan?'

'Yes. The Falcon Inn only has four rooms but we will cope somehow.'

'One for you,' Newman said, 'one for Paula. I'll share with Cardon and Butler and Nield won't mind sharing the other. It's a nice place, the Falcon, Paula, and just about the most difficult place on earth to find.'

'The latter being the main reason why you chose it?' Paula asked Tweed over her shoulder.

'Partly,' he said and relapsed into silence.

Paula guided them to the right on to the A39, another good wide road, and they drove on through the night, meeting no other traffic, the wind still hammering the car. Later she guided them off the A39 with a fresh right turn on to the Newquay road, the A3059. She soon warned Newman they had to keep a lookout for a side road. It was Tweed who spotted the turning.

'Right here,' he called out. 'We're getting close now to where we turn off yet again . . .'

Paula was conscious they were getting into very remote

country. They drove down a steep narrow winding hill and Tweed warned Newman to crawl. He then completed answering Paula's question.

'St Mawgan is close to what is called Newquay Airport. We are booked to catch the 11.05 flight to Heathrow. It arrives at 12.15 p.m. During one of my visits to that phone box I called this airport, booked our seats in our own names.'

'Was that wise?' Paula ventured.

'It was deliberate. I am leaving a trail for the enemy to follow. I want him out in the open, where I can see him, identify him – and deal with him,' Tweed concluded grimly.

At St Mawgan it was nine o'clock at night. In Washington it was four in the afternoon as Jeb Calloway, Vice President, paced slowly round his office while his aide waited for him to speak.

'I'm secretly in touch with someone in Europe to find out what the hell is going on, Sam,' Calloway said eventually. 'The difficulty was to find someone I could totally trust, but I think I found the man.'

Calloway, forty-five years old, was six feet tall and heavily built. Clean-shaven, with fair hair, he was dressed immaculately in a blue Brooks Brothers business suit. Strong-featured, he had a long nose, grey eyes and a determined mouth and well-shaped jaw.

'That could be dangerous, sir,' Sam suggested. 'You've sent this emissary to Europe on a secret mission without the President's knowledge?'

'He was there already. He contacted me. I've also had a talk with a top gun in the establishment. He also approached me. He's as worried as I am about the mounting world crisis. And March doesn't give a damn.'

'Isn't this possibly a catastrophic move?' Sam persisted.

'If Brad March ever finds out he'll close all doors to you.'

Calloway smiled wryly, a smile which had made him very popular. It was the smile of a man of integrity and conviction. He waved a large hand as he went on.

'All doors are closed to me now. March doesn't tell me a thing that matters. And I've heard a whisper that he's assembled a secret paramilitary force, his own Praetorian Guard – like a Julius Caesar.'

'Whispers! Sounds like a load of crap. March wouldn't do that – it's against the Constitution.'

'Brad isn't too hot on obeying the Constitution – if some overt move helps him to increase his power.'

'Who are you in contact with in Europe?' Sam asked.

Sam was a short plump man of fifty-eight. He'd had experience of serving under more than one president, knew the pitfalls of the Washington power game. Calloway mentioned a name. Sam looked dubious.

'Wouldn't play poker with that guy. I heard he had to flee to Europe overnight. Some mysterious investigation his new boss in Memphis chopped. That guy is trouble.'

'I'm still keeping in touch. Rare type, Sam – an honest man.'

The Falcon Inn at St Mawgan was a compact building of old grey stone. It stood on the edge of the lane at the very bottom of the steep winding hill. Newman drove the Merc. slowly past it, turned right down a narrow lane alongside the inn.

'The car park is a little way from the Falcon,' he explained to Paula. 'Hidden well away behind it.'

His headlights swept over a small village shop, swung to the right. They shone down an even narrower track with ramps.

'This is a pretty lonely spot,' Paula commented.

They had reached a dead end, a forest-shrouded bowl

133

which was the car park. No other vehicles were parked. Behind them Cardon followed in the Escort while Butler and Nield brought up the rear end of their small cavalcade in the Sierra. Newman had switched off his engine but he left on the headlights so Tweed and Paula, climbing out of the car, could see. Paula adjusted her shoulder-bag as she stood in the bitter cold, staring round at the bowl overhung with dense trees rising up slopes.

'Don't like this,' she said. 'It's creepy. And anyone could tamper with the cars while we're asleep in the Falcon.'

'You have a point there,' Tweed agreed. He looked at Butler, Nield and Cardon who had joined them. 'I think we ought to organize a roster among us so someone is always here to guard the cars.'

'You and Paula can get your beauty sleep,' Newman decided. 'The four of us will take it in turn through the night to sit in the Merc.'

'I've got a better idea,' suggested Butler. 'The four of us split into twos. I take the Sierra back, park it out front of the inn. That way we have the back and the front under surveillance.'

'Agreed,' said Tweed. 'Now let's go and see what we can get for dinner . . .'

It was the middle of the night when Butler, slumped behind the wheel of the Sierra parked outside the Falcon, heard a car approaching down the steep hill. He sat up, took a bottle of beer he'd kept for the purpose, swilled some round in his mouth, spat it out of the window he'd opened.

Newman was taking his duty stretch in the Merc. in the park behind the inn where he could also keep an eye on the Escort. In the wing mirror Butler saw the headlights of the oncoming car dip. When it stopped close to him he saw it was a cream Chevrolet. He recognized the driver as soon as he stepped out and came over.

134

It was the big American with dark brows which almost met across his boxer's nose. The American who'd tried to pick a quarrel with Newman in the bar at the Metropole in Padstow. Butler had seen the Yank as he slipped past the bar entrance on his way with the others to the elevator. But the Yank had *not* seen him.

'You been here long, buddy?' the American asked.

'Hours. What's it to you? I had a skinful back in the inn and I'm not risking getting caught by a patrol car. So *you* have a problem, mister?'

'Maybe my approach was wrong.'

'So, we've got that settled. You lost?'

'You know the area?'

The American was eyeing Butler carefully. He leaned inside the window. Butler chose that moment to manufacture a large belch. Beer fumes assailed the American's nostrils. His brutal face showed distaste.

'I asked you a question.'

'I know the area. And I asked you a question, mate.'

'You been here long?' the American persisted.

'I told you. Something wrong with your memory?' Butler snapped.

'Sorry. Wrong approach again. It's a friggin' cold night. I'm looking for a Mercedes 280E. Blue colour. Seen a car like that around here?'

'No.'

'Sure?' the American persisted further.

'There you go again. Asking the question I've answered. And you still haven't answered mine. You lost or something?'

'My pal and I – the one in the Merc. – were going to meet with each other. I've lost the note he gave me of the name of the hick place he said he'd wait.'

'I was right, mate,' Butler jeered. 'You are lost.'

'How do I get out of this dump?'

'This is a very small and attractive village. You piss off

135

out of it by driving straight on. Get it?'

The American gave him a savage look, walked back to his Chevrolet, clashed the gears and gunned the motor as he drove off, not giving a damn how many people he woke in the middle of the night.

'And you just missed getting a bullet in your gullet,' Butler said aloud.

He holstered the Walther he'd been holding in his lap under his windcheater. Checking his watch, he saw it was 3 a.m. Nield would be coming to take his turn while Cardon relieved Newman at any moment. He grabbed for his Walther again as a slim figure appeared next to his window. It was Nield.

'Time for your beauty sleep, Harry. Had a restful doze?'

Newquay Airport – several miles outside Newquay itself – was one of the bleakest departure points Paula had ever seen. Perched on a lonely plateau in the middle of nowhere, it was little more than a grassy field crossed by concrete runways. An eight-foot wire fence surrounded it and 'reception' was little more than a single-storey shed. They had found a place they could leave the cars and Tweed had reassured the attendant.

'It's a business trip and we might not be back for some time. All right to leave our cars?'

'At your own risk, guv'nor . . .'

Newman asked the girl behind the counter the question after they had checked in with their luggage when Tweed had collected and paid for the tickets.

'Yesterday a helicopter buzzed us as Padstow, nearly sank the boat we were in,' he lied smoothly. 'Does anyone ever hire choppers from here?'

'It happens occasionally, sir. Yesterday? I heard two Americans hired a machine for a few hours. It caused a bit of gossip – one of them had a British pilot's licence, which is unusual. And your flight is ready for departure . . .'

Newman exploded after they had all trudged across to the waiting machine with their luggage. It was a sizeable plane but he pointed at the nose.

'Look at those things!'

'They're propellers,' Tweed said quietly, knowing Newman disliked prop aircraft. 'It will fly, you know.'

'Yes, but will it get there? And we seem to be the only passengers for the 11.05 flight . . .'

The Brymon Airways aircraft was in mid-air before Paula looked down on the grey landscape. She was seated next to Tweed who stared ahead grimly.

'A penny for your thoughts. You've been very quiet since Harry Butler told us at breakfast about the reappearance of the American brute.'

'I'm worried and relieved at the same time,' Tweed admitted. 'Staggered that one of them should turn up at an out of the way place like St Mawgan. You realize what that means?'

'No, but you might tell me. I expect you will anyway.'

'For one to arrive in St Mawgan they must have an army of them combing Cornwall for us.'

'That's the worry. What's the relief?'

'That I guessed right early on in this sequence of macabre and mass-murder campaigns against us. To operate on such a scale calls for an organization of enormous magnitude. With all this firepower against us the ultimate enemy can only be one source.'

'You're not going to tell me what it is, are you? Before you say it, I'm sure you need more data to be absolutely sure. But where are we going now? London could be a death-trap.'

'It would be exactly that,' Tweed agreed. 'Which is why we're flying on to the one safe haven.'

'I suppose I shouldn't ask where?' Paula remarked.

'Switzerland. Where we have a powerful friend.'

15

'Norton is on the private line, Brad,' said Sara Maranoff.

'OK. Put him through. Time that street bum got results.'

'Brad, Norton is the best we've got. Hold yourself in. I also have Ms Hamilton waiting to see you.'

Sara knew what Ms Hamilton was about. She glanced round the Oval Office, checked that there were plenty of cushions on the large couch stood against one wall. She waved her index finger at him, warning him to cool it with Norton.

The President often omitted to shave until the end of the morning. His jaw and upper lip would be covered with a black stubble. But this morning he was freshly shaved, wore a smart blue suit with a crisp clean shirt and a tie. Ms Hamilton, Sara thought. Had to be at his best for *her*.

'I'll leave you to take your call,' she said.

Alone, March pushed back his chair, planted his feet on the desk top, crossed his ankles. He picked up the phone kept in a drawer.

'That you?' he barked.

'Norton here. I need those reinforcements . . .'

'They're aboard United flight 918 flying non-stop to London. Over the Atlantic as I speak with you. That's all the rest of Unit One we had in reserve here. Marvin Mencken is in charge.'

'That barracuda . . .'

'He's the best . . .' March remembered Sara's warning.

'I mean the best next to you. Now where are we with this goddamn problem? Where is Joel Dyson? Where is *Special Agent*' – his tone was savagely sarcastic – 'Barton Ives? Give.'

'In Zurich . . .'

'You've traced those bastards? Well, well. Miracles still happen. They're six feet under the ground now?'

'Not exactly. Not yet . . .'

'Don't give me no smoke, Norton. You sittin' on your thumbs out there? What the hell is the position?'

'We know both men are in Zurich. They've been seen but they disappeared again. Temporarily . . .'

'Temporarily is too long. What about the CIA shyster – Cord Dillon?'

'No sign of him yet, but we'll track him. An operation like this doesn't happen overnight.'

'I want all three of them put away for good. Norton, your head is on the block. There's always Mencken . . .'

March slammed down the phone, inserted a thick finger inside his neckband, loosened it. The phone rang again as he stood up to go to the door. He snatched it up.

'Yes?'

'Norton here. We got disconnected. I'm handling this my way. I'll be meeting Mencken's flight at London Airport. I'm flying to Zurich to take personal charge. How many reinforcements are aboard that flight? I need specific information.' A brief pause. 'Mr President.'

'Forty men. With what you've got you should be able to check everyone in Switzerland.'

'I said I'd handle this my way . . .'

The line went dead. March stared at the phone. Norton had had the balls to hang up on him. He remembered what Sara had said. Norton is the best. So maybe he was.

He checked his appearance in a mirror, went to the door, opened it, beaming his famous smile. The elegant blonde woman waiting on a seat outside returned the

139

smile, walked in, he closed and locked the door. Taking her by the arm he led her to the couch, turned her round, lowered her gently.

'You've got too many clothes on, Glen. I'll start by undoing this top button . . .'

Swissair flight SR 803 had departed from London on schedule, taking off for Zurich at 13.50 hours. Tweed and his team were aboard in first class and had that section to themselves. One of the advantages of flying in February.

The Brymon Airways flight from Newquay Airport had arrived on time at London at 12.15 p.m. Tweed had collected and paid for the tickets by calling on Jim Corcoran. He had then had a tough conversation with Chief Inspector Roy Buchanan when he phoned him at the Yard.

'Where are you?' Buchanan had snapped.

'My whereabouts are not important. I see there has been not a single report of the massacre at Tresillian Manor in the press. Nine corpses and the press isn't interested? I suspect a "D" notice has been issued to the press. What excuse was used this time? A matter of national security?'

'This is a major anti-terrorist operation, Tweed. Which is all you're getting out of me. And there were ten corpses. A Tresillian Manor servant girl called Celia Yeo was found at the foot of High Tor. An anonymous caller alerted me. You wouldn't know anything about it, I suppose?'

Buchanan's tone dripped sarcasm. Tweed made him stick to the point.

'A major anti-terrorist operation? You really swallowed that? So they've got at you too . . .'

'My patience has run out with you, Tweed. I want you here at the Yard yesterday.'

'You're a man of integrity,' Tweed said quietly. 'You know you should be investigating a case of mass murder.

140

And not by terrorists. Don't take it out on me because they've fenced you in.'

'I said I expect you here at the Yard at the earliest possible moment. Needless to say, you don't leave the country.'

'You're still evading the main issue. Check up on the mass murder in Cornwall. Check on who set up fake roadblocks one night recently. Get a description from anyone who was stopped by them. Make sure you ask what nationality they were . . .'

'Are you telling me how to do my job?'

'I'm simply suggesting you actually *do* your job. Have to go. Goodbye . . .'

Sitting next to Paula in mid-air he had relayed his conversation with Buchanan to her. He made his comments after he told her how he had ended the call.

'The significance of that verbal duel was what Buchanan *didn't* say.'

'What was that?'

'He didn't deny he'd been told to pigeon-hole the case. I expect he was ordered to by the Commissioner. After the Commissioner had taken a call from Downing Street. They have thrown a tight net round the whole horrific business.'

'But why? I'm getting scared the way Howard can't contact the PM.'

'Someone with immense power has thrown out a smoke-screen. By labelling these violent events as the work of a major terrorist organization it gives the people at the top a perfect excuse for their inexcusable actions. I know I've just contradicted myself, but you grasp what I'm getting at.'

'Except I can't grasp who could have such an evil influence over our Prime Minister.'

'Read the papers – the international news. That's where one of the keys lies. Now I want to give a message to the pilot to be radioed ahead of us.'

'Can I see it?' Paula asked, her curiosity aroused.

While Tweed was writing on a small pad he'd taken from his pocket Paula glanced beyond him from her window seat at Newman and Cardon who were seated opposite across the aisle. Newman grinned at her, gave a thumbs-up signal. Tweed and Paula occupied the front seats where there was plenty of leg room. Immediately behind them sat Butler and Nield who had refused drinks and remained very alert.

Tweed finished writing, showed her the message, put it in an envelope, sealed it and called to the stewardess.

'Could you please hand this to the wireless operator? It's very urgent.'

'Certainly, sir . . .'

Paula sat frowning. She asked her question as the plane flew on over dense clouds which looked just like the Alps, shining in the brilliant sun. At that moment the aircraft was barely midway between London and Zurich.

'I thought you said Switzerland would be a haven of safety?'

'It won't be,' Tweed said with a face like stone. 'Not for the opposition once I locate them.'

The radio message, addressed to Tweed's old friend, Arthur Beck, Chief of Federal Police, had been terse and to the point.

Urgently request full protection six people aboard flight SR 803. ETA Kloten Airport, Zurich, 1625 hours your time. Tweed.

The plane had begun its descent to Kloten when Paula saw out of the opposite window a breathtaking panorama of a great range of snowbound mountains. Massive in their continuity, she realized she was staring at the Bernese Oberland, the most spectacular mountains in all Europe.

She continued gazing at them. They reminded her of

142

some enormous tidal wave about to engulf the entire continent. The descent increased in angle, the view vanished. Beyond her own window there was nothing to see but a curtain of clouds drifting past, growing denser as they dropped lower and lower.

Suddenly the clouds cleared and the lights of Switzerland were coming up to meet her. The stewardess returned again, whispered to Tweed.

'We've had instructions from Zurich Control that you and your party will leave the plane first after landing.'

'I'm glad you added "after landing",' Tweed joked.

Paula sensed his sudden change of mood – Tweed was looking forward to the opportunity to take action. She felt her own spirits rise. For days she had lived in a state of suppressed terror. She stared eagerly out of the window again.

They were landing – she could see the forest of evergreens which surrounded Kloten Airport. The Swiss pilot brought the machine down so smoothly the wheels barely kissed the concrete runway. As they emerged Paula saw a familiar figure waiting just beyond the metal platform leading from plane to airport building. The Chief of the Federal Police. He took hold of her in both arms and hugged her.

'Welcome to Switzerland, Paula.'

'I'm here too,' said Tweed, amused because he knew Beck was very fond of Paula.

Arthur Beck, in his forties, was slim and plump-cheeked. His most arresting features were his alert grey eyes beneath dark brows and his strong nose above a trim moustache. Of medium height, he moved his hands and feet quickly, his complexion was ruddy and he wore a smart grey suit, a blue striped shirt and a blue tie. Tweed quickly introduced him to Philip Cardon: Beck had met the others before and knew Bob Newman well. He led the way, talking rapidly to Tweed and Paula in perfect English.

143

'We're bypassing Passport Control and Customs. I have limos outside waiting to take you wherever you want to go.'

'The Hotel Schweizerhof opposite the Hauptbahnhof. It will be our official residence but we won't actually be staying there. We'll be at the Hotel Gotthard just behind the Schweizerhof,' said Tweed.

'You are taking great precautions, my friend,' commented Beck. 'This must be a very serious affair.'

'A matter of life and death – for all of us. I'll tell you what's happened while we're driving into Zurich.'

'Our bags,' Paula intervened. 'They'll be delivered to the carousel . . .'

'We travelled first class and were the only passengers,' Tweed said quickly.

'Easy.' Beck grinned. He spoke to an aide in plain clothes who had walked alongside them. As the man dashed off he explained. 'I've told him to collect all the first-class luggage off the carousel. He'll bring it to the cars . . .'

They were escorted via a devious route which bypassed Passport Control and Customs. Striding across the concourse, Beck guided them to a convoy of three waiting stretched Mercedes, all black in colour. Near by uniformed motorcyclist police waited, straddling their machines. Beck gestured towards them as he opened the door of the first car.

'Outriders. Our escort. After receiving your message I decided to take no chances. I drop you outside the Schweizerhof?'

'Yes, please,' said Tweed. 'Later we make our way on foot one by one to the Gotthard. I've booked rooms in both hotels . . .'

It was a twenty-minute drive from the airport into the centre of Zurich. Beck sat next to Tweed in the rear of the limo while Paula was seated alongside Tweed. The driver

144

wore civilian clothes, as did the tough-looking individual in the front passenger seat.

Newman, Butler, Nield and Cardon occupied seats in the limo behind them and the third car was full of more men in plain clothes. The outriders on motorcycles led the way into the Swiss city while two more brought up the rear.

Beck listened in silence as Tweed told him concisely everything that had happened to them – including the bombing of SIS headquarters in London and the events in Cornwall. Frequently the Swiss glanced back through the rear window. At one moment he interrupted Tweed for the first time.

'Excuse me, I have to radio a message to the rear car. We were followed from the airport by an Impala – significant, possibly, that it is an American car . . .'

Picking up the microphone slung from the side of the car he spoke in Switzer-Deutsch, the dialect understood only by the Swiss. Tucking the microphone back on its hook, he explained after again glancing through the rear window, 'I ordered interception. The third car has just stopped that Impala. They'll think up some fictitious traffic regulations the driver's broken to delay him. And all these cars are bulletproof. Your story, Tweed, is very strange, but of course I believe you. It might interest you to know there are too many Americans arriving in Switzerland – especially in Zurich.'

'Too many?' Paula leaned forward. 'How do you know that?'

Beck smiled cynically. 'Oh, we do know what is going on in our country. In late February you might expect a few businessmen, even the odd wealthy tourist from the States. But these men – and we don't like the look of them – all carry diplomatic passports. From my headquarters in Berne I've already phoned their embassy and complained that they're exceeding their complement of diplomatic staff. The Ambassador, an old friend – and one of the few

145

President March has not replaced by some of his cronies and backers – was embarrassed. I found it significant. He told me these men were soon to be routed to other embassies in Europe. Both of us knew he was not telling the truth.'

'So Zurich could be dangerous?' Paula suggested.

'Yes, it could.' He smiled again. 'But not as dangerous as Britain, from what Tweed has told me. How are you going to proceed, Tweed? Or is that top secret?'

'Not at all. I want to locate three men. Joel Dyson – I think it may have all started with him. Then Special Agent Barton Ives and Cord Dillon. One of them has to tell me what the blazes is happening.'

'I do find' – Beck paused to ruminate – 'the most unexpected of those three people to be running is this Barton Ives. FBI – why should someone be after his blood?'

'That mystifies me too,' Tweed admitted.

'A pity you don't know what this Norton looks like,' Beck commented.

'I gather no one knows that. Which I find sinister . . .'

Tweed, carrying his bag, led the way into the Schweizerhof, where he had stayed on previous visits. The same concierge greeted him warmly. As they went up in the lift after registering, Tweed told Paula to come and see him urgently when she'd left her bag in her room.

'I have room 217,' he reminded her as he left the elevator.

She was tapping on his door within three minutes of his arriving in the large corner room overlooking the main station at the front. The side windows looked down on the famous Bahnhofstrasse – the street of great banks and some of the most luxurious shops in the world. He went out of the spacious living-cum-bedroom into the lobby to let Paula in.

146

'I'm afraid I've got rather a lot for you to do,' he said.

'Fire away!'

'All of us must leave in our rooms here convincing evidence that this *is* where we are staying. Toothbrushes, toothpaste, shaving kit, et cetera in the bathrooms . . .'

'The ones we're using now would be most convincing . . .'

'Agreed. Plus about half our clothes in the wardrobes. Now that means I want you to . . .'

'Go out and buy six toothbrushes, six tubes of paste, five electric shavers, more make-up for myself,' she interjected.

'Why more make-up?'

'Because you expect to find some in a room occupied by a woman. While I'm buying I'll have to collect a load of large carrier bags. Presumably we need those to sneak out of here to the Gotthard with the clothes we take. I foresee one other problem.'

'Which is?' Tweed enquired.

'We would look suspicious turning up at the Gotthard without suitcases. I know – two of the men wait with new suitcases we buy in the men's lavatory down in Shopville.' Paula peered out of the side window at the escalator leading down into the underground shopping centre. 'Two more of us, say Bob and Philip, can take the carriers with the clothes into the lavatory and they can be put inside the cases in cubicles.'

'I don't know why I bother planning things like this out,' Tweed said, raising his hands in mock frustration. 'Not when I have you with me.'

'I'll be away for a while on my shopping expedition,' she warned. 'It would look funny if I bought six of everything at one shop.'

'I'm not letting you go alone,' Tweed said firmly. 'I'm calling Butler to accompany you as bodyguard.'

'Harry is a perfect choice. And he can help to carry

147

my purchases. What about the suitcases?'

'I'll phone Newman and Cardon. They can buy the suitcases and call me back when they've done the job. Then they can get coffee at Sprüngli and call me again. By then you and Harry should have done your shopping. I'll fix a precise time for Pete Nield and myself to meet you, collect the carriers and make the switch in Shopville. Have you got enough Swiss money?'

'You gave me sufficient at London Airport to go out and buy an outfit Elizabeth Taylor would be happy to wear. Come to think of it, I rather fancy a Chanel suit,' she teased him and left the room.

Tweed summoned Newman and Cardon and gave them their instructions. As they left, the phone rang. Tweed frowned, lifted the receiver cautiously.

'Yes. Who is it?'

'Beck here,' the familiar voice opened. 'I have bad news. Remember that Impala my men stopped on the way from the airport? They found him just ending a conversation on a mobile phone. He undoubtedly warned his chief that a competitor had arrived.' Beck was phrasing his message carefully, knowing it was passing through a hotel switchboard. 'You might have company from the opposition earlier than you expected. Keep in touch. I'm staying in Zurich.'

'Thank you.'

Tweed put down the phone with a sense of foreboding.

16

The move to the Hotel Gotthard, only a short distance behind the Schweizerhof, had been completed by eight in the evening. Tweed arrived in his room, threw back the lid of his case, went down to the bar. He ordered a glass of champagne, paid for it and began exploring the hotel.

With the glass in his hand he appeared to be looking for someone. He tipped some of the contents into a plant pot and continued checking on the few people who sat in the lounge area. No one suspicious anywhere, no sound of an American voice.

Strolling slowly along he passed a man sitting in a chair reading a paper. A slim individual, smartly dressed, he glanced up, folded his paper, followed Tweed to a quiet area near the cheaper restaurant fronting on the Bahnhofstrasse.

'Excuse me, sir. Have you a light?'

Tweed tensed, turned round slowly. The slim man was clean-shaven, his dark hair slicked back over his head. About thirty years old, he held a cigarette in his hand. Tweed continued staring at him as he reached for the lighter he carried for other people's cigarettes.

As he ignited it the man leaned forward, holding one hand to shield the flame although there wasn't a current of air in the place. The man took his time getting his cigarette lit and it was then Tweed saw the open folder held in the palm of the extended hand, the printing inside below a photo of himself.

Federal Police. P. Schmidt. A visiting card had been

149

attached in the lower half with Sellotape. *With the compliments of Arthur Beck.*

'Thank you, sir,' the slim man said. 'It's very quiet here. February, I expect . . .'

Tweed went back up in the lift with mixed feelings. It was very good of Beck to post one of his men inside the hotel. But it also indicated that Beck was worried about their safety.

He inserted the key into his door, opened it, reached for the switch to illuminate the room before entering it. On the carpeted floor was a long white envelope which had been slipped under the door.

Tweed closed and locked the door. Using a penknife, he slit open the envelope carefully. There was one sheet of folded paper inside. No address at the top and a brief hand-written message.

Call me from a safe phone at this number . . . Between 8 p.m. and 8.15 p.m. this evening. Dillon

He was startled. Dillon must either be staying in the hotel, as he had suggested he should – or he had observed their arrival. Tweed checked his watch. 8.08 p.m. He had seven minutes to reach an outside phone. Picking up the phone he dialled Butler's room number.

'Tweed here. Harry, we have to go out. Very fast . . .'

'I'm on my way . . .'

Tweed had his overcoat on when Butler arrived wearing a padded windcheater. He opened the front, whipped a 7.65-mm. Walther automatic out of a hip holster, grinned and replaced the weapon. Tweed waited until they were hurrying on foot up the Bahnhofstrasse in a bitterly cold night before he asked the question.

'Where the hell did you get that? We ditched all weapons on our way to Newquay Airport.'

'By courtesy of Chief of Police Beck. You didn't see

150

the canvas hold-all he handed to Paula after you'd left the car outside the Schweizerhof?'

'No, I damn well didn't.'

'It contained Walthers for Pete Nield and me, a .32 Browning automatic for Paula and a Smith & Wesson for Newman. Plus ammo for all the guns. Paula guessed what was in the hold-all, passed it to Newman before she followed you inside. There were also special certificates to carry a firearm, signed by Beck, for each of us.'

For Butler it was a long speech. By the time he had ended it they had arrived at the down escalator into Shopville. Tweed's only reply was a grunt. He liked people to keep him informed but it *had* been a rush, moving to the Gotthard.

At that time of night the underground complex was quiet and few people were about. Tweed deliberately didn't glance inside the phone cubicles which were occupied. If one contained Cord Dillon he wasn't risking drawing attention to him.

'I won't be long,' he told Butler as he entered an empty cubicle.

He dialled the Zurich number, standing sideways. Butler was taking an apparent interest in a closed vegetable shop opposite.

'Who is it?' Dillon's voice asked brusquely.

'Tweed here. Got your message . . .'

'Just listen. Special Agent Barton Ives is in town. He will try to contact you if it's safe . . .'

'Why did he leave the States? I need some data . . .'

'He was investigating a chain of serial murders in Tennessee, Mississippi, Louisiana, Alabama, Georgia and Florida. All of them women. Raped, murdered . . .'

'So why would he need to flee to Europe?'

'Ask him. Got to go now. Zurich is swarming with Norton's gunmen. I have a hunch Norton will be here soon, may be already. Then the earthquake rocks Zurich.'

151

'Cord, how on earth do these serial murders link up with what's going on . . .'

'Not over the phone. Ask Barton. Stay under cover. I'm doing just that . . .'

'Since we don't know what Norton looks like it doesn't help to know we may be enjoying his company . . .'

'No one enjoys that. They just end up dead. Got to go . . .'

Again the line was cut before Tweed could ask him a vital question. The abrupt termination of the call worried Tweed as he walked back to the Gotthard with Butler. Dillon was a tough character and he'd never known him be scared of anyone before. This Norton must be quite something.

Norton was waiting at London Airport when United flight 918 landed from Washington. He stood among a small crowd of people who were waiting to greet arrivals. Alongside him stood a porter holding a large heavy envelope Norton had given him together with a £20 tip.

Marvin Mencken appeared first followed by four of his men. A tall well-built man, Mencken had a cadaverous face and behind his back he was nicknamed 'the Skeleton'. Wearing a dark blue trench coat and carrying his bag, his narrow foxy eyes swept the concourse as he paused.

'That's him,' Norton told the porter. 'The one in a dark blue trench coat.'

The porter, who had been given very precise instructions, hurried forward. Sidling his way between people he stopped in front of Mencken, presented him with the envelope.

'I've been asked to hand you this.'

'Who by?' Mencken flashed back, his eyes darting round the concourse as he took the envelope. 'Point him out to me.'

'Not part of my instructions, sir . . .'

'Look, you bum . . .' Mencken had dropped his bag, his hand grasped the porter by the shirt collar. 'You're goin' to point him out to me. Then you get fifty dollars. Play dumb and I'll tear your throat out.'

The porter, scared stiff, gulped. Indignation overtook fear. This was his airport. Reaching up, he dug his fingernails deep into the back of the hand holding him. Mencken let go, was about to tread hard on one of the porter's feet when his victim spoke.

'Any more of this and I'm calling Security. I can see the Chief over there.'

'Get lost,' Mencken snarled.

He couldn't afford trouble here – especially if Norton was watching him. He ripped open the envelope. Inside were forty one-way Swissair tickets to Zurich, a wad of banknotes, high Swiss denominations, and a typed instruction.

Board the flight with your friends. At Zurich you receive fresh orders.

The instruction ended with a flourishing 'N' written in ink. Norton. Mencken gritted his teeth. Sara Maranoff had told him in her curt way that he was second in command to Norton. Which was something he didn't appreciate. Especially as he had no idea what Norton looked like. Always just an abrasive voice on the phone.

Mencken had divided his group of forty men into sections of five, each with a leader. He began to distribute five tickets to each section leader, gave them the instruction for arrival in Zurich.

'You hang around the carousel at Kloten. I may give you orders then. Or I may wait till we hit the concourse. Just depends the mood I'm in. Well, look at the time – move ass . . .'

*　　*　　*

153

'I've made an appointment to see Walter Amberg at the Zurcher Kredit Bank in Talstrasse,' Tweed announced.

They were all having an excellent breakfast at a long table in La Soupière. This was the high-class dining-room on the first floor of the Schweizerhof. Having slept at the Gotthard they had wandered round to the Schweizerhof in pairs. It confirmed the impression they were staying at the hotel.

At Tweed's suggestion, the previous evening at nine o'clock Newman and Butler, carrying keys to all their six rooms, had paid a brief visit to the Schweizerhof. Each had taken three rooms, had then pulled back the covers, kicked off their shoes and rolled in the beds, rumpling sheets and pillows. This further confirmed the impression to the management that they were sleeping there.

'Walter is the twin of poor Julius,' Paula recalled in a whisper.

'The identical twin. Seen together you couldn't tell them apart,' Tweed agreed. 'The Swiss do have a sense of humour. Julius and Walter used to wear exactly the same outfits – so often their own staff got them mixed up.'

'And does Walter know about Julius's murder?' Paula asked in the same low voice.

'No. Which is unfortunate. No one – even Buchanan – had thought of asking who should be informed. I think the Chief Inspector was too appalled by the scale of the massacre. I shall have to break the news to Walter. Would you like to come with me?'

'Yes, please,' said Paula. 'Had Julius a wife?'

'He had, but I don't know her address. I did think of trying to get hold of it – but it's hardly the type of news you want to tell people over the phone.'

'A Swiss wife?' queried Paula, her curiosity aroused.

'No, English as a matter of fact. Much younger than her husband was. I think her name is Eve. Walter will have to undertake that unpleasant task. Walter is Chairman –

Julius was Chief Executive, the man who really ran the bank and its various branch offices.'

'Is Walter up to it?' asked Newman. 'To taking over and running the organization?'

'No idea.' Tweed polished off his bacon and eggs, pushed his plate back. 'You know, Paula, among all the things which have happened one stands out, puzzles me.'

'And that is?'

'Why, after shooting down Julius Amberg at Tresillian Manor, did the assassin throw acid all over his face? Not for revenge – we're not dealing with that kind of enemy. So why the acid?'

17

Norton travelled on the same flight to Zurich as Mencken and his large team. But whereas the forty men who were reinforcements occupied economy seats Norton was in the first-class section.

He wore an English suit and spoke with an English accent without a trace of his native American. When he had boarded the plane at London Airport he had chosen the aisle seat next to an elegantly dressed Swiss woman. He was careful that nothing in his manner suggested he was trying to pick her up.

'May I sit here, if you don't mind?' he had enquired courteously. 'There is more leg room and I have business papers I must study before we arrive.'

'The seat is vacant,' she replied after glancing briefly at him.

The plane took off and Norton extracted a folder of

papers with statistics about computers. He didn't understand any of it but if Mencken peered into First Class it would seem they were a couple travelling together.

Holding his briefcase, he moved quickly when the plane landed at Kloten. By the time Marvin Mencken arrived at the carousel a uniformed porter was waiting for him. He handed him a large envelope.

'I was asked to give this to you, sir. Your baggage will arrive very shortly.'

Remembering his experience at London Airport Mencken made no attempt to question the porter who was walking away. He glanced round at the passengers – not a chance of identifying Norton, assuming he was near the carousel, which he doubted. Mencken opened the envelope. Another sheet with no address and detailed instructions.

Distribute your men among the following four hotels – two groups should occupy the first hotel listed. Golden Bay Tours have booked accommodation. I will call you at your hotel telling you where to pick up special equipment. Hotels – Baur-en-Ville, Eden au Lac, Dolder Grand, Baur au Lac.

The sheet was again signed in ink with the flourishing 'N'. Mencken swore to himself at the familiar abrupt commanding tone of the instruction. He began strolling among the passengers, giving each section leader the name of his hotel. As he did so the luggage started moving along the carousel.

'Special equipment' – Mencken knew that referred to guns and explosives.

Newman had decided to accompany Tweed and Paula to meet Walter Amberg at the bank headquarters in Talstrasse, which ran parallel to Bahnhofstrasse. Paula was intrigued and a little nervous. She couldn't get out of her head 'snapshot' pictures of Julius Amberg before the attack – and how he had looked with his face destroyed by acid. Now she was going to meet the identical twin . . .

Prepared as she was, it came as a shock when a Swiss personal assistant showed them into a large office and a man came forward, hand extended, to greet them.

'Welcome back to Zurich, Tweed. Always good to see you.'

Small and portly, in his fifties, he also wore his black hair without a parting, slicked back from his high forehead. Under thick brows his blue eyes were shrewd, his face clean-shaven and plump. Inwardly, Paula gasped. She was staring at a mirror image of the banker she had met at Tresillian Manor. He even wore the same dark suit with a red silk display handkerchief protruding from his breast pocket.

Tweed introduced Paula, who gathered that Newman had met the banker before. Amberg escorted them to comfortable chairs round a long polished antique board-room table.

'I'm sure you would all like coffee,' he suggested and gave the order over an intercom. 'I understand you have met Julius down in Cornwall,' he went on, addressing Tweed as he sat down with Paula on his right and Tweed and Newman facing him. 'I haven't heard from him – not unusual since Julius often told me little about his affairs. I trust all went well.'

Tweed took a deep breath. He had not looked forward to this moment.

'I'm afraid I have bad news for you about Julius.'

'He's ill?' Amberg looked surprised. 'He's hardly ever ill. Always says he hasn't the time.'

'The news is worse than that, much worse,' Tweed warned.

'You can't mean he's . . . dead?'

'I mean just that . . .'

157

Tweed began to give a terse account of the events which had taken place in Cornwall. Amberg listened, his face blank of emotion, but Paula noticed his lips had tightened as the gruesome tale unfolded. The Swiss listened with his hands steepled, fingertips of each hand touching – a mannerism she had noticed at the dining table in Tresillian Manor.

'It's a grim tragedy,' Tweed concluded, 'and we have no idea who made the fatal attack – or why. I was hoping you might have some inkling.'

'As I told you, Julius handled his own affairs. Which makes it difficult for me to help. I don't – didn't – even know why he was going to Cornwall to meet you.'

'Have you ever heard of a man called Joel Dyson?' Tweed enquired.

'Yes. Not an individual I took to – I'm sorry, is he a friend of yours?'

'He most certainly isn't. Do go on.'

'This Dyson arrived recently with a suitcase and asked to see Julius. He was quite aggressive and I was surprised when my brother agreed to see him.' Amberg looked at Newman. 'I understand you once did Julius a great favour. which involved this individual.'

'It was nothing,' Newman said, dismissing the incident.

'Dyson seemed frightened on his second visit here,' the banker continued. 'After seeing my brother he asked to be let out by the rear door. Later Julius told me Dyson had handed him a film and a tape recording for safe keeping. I haven't seen Dyson since.'

'Where were the film and the tape stored?' Tweed asked casually.

'In the vault, of course. Then Julius had them transferred to the vault in our Basle branch. I've no idea why.' He clapped a hand to his forehead. 'Oh, God, I had forgotten about Eve. Since this is the first I've heard of this dreadful news she may not know. Eve is his estranged English wife.'

158

'Estranged?' Tweed enquired delicately.

'Yes. Julius had his final quarrel with Eve just before he flew to London on his way to Cornwall. They had not been getting on well for some time. Foreign wives . . .' He tilted his head towards Paula. 'Please do excuse my phraseology. Foreign wives,' he continued, 'are often a disaster when they marry Swiss men. Julius told me just before he left for London they had agreed on a separation, that he never wanted to see her again. But someone must tell her . . .'

Amberg trailed off, looked all at sea. The shock of what happened is beginning to sink in, Paula thought. It was Tweed who intervened.

'If you would like to give me her address, Walter, I will go and see her myself. I was at Tresillian Manor shortly after the tragedy occurred.'

'As her brother-in-law I suppose I should, but . . .'

'Give me her address, if she's still in Switzerland,' Tweed urged.

'She's here in Zurich.' Amberg extracted a white card from a box, wrote down the address and phone number, handed it to Tweed. 'She lives in the villa Julius has – had – in the Dolder area. He was moving into an apartment when he came back. I'm very grateful to you.'

'One more thing.' Tweed had stood up after draining the excellent coffee his assistant had brought in earlier. 'I expect you know whether Julius had viewed the film, listened to the tape Joel Dyson delivered before having them sent to Basle?'

'No idea. Why was Dyson so frightened when he brought them to us?' Amberg asked.

'Oh, that's simple. There are assassins here looking for him – to kill him. At least ten people have so far been murdered over this business. Maybe you should have a guard, Walter.'

'This *is* Switzerland,' the banker said indignantly.

*   *   *

159

'Something's very wrong about the sequence of events,' Tweed said as they left the building and headed for Bahnhofstrasse.

Butler and Nield appeared out of nowhere as they walked along. Newman was walking on the inside nearest the shops with Paula between him and Tweed on the outside. Butler strolled slowly past Tweed, staring ahead as he spoke out of the corner of his mouth.

'You've been followed. Chap in ski gear. Peaked cap with tinted visor . . .'

He continued on ahead of them while Nield remained behind the trio. Paula stopped for a moment, apparently to glance into a shop window. In the reflection from the brilliant sun she saw the man in a ski outfit walking ahead of Nield. She resumed her conversation as they approached Bahnhofstrasse.

'What is wrong about the sequence of events Walter described to us?'

'Dyson arrives with film and tape. Who could resist the temptation to watch, to listen? This coincides with Julius leaving his wife, Eve. It further coincides with his urgent call to me to meet him, followed by his flight to Tresillian Manor. Plus the fact he transferred film and tape to the bank vault in Basle. Dyson asked to be let out by the back exit. The only reason for that is he suspected he'd been followed, which he probably told Amberg. Even if he didn't, Amberg would guess the reason.'

'Why do you think Julius left his wife so suddenly?'

'I can only guess. But I know he had a mistress in Geneva. Normal lifestyle for *some* Swiss bankers. Live in one city, have your mistress in another, visit her at the weekend on a fictitious business trip. Maybe Eve found out – being English she might not have appreciated old Swiss bankers' customs. That's why I want to see her. I'm hungry. Let's have a coffee and cake at Sprüngli before we start checking . . .'

*   *   *

160

The tea room at the famous Sprüngli was on the first floor, overlooking Bahnhofstrasse. It gave Paula an eerie feeling when she recalled the package the 'postman' at Tresillian Manor had delivered before murdering eight people – a box of chocolates from Sprüngli.

'Excuse me a moment,' Newman said.

They ordered coffee from the waitress as Newman peered out of the window down into the boulevard-like street. He joined them as they went to the counter to select a cake, waited until they were seated again.

'We still have company. Ski-man with his tinted visor is leaning against a tree on the far side where he can watch the entrance to this place. No sign of Pete Nield or Butler.'

'There wouldn't be, but they'll be out there,' said Paula as she dug her fork into a cream pastry. 'This is super.' She glanced round the long room where wooden-topped tables were carefully arranged, at the hygienic counter they had visited for their cakes. 'I think this is where the Zurich *grandes dames* meet each other to natter about the latest gossip. Bet there's plenty of that if they have bankers for husbands.'

'Why should they be bankers' wives?' Newman asked.

'Just look at them. Dripping with pearls, three or four solid gold bangles round their wrists. Dripping with wealth.' She looked at Tweed. 'What's next on the programme – and why did we register in our own names at the Gotthard?'

'To smoke out the enemy,' Tweed said, his expression determined. 'This is the battlefield. When we leave here we'll go to police headquarters, hope to find Beck there. Philip Cardon wants a weapon. Then we'll take a taxi up to that villa in the Dolder area in the hope I can talk to Eve Amberg. That could be interesting . . .'

*   *   *

161

Sara Maranoff walked into the Oval Office, closed the door, locked it. She ran a finger over her lips as she tried to assess her boss's mood. Bradford March was twisted sideways in his chair, staring out of the windows, his thick lips pressed together. A black stubble covered his jaw and she didn't like the look of his expression. She took a deep breath as he turned to glare at her.

'Bad news won't wait, Brad. I just took a call from Zurich – whoever it was cleverly insisted on speaking to me. You may be glad about that.'

'More bad news I can do without. Get to it. Norton telling us he hasn't achieved one friggin' thing?'

'Norton is holding on the line, but this call came from a no-name guy. Said he had a couple of items you might not want him to go public with – not how he phrased it but that's what he meant. He's demanding twenty million dollars for them – whatever they may be. Could be a crank . . .'

She was watching March's reaction closely. The President leaned forward, folded his hairy-backed thick fingers, rested them on the desk. He had a look of thunder and she was careful to keep quiet.

'You traced the number he was calling from?' snapped March.

'Tried to. He wasn't on the line long enough. All they could get was a Zurich call. Is there something I should know, Brad?'

'You should put Norton through *now* . . .'

'Norton here, Chief. I've taken personal control of the operation on the spot. I'm in Zurich. I've traced Tweed and company, got the bastard in my sights.'

'Handle that your own way.' March's tone became tough. 'This is an order. Track down Dyson, Ives and Dillon. Take them out. Got it? No more friggin' around. Just do it . . .'

He slammed down the phone, stood up and began

162

prowling. Wearing an open-necked shirt which exposed his hairy chest he was also clad in jeans and sneakers – the outfit he wore when mixing with the 'common folk'.

'What about this crank?' Sara pressed. 'We ignore him if he calls again?'

'He calls again, say we'll pay. Ask him where the money is to be deposited. Then call Norton, tell him the location. He's to surround it with an army of concealed and armed men. Tell him to make up a bundle which looks like it contains banknotes as bait. Just do it – and it isn't anything you need to know about.'

Tweed had left Sprüngli with Newman and Paula and they were walking up Bahnhofstrasse *en route* to police head-quarters. Despite the brilliant glare of the sun it was bitterly cold and there were few people about. A small crowd stood waiting for a tram.

They heard one rumbling from behind them and had just reached the crowd when the Ski-man brushed close to Tweed. Newman had gripped his Smith & Wesson and behind the skier Butler held his Walther concealed in his hand. The Ski-man had white hair projecting from under the back of his cap. Tweed laid a restraining hand on Newman's arm.

'It's all right . . .'

'Tweed' – the Ski-man spoke rapidly in an American accent – 'one thing I forgot. My office safe at Langley was raided – they have photos of yourself and Paula . . .'

He leapt aboard the tram just as the automatic doors were closing. Newman and Paula stared at Tweed.

'That was Cord Dillon,' he told them. 'Wearing a white wig. Well disguised. And now we know the worst. Paula and I are recognizable to the opposition. Bob, stay close to Paula.'

'And I'm staying close to you,' Butler told him. 'I was

163

expecting Dillon to produce a knife. If he had done he'd have got a bullet through the spine.'

'Don't think badly of him. He's on his own and running. He just did us a big favour. Now for Beck and then Eve Amberg . . .'

Amberg's estranged wife lived in a large old grey villa perched high up above the city. As they'd climbed higher and higher a panoramic view of Lake Zurich and the city had appeared below. The three-storey villa stood back from the road behind tall railings rising up from a low stone wall. A short distance behind their taxi a black Mercedes slowed, parked by the kerb.

Behind the wheel, Butler, who had hired the car, looked at Nield seated alongside him. He checked his rear-view mirror again.

'No sign of a tail, Pete. So I suppose we just wait.'

'Someone in the BMW parked in front of the villa. A girl, I think. Tweed and Co. are approaching her . . .'

After paying off the cab driver, Tweed, with Paula and Newman, was approaching the wrought-iron gates when Tweed stared at the BMW. He paused, spoke half under his breath.

'I don't believe it. I think a word with her would be a good idea before we go barging in.'

The girl sitting in the front passenger seat by herself wore a pale blue woollen helmet but it didn't conceal the wave of golden hair falling to her shoulders. She wore sun-glasses and turned as Tweed bent down to speak to her. Paula was stunned. It was Jennie Blade, last seen in Padstow.

'You're a long way from Cornwall,' Tweed greeted her genially. 'You flew to Zurich?'

164

'Bloody hell, no. Look, it's freezing out there. Bob, come and sit beside me. Tweed, you and Paula climb in the back. It's warm as toast in here. Then we can talk.'

She flashed Newman a warm smile as he settled in the front passenger seat. She had the heaters going full blast and the warmth hit them. Jennie twisted round to talk to Tweed.

'We sailed here in the flaming *Mayflower*. Across the North Sea, up the Rhine and berthed at Basle. Then by train to here. I was thrown all over the place during the sea crossing. His lordship is mad keen on sailing.'

'His lordship? Gaunt, you mean?' Tweed queried. 'Where is he now?'

'At this moment? He's inside that villa. Enjoying himself.' She gazed fixedly at Tweed. 'Could you and I meet for a drink this evening? I'll tell you the story of my life.' She grinned wickedly. 'You'll find it a rather lurid tale.'

'Certainly,' Tweed agreed promptly. 'Six o'clock at the Hummer Bar in the Gotthard? You'll find the main entrance in Bahnhofstrasse a stone's throw from the Bahnhofplatz.'

'I'll look forward to that.'

'What did you mean when you said Gaunt was enjoying himself inside that villa?'

'Oh, didn't you know? Eve Amberg is one of his girl friends.'

18

Tweed hauled on the long chain bell-pull inside the massive porch of the villa. Turning round, he waved to Jennie Blade, who waved back. Newman stared at the door.

'Is this a good time to call?' Paula asked. 'What on earth are Gaunt and Jennie of all people doing in Zurich?'

'That's what I hope to find out . . .'

He broke off as the massive door was unlocked, unchained and swung inward by a maidservant in uniform. A Swiss girl, Paula thought when she heard her speak in English.

'Is Madame expecting you?' She studied the card Tweed had given her. 'You are an insurance salesman?'

'Hardly. I'm Chief Claims Investigator. Just take the card to your mistress and tell her we've travelled here all the way from Cornwall to see her.'

'I suppose she has to get dressed quickly,' Paula said in a low voice.

'Not necessarily,' Tweed replied.

In less than a minute the door was opened again, the maid informed them that Madame would see them now. The hall was very large and something about the atmosphere repelled Paula. The old woodblock floor was highly polished and a large over-ornate grandfather clock against one wall ticked ponderously. Leading them to the rear of the hall, the maid opened a door, stood aside. Tweed, sensing Paula's reluctance, marched straight into a vast living room with windows overlooking a neglected back garden which was a tangle of undergrowth and stunted evergreens.

'Mr Tweed? I believe you have met Mr Gaunt. I don't know about your friends . . .'

'They all know me. Naturally,' boomed Gaunt. 'We've had drinks together in the local pub. Right, Tweed? You following me around? Want to know what I'm up to, I expect. Eh? Let me introduce you all. This is Madame Eve Amberg, wife of the late lamented Julius Amberg.'

'Not all that lamented, Mr Tweed. Do sit down, all of you. Gregory is just leaving.'

166

Eve Amberg was an attractive woman in her mid-thirties. She had long titian hair and looked as though she had just returned from an expensive hairdresser. She had greenish eyes, strong features, a full mouth and a shapely chin. Her complexion had the marble-like glow Paula knew came from careful and lengthy make-up. She wore a bolero jacket over a green dress which emphasized her shapely figure. Her long legs were crossed elegantly. She had an aura of a strong personality and her voice was soft and appealing.

She patted the empty seat beside her on a couch inviting Tweed to sit next to her. The vacant cushion showed no sign of recent occupation. Gaunt was standing under an elaborate chandelier, clad in a houndstooth jacket and cavalry twill trousers with a blue silk cravat under his jaw. Very much the country gent, Paula thought.

'Eve, I really must go. I regret the reason for coming to see you.' He looked at Tweed before leaving. 'I now leave you to the tender mercies of Eve. Survive her charms if you can . . .'

Newman, seated next to Paula on another large couch, detected a note of irony in the remark. Eve chuckled good-humouredly, called out to him as he reached the door.

'You really are a horrible man, Gregory – leaving my new guests with the impression that I'm a monster.'

'But she is, she is,' Gaunt shot over his shoulder and closed the door behind him.

'I gather, Mrs Amberg, that you have heard the tragic news about your husband,' Tweed began. 'I was actually at Tresillian Manor shortly after the massacre had taken place.'

'Don't think I am a monster, Mr Tweed.' Eve stretched out a bare arm below her short-sleeved dress along the couch behind him. 'Julius and I had parted company for good before he left for England. But the manner in which

167

he died has shocked me. I can tell you that – the Squire has a tendency to despise women who can't stand up to a shock.'

'You are thinking of going back to England?' Tweed asked.

'Not bloody likely.' She reached for a cigarette out of a pearl-encrusted box, lit it with a gold lighter. 'Not yet. During the final blazing row Julius let slip he was expecting to make a fortune within days. Think I'm mercenary if you like, but I'm entitled to something after enduring his way of life for two years.'

'His way of life?' Tweed probed.

'Some bankers have their girl friends in other cities – are discreet. Not Julius. He visited a high-class call-girl on his doorstep. She has an apartment in Rennweg – in the middle of Zurich, for God's sake.'

'You know her name?'

'Yes. I had him followed by a detective. Helen Frey is her name. Rennweg 590. An apartment on the first floor. A bit too close for comfort. My comfort.' Her expression clouded over. 'I still think it's beastly the way he died. Damned weird, too.'

'Have you any idea where this fortune he spoke of was coming from?'

'No real idea at all. He speculated successfully on a large scale buying and selling foreign currencies. It might be that – although I gathered it was some new and unique deal. God knows how the bank will fare under the guidance of Walter.'

'He wasn't as competent as Julius?' Tweed ventured.

'I can never make him out. He's devious, gives the impression he's just chairman to preside over meetings. Sometimes I wonder about Walter.' Her arm touched Tweed's neck, her voice very soft. 'Did Julius suffer before he died? Gaunt gave a perfectly horrific description, but he's not known for his subtlety. He thinks *finesse* is a French pastry. Do smoke if you want to, Mr Newman. I

168

saw your hand reaching towards your pocket. May I call you Bob?'

'Please do.'

Paula had taken an instant dislike to Eve Amberg at first sight. Now she was changing her mind about her: she was only human after all, had shown genuine distress at the manner of her husband's death. Newman reached down for a crystal glass ashtray on the lower shelf of a small table.

Inside it was a crushed cigar stub. Gaunt must have spent some time with Eve to have smoked a whole cigar. Which reminded him of the cigar ash sample which Paula and Tweed had left at police headquarters for analysis – the sample Tweed had collected off the window-ledge in the no-name house at Rock in Cornwall. Eve jumped up, brought him another ashtray.

'That one is messy.'

She returned to her place on the couch beside Tweed. She was smoking her own cigarette in a long ivory holder and waved it to make a point. Her other hand clasped Tweed's and squeezed it.

'It really was very sweet of you to come here to tell me about Julius's tragic death. It just happened Gregory Gaunt got here first. I'm grateful to you. Now I am wondering whether po-faced Walter knows. Hardly ever see him but I'll have to call him.'

'I've saved you the trouble,' Tweed informed her. 'We visited him at the Zurcher Kredit . . .'

'Ah! And rather than come to see me himself he agreed you should perform the horrid task. Typical of him. But Walter and I are practically strangers.'

You catch on quick, Paula thought. You have got all your marbles. Julius was a fool to play around with other women. They chatted for a little longer, then Tweed said they must go. Eve accompanied them to the door, her arm looped through Newman's.

'Please do come and see me again before you leave

169

Zurich. Promise.' She looked at Paula. 'That invitation does include you, Paula. I'm sorry that I haven't paid you the attention a perfect hostess should have done.'

'Think nothing of it,' Paula assured her. 'This really is the most difficult time for you.'

'The maid said you came by taxi,' Eve recalled suddenly. 'There aren't any as high up as this. I'll phone for one. Be here in no time . . .'

As the taxi was driving them away from the villa Tweed glanced back through the rear window. The BMW was still parked further up the hill and there were two people inside. He had told the cab driver to drop them on the Limmat quai, close to the Rudolf bridge.

The sun was still shining out of a clear blue sky as he led the way across the Rudolf-Brun-Brücke. Looking back to the Altstadt – the Old Town on that side of the river – Paula drank in the ancient stone buildings, the green spires of churches which had once been gleaming copper. Butler's black Mercedes was just turning on to the bridge.

'We're going first to police headquarters again,' Tweed told them. 'Let's hope Beck is in this time.'

'Talk of the devil,' Paula said as they turned right up a steep incline. 'There is Philip – staring at police head-quarters.'

'You must be psychic,' Tweed told Cardon as he joined them. 'Where have you been?'

'Exploring Zurich, sniffing the atmosphere. You might be interested that the city is crawling with Americans who appear to be drifting round to no purpose. I stress the word "appear". All of them men and all carrying handguns. In this weather in a tight overcoat – topcoat as they call it – a holster is a giveaway.'

'Significant,' Tweed commented, and left it at that.

* * *

170

Arthur Beck, whose Federal HQ was in Berne, had an office in the solid four-storey building which is Zurich Police HQ. His large first-floor room overlooked the Limmat and the university perched high up on the opposite bank. He greeted Tweed and his three companions gravely and smiled briefly at Newman.

Paula sensed Beck's change of mood as he squeezed her arm, escorted her to a chair at a table. Cardon sat beside her. Newman and Tweed were seated as Beck took his place at the head of the table. The atmosphere was tense. Beck unlocked a drawer, took out a certificate signed by himself, a Walther with ammo, pushed everything across to Cardon including a hip holster.

'I fear you are all in great danger,' Beck began. 'And I have to warn you I cannot guarantee your protection. You have been followed by armed men since you left the Gotthard this morning. Your unknown adversary appears to be employing American gunmen – many dressed in Swiss clothes. They work in teams which alternate frequently. Only a very smart detective observed that you were followed again when you left the Zurcher Kredit Bank. I was informed because my people carry walkie-talkies. I took action.'

'What was that?' Tweed asked quietly.

'When you took a taxi to somewhere across the Limmat a car attempted to tail you. One of my patrol cars blocked this car. You had disappeared by the time the car was free to proceed.'

'Thank you for that,' Tweed said.

'Even so, I cannot guarantee your protection,' Beck repeated. 'The situation is exceptional.'

'Exceptional in what way?' Tweed enquired. Lord, he thought, are we back to square one? Is it possible that this huge organization we are up against can reach out and taint the Chief of Swiss Federal Police? Beck's next words in response to his question told him how wrong he

171

had been to doubt the Swiss.

'No fewer than forty more Americans – all carrying diplomatic passports – have arrived via Kloten. I do not have the manpower to track them – bearing in mind those who arrived earlier.'

'If they are carrying guns . . .' Paula began.

'I understand your thinking. But they have diplomatic immunity. We cannot arrest or search any of them. It is against international law.'

'You are powerless,' Tweed commented.

'There is a further difficulty. Last night in Munich an American diplomat was shot down, murdered. A woman got in the way of the assassin who shouted and threatened her with his gun. She reported that the killer spoke with a strong American accent before he escaped. So for the moment all American so-called diplomats in Europe have an added excuse for carrying a gun.'

'You're suggesting the Munich diplomat was murdered to provide this excuse?' Newman asked.

'I think these are very ruthless people we are dealing with. Yes, that is what I was suggesting. It conjures up nightmares, does it not?'

There was a heavy silence after Beck's words. Paula sat stunned. Newman looked thoughtful. Cardon, after checking the Walther, slid it inside the hip holster he had strapped on. He looked at Tweed and grinned, quite at ease with the situation.

'This calls for a Swiss protest to Washington,' Tweed said eventually. 'All these pseudo-diplomats flooding in.'

'Which is exactly what I have done,' Beck said in a very different tone. 'You think I remain passive regarding this invasion of our territory? I have already phoned Anderson, the American ambassador in Berne. You would like to guess what he said to me?'

'No. What did he say?'

'The same old phoney story as when I contacted him last time. The March administration is recalling diplomats from all over Europe. These men are supposed to be the replacements. Anderson, a friend of mine, sounded most embarrassed. He has already protested to Washington.'

'So that road is closed. But it tells me something.'

'But I am a fox.' Beck smiled at Paula. 'Today I fly to Berne to confront Anderson with evidence. I shall be taking with me one of the new arrivals' so-called diplomatic passports. My experts tell me it is forged.'

'I'd better not ask you how you got hold of the passport,' Tweed remarked.

'Oh, he dropped it in the street after leaving the Hotel Baur-en-Ville. By chance one of my men picked it up when the owner had disappeared.'

Newman grinned and Tweed smiled. They had guessed that Beck's man who was there 'by chance' had picked the American's pocket. Yes, Beck was a fox, Tweed said to himself. He stood up to leave.

'Sit down for a moment more,' Beck urged. 'Since that episode I had a call from another visitor at the Baur-en-Ville – an individual I suspect could be the leader of the new contingent. A Mr Marvin Mencken.'

'And what did this Mencken want?' Tweed asked.

'To report the loss of the diplomatic passport. He said his assistant had had his pocket picked, that I should know which petty thieves patronized Bahnhofstrasse and would I trace the criminal and return the passport within the next twenty-four hours. A very unpleasant man, this Mencken. One of my men, disguised as a street photographer, tried to take his picture and he smashed the camera.' He paused. 'The photo is a good one.'

'But you said the camera was smashed,' Paula reminded him.

'I said just that. But the first man in civilian clothes was a

173

decoy. While his camera was being smashed a backup man took another picture. You might like copies . . .'

Opening a drawer, Beck took out an envelope and extracted four glossy prints. Paula studied her copy. The slim man's face came out clearly, a foxy face twisted into an expression of cold fury.

'A savage-looking brute,' she commented.

'Not the sort of chap you'd invite to your London club,' Newman remarked ironically.

'Keep those pictures,' Beck advised as his guests prepared to leave. 'They might save your lives . . .'

'Who is it?' Norton answered the phone in his usual abrasive tone.

'Marvin here . . .'

'Get to it, Mencken. Any news? There should be by now, for Christ's sake.'

'It's Tweed. He's just returned from a visit to Amberg's wife, Eve. I had the news ten minutes ago . . .'

'Why the hell didn't you report earlier, then? Tweed? I want him taken out – before he reaches Dyson, Dillon or Ives. Especially Ives . . .'

'Tweed's at Zurich police headquarters now . . .'

'Then organize it. I want him carried away in a box before tonight. Just do it . . .'

Outside police HQ a black Mercedes was parked. Butler sat behind the wheel. A short distance away Pete Nield stood, taking a great interest in the River Limmat.

'Our next port of call is Helen Frey's apartment at Rennweg 590,' Tweed told Paula and Newman. 'It's only a short distance on foot.'

'Our next port of call is lunch,' Paula said firmly. 'My stomach is rumbling.'

Tweed agreed reluctantly. He seemed to be able to go for hours without food once he'd picked up a scent. Newman said he was starving too.

'The Baur-en-Ville is close,' Tweed said. 'We'll get a quick meal there.'

'I'll trail along behind you,' remarked Cardon, who had heard every word.

'Then first go over and tell Butler to take Nield back to the Gotthard for something to eat . . .'

The Baur-en-Ville's lunch bar is entered by climbing curved steps just off Bahnhofstrasse. Newman led the way as the automatic doors slid back. He scanned the few customers as he walked inside. The bar is a split-level room with a curved bar on the ground level. At the back steps lead up to the second tier which is separated from the lower level by a low wooden wall topped with a gleaming brass rail.

Newman walked up the steps, chose one of the blue leather banquettes with its back to the wall. Illumination came from lights recessed in the ceiling. Paula thought the atmosphere was luxurious and welcoming. While she sat with Tweed on the banquette Newman went back down to the bar for a pack of cigarettes.

Tweed was studying the menu when Paula nudged him. He looked up.

'That man who has just come in from the hotel entrance and stopped at the bar. The tone of this place has dropped to zero.'

At that moment, Mencken, standing at the bar, glanced up at the second tier. His cadaverous face froze for a second in an expression of vicious hardness, his foxy eyes bored into Paula's. She slowly switched her gaze as though interested in the other customers. Tweed noted the soulless blank eyes as he also looked round the bar.

Seated at a small table by the door, Cardon's right hand had slid inside his windcheater, was gripping the butt of his

175

Walther. Mencken appeared to change his mind and walked rapidly back into the hotel. He had not noticed Newman.

Later, Tweed ate his club sandwich of smoked turkey, egg and bacon with great gusto. His manner was buoyant.

'It's starting – what I hoped for. The enemy is crawling out from under the rocks. Remember Cord Dillon warned us photos of myself and you, Paula, had been taken from his safe in Langley? That walking skeleton recognized us,' he said with great satisfaction.

'What a perfectly horrible thug,' Paula commented. 'And while I remember it, why are we visiting Helen Frey? I've always wanted to see a call-girl's apartment, particularly a high-class one. It will add to my experience.'

'Helen Frey may have vital information,' Tweed explained. 'During one of his visits Julius Amberg may have indulged in pillow talk . . .'

Only one person noticed something unusual as they entered Bahnhofstrasse. Philip Cardon, strolling well back from them, observed a cripple in a battery-operated wheelchair emerge from an alley-way. The wheelchair kept pace behind Tweed and his companions.

19

Rennweg was a narrow street of shops which led off Bahnhofstrasse at a slanting angle. No. 590 had a closed door with a metal grille speakphone beside it. Tweed pressed a button below the grille, wondering what he was going to say to a professional call-girl. Best to improvise on the spur of the moment.

'*Ja?*' a soft feminine voice answered in German.

'Helen Frey?' he asked.

'*Ja.*'

'I only speak English. I'm a friend of Julius Amberg, the banker. Zurcher Kredit, Talstrasse. I was given your name.'

'You sound OK,' the voice replied in English. 'Come up – push the door when the buzzer goes . . .'

Tweed leaned against the door and it swung inward, revealed a straight staircase. Followed by Paula and Newman, he mounted the stairs quickly. A door opened at the top landing and Paula stared at one of the most attractive women she had ever seen.

A natural blonde, Helen Frey had a long face, a shapely nose and full lips, emphasized with red lipstick. She gazed back at Paula, turned her attention to Tweed and spoke in English again.

'What the hell is this? I don't do foursomes.'

She was closing the heavy door. Tweed used shock tactics. He rammed his foot between the door and the frame. The girl, twenty-eight or so, Paula guessed, wore a smart blue figure-hugging suit. Her other hand appeared, holding a wide flick knife. There was a loud click as the blade shot out.

'Julius Amberg is dead, murdered in England,' Tweed said quickly. 'I'm concerned about a lot of money. This is my assistant, Paula, and my adviser, Newman. A lot of money,' he repeated.

She studied Paula again, then Newman, who stared back with no particular expression. Tweed folded his arms, a pacific gesture, and kept his foot in the door. She nodded as though answering a question she had asked herself.

'You'd better come in, then.'

'I'd feel happier if you put away that knife,' Tweed told her. 'All we want is a discussion. I am willing to pay a reasonable fee. I appreciate your time is valuable,' he ended without a trace of sarcasm.

'I did say you could come in.' She held up the knife and there was another click. The blade shot back inside its sheath. 'Feel more comfortable now, Mr . . .?'

'Tweed. Now we're all introduced.'

Discreetly, Paula glanced curiously round the large sitting-room. The main colour motif was pink, which normally would have seemed over-ornate, but instead the effect was welcoming. Curtains drawn over the window protected the room from the outside world.

It was illuminated by soft pink wall-sconce lampshades. The deep-pile carpet was off-white and against one wall stood a vast couch – large enough to take two reclining people. Comfortable armchairs were scattered about the carpet and an antique desk occupied one corner near the curtains. A huge wall mirror faced the couch.

Presumably some men liked to watch what they were doing while others didn't – a long brass rod ran full length along the top of the mirror flanked by pink curtains, held in place with tie-backs. A silver champagne bucket perched on a metal tripod stood at one end of the couch.

Helen Frey walked slowly over to the couch, sat down, waved her hand towards the chairs.

'Well, make yourselves at home, everyone. And tell me what this is all about. You're sure Julius is dead? He was my most profitable client.'

'Oh, he's very dead, I assure you,' Tweed said with rare brutality. 'I myself saw his blood-soaked body. A machine-gun makes an awful mess fired at point-blank range.'

'I can hardly believe it,' Helen said.

'You'd better believe it,' Newman told her.

'It must be a shock to you,' Paula intervened. 'I also saw poor Julius, Miss Frey. It gave me one hell of a shock.'

'Call me Helen, everyone. You seem decent people. But

178

I'm wondering what your interest is in the tragedy. You've shaken me.'

Tweed changed tactics. He had assumed Helen Frey would be as hard as nails, but Paula's more sympathetic approach had altered Helen's attitude.

'You could call me an investigator,' he began. 'Julius was a friend of mine and I'm trying to find out who murdered him. If I can find out why this hideous crime was committed I'll be closer to the murderer. Was Julius expecting to make a great deal of money in the near future?'

Helen sat very erect on the couch, her long legs crossed. She reached for a silver cigarette box on a table, offered it to her guests.

'Thank you, but I prefer my own,' Newman said, producing his pack. 'My friends don't smoke. This is a lovely room you have.'

He stood up and lit Helen's cigarette. She was concentrating on Tweed as Newman then wandered round, looked at a portrait of Helen, moved a few paces apparently to look at a framed landscape above the desk. A diary lay open at the day's date, reminding him that they were at the beginning of March. What caught his attention was Helen's next appointment.

4.30 p.m. Emil Voser.

'Was Julius expecting to make a great deal of money in the near future?' Helen said, repeating Tweed's question after she'd taken several deep drags on the cigarette, blown smoke rings into the air. 'Yes, he was.'

'May I ask how you know that?' Tweed asked gently.

'You may.' She gave him a bewitching smile. 'It was on the day before he left for Cornwall.' She phrased her next remark delicately. 'He was here with me. He'd lost a big sum investing in foreign currencies. But he said he would more than make up the loss and end up with a fortune.'

179

'Did he give you any idea where this fortune was coming from?'

'He said fate had handed him a gigantic royal flush. I remember his exact words – they were so graphic. Julius was an enthusiastic card player.'

'May I also ask what his mood was like when he was here for . . .' Tweed trailed off.

She smiled wanly, took another drag on the cigarette, blew another perfect smoke ring.

'You were going to say when he was here for the last time. And you are right, Tweed. That *was* the last time I saw him alive. His mood? It was rather strange – a mixture of excitement and . . .'

'Fear?' Paula suggested.

'Yes! That was it. He was very nervy as though what he had in mind was dangerous. I even told him not to take too great a risk.'

'And how did he react to that?' Tweed enquired.

'He said that making a lot of money always involved taking a risk. He added that also it was too late for him to change his mind, so he was going ahead to push the deal.'

'Thank you for being so frank, Helen. Now, I owe you a fee for your time. Business is business.'

'I normally charge one thousand Swiss francs.'

Tweed was reaching for his wallet when Helen thrust out a hand to stop him. Her tone of voice had an appealing quality which touched Paula.

'I don't want your money, Tweed. I'm convinced you are telling the truth – that you are determined to track down the monster who murdered Julius. A woman in my profession becomes an expert in knowing when men are lying. Regard it as my contribution to bringing the swine who killed him to justice.'

'If you insist . . .'

'But I do.' She stood up to unfasten the two deadlocks on her door. 'By the way, as you leave the opposite door on

180

the landing may open. It will be Klara. We are in the same business but good friends. She is often curious about my cleints.'

Tentatively, she held out her hand to Paula. Without one moment's hesitation Paula grasped it warmly and stared into Helen's steady blue eyes. She felt that they were, when all was said and done, sisters under the skin.

Newman walked out on to the landing first to make sure it was safe. The door opposite opened and a tall brunette peered out. She wore a housecoat loosely tied and grinned wickedly at Newman.

'I'm Klara,' she said as Helen closed her door. 'Have you the energy left to come and play with me?'

'A tempting proposal.' Newman smiled at her. 'There are two things against the idea. I've just had a very large lunch recently. And I'm late for an appointment which could be profitable.'

'Come back later, then. Spend a little of the profits on me. You and I could make music together.'

'I'm sure of it,' Newman agreed. 'I may see you later,' he lied.

'You should have accepted her invitation,' Paula teased him as they got to the bottom of the stairs. 'I liked Helen, but I think Klara could be great fun too . . .'

Rennweg was quiet as they stepped back into the street. Opposite Helen Frey's doorway was a small café. Inside, close to the window, Cardon sat with a soft drink in front of him. He stroked a hand across his forehead to signal he had seen them.

'I want to call Eve Amberg,' Tweed said. 'I need a public phone box.'

'There's one near Bahnhofstrasse,' Paula told him. 'I

181

remember seeing it on our way here . . .'

As the three of them walked off Cardon waited for a few minutes inside the café. He had seen the cripple in the wheelchair taking an unusual interest in shop windows near Frey's doorway. The invalid man wore a peaked shabby cap like those once sported by German students. His face was muffled in a woollen scarf, but it had slipped for a moment and Cardon had a good look at his face.

The nose curved downwards over his upper lip, reminding Cardon of an evil parrot. In his forties, Cardon had estimated. A worn rug covered his lap and his hands, on the controls, remained concealed underneath it. The wheelchair now began to follow Tweed and his companions. Cardon walked slowly after it.

Tweed entered the phone cubicle, looked up Eve Amberg's number in the directory. He inserted coins, dialled and she answered quickly.

'Amberg. Who is calling?'

'Tweed here, Eve. Sorry to bother you again but there are one or two personal questions I didn't ask when we met.'

'Ask away. It's a relief to talk to someone English. I come from Cornwall. I'm reverting to my maiden name – Eve Royston. Now, the stage is yours.'

'Would you mind confirming how close it was to Julius's departure for England that you separated?'

'Two days before,' she said crisply. 'I'd challenged him earlier about his visits to Helen Frey. She may be a call-girl but I sensed their relationship was close. He then phoned me, as I said, two days before he flew to Britain. Said he wanted a separation and a divorce in good time. We had a helluva row over the phone. I told him I'd already decided to walk, so his suggestion was a bit late in the day.'

'You mean you never saw him again before he left? All this was over the phone?'

'It was,' she said emphatically. 'Something else I did not

appreciate. He might have come to see me.'

'May I also ask how you first knew about Helen Frey?'

'Like something out of a cheap play. He was careless. Came home with traces of lipstick on his collar and he smelt of the wrong perfume. Despite smoking, I have a good sense of smell. I didn't say anything. I phoned the best private detective in Zurich to follow him. A bit sordid, but I was desperate to know the truth. He – the detective – followed him three times to Frey's place in Rennweg. That was it.'

'Would you be willing to give me this detective's name, address and phone number?'

'Of course. Name is Theo Strebel. He has a small apartment in the Altstadt – on this side of the Limmat. Here are the details . . .'

Tweed had his notebook and pen ready, scribbled down the information. Outside the phone cubicle Newman was leaning against a wall as though waiting to use the phone. Paula appeared to be window-shopping.

'Thank you, Eve,' Tweed said. 'I'm most grateful.'

'Did you want to interview Strebel? If so, ten in the morning is the best time. He's going through his post. Would you like me to call him, introduce you, arrange a time?'

'That would be helpful. Ten in the morning tomorrow would be fine. And thank you again . . .'

Tweed emerged and continued walking with Newman and Paula into Bahnhofstrasse. Behind them the wheelchair began moving again.

Tweed told them about his conversation with Eve. Paula guessed why he wanted to talk to Strebel, but asked him, to see if she'd guessed right.

'He's a detective – a good one, Eve said. I want to see whether he took any photos of Julius entering Helen's place.'

183

'Why?' Paula persisted.

'Just an idea I have. Helen said Julius was in a strange mood.'

'But she explained that,' Paula recalled.

'So she did,' Tweed agreed, and Paula knew he wasn't going to tell her any more. In Bahnhofstrasse commuters on their way home were clustered in a crowd round a tram stop twenty yards or so away. Cardon came up behind them.

'Freeze. Don't move . . .'

They obeyed his instruction instantly. Newman saw out of the corner of his eye that Cardon was gazing at something. He looked in that direction. A man in a wheelchair was backing it inside a side-street where there was a small modern white church Paula admired. When the wheelchair was alongside the street's far wall it stopped moving.

The man huddled inside the chair whipped back his lap rug. He showed startling agility. His right hand, holding something, was hoisted high, like a bowler in a cricket match about to throw the ball. A cylindrical object sailed through the air in an arc, descending to land at Tweed's feet. Cardon's left hand, clawed, caught the object before it landed on the pavement. In a blur of movement he lobbed it back. It landed in the lap of the man in the wheelchair. The 'cripple' jerked upright, had one foot on the street, when there was a loud explosion.

The man who had hurled the grenade disintegrated. The relics of his body were smashed against the white wall where a red lake appeared. The wheelchair became a shambles. One wheel rolled up Bahnhofstrasse, leaving a trail of dark red blood in its wake. Paula saw a severed hand lying in the street.

As the commuters jerked their heads round Newman suddenly dropped into a crouch, his Smith & Wesson gripped in both hands. Behind them, five feet or so away, a man in a belted raincoat had opened a violin case, extracted a snub-nosed Uzi machine-pistol. The muzzle was aimed at Tweed as Newman fired three times in rapid succession. The sound of the shots was masked by the screeching stop of an approaching tram – the driver had seen the lake of blood spilling into the road. The man holding the Uzi was hurled back against a plate-glass window with such force it fractured as he sagged to the ground.

'Scatter!' Tweed ordered. 'Meet up at the Gotthard . . .'

20

Paula sat on the edge of the bed in Tweed's room at the Gotthard. Her feet were pressed hard on the floor to prevent them from trembling. She was suffering from delayed shock brought on by the events in Bahnhofstrasse. Also in the room, seated in chairs, were Newman and Cardon. Paula's mood was not helped by Tweed's – she sensed he was puzzled by something. His first words didn't help her to detect what was bothering him.

'Let's sum up what happened. While we were in the bar at the Baur-en-Ville that villainous-looking type – I'm going to nickname him the Skull – spotted Paula and myself and then hurried back into the hotel.'

'I don't see what you're getting at,' Paula said, forcing herself to speak in a calm voice.

'Have patience. We didn't spend long over lunch but when we left to walk to Helen Frey's place in Rennweg the fake cripple was waiting for us, presumably already armed with his grenade. The speed with which the Skull and his associates move is incredible. Professionals of the top rank, I fear.'

'I still don't really see what you're driving at.'

'Communications. I feel sure the wheelchair man also had a mobile phone under the lap rug which concealed his grenade. He could have used that phone without Cardon seeing him. I'm worried about Helen Frey.'

'What on earth for?' Newman intervened.

'Because the cripple must have used the phone to report we were nearing that tram-stop. Hence that man with the Uzi you dealt with was waiting for us.'

'I see that,' Paula agreed, 'but why this anxiety about Helen Frey?'

'The cripple could have reported our visit to her to the Skull. She could be in danger. Time for me to call her.'

'She has a 4.30 p.m. appointment with an Emil Voser,' Newman recalled. 'I noticed it in her desk diary. So she may be busy.'

'Then she'll indicate that on the phone.'

While Tweed was checking Frey's number in the directory Paula began talking to Cardon. She kept her voice down as Tweed dialled the number.

'Philip, I still can't understand how you were able to catch that grenade in time and lob it back. Or, Bob, how you spotted the second assassin.'

'Easy.' Cardon grinned. 'First I'm good at cricket as a bowler. But mainly it was Butler's training me on a course down at the Send manor in Surrey. In the grounds he'd throw me a live grenade with the pin out – I had to lob it over the other side of a brick wall before it detonated. He tested me first with a cricket ball. Just one of the many contingency attack situations he trained me in. So, easy.'

'You make it sound so simple,' Paula remarked, her hands pressed against the bed. 'What about you, Bob?'

'Oh, I'm getting the measure of this mob. Organized up to the hilt. It occurred to me the grenade thrower might

186

well have back-up, so I checked all round, saw this character with a violin case. Rather old-fashioned technique – a
method used by Chicago gangsters at one time, carrying a
sub-machine-gun in a violin case.'

He stopped talking as Tweed put down the phone. His
expression was serious. He began to put on his overcoat.

'I don't like it. I called Frey's number. No reply for a
number of rings, then the phone was lifted, no one spoke,
the phone was put down again. I just asked to speak to
Helen Frey, gave no name. We're going back to Rennweg.
I'm really worried now . . .'

It was dark as they approached Rennweg 590 for the
second time. Again Paula and Newman walked with
Tweed while Cardon trailed behind them. On opposite
sides of the street Butler and Nield strolled along, pausing
to gaze into shops. The café opposite the entrance to No.
590 was still open and Cardon slipped inside it.

Tweed was about to press the speakphone button when
he stiffened. The door was not closed properly – its automatic lock had failed to work. Glancing up and down the
street, he pushed gently and the door swung inward. No
light on the staircase. Odd. He stepped inside, produced a
pencil torch, shielded it with his hand so it gave just enough
illumination to see the stair treads.

'I'd better go up first,' Newman whispered, the Smith &
Wesson in his hand.

He squeezed past Tweed who gave him the flash. Their
rubber-soled shoes made no sound as they slowly mounted
the staircase. Paula, who had quietly closed the front door,
brought up the rear. The atmosphere of the dark staircase
was eerie: she felt as though the walls were closing in on
her. The closed front door shut out all sounds from the
outside world. A stair tread creaked loudly as Newman
stepped on it. He climbed higher, shone the torch back to

187

illuminate the giveaway tread. Tweed and Paula stepped over it.

Arriving at the landing, Newman first pressed gently against Klara's door. It held firm. He walked over to Helen's door, saw that it was open half an inch or so. Someone had left in a hurry – so why hadn't she secured it afterwards?

With his gun still in his right hand, he used his left to push the door wider open, waited, listened. He had switched off the torch. He was listening for sounds of breathing, any sound. Nothing. He switched on the torch again, shone it slowly round, then held it motionless. With a swift movement he shone it towards the window: the curtains were still closed. He spoke over his shoulder.

'Paula, I wouldn't come in if I were you.'

That was just the sort of remark which made her determined to go inside. She followed Tweed, who took two steps inside and stopped. She saw him reach inside his jacket pocket under his raincoat, produce a pair of surgical gloves and put them on his hands. She extracted her own pair from her shoulder-bag. Newman stood very still inside the room, his torch beam held steady. He had pushed the door open with his knuckles. No fingerprints.

Tweed reached for the wall switch he'd noticed on their earlier visit, pressed it down. The pink wall-sconce lights came on and Paula saw what Newman had been staring at.

'Oh, no!'

Helen Frey, clad only in underclothes, lay sprawled back in an armchair. The front of her white slip was drenched with dark red blood. Her head flopped against the back of the chair at an unnatural angle. A savage crescent moon, blood red, circled her throat. She had been garrotted.

Tweed went close to the armchair followed by Paula. He guessed that a strong sharp wire had been used. The head had been almost severed from the body. She looked hideous with her lipsticked mouth open and her tongue

188

protruding. The weird angle of the head was now explained. Very little remained to attach it to the body.

'Emil Voser. 4.30 p.m.,' said Paula, recalling Newman telling them about the desk diary.

'Which is probably not his real name,' Tweed commented, his eyes scanning the apartment. 'I don't think that we ought to linger here. What is it, Paula?'

She was crouched near the side of the chair. She used her index finger to point and Tweed crouched beside her. On the carpet lay a blood-stained pearl, pierced at either end as though it belonged to a string.

'Bring it with us,' Tweed ordered.

'Which means we are tampering with evidence.'

'Which means exactly that,' Tweed agreed. 'But we know more about these people than anyone.'

Paula was already extracting a Cellophane specimen wallet from her shoulder-bag. She fumbled in her bag again and her right hand came out holding a pair of tweezers. She used them to tease the pearl, split along one side, into the wallet and sealed it. With a pen she wrote on the attached tab the date and *Rennweg 590*, and slipped the wallet inside her bag. She was sniffing the air as she stood up. She began prowling round the apartment.

'Can't you smell the faint whiff?' she said to Tweed. 'I caught it as soon as we came in – someone has been smoking a cigar. Got you . . .'

From a low table concealed by the arm of the couch Paula lifted up a large glass ashtray. Inside nestled an intact roll of cigar ash. Extracting another wallet, she carefully tipped the roll of ash into the second wallet. Sealing it, she wrote only *Cigar ash specimen No. 2*, and put this wallet into her bag.

'I missed that. Good work,' Tweed told her.

Newman was standing by the desk near the curtained window. He was staring down at the open desk diary.

'She had no other appointments today. Only this Voser.'

'We'll go now,' Tweed decided. 'I'll leave the door, half an inch open as we found it. Move silently – mind that creaking stair. We don't want to attract Klara's attention . . .'

They stepped into a quiet street, Tweed leaving last to pull the door almost closed, his hands now wearing leather gloves. Again Cardon signalled to them from the window in the café. This time Newman went inside, then turned to beckon Tweed and Paula to follow him. Tweed understood his motive when he saw Klara sitting by herself at a side table with a cup of coffee in front of her.

'I'm going to talk to Klara,' Newman said. 'She might have information.'

'Good idea,' Tweed agreed after a moment's hesitation.

'So you've come back again for a frolic?' Klara greeted Newman.

Tweed smiled as they sat at her table. He ordered coffee from the waitress for himself and Newman after Paula shook her head. Her stomach was queasy. Like Tweed, she kept quiet while Newman and Klara talked.

'I'm afraid I haven't,' Newman began. 'Maybe you ought to put that cup down. I have some rather shocking news for you. Just about as shocking as you can get.'

'I've got strong nerves,' Klara told him, her expression serious. 'You need them in my business. Some of the men who come to see you.'

'That's really the tragedy in Helen Frey's case.'

'Tragedy?' Klara looked down as she slowly drummed the pink-varnished nails of her right hand on the table. She looked up again direct at Newman. 'I'm tough – so don't treat me like a kid. Just tell me what's happened to Helen.'

'We came back a few minutes ago to ask her some questions we'd overlooked earlier. The front door was open, her door was open a bit. We found her inside. Murdered.'

'Oh, hell. I was always telling her to be more careful.

190

Which is why – if I hadn't a client – I used to open my door a crack when one of the stairs creaked. Not to be nosy, believe me. Just to try and look after her. I hope it wasn't a pervert. Did she suffer?'

'I'd say it was pretty quick. He slashed her throat open. It's not a nice sight. Did you by any chance see her four thirty appointment arrive this afternoon?'

'Yes, I did.'

'But there's no light on the staircase. In daytime the fanlight at the top gives enough illumination to see your way, but now . . .'

'There's a time switch, lasts one minute. If you know where to find it you can switch it on from just inside the front door. Then Helen and I have switches inside our apartments we can operate. When he came upstairs she'd obviously operated her time switch.'

'So you can describe him?'

'Well, yes and no. I only open my door a crack so her client won't spot me. I'd say he was taller than you are. His feet seemed to hurt him a bit the way he was walking slowly and carefully.'

'Slim?'

'No. Pretty fat, I'd say. His black overcoat was tight across his waist and the buttons looked as though they could fly off at any moment.'

'Colour of hair?'

'No idea. He also wore a black broad-brimmed hat pulled well down. Couldn't see his hair.'

'Describe his face.'

'That's difficult too. He had a pair of those wrapround tinted glasses which covered a lot of his face. And a white silk scarf which covered more of it. I do know his feet hurt him.'

'What about his age?' Newman pressed. 'Thirty, forty, older?'

'I honestly couldn't tell. I judge a man's age by the way

191

he moves – but coming up unfamiliar stairs with tender feet throws any body language.'

'Would you recognize him again if you saw him?'

'Only if he was dressed exactly as he was when he came up those stairs.'

'Then you'd really just be identifying the clothes,' Newman pointed out.

'I suppose you're right.'

'Sitting here, did you see him leave, get a better view?'

'No, I didn't. But just before you came in I was chatting with a girl friend. I didn't even see the three of you go back inside.'

'You're English, aren't you?' Newman suddenly shot at her.

'Yes, I am,' Klara said after a pause. 'So was Helen – her real name is – was – Helen Dane from Cornwall. We teamed up to come out here, hoping we'd have a novelty value for Swiss men. And we do. But they prefer you to have a common Swiss name. Don't ask me why. And don't ask my real name.'

'What's your Swiss surname, then? Klara who?'

'I'm not telling you that either. I'm clearing out of my apartment within the hour. Do the police know about Helen yet?' Klara asked.

'No, they don't. I'd just as soon you didn't mention our visits.'

'You can count on that,' she assured him. 'First, I simply couldn't stay in a building where poor Helen was murdered. Second, what clients are going to come back to me here? Rennweg 590 will become notorious once the press get hold of the story. That girl friend I was chatting to is about to vacate her apartment to take up a job in Geneva. I'm also not giving you the address.'

'Fair enough.'

Klara looked at Paula. 'Would you do me a great

favour? Come back with me to my apartment while I pack? *Please.*'

Paula looked at Tweed. He checked his watch. His six o'clock appointment with Jennie Blade at the Hummer Bar was coming up soon. Klara sensed his problem – time. She gazed at Paula.

'I'm the world's quickest packer. One suitcase and in five minutes we'll be in the street again.'

Tweed, reluctantly, nodded agreement to Paula. Newman warned Klara as she stood up, door key in her hand: 'When you're going to this new address I'd take a taxi. You know Zurich well? Good. Think of two fake destinations. Then get a third taxi to take you where you're going.'

'Good idea. Thanks . . .'

Tweed checked his watch again as the two women left the café. He doubted Klara's statement that she could pack in five minutes. Paula could but how many other women achieved that speed?

'Her description of Voser was pretty distinctive,' Newman commented. 'A tall fat man with tender feet.'

'I found two aspects of her description intriguing,' Tweed remarked.

'Which two aspects?'

'I want to chew them over in my mind,' Tweed told him cryptically. 'I did notice Klara is very tall.'

Newman gave up trying to penetrate the subtle recesses of Tweed's mind. He sat watching the closed door opposite.

Tweed had time to call Monica after he arrived back at the Gotthard. Klara had been as good as her word – she had packed the suitcase and emerged back on Rennweg with Paula in five minutes. Newman saw her safely into a taxi before they hurried back to the Gotthard . . .

'Monica, Tweed here. Are you alone? I do not want to

get in touch with Howard now. I'm speaking from my hotel.'

'All's quiet down here in Surrey . . .' Monica was wording what she said carefully. Anyone could be listening in. 'I have the details of the Gaunt concern. The top man is a millionaire. He likes to spread it round that he has no idea where the next penny is coming from. He owns the manor – no mortgage – a property in Rock with no name and has considerable assets in Switzerland. No details about them, of course. He was once a captain in the SAS. Had to resign – too independent-minded. A bit of an adventurer, like the old buccaneers. Popular with women. Has had a lot of girl friends. That's it.'

'Thank you. Now, two women have applied to me for jobs. I need to have detailed references. Ready to take down their names? Good. Jennie Blade. And Eve Amberg – maiden name Royston. I'll spell that last name. Got it? I suggest concentration on the Padstow area. I must go now. I'll call you in the near future. Take care . . .'

Paula was intrigued as Tweed put down the phone. Waiting while he loosened his collar, she asked her question.

'Why especially do you want to know about those two women?'

'Both of them have connections with Cornwall. Which is where it all started.'

21

Walking briskly into the Oval Office Sara Maranoff knew the moment she saw the President that he was expecting a visit from his latest girl friend, Ms Hamilton. Bradford

March was freshly shaven, wore a smart grey suit, had a bottle of champagne in the ice bucket.

'Senator Wingfield has asked to come and see you.'

'That friggin' wooden Indian? Stall the bastard. Tell him I'm up to my neck in paperwork for a new bill. Oh, I didn't tell you, Ms Hamilton is calling on me in half an hour. See I'm not disturbed while we talk.'

'Sure, boss.' Sara's expression suggested it was news to her. And she liked the word 'talk'. He wouldn't waste time talking to her. 'Norton is on the line,' she went on. 'Sounds to be in a hurry.'

'Does he? I'm in a hurry – for him to finish the jobs he was sent out to do. Put him on the line . . .'

'Norton here. We're closing in on Tweed. Nearly got him today . . .'

'*Nearly!* You mean the pest is hospitalized?'

'Not exactly. I've thought up a new angle to fix him for all time. Thought you'd like a bulletin . . .'

'Oh, you're issuing bulletins now, are you?' Livid, March leaned across the desk, shouting down the phone. 'For bulletin I read bullshit. The only bulletin I want from you is that Tweed, Dyson, Ives and Dillon are all gone to join the fathers they never had. How is Mencken working out?'

'He takes orders . . .'

'More calls like this and *you* will be taking orders from *him* . . .'

He crashed down the phone and Sara shuddered inwardly. If Brad went on like that he was going to shatter the instrument. It would be expensive replacing that special private phone. Sara was money-conscious. She tried another tack.

'I just heard you've recalled Ambassador Anderson from Switzerland. That you're sending out Mike Gallagher in his place.'

'I congratulate you on your source of information,' March said sarcastically.

'Anderson is an experienced diplomat. Gallagher is raw, a rough diamond. He could cause trouble, the language he uses.'

'Gallagher is a man I trust. Anderson has been interfering with things that don't goddamn concern him. He is out. *Out!*'

'Gallagher hasn't left the States yet. You could change your mind. I would if I were you . . .'

'But you're *not* me!' March roared at her. 'When you're sitting in this chair you can decide who goes where. And Gallagher contributed plenty to my election campaign.'

She sighed. Normally she could handle Brad, but there were times when he acted like a maddened bull. This was one of them. Time to change his mood. A reference to Ms Hamilton, bringing her back into his thoughts, should do the trick.

'Another bottle of champagne – to oil the works?' she suggested.

March glared at her and Sara realized her tactic had misfired. He pointed a short stubby finger across the room.

'The door is there. Walk. Preferably through it without opening it . . .'

'Thank you, Sara,' said Senator Wingfield. 'Don't worry about it. I know you tried.'

He put down the phone in the room at his Chevy Chase residence where the Three Wise Men were gathered. The banker and the elder statesman, nursing their drinks at the round table, watched the Senator as he joined them. Wingfield shook his head regretfully.

'I'm sorry, gentlemen. The President refuses to see me at the Oval Office. Some nonsense about paperwork piling up. It's a ploy to avoid meeting me. He probably guessed the subject I was going to raise.'

'Gallagher,' snapped the statesman. 'From my own experience I know the Berne embassy isn't a plum job. But Berne is a good listening post. How can he contemplate appointing a man who may come under investigation by a Senate sub-committee – for corruption in obtaining government contracts?' He lapsed into unusual vulgarity. 'When the shit hits the fan, when the press gets a whiff of it – which they will – the US government is going to be a laughing-stock all over the world.'

'You may be right,' Wingfield agreed.

'He is right!' the banker burst out. 'On top of that he is spending money on programmes like there's no tomorrow. Face up to it, March has become a menace.'

'Thank God Jeb Calloway is waiting in the wings,' said the statesman.

'Don't let's get excited,' Wingfield urged. 'Timing is everything in politics. We'll wait and see how it all pans out . . .'

Jeb Calloway paced his office, his six-foot frame taking long strides while his closest aide, Sam, watched him. Calloway sat down suddenly, pounded his clenched fist on the table where Sam sat.

'The rumours are growing about this private army March has organized. Ever heard of Unit One, Sam?'

'Maybe the odd whisper.'

'You have?' Calloway looked surprised, annoyed. 'Is that the name of the secret paramilitary force Brad March is rumoured to have built up?'

'Brad,' Sam remarked, watching the Vice-President closely, 'is wily, throws out smokescreens, spreads rumours. Best forget all about this thing, even if it did exist.'

'You seem to know one helluva lot. Most Americans

197

here in Washington have never heard of it.'

'Jeb, I'm not "most Americans". I've been on the Hill for quite a few years. Stay cool. What about that guy you contacted secretly?'

'He's already been in place for some time,' Calloway snapped. 'I heard a rumour that forty more invisible men were being flown to London aboard a United flight.'

'What source fed you that dangerous info., Jeb?' enquired Sam quietly.

'I don't name informants.'

'OK, clam up. We're just talking.'

'When I heard that,' Calloway rattled on, 'I called someone I know inside the American Embassy in London. He was at London Airport when the flight landed. They transferred to a Swissair flight for Zurich. So-called diplomats.'

'And the guy you have in place – to quote your own words. Where might he be?'

'In Zurich, of course,' Calloway said with a smile of self-satisfaction.

Sam lit a cigarette. Calloway pursed his lips. He didn't allow smoking in his office, but Sam was a law unto himself. Sam eyed Calloway shrewdly. He was wondering how he could persuade him to stop playing the power game.

'Better watch your step, Jeb,' he advised. 'All this intrigue you're tangled in. If Brad gets just one hint of what you're up to your ass will end in a sling.'

'I know what I'm doing. I need to know what's going on.'

Sure you do, Sam thought, but what *are* you doing?

The phone message which had come through while Tweed was talking to Monica was slipped under his door by a member of the Gotthard's staff. Tweed opened the

198

envelope, read the typed sheet inside and half-closed his eyes. Paula knew something had happened which was making him think furiously. He handed it to her.

'Read it, then show it to Bob and Philip.'

I am sorry I have to cancel our date for tonight. Something urgent cropped up. Can we meet same place same time tomorrow instead. Again, apologies. Love. Jennie Blade.

'She does leave it till the last minute,' Paula remarked as she handed it to Newman, who scanned it, passing it on to Cardon.

'The last minute is the significant factor.' Tweed went on talking before she could react. 'One key to this whole grim business is Newman's friend, Joel Dyson. I suspect everything started with him . . .'

'Acquaintance, not friend,' Newman said sharply.

'Just listen, I hadn't finished. Paula was always good at art, drawing portraits. Do you think, Bob, you could describe Dyson to Paula while she makes a sketch, an identikit picture?'

'I could try,' Newman agreed.

'I can use some of the good notepaper in that hotel folder,' Paula suggested. 'Pity I haven't a piece of charcoal. I'd get a much better result with that . . .'

'This do?' Cardon produced a short stick of charcoal. 'I use it to darken my eyebrows when I'm changing my appearance.'

'Now I can get to work. You seem to carry everything on you . . .'

Newman sat on the arm of the chair Paula occupied, began to give her a description and she made bold strokes on her paper with the charcoal. 'Nose a bit longer,' he said at a later stage.

While they were working on the identikit sketch Tweed took out his notebook, started writing down

199

names and linking them. Cardon watched over his shoulder, fascinated.

Joel Dyson – Julius Amberg – Gaunt – Jennie Blade – Eve Amberg (Royston) – Amberg – Helen Frey – Klara – Theo Strebel, Eve's detective – Gaunt? – Norton. Cornwall: Gaunt – Eve Amberg – Helen Frey. Washington: Dillon – Barton Ives, Special Agent FBI – Norton.

'It's beginning to link up,' Tweed remarked.

'Darned if I can see how,' Cardon commented.

'You might – if you bear in mind most of them are not what they seem.'

'You've lost me . . .'

'Bob says this is Joel Dyson,' Paula said, bringing her third sketch.

'The very image of the little creep,' Newman said, joining them.

'Good,' Tweed told Paula. 'You've done very well. Now tomorrow we need six small photocopies of that sketch.'

'I noticed there was a photocopying firm in Rennweg,' she recalled. 'I'll go there and get six reduced in size copies.'

'Why reduced?' Cardon asked her.

'Because the result will be clearer if you reduce it. If you enlarged it the detail would begin to disappear.'

'And,' Tweed told Cardon, 'I want every one of us to have a copy. I'm convinced Dyson is still in Zurich. This way whoever encounters him – if anyone does – will recognize him instantly. Paula, could you make a second copy of that sketch?'

'I'm sure I can. Why?'

'Joel Dyson is on the run. My guess is he's running for dear life. So he may well try to disguise himself. He's had time to take the obvious precaution – to grow a small moustache. Can you add that to the second sketch? Then

200

get the Rennweg printer to run off six copies of each version?'

'It will only take minutes,' she said.

'And I'll accompany her,' Newman announced. 'Dillon told us before he leapt aboard that tram that the opposition has photos of Tweed – and of Paula.'

'Don't leave her side for a moment,' Tweed ordered.

Cardon had just left the room after saying he was going to have a quick bath when the phone rang. Tweed raised his brows, glanced at Newman, let it ring several times before he answered.

'Yes, who is it?'

'Tweed?' a hoarse voice said. 'Cord here. I've got a bad cold, goddamnit . . .'

'You do sound awful . . .'

'Tweed, do you want to meet Barton Ives or is this a bad time? I can send him along to the Gotthard now.'

'Do it,' Tweed agreed and then the connection was broken.

He put down the phone slowly. 'At long last we are about to meet Barton Ives, unless he changes his mind. He's also running for his life. We mustn't overwhelm him with too many people.'

He reached for the phone, called Cardon, Butler and Nield in their rooms. He gave each the same instruction.

'From now on don't come to my room or approach me. Your first priority is still our protection – but stay in the background . . .'

They waited thirty minutes and no one arrived. Tweed was still studying his list of people whom he had linked together. He checked his watch, folded the sheet he had torn from his notebook, slipped it into his wallet and stood up.

'You don't think he's coming after all?' Paula suggested.

'I was doubtful from the beginning. He's survived so far by staying in deep cover. It takes a great effort of will to emerge into the open in that sort of situation. I'm hungry. They serve marvellous food in the Hummer Bar restaurant. We'll go down, the three of us, and eat . . .'

Tweed was locking his door as Newman strolled slowly down the corridor. He stretched a hand across his face, a mannerism Paula had noted when he was puzzled by something.

She brought up the rear as Tweed followed Newman. It was very quiet in the corridor as they headed for the lift. A man was walking towards them with a deliberate tread. As he passed Newman Paula automatically noticed that he was of medium height and athletic build. He had a large head, was clean-shaven and his dark hair was cut short. His eyes, under thick brows, were blue and penetrating. He reached out a hand as Tweed was passing him, grasped his arm.

Paula's hand was inside her shoulder-bag, gripping the butt of her .32 Browning in a flash. Newman had swung round, had taken three swift strides and pressed the muzzle of his Smith & Wesson into the stranger's spine.

'You wanted something?' Newman snapped.

'Hold it, fellas,' he whispered. He stretched out both hands and his square-tipped fingers touched the walls. 'Cord said it would be OK. I'm Special Agent Barton Ives, FBI.'

22

Tweed unlocked the door, Paula backed into his room, gun pointed at the American, and Newman nudged him inside with the Smith & Wesson muzzle. As Tweed followed them, locking the door again, Newman slipped his revolver into his holster, began to feel the captive all over for concealed weapons.

'I'm loaded,' Ives told him. 'Under the left armpit.'

Newman hauled out the weapon. The American also favoured a .38 Smith & Wesson. Paula noted that all his clothes, a business suit under his open trench coat, were of Swiss make. With his neatly trimmed short hair he reminded her of a tough teddy bear.

'I'll need to see some identification,' Tweed told him.

'Can I reach into my breast pocket? You folks sure don't take any chances. That's good . . .'

'He's clean now,' Newman said, checking the revolver and slipping it inside his large jacket pocket.

Ives produced a folder, handed it to Tweed, looked at Paula and grinned wearily.

'I could do with a glass of water, if that's permitted.'

She poured him mineral water, handed him the glass. He swallowed the contents with one gulp, sighed with relief. Tweed examined the folder carefully, checked the photo, the details printed behind the plastic cover.

'You do appear to be Special Agent Barton Ives,' he said, handing back the folder. 'Welcome to Zurich. And sit down.'

'You make it sound like I just arrived,' the American commented as he sat in an armchair and crossed his legs. 'Fact is I've been here a while, never staying in one place for more than a night. That gets kinda tiring, I can tell you. Cord sends his regards.'

'Do you mean you've been moving round Switzerland or just inside Zurich?' Tweed enquired, still standing up.

'Zurich and some of the hick places just out of town. I was real worried about this Swiss system which means you've gotta register at a hotel, give them your details.'

'So you were compelled to register under your own name?'

'You think I fled from the States with a bundle of phoney identities?' Ives asked aggressively. He leaned forward. 'I had to run like hell to stay alive, packed one bag and boarded the first flight.'

'How did you recognize me in the hall?' Tweed pressed on. 'There are hardly any photos of me in existence.'

'That was Cord. He described you from your hair down to your toetips. Only way I agreed to take the chance, to come and see you. Cord was very pushy about me seeing you, Tweed.'

Tweed sat down. He took off his glasses and cleaned them with his handkerchief. He took his time and Ives, sitting erect, clasped his hands in his lap, waiting patiently. Apart from his Swiss outfit, he was Paula's idea of an FBI agent. Wary, watchful and controlled. Tweed put on his glasses, studied Ives for a moment before he spoke again.

'You said you fled from the States, that you had to run like hell to stay alive. Why? And who was pursuing you?'

Ives looked pointedly at Paula. He switched his gaze to Newman behind him who still held his gun in his hand.

'I can't answer those questions unless we're alone. I know the guy is Robert Newman – seen enough of his pics at one time in papers over pieces he wrote and he hasn't changed.'

'Did Cord advise you to take that attitude?' Tweed asked.

'No, I'm taking the attitude.' Aggressive again. Paula thought she understood: Ives had been staying under cover for some time. This was his first excursion into the open. Despite his outward air of self-control he was probably a bit trigger happy. 'What I have to tell you is confidential, top secret – you name it.'

'Both Paula and Bob are trusted members of my team. You talk in front of them or you just go away somewhere . . .'

'Cord said you were tough.' Ives waved his hands in a gesture of resignation. 'God help you if any of this strays beyond this room.'

'Is that a threat?' Tweed enquired mildly.

'No, it's stating the situation. You'd become targets for people who never miss.'

'They do sometimes,' Tweed observed. 'I'm still waiting. Would you like some coffee? There's plenty left in the pot.'

'I'd be grateful for that.' Ives looked at Paula. 'Very grateful. My mouth feels like the Sahara . . .'

Tweed waited again while Paula poured a cup. Ives refused sugar or milk. He took the cup and saucer from her and gulped half the contents down.

'That's better, a whole lot better.' He seemed to relax for the first time since he'd entered the room. 'Well, here goes. I was born and raised in New York, but I was stationed in Tennessee in the South. I was investigating the disappearance of huge sums of money. We thought at first someone was laundering drug money, but now I think the money went into a political fund . . .'

'Are you talking about bank robberies?' Tweed asked.

'Hell, no. Creative accounting. I'd interview a key witness, get a tape recording of what was said, then the witness would disappear off the face of the earth. I never did find where the bodies were buried.'

'Bodies? Plural?'

'Ten. Including three women.'

'That's mass murder,' Tweed said slowly. He paused. 'But why would the FBI be called in if the crimes were all committed in Tennessee?'

'They weren't. They crossed state lines. That's when the FBI is called in. I'm sure you know that. The trail led me from Tennessee to Mississippi, Louisiana, Oklahoma, New Mexico and Arizona.'

'That's a lot of territory. Earlier you said you thought at first *someone* was laundering drug money. Who did you mean?'

Ives took a deep breath, sighed. Again he looked at

205

Paula and Newman who were hanging on every word.

'I'm talking about Jeb Calloway, now Vice President of the United States.'

There was a hush in the room. Tweed walked across to the closed curtains, opened them a little, peered out. It had begun to drizzle and the street had a sweaty look. He went back to his chair, sat down and stared at Barton Ives.

'Are you sure about this?' he asked.

'Positive,' Ives snapped.

'I understood Calloway came from the Philadelphia area in the north-east.'

'He does.' Ives smiled bitterly. 'Which was why Bradford March, who is a Southerner, had him on the ticket for the election as running mate. Calloway was able to deliver New York, Pennsylvania and other key states.'

'So what was Calloway's connection with the Southern states where you carried out your investigation?'

'Quite a few years ago Calloway moved his electronics outfit to Phoenix, Arizona. It was the trend. The climate in Arizona was unpolluted, the unions hadn't the tight grip they exercised in the North. The money-laundering operation was controlled from that outfit in Phoenix.'

'And you say this money ended up . . .'

'In Bradford March's war chest to fight the election. I doubt he knew it was stolen money. What politician enquires too closely the origin of desperately needed funds for a presidential election?'

'And the ten witnesses who disappeared?'

'Were murdered,' Ives corrected. 'Any one of them could have testified to the illegality of the operation. Most of them were married, had families. I even had a witness who saw a woman I'd interviewed dragged into a car late at night. Neither was ever seen again. I was closing in on

Calloway when the election took place. That was when I found myself dodging bullets.'

'You mean that literally?'

'I do,' Ives assured him. 'I'd driven back to Memphis to report my findings to my chief, Murcall. I found Murcall had been replaced by a guy I didn't know called Foley. He told me to close my investigation. Orders from Washington. That was just after the election . . .'

'You mentioned bullets,' Tweed reminded him.

'Goddamnit! Let me finish my story. It was night. On my way home to my apartment from FBI HQ a red Caddy was following me. In a quiet street it drew alongside. I ducked just in time – they machine-gunned my car. When I got to my apartment a guy slipped into the elevator with me. I shoved my gun into his side, searched him, found he had an automatic. He tried to grab it and I hit him on the head. That was when I packed and took off for the airport.'

'And flew here?' Tweed enquired. 'Why?'

'Switzerland seemed a safe place, but they followed me. Don't ask me how. I'm pretty good at spotting tails. But Calloway has plenty of money. He's used it to hire a lot of people to come after me—'

Ives broke off as the phone rang. Tweed jumped up, answered it.

'Sorry to bother you,' Butler's voice said quickly. 'But I think you'd better come to my room pretty damn fast.'

'I'll come down and collect it.' Tweed turned to face the others. 'There's someone arrived downstairs I must see. But they'd better not see you, Ives. I may be a little while.'

'I'd like to visit the bathroom,' Ives said.

'Certainly,' Newman agreed. 'But I'm coming with you – for protection after what you've told us . . .'

Tweed waited until the door had closed and he was alone with Paula.

'That was Butler,' he whispered. 'Could be bad news. I want you to have your Browning in your hand the whole

207

time I'm away. Anyone knocks on the door after I've gone – don't answer it. When I get back I'll rap on the door like this . . .' He beat a short tattoo on the top of a desk.

'Is it closing in on us?' Paula asked calmly. 'Maybe since we have Barton Ives.'

'It could be, I fear . . .'

Afterwards, Tweed was never sure what instinct had made him grab hold of his raincoat before he hurried to Butler's room. He knocked on the door, which was opened a few inches. Butler peered out, swung the door wide open and closed and locked it the moment Tweed was inside. In his right hand he held his Walther.

The room was in darkness. Tweed remained quite still as Butler touched his arm.

'I'll guide you over to the window. Then I'll open the curtains a fraction. You won't like what you see . . .'

Arriving at the window, Butler pulled open the curtains a few inches. Tweed peered down into Bahnhofstrasse. It was still drizzling, a fine veil which blurred the street lamps. Tweed counted four men standing in the rain and all wore American-style trench coats.

'I see them,' he said grimly.

'There are more,' Butler warned him. 'Pete spotted them first from his window. We count ten men leaning against tree trunks, walls, just inside shop doorways. We are surrounded.'

'So we are.' Tweed mused in the dark. 'We do have in our room a fugitive from the States they've attempted to kill at least twice.'

'I'd like to do something about this,' Butler said. 'We are surrounded,' he repeated.

'Perhaps not. Get your coat on, Harry. I have a phone call to make. From Shopville.'

208

'They'll see you come out. They could be waiting for *you*.'

'We may not be as surrounded as you think. Ready? Good. There's an exit they may well not know about. A single door leading direct into the Hummer Bar – well away from the main entrance . . .'

Tweed was proved right. No one waited in the deserted side-street beyond the door leading from the Hummer Bar. They descended into Shopville, Tweed walked into the first empty phone cubicle, dialled Beck's private number at his Berne HQ. The Swiss answered the phone at once.

'Beck . . .'

'Arthur, Tweed here . . .'

'There has been a lot of violence in Zurich since I left—'

'I know,' Tweed interrupted him. 'Talk about that later – an emergency has arisen . . .'

'Details?' Beck demanded.

'The Gotthard, where we are staying, is practically besieged by ten Americans standing in the drizzle. Wearing belted trench coats, leaning against trees, walls. It may be because someone new has arrived, but I'm not sure about that.'

'They saw you leave?'

'No, they've missed the side-door exit from the Hummer Bar. I'm talking from a Shopville phone.'

'Bloody nerve!' Beck prided himself on his command of the English language. 'I've had enough of them. Fortunately Zurich police HQ is close to the Gotthard. They'll find themselves moved pretty damned quick, and their so-called diplomatic passports won't help them. That's it? Right. I'm calling Zurich now . . .'

Tweed and Butler returned the way they had come, entering the hotel via the Hummer Bar. They heard the sound of police car sirens before they'd closed the side door. Tweed thanked Butler, went up to his room. When Newman opened the door Ives was standing at the window, peering through a crack in the curtain. Paula sat a distance away, gun in her hand.

'That's sorted out,' Tweed announced. 'So we'll all have a decent meal in the Hummer Bar restaurant . . .'

A patrol car full of uniformed police stopped in a side street just off Bahnhofstrasse. A lieutenant, followed by his men, ran into Bahnhofstrasse, paused, glanced round. The lieutenant unbuttoned the flap of his holster before he approached a tall, heavily built man wearing a coat and a slouch hat, brim pulled well down against the persistent drizzle. Uniformed police from other patrol cars were flooding into the street.

'You can't stand loitering here,' the police officer told the man. 'We've had a complaint from a Swiss woman – she's frightened to walk along here.'

'Don't ruffle the feathers, buddy,' the man replied with a pronounced American accent. 'I'm a diplomat. You can't touch me.'

He reached inside his pocket, the officer whipped out his gun.

'No call to get nervy,' the American continued. 'I'm showing you my passport.'

The officer flipped open the folder, closed it, handed it back.

'We're not convinced those are genuine. Where are you staying?'

'Baur-en-Ville. Now look here, buddy . . .'

'Then get back inside your hotel now. And don't come out again tonight.'

'Christ! You can't do this . . .'

'The Baur-en-Ville. Now! Or I'll haul you off in that

police van over there and you can spend the night in a cell. Arrested as a suspect character . . .'

The American swore foully, pulled up his collar, walked off in the direction of the hotel. Other Americans, similarly accosted, were leaving, trudging off through the drizzle which had given the street a surface like a band of wet blue leather. All was quiet in minutes.

In the restaurant Paula sat opposite Ives. She thought he looked more like a teddy bear than ever with his ice-blue button eyes, his closely trimmed brown hair. He looked up from his menu and smiled, the most charming smile. So why did she feel disturbed?

Tweed sat beside her with Newman opposite him. They had a table by the wall with no one near them. Tweed was studying his menu when he asked Ives the question.

'I heard a rumour that while you were in Memphis you had another job, investigating a spate of serial murders in different states.'

Ives hesitated for a fraction of a second. Paula was watching him, felt he was unsure whether to reveal dangerous information.

'Hell,' Ives addressed Tweed, 'that was one of my failures. I spent months on that grim case, got nowhere. Serial murderers are the most difficult to catch. Murcall, my old boss, switched me to checking Calloway, the embezzlements.'

'Which was not one of your failures,' Tweed observed, 'even though you were later removed from that case.'

He ordered the same as Paula had chosen, *filet de fera* with boiled potatoes, a fresh salad and mineral water to drink. Ives plumped for lobsters – this was a lobster bar and the German word for lobster was *Hummer*. Newman once again ordered his favourite dish which he had lived off at main meals since they arrived – *émincé de veau* with *rösti*

211

potatoes. He drank white wine while Ives ordered half a bottle of Beaujolais. When the waiter had gone Tweed continued asking questions, gazing at Ives.

'Why would Calloway want you killed since you had no evidence strong enough, no witnesses left alive to confront him with in an American court of law?'

'Calloway,' Ives responded promptly, 'is a success in both business and politics. He made it by taking no chances, leaving no loose ends. I'm a loose end.'

Paula sensed Ives was tense. Whenever a new customer entered the restaurant he glanced quickly over his shoulder. Newman was unusually silent. Only Tweed seemed completely relaxed as he glanced slowly round the restaurant.

The dining-room was oblong, divided from the bar with sheets of frosted glass which had Edwardian couples etched on its surface. The main colour motif of the room was red. The ceiling was divided into large crimson panels, the walls were covered with carmine velvet. The small table lamps which provided the main illumination had crimson shades and the tablecloths were pink.

Paula thought it was a daring decor which could so easily have been chichi. But it worked: the whole atmosphere of the Hummer Bar suggested a warm and welcoming intimacy. She felt relaxed – except for an aura of tension which seemed to originate from Barton Ives. She thought she now understood it – Ives probably hadn't relaxed for a second since leaving the States. Now he was finding it difficult to adjust to the pleasant and secure surroundings. Other tables were full but the restaurant wasn't noisy. Just a gentle chatter and the occasional chuckle of pure enjoyment.

'I wonder who those guys were standing about outside in the rain,' Ives said suddenly.

'Doesn't matter now,' Tweed told him. 'They've all gone, I heard. Chased away by the police.'

'The police?'

'That was what I heard at reception.'

'You think those characters knew I'd arrived here?'

'I very much doubt it,' Tweed reassured him. 'I expect they were looking for me. Oh, by the way, have you taken a room here in your own name?'

'Had to, didn't I?' Ives flared up. 'I told you – I'm not carrying any phoney papers.'

'I check details,' Tweed told him quietly. 'Our job is to protect you. How is Dillon? And how did you happen to meet him here in Zurich?'

'Jesus Christ! One question at a time.' Ives quietened down. 'Cord is restless, jumps at his own shadow. I met him by accident in Sprüngli. He didn't immediately know who I was when I sat opposite him. I was wearing tinted glasses. Damned near fell off his chair when he realized it was me.'

'How did you two first meet?' Tweed went on. 'The Deputy Director of the CIA doesn't normally have contact with the FBI. The CIA isn't supposed to operate inside the United States.'

'But they do when it suits them. I found the head man of a sabotage ring Cord was looking for. He was always grateful for that.'

'He would be . . .'

Their meal arrived and no one spoke as they consumed the excellent food. Paula, who ate quickly, as usual finished first. She watched Ives handling his lavish helping of lobster. When they had all finished Ives reached into his pocket.

'Goddamnit, I've left my cigarettes in my room. Won't be long.'

Newman offered his pack of Silk Cut.

'Thanks,' Ives said, 'but I only smoke Lucky Strike . . .'

'Seems very edgy,' Newman commented after Ives had gone.

'You can understand it – after what he's been through,' Paula countered. 'Who wouldn't be?'

'We'll wait for coffee until he gets back,' Tweed said and checked his watch.

Ten minutes later Tweed suddenly stood up. He put his hand on Paula's shoulder to keep her in her chair.

'Bob, I want to make an urgent call. Your room is much closer than mine. Could I borrow your key?'

He was absent for longer than Paula had expected. When he came back into the restaurant he asked the waiter for the bill, scribbled his room number and signature. Hurrying to the table, he remained standing, leaning forward and keeping his voice down.

'Did Ives return?'

'No, he didn't,' Paula said, alarmed. 'Is something the matter?'

'You could say that. I've phoned police headquarters – luckily Beck had flown in from Berne to check the situation after my first phone call. He's on his way over with a team of specialists.'

'Specialists?' Newman queried. 'What kind?'

'His top man with a machine-pistol. And a chemist with his equipment. Plus a bomb squad team.'

'What on earth for . . .' Paula began.

'Beck is in the entrance now,' Newman told Tweed.

They walked over to where the Swiss police chief waited, fresh as paint in his business suit, calm in a crisis.

'I have this Barton Ives' room number from reception and a master key,' Beck said as he ushered them out of the restaurant.

'I could be wrong about this,' Tweed warned.

'Never known your instinct to be wrong yet. I have armed guards at either end of the corridor where his room is. And I'd like to have your room key for the chemist and the bomb squad. Thank you . . .'

Mystified, Paula and Newman stood with Tweed and

214

Beck as the lift ascended. Beck stepped out first, looked in both directions, waved for them to follow him out. He was striding ahead of them when Newman asked Tweed what the devil was going on.

'For one thing, my room lock has been tampered with since we came down to dinner. I was careful not to turn the key, let alone go inside. Also the so-called Barton Ives had the wrong answers to quite a few questions.'

'So called?' Paula repeated.

She got no reply. They had come close to the room taken by Ives. Beck's hand gestured for them to keep well back. Standing against the wall opposite the closed door was a uniformed policeman. He wore a flak jacket and was aiming a sub-machine-gun at the door. Two other men, pistols in hand, were flattened against the wall on either side of the door. A fourth man stood close by, holding a short wide-barrelled gun. Tear-gas. Beck was on red alert.

Taking out his own pistol, Beck leaned past one of the men against the wall, rapped on the door with the muzzle.

'Police. Open up. A team of armed men are outside.'

He waited. A long silence. Eventually Beck pressed an ear to the door, listened. Stepping back, he tossed the master key to the other man pressed against the wall. Paula saw the man with the machine-gun stiffen. The policeman with the key quietly inserted it in the lock, turned it, took hold of the handle, glanced at the man with the flak jacket, who nodded.

The door was hurled wide open. Flak Jacket literally dived into the room, sprawled on the carpet, swinging the muzzle of his weapon in a wide arc. He called over his shoulder to Beck, who had stepped in behind him, his gun ready.

'Empty, Chief . . .'

'Check the bathroom. Same approach . . .'

A minute later they realized the bathroom was also empty. Beck looked at Tweed.

215

'The bird has flown. So you were right. Now for your room. You all stay here, standing where Stefan sprawled. You don't touch anything. You don't drink anything.' He pointed to a half-empty bottle of mineral water. 'You don't use the bathroom . . .'

A policeman with his pistol in his hand stood outside the room while they waited. Newman asked the question in a low tone.

'Look, Tweed, what is this all about?'

'I am certain we've just dined with a man Dillon warned me against for fear of our lives. A man called Norton.'

23

Beck reappeared after about ten minutes. He waved for them to follow him. As they left the room two policemen wearing protective clothing, one carrying a tool-kit box, arrived, slipped inside the room.

'Bomb squad boys,' Beck remarked. 'Your room is clean – as regards explosives . . .'

When they entered Tweed's room a small gnome-like figure in civilian clothes was waiting for them. On a table a compact leather case was open and inside lay a collection of instruments. The only one Paula recognized was a calibrated dropper – like an eye dropper. A small container made of thick glass with a screw top stood next to the case. Inside it was half full with a crimsom liquid. Beck introduced the gnome.

'This is our chemical specialist, Dr Brand.'

'After what I found, Beck,' the gnome said, 'you might be interested to take them into the bathroom.'

Tweed stood with Beck just inside the bathroom doorway. Paula peered over Tweed's shoulder.

'Now have a good look round,' Beck suggested to Tweed. 'You're exceptionally observant. Notice anything not the way you left it before dinner?'

Tweed stared slowly round. His eyes lingered on items from his spongebag he'd placed on a glass shelf over the basin. He shook his head.

'It appears to be the same. I can't see anything unusual.'

'When do you use the mouthwash?' Beck enquired, pointing to a bottle.

'First thing every morning. It freshens me up for the day.'

'In that case,' Beck said cheerfully, 'you had only a few hours to live. Come back into the bedroom.' He looked at the gnome. 'My friend here uses the mouthwash every morning when he gets up.'

'I gargle with it,' Tweed added.

'Then maybe you would sniff this,' Dr Brand suggested and unscrewed the cap on the small thick glass container. He held it a moment before handing it to Tweed. 'Be very careful. It contains a small quantity of the mouthwash and a certain solvent I tested it with.'

Tweed raised the container, took a cautious sniff. Paula saw his facial muscles stiffen for a second. He handed it back to Brand, who immediately screwed on the cap.

'A faint aroma of bitter almonds,' Tweed said slowly.

'That's right,' Brand said agreeably. 'Prussic acid. I calculate you'd have gargled for two seconds. I placed the mouthwash bottle back exactly as I found it after I tested.'

'So did someone else,' Beck said grimly, 'after he used a pick lock to get into your room.'

'Prussic acid. Oh, my God,' Paula said half to herself.

She had a sudden vivid picture of Amberg at Tresillian Manor in Cornwall, his face destroyed with acid.

Beck and his team had left as Tweed sat with Newman and Paula in the bedroom. Before leaving he'd reported to Tweed that not a single fingerprint had been found in the room occupied by the man who'd registered as Barton Ives.

'Probably wore surgical gloves before he even entered the room,' he commented. 'And all the glasses and cutlery he used at dinner has been washed. His case also has disappeared. It's as though he'd never been here. And Brand has taken the mouthwash bottle with him. Take care . . .'

Newman had ordered a double Scotch from room service when they were alone while Paula decided she needed a glass of white wine. Tweed stayed with mineral water.

'God! That has shaken me,' Paula said. 'How on earth did you spot that it wasn't Barton Ives?'

'An accumulation of things,' Tweed told them. 'First the phone call from a hoarse-voiced man asking if Barton Ives could come. He opened up with "Cord here" – something like that. Unlike many Americans, Dillon is very formal, always introduces himself by his surname. Not conclusive.'

'Why phone at all?' Paula asked.

'To make sure the real Barton Ives hadn't already come to see us. After he'd arrived he kept referring to Dillon as Cord, which increased my suspicion. From his own made-up story about how they met, he was only an acquaintance. Still not conclusive . . .'

'So what was – conclusive?' Paula persisted.

'An accumulation of implausible things, as I just said. The real giveaway was no reference on his part to pursuing the serial murderer – and that information came from Dillon, so has to be true. Then I bring up the subject over dinner – and he dismisses it in two or three sentences! A gory long-drawn-out case like that. Then there was the story he'd thought up as to why he *had* fled the States. Why should Calloway send over an army to kill "Ives" when he'd admitted he had no evidence that would be accepted in court? A rubbish story. Then at dinner he kept checking every customer who entered the restaurant.'

'What was the significance of that?' Paula enquired.

'Link it with his nervousness about the men who'd been watching the hotel . . .'

'Yes,' Newman intervened, 'he was obsessed with them. While you were away he kept peering out to see if they had gone away.'

'No,' Tweed contradicted. 'To make sure *they were still there!*'

'Don't follow that,' Paula commented, frowning.

'You're usually quicker,' he gently chided her. 'The men outside were Norton's. Placed there in case the real Barton Ives arrived and tried to enter the hotel. That would have been a disaster for Norton, impersonating Ives. His men were there to take care of the real Ives for good if he showed up.'

'So when you came back from phoning Beck . . .' Paula began.

'*My* story,' Tweed interjected. 'Yes, it was my remark – invented – that reception had told me the police had removed the watchers which told Norton he was in trouble. Again, the real Ives could have walked in on us. Hence his exit to his room, supposedly for cigarettes.'

'And to your room,' she reminded him.

'Well, that's why he came here – to kill me. But for Beck bringing Dr Brand he'd have succeeded. I find the method he chose interesting.'

'Not the word I'd have used,' she remarked. 'But using acid does make me wonder if Norton was the fake postman who committed the massacre at Tresillian Manor.'

'I was going to say interesting because it's a measure of the ruthlessness of the man – and his determination. He was worried stiff Ives himself might turn up but he still went ahead and tried to murder me.'

'What is the programme for tomorrow?' Newman asked impatiently.

'I have a ten o'clock appointment with that detective of Eve Amberg's, Theo Strebel,' Tweed reminded him. 'I'm hoping he'll lead me to wherever Klara, Helen Frey's friend, has moved to. I want to talk to her again. I have an idea she knows more than she realizes. Then in the evening it's drinks with Gaunt's girl friend, Jennie Blade, at 6 p.m. downstairs in the Hummer Bar.'

'I wonder how Squire Gaunt fits into all this,' Paula mused.

'He was in Cornwall at the time of the massacre,' Tweed reminded her. 'He could be a key figure.'

While it was dark and drizzling in Zurich, it was still daylight in Washington. 'A kinda daylight,' March reflected as he gazed out of the window. It was snowing heavily. The traffic down on Pennsylvania Avenue was already getting snarled up. He pressed a button on his intercom.

'Sara, get hold of the shit-kicker who's supposed to send out snow ploughs. I want them on Pennsylvania Avenue in ten minutes. When the machines get moving let the press know I gave the order.'

'Good thinking, boss . . .'

'Sure is. Let the folks know their President is lookin' after them.'

'There's a call, long distance, on your private phone. The caller won't give a name. Said you might be interested in a couple of items you were searching for . . .'

'Put them through. And put a trace on the call . . .'

'They're leery, boss. They rang off, said they'd call again shortly. I'll try a trace . . . Hold it, I think they're back on the line . . .'

'Who is this?' March barked when the connection was made.

'No names. Got a pad and pen? Good . . .' The voice was husky. 'I have a film and a tape recording for sale. The price is still twenty million dollars . . .'

'A courier is on the way to Zurich with the pay-off. I need first to be sure . . .'

'You need to shut your trap . . .'

March's mouth became ugly. You didn't talk to the President of the United States that way.

The voice went on: 'I know you're trying to trace this call. Write this down. The three possible rendezvous for the exchange – money for film and tape. On the Zurichberg, Orelli-strasse by the hotel. I'll spell it . . . Next possible place, airfield at Hausen am Albis. Here's that spelling . . . Third is Regensburg, outside Zurich . . . I'll be in touch again with specific details . . .'

The connection was broken. March was puzzled by the voice. Husky, yes. Growly, yes – very growly. But twice it had become high-pitched, sounded like a woman. Sara came on the internal line a few minutes later.

'No luck, boss. Trace took us to Zurich in Switzerland. Couldn't get the number in Zurich . . .'

'Hell! Don't know why we bought that trace equipment . . .'

March slammed down the phone. He'd pass this info. over to Norton when he next came through.

In Zurich the woman who had called March smiled at the man who had listened. She had disguised her voice by speaking from the bottom of her throat.

'March would never recognize your voice even if he ever

met you,' the man said, wrapping his arm round her.

'I *growled*. That's the trick. Twenty million dollars. That should enable us to live in style.'

'You were great. What about going to bed to celebrate?'

'Why did I think you had that in mind?'

The following morning Tweed had breakfast with Paula and Newman in the first-floor dining-room, La Soupière, at the Hotel Schweizerhof. Butler, Cardon and Nield sat by themselves at separate tables. The previous evening Butler and Nield had visited the hotel, entered all six rooms and rumpled the bedclothes.

'Since Norton knows we're staying at the Gotthard,' Paula suggested, 'is there any point in us remaining there?'

'None at all,' Tweed agreed. 'Which is why we're moving our things back here after breakfast. I've already paid our bill at the Gotthard, told Harry, Pete and Philip to do the same thing.'

'What is the next move?' Newman asked. 'I'd like to get to grips with Norton and Co.'

'If he *is* the real enemy,' Tweed remarked. 'Nothing is certain. I'm now convinced few of the people we've met here – and in Cornwall – are what they seem.'

'That's reassuring,' Paula said ironically. 'Anyone in particular you're after?'

'I need more data before I can plan an elaborate trap. Elaborate because someone is masterminding a complex plot. I only realized that after we arrived here.'

He was keeping his thoughts all to himself once again, Paula said to herself. She tried another tack.

'Well, we're staying in Zurich, then.'

'No, we aren't,' Tweed told her. 'Tomorrow we catch an express train from the Hauptbahnhof to Basle.'

'Why Basle?'

'I phoned the Zurcher Kredit before breakfast to speak

to Amberg. Luckily I got Amberg's personal assistant. She told me he had left suddenly for Basle in a great rush.'

'I remember – Zurcher Kredit has a branch in Basle. But why are we following him there?' Paula asked.

'Maybe you've forgotten. Amberg told us Julius had moved the film and tape Dyson delivered to the bank vault in Basle.' He checked his watch. 'I'll have to leave soon for my appointment with Theo Strebel.'

'Well, at least we know now what Norton looks like – the man who up to last night no one had ever seen.'

'I wouldn't count on that,' Tweed replied.

Inside the apartment he had rented, Norton returned to the bathroom. Thirty minutes earlier he had rubbed grey colourant into his normally light brown hair. Now he rinsed off the surplus with water and examined the result in the mirror.

His appearance was changing already. He'd forget his weekly visit to a barber, and let his hair grow longer. It grew very rapidly. Satisfied with its progress, he put on his jacket, checked the time.

Timing was everything. He had his whole day planned out with the precision of a general preparing for a major battle. He was whistling a tune as he left the apartment.

Tweed was accompanied by Paula when he climbed ancient stone steps inside the old building in the Altstadt which housed Strebel's office. Newman followed a few paces behind, waited in the corridor as Tweed opened a door with a frosted-glass window in the upper half. Etched into the glass was a simple legend. THEO STREBEL. No indication of his profession.

They walked into an empty ante-room. A solid oak door in the opposite wall with a glass spyhole. Paula was

223

suddenly nervous – the atmosphere on the old stone staircase had been eerie, the smell of a musty building barely occupied for years had assailed her nostrils.

Here the atmosphere was even more sinister. A heavy silence filled the room which was furnished only with an old empty desk. She was sure no one had occupied the room for ages. She slipped her hand inside her shoulder-bag, gripped her Browning automatic.

'Announce yourselves. Your names, please.'

The disembodied voice seemed to come out of nowhere. Tweed pointed to an ancient cone-shaped speaker fixed to a corner high up. The voice had spoken in English.

'Is that you, Mr Strebel?' demanded Tweed.

'I said announce yourselves. Your names and business.'

'I have an appointment with Theo Strebel. For 10 a.m. Eve Amberg said she would phone you. My assistant, a woman, is with me.'

'Tell her to say something,' the disembodied voice commanded. 'Anything. Apples are green.'

'Only when they are not normally ripe,' Paula called back.

'Enter.'

There was a sound like the buzzer Helen Frey had operated on the front door in Rennweg. Tweed pushed at the heavy door and, reluctantly, it swung inward.

'Good morning, Mr Tweed. Don't just stand there. My greetings to you, Fraulein.'

A very fat man dressed in a black suit sat behind a desk. His hair was dark and brushed back over his high forehead without a parting. Below a short pugnacious nose he sported a trim dark moustache. The door closed automatically behind them as they walked inside the office. Paula heard the lock click shut, felt trapped.

'You are Mr Tweed. You fit Mrs Amberg's description. Do sit down, both of you. Now, what exactly can I do for my latest client?'

224

'You are Theo Strebel?'

'The great detective himself. No impersonations here.'

As Paula followed Tweed's example, seating herself in the other hard-backed chair facing the Swiss, she found she rather liked Strebel. He radiated energy and the good humour often associated with fat men. He leaned both elbows on the desk, clasped his surprisingly small hands under his jowly chin and smiled.

'The ball is in your court, Mr Tweed.'

'I am trying to locate the new address of a brunette who lived in the apartment opposite Helen Frey . . .'

'Whose ghastly murder is written about at length in the newspaper. So?'

'I have just said what I wish you to find out. Where Helen Frey's friend went to. I only know her first name. Klara.'

'And have you any clue as to her profession? Clues are my lifeblood, Mr Tweed.'

'She was a high-class call-girl. Like Helen Frey.'

'I appreciate the description. Everyone has to earn a living. That profession can be highly dangerous – as the latest news indicates. They are entitled to charge the high fees they do for their services. Danger money, Mr Tweed.'

'I need to locate her urgently.'

'First things first. Would you be so kind as to show me some identification? Your description may fit, but I am known as the most careful man in all Zurich.'

Tweed could have produced his driving licence. Weighing up Strebel, he produced instead his Special Branch folder, a document forged in the Engine Room basement at Park Crescent – when it had existed. Strebel raised his thick eyebrows as he studied the folder, looked at Tweed while he handed back the document.

'Special Branch? I am honoured,' he said gravely. 'You are a new experience for me.'

225

'I realize I have no jurisdiction here,' Tweed commented quickly.

'I was not about to make that remark.' He clasped hands under his jaw again. 'Unprecedented movements of certain people are taking place in Zurich. I get a hint of why you are here. There could be danger for me.'

'Why do you say that?' Tweed asked.

'That I cannot tell you.'

'Mr Strebel, I know you watched Rennweg 590. Could you tell me who called on Helen Frey recently – apart from Julius Amberg?'

'Ah! Julius . . .' The Swiss paused. 'I cannot reveal information confidential to clients of mine.'

'This is now a murder case – a particularly horrible one.'

'True, Mr Tweed. True. Let us say I observed someone from your country entering that door and leave it at that.'

'You won't even give me a hint?'

'I have already done that, Mr Tweed.'

'Thank you. Now I still need to locate Klara urgently.'

'That could take some time. Zurich is an intricate city. It has two Altstadts – the one you are now in and then another equally complex area on the other side of the River Limmat.'

'I haven't got the time, Strebel.'

'Obtaining information quickly is more expensive. My fee would be one thousand Swiss francs.'

Tweed produced his wallet. Extracting a 1,000 Swiss franc note, he laid it on the desk, his hand still resting on top of it. Strebel gave him his warm smile and included Paula in his hospitality. He was reaching into a drawer when Paula spoke for the first time.

'I've never seen such a tidy office. Not a single filing cabinet, no cupboards – just yourself and your desk.'

'Also my head.' He smiled at her again as he placed a notepad on his desk. He wrote something on the top sheet with care in a neat legible script. 'My files are stored in a bank vault. I respect my clients' confidences. Also I carry a

226

secret filing cabinet in my head.' Strebel tore off the sheet, folded it, handed it across the desk to Tweed.

'That is the new address of Klara. She is in this Altstadt. Not five minutes' walk from the front door to this building.'

Tweed smiled, pushed the banknote across the desk. The Swiss picked it up, inserted it carefully inside a slim wallet.

'So,' Paula teased him, 'you knew all the time?'

'In my profession I charge for providing the information a client requires. Mr Tweed is paying for what I know.'

'I've said this before, Paula,' Tweed reminded her. 'It is not always what you know, it's where to find it.'

'Were you once a police detective?' Strebel asked.

A perceptive man, Tweed thought. It was the first time he'd ever been asked the question in that form.

'I was with the Murder Squad at Scotland Yard once,' he said.

'And he was the youngest superintendent the Yard had ever had up to that time,' Paula told Strebel.

'No need to go into details,' Tweed snapped.

'I can well believe it,' Strebel told Paula. 'Mr Tweed, maybe before you leave Zurich you would join me for a drink. We could exchange experiences – I mean from when you were at the Yard,' he added hastily.

'It would be my pleasure.'

Strebel accompanied them to the door after pressing a button underneath his desk. He shook hands formally with both of them and when Paula glanced back as they reached the outer door he smiled again, bowed his head.

'What a nice man,' Paula said as Tweed closed the outer door. 'I always picture private detectives as nasty little men in shabby raincoats.'

'I suspect Strebel was once a member of the Swiss police. He may well know Beck.'

227

Newman was waiting for them at the end of the dark corridor. He spoke to Tweed immediately.

'Someone started to come in downstairs, opened the door. I think they saw me and changed their minds. Didn't get a glimpse of who it was.'

'People calling on private investigators are often shy of being seen. We've got Klara's new address . . .'

Outside on the uneven pavement which, like the buildings, looked as though it had been there for centuries, Paula consulted her map. She looked to the end of the deserted square from the edge where they stood. The square was surrounded with six-storey buildings as old as time.

'Klara is living at the far side of the square. No. 10.'

The entrance hall was similar to the one they had just left. As they entered a door opened on the ground floor. A hook-nosed woman with beady eyes and dressed in a black dress peered at them.

'You want the girl who's just moved in upstairs?' Her thin lips curled. 'Some people don't care how they make their money. Mixed doubles this time, is it?'

She slammed the door before Tweed could retort. Newman led the way up the old iron-railed stone staircase. Close to the only door on this landing he stopped. Tweed and Paula stared past him. The door was open a few inches.

Newman had his Smith & Wesson in his hand as he moved silently to the door, paused to listen, pushed the door open wider with his left hand, took a step inside, froze. He called over his shoulder.

'Paula, for God's sake don't come in here . . .'

24

It was a replay of the grim tragedy in Helen Frey's apartment. Klara, fully dressed, lay back in an armchair, her head flopped at an unnatural angle. A dark crimson sickle gash curved round her throat, disappearing round the back of her neck.

'He's been here,' Paula said quietly.

Despite Newman's warning she had followed Tweed into the apartment. She pulled on her surgical gloves as Tweed walked slowly round the back of the chair. Again the head was almost severed from the neck. Someone favoured garrotting.

Paula stood sniffing the air. She frowned, began prowling round the apartment, careful not to disturb anything.

'What is it?' Tweed asked Paula sharply.

'Cigar smoke . . .' She continued walking slowly, weaving her way among armchairs, passing a large couch. 'Got you,' she called out.

She was extracting a specimen wallet from her shoulderbag when Newman stood alongside her. On top of a small piecrust table, hidden by the arm of the couch, stood an ashtray. Inside it rested a thick roll of cigar ash. Tweed joined them as she lifted the container with her gloved hand, skilfully tipped the ash roll inside the wallet. Sealing it, she wrote the date, the second of March, and a name. *Klara*.

'She had a customer at nine thirty a.m. according to her desk diary,' Newman said.

He took them over to a table where a new diary lay open.

9.30 a.m. *E*dwin *A*llenspach. Tweed and Paula stared down at the entry.

'Strange she underlined the initials of each name,' Paula remarked.

'Could have been any reason,' Newman reacted dismissively. 'Maybe it was a new client and she was reminding herself to check up on him.' He glanced at Paula. 'Or maybe he had certain tastes she catered to,' he suggested, phrasing it carefully.

'You mean kinky,' Paula suggested. 'Somehow I don't think Klara went in for that sort of thing. And nine thirty in the morning seems rather early for . . . although I suppose some men . . .'

She trailed off as she saw Newman watching her. She grimaced at him.

'You know what I mean.'

'I wonder whether either of you are right,' said Tweed.

He was still gazing at the entry. He made no attempt to explain what had crossed his mind. Standing in the centre of the apartment he scanned it swiftly, taking in everything.

'Again no sign that the place has been ransacked, searched in any way.' Paula realized he was talking to himself as he continued: 'So, whoever is the murderer came for that specific purpose. Murder. He's systematically exterminating everyone who might provide vital information.'

'Maybe it's just become a habit with him,' Newman said, attempting to lighten the traumatic atmosphere with a little black humour. 'Could be a psychopath, I suppose.'

'I think not,' Tweed objected. 'But yes, systematically exterminating all potential witnesses,' he repeated.

'Well, the bastard's doing a damn good job,' Newman remarked.

Tweed was strolling round the apartment. Paula, watching him, saw him suddenly clap a hand to his forehead. He grunted. He stiffened.

'On our way out, I'll try out my German again on Old Nosy downstairs. I did understand the dirty remark she made. She may have seen him arrive or leave. She has the mind of a concierge who can't abide not knowing what people are doing. I also suspect she's greedy.'

'We must report this crime,' Newman said. 'I know we skipped out of Helen Frey's place . . .'

'It was important we didn't get tangled up in an inquiry, slowed down. But this I was going to report,' Tweed agreed. 'Something else is worrying me though. We'll report it to the police shortly.'

As they made their way back down the stone stairs the door on the ground floor opened and Old Nosy stood in her doorway, arms akimbo. Both Paula and Newman also understood German.

'That was a quick one,' she sneered. 'Must have been easy money for that new girl.'

'I have a question to ask you,' Tweed said in German.

'Ask away. Don't promise you'll hear anything from me. Not as though I'm the local gossip.'

'I'm sure you're not,' Tweed said amiably. 'The new girl had someone who called on her before we arrived. Did you by chance see them? Could you give me a rough description?'

Between his fingers he held a hundred-franc note. She was eyeing it with great interest. She tossed her head.

'Information costs money in Switzerland.'

'Which is why I'm willing to pay – if I'm convinced you're not making it up.'

'Me make something up for money?' she blazed indignantly. 'Who do you think you're talking to?'

'Someone, apparently, who isn't interested in accepting a fee in good faith,' Tweed replied, his tone harsh.

231

'Didn't say that, did I?' She simpered and Paula felt nauseated. 'I didn't see them go up,' the woman said in a regretful tone. 'I was listening to my favourite radio programme. But I did hear them leaving. Tiptoeing down those steps pretty fast.'

'You saw who it was?' Tweed asked, mentally crossing his fingers.

'Only saw the back of the caller. As they was leaving, going out the front door.'

'Describe them for me as best you can,' Tweed coaxed.

'He had a black wide-brimmed hat on, pulled well down . . .'

'Colour of hair?'

'I just told you – he had the hat pulled well down. So how could I see the hair? One thing I can tell you is his height. I always notice how tall someone is. About as tall as her.' She nodded towards Paula, looking her up and down. Paula's gaze remained steady as she stared back at the ferret-like eyes. 'Wore a long black overcoat and a thick woollen scarf.'

'A fat man?' Tweed enquired.

'No. He was tall and fairly slim. Had a funny walk.'

'Funny in what way?'

'Took quick short steps. Like a pansy.'

'Did he move like a pansy then?' Tweed pressed.

'No, I don't think he did. Didn't mince, if that's what you mean. I only got a glimpse as the door was closing.'

'A thick neck?' Tweed probed.

'No idea. How could I? He was wearing this thick woollen scarf. I just told you that.'

'So you did,' said Tweed, who was checking her powers of observation. 'Was he carrying anything?'

'Not in his hands. But he had something pretty heavy in his coat pocket. Weighed it down, it did.'

'Thank you,' said Tweed and handed her the banknote. 'I congratulate you on your powers of observation.'

'Something funny has happened up in her apartment?' she asked, her eyes gleaming at the prospect.

'According to you something funny is always happening in that apartment.'

Tweed left the building before she could think up some vicious retort. He began walking rapidly across the square, returning to the side they had come from. His legs, despite his shorter stature, moved like pistons and Newman had trouble keeping up with him. Paula was running when they reached the entrance to Theo Strebel's building.

'What is wrong?' Paula asked.

'Nothing, I hope. But I am very much afraid . . .'

Newman managed to get alongside Tweed as he took two steps a time up the staircase to the first floor. On the landing Tweed stopped suddenly, pointed. The door with frosted glass in the upper half leading to the ante-room was open several inches. Behind them, Paula froze briefly. Doors partly open were beginning to fill her with terror.

She grabbed for her Browning as Newman, Smith & Wesson in his hand, used his other hand to hold Tweed back. Paula caught up with them.

'Strebel is so careful about security,' she whispered.

'Exactly,' Tweed responded in a grim tone.

'You're not armed,' Newman reminded Tweed. 'We'll go ahead, check the lie of the land.'

Paula had slipped off her gloves, held the Browning in both hands as she followed Newman into the ante-room. It had the same long-uninhabited feel she had sensed last time. But there was one difference. The heavy oak door to Strebel's office was open several inches.

Tweed had followed closely on their heels. He stood for a moment, fists clenched out of sight in his trench coat pockets. Newman, on the hinge side of the door, reached out his left hand, pushed it hard. It swung open slowly, noiselessly on its well-oiled hinges. There was a terrible silence pervading the atmosphere, a lack of life. Paula, awaiting a signal from Newman, was pressed against the wall on the other side of the door.

Tweed, standing very still, watched the door expose more and more of the room beyond. There was something theatrical about its movement. Then he had a clear view of the interior of the room.

Without hesitation, Tweed marched straight inside. Newman, inwardly cursing what he regarded as fool-hardiness, jumped in after him, stopped. Paula, Browning aimed for instant firing, stood in the open doorway, slowly lowered the angle of her gun until the muzzle pointed at the floor.

'Dear God, no!' she exclaimed in anguish. 'Not again.'

'Yes, again,' Tweed said in a voice which held no emotion. 'Exactly what I expected. Except for the method of execution . . .'

Theo Strebel lay back in his chair behind the large desk. His jacket was open, revealing his white shirt front. A large red rose shape decorated the white shirt to the right. Over the heart. A red rose which blossomed and spread slowly as Paula watched, almost hypnotized.

Tweed walked swiftly round the desk. He felt the carotid artery, shook his head.

'He's dead,' he said simply. 'Shot through the heart. One bullet, I suspect. And I blame myself. I was so looking forward to having that drink with him. Some people – a rare few – make an instant impact on you – he was one of that rare breed. Such a bloody waste.'

Paula had seldom heard Tweed swear. And he had spoken with a ferocity that startled her.

'Where's the flaming phone?' Tweed demanded.

'Why, for Heaven's sake, blame yourself?' she enquired.

'Because the murderer arrived while we were talking to

Theo Strebel.' He looked at Newman. 'You gave me the hint and a faint alarm bell rang. I was fool enough to ignore it.'

'What hint?' Newman, puzzled, asked.

'When we were leaving here before you said someone started to come in through the front door. You thought they'd seen you and changed their minds. That was the murderer. He'd just committed one and was on his way here to kill Strebel.'

'Committed one?' queried Paula.

'Yes. The garrotting of Klara. I only realized Strebel was probably in great danger when I said aloud that the murderer was exterminating everyone who might provide information. I shouldn't have delayed our departure by questioning that awful woman. But on the other hand she did say something very significant, and Strebel was by then probably already dead.'

'What was very significant?' Paula asked.

'So where *is* the phone? I must call Beck . . .'

It was Paula who found out where Strebel hid his phone. Wearing her surgical gloves, she began opening drawers in his desk. Hauling open a deep drawer at the bottom, she lifted out a telephone. She dialled police headquarters, then handed the instrument to Tweed who was wearing gloves. He asked for the Swiss police chief, giving his name.

'Tweed here, Arthur . . .'

'I have news for you,' the familiar voice broke in. 'I have at long last received the expert's report on that cigar ash specimen you gave me. Whoever smoked the cigar has expensive tastes. It is a Havana.'

'Thank you, I have another specimen for you to check – but that can wait. There have been two more murders . . .'

'Two more?' Beck's tone was ironical. 'You know then about the killing of a certain Helen Frey?'

'Yes, we can talk about that when we meet. One victim is

235

Klara, the girl who had the apartment opposite Helen Frey's. The other is a private detective. I'm speaking from his office now. A Theo Strebel . . .'

'Strebel! Oh, no, not Theo. He worked in the police force just before I got the top job. I wouldn't have thought anyone could have murdered Theo. You said you were at his office?'

'Yes. The address is—'

'I know it. I'm on my way there now . . .'

25

Paula sat in the front passenger seat next to Butler as he drove them up the steep hill to Eve Amberg's villa. Nield was in the back. The two men had discreetly followed Tweed to the Altstadt address when he had first visited Theo Strebel.

Before Beck arrived at Strebel's office, Tweed had given Paula careful instructions as to the information he wanted her to obtain from Eve Amberg. He had warned her not to mention the murders of Klara and Strebel, had then taken her down into the street to find a taxi. Relieved to see Butler and Nield, he had left her in their safe hands while he waited with Newman for Beck.

'Shouldn't you have phoned her first to make sure she is in?' Butler suggested as he pulled up in front of the wrought-iron gates.

'I did think of that but Tweed was anxious for me to get clear before Beck arrived.'

'Makes sense – under the circumstances,' Nield remarked.

On the way Paula had told them about the two murders. They had listened in silence as she put them concisely in the picture.

'A pretty grisly experience,' Butler had commented when she had finished. 'The murder count is climbing. Tweed could be next if he's not careful.'

'Bob stayed with him. Tweed will be all right. Now, if you don't mind, I'll go in by myself. I shouldn't be long . . .'

Tweed had made that point – that she should talk to Eve on her own.

'She may tell you more on a woman-to-woman basis . . .'

Pushing open one gate, Paula walked past an Audi parked in the drive, bonnet pointed towards the garage, caught a whiff of petrol in the fresh clear morning air. She hauled on the ancient chain bell-pull and the door was opened almost at once by Eve Amberg.

The Englishwoman wore denims, a padded windcheater and a knitted blue woollen cap. Her titian hair cascaded down her back. She gave Paula a warm smile, invited her inside, took her into the living room.

'I was just going shopping. Hateful task but it has to be done. Just before I left a Swiss woman friend called on the phone. She's nice but once she gets talking her mouth is glued to the phone. Goes on and on. Would you like some coffee? It's bitterly cold out there.'

'No, thank you just the same. Am I throwing your whole schedule out of gear? I tried to phone but the line was engaged,' she lied to cover up what might appear to be lack of manners.

'Not at all.' Eve pulled off her woollen cap, took her guest's coat, laid it neatly over a chair and sat down facing Paula. 'It's a relief for me to talk to someone English. The shopping can damn well wait.'

'Tweed is still trying to find out who committed those terrible murders – the ones at Tresillian Manor and now Helen Frey. We went to see her yesterday.'

'What happened to her was horrific. I read about it in the paper. What was she like? I am still wondering what Julius saw in her.'

'I thought she was rather ordinary,' Paula said tactfully. 'You mentioned to Tweed you knew Cornwall. He wondered what part of it you come from?'

'Launceston, just beyond where Bodmin Moor ends. That's how I know Gaunt.'

'And he came all this way to tell you about Julius? A nice gesture. Tweed is intrigued by Gaunt.'

'I don't wonder. He has such a strong personality. No, he didn't come just for that. He has business interests in Zurich. Don't ask me what they are. I'm hopeless when it comes to money. That's why the fact that Walter now controls the bank is a worry. What money I have is in that bank.'

'Walter is still in Zurich?'

Eve produced her ivory holder, inserted a cigarette, lit it. She waved the holder.

'I imagine so. Haven't heard a word from him, let alone seen him. Strange man.'

So she didn't realize Walter was now in Basle, Paula thought. He obviously doesn't let his sister-in-law know a thing.

'Lucky – from your point of view – that you didn't think of going to Cornwall with Julius,' Paula suggested.

'I can't make up my mind about that. He might still be alive if I'd gone.'

'I think that's highly unlikely – considering what took place. *I* was there – and only escaped with my life by pure chance.'

'Frightening,' Eve said. 'You lead a charmed life. I expect I shall go back to Launceston when this is all over.'

'They didn't try to get you back to attend to the funeral arrangements?'

238

Eve took a deep drag on her cigarette, blew out smoke. Again she brandished the holder.

'It was all settled by phone. Julius always said if anything happened to him he wanted to be buried in Cornwall. He loved the place, hoped to retire there. I suppose in a macabre way he got his wish. I didn't go – it would have been too upsetting. I'll visit his grave when I do go back.'

The phone began ringing. Eve made a moue, crossed the room with brisk steps. She picked up the phone, her back to Paula.

'Yes, who is it?'

She listened, then replied, her voice high-pitched.

'Not now. It's not convenient. I'll get back to you this afternoon. At least, as soon as I can. Goodbye.'

She waved the holder a third time as she sat down again. Paula thought she detected a trace of annoyance in Eve's manner.

'That was Gaunt,' Eve said. 'Wanted to come and see how I was getting on. Very considerate, but you can have too much of a good thing.'

'Sorry, I'm not with you.'

'Just between you and me, he's a nice man. But I find him overbearing at times. Wants to order your life for you.'

'Where did you first meet him?'

'In Padstow, where I was born. That was when I was long grown up. Quite a while after I'd left Roedean School and started to live a normal life. You won't believe this, but I was Head Girl for a short time – and hated every minute of it. Felt like a fish in an aquarium. I bought a house outside Launceston when my father died – I'd had enough of Padstow. The summer, the best time, was ruined with ghastly trippers.'

'I've taken up a lot of your time. I think I'd better go, let you get on with that lovely shopping.'

239

'Excuse my attire. Don't like women who frolic about in denims. You see a lot of that in Padstow these days. But they're practical for shopping.'

Paula was standing up to go when she turned round as Eve prepared to see her to the front door.

'One more thing Tweed wanted to know, if it's not too personal. He gathered Julius decided on his trip to Bodmin Moor at short notice. So he must have phoned Gaunt to see if Tresillian Manor was available for him. It really was very short notice for Gaunt to clear out to his cottage at Five Lanes. How did Gaunt react?'

'Said Julius could have the manor for as long as he liked, that he needed the money.'

She opened the front door and came out into the porch as Paula thanked her. Eve looked at the parked Audi.

'I'm glad to see that. It's just been returned from our service garage after a maintenance check. Something about the brakes. Arrived just before you did.'

'In time for your shopping. Again, many thanks . . .'

Butler waited until he had turned the black Mercedes in the road and was heading back for Zurich, before he asked Paula: 'Did you get what Tweed wanted?'

'No idea. I won't have until I've reported our conversation to him. You never know what he's really after.'

Tweed arrived back in the late afternoon from police headquarters with Newman. He went straight to Paula's room and Butler left them alone.

'Tell me,' Tweed requested.

Paula began to speak by rote. She spoke with her eyes closed, seeing and hearing all that had happened from the moment she had left the car and walked up the drive to Eve Amberg's villa.

Meticulously, she recalled every detail – the Audi in the drive, Eve answering the door quickly, dressed to go out

240

shopping. Her clothes, her manner, every word she had said. Tweed sat in a chair facing her, recording every word Paula said.

'That's it,' she eventually told him.

'Word for word?'

'That's what you asked for. That's what you got.'

'What was her mood after she'd taken that phone call?' he asked.

'I told you. Annoyed. Irked. A bit put out.'

'Gaunt. Gaunt. Always Gaunt,' he repeated.

'No point in asking what you're after?' she suggested.

'A link, between Cornwall, Zurich – and Washington.'

'Norton here . . .'

President Bradford March lounged in his chair, his feet clad in sneakers perched on his desk. He wore jeans and an open-necked shirt exposing the hair on his broad chest. A leather belt encircled his waist in an attempt to hold in his ample belly.

'Norton here,' the abrasive voice repeated. 'I got the code-word on my answerphone to call you . . .'

'So squat on the butt and listen. The courier with the big bucks is on his way. He hits Zurich airport tomorrow certain. Aboard Swissair flight SR 805, ETA Zurich 4.25 p.m. He takes a cab to Hotel Baur-en-Ville. That right? Where Mencken is shacked up?'

'I don't want Mencken in on this . . .'

'Shut your trap. I said listen. OK? Great. You'll make it yet. Courier's name is Louis Sheen. Got it? He'll carry a suitcase, brown in colour. When he arrives at this Baur place 5.30 p.m. Zurich time, he goes to reception, tells them at the top of his voice that he's Louis Sheen, that they have a reservation, which they won't have. You contact him immediately with the code-words Lincoln Memorial. Got that? Then you take him to a safe place, wait for instructions from the creep who calls me.'

'I'm not showing my face . . .'

'Your problem. The creep demanding the dough pho-ned, gave three possible exchange points. Note them – I'll spell them out . . . OK? Something else – Sheen will be handcuffed to that suitcase. It stays that way until you meet the bastard who tries to collect. The case has combination locks. Only Sheen knows the numbers which open it. Try opening that case without operating the combination, a small thermite bomb inside explodes, burns the contents to crap.'

'I ought to know that combination,' Norton demanded.

'All those big bucks? You're a joke, Norton. One more thing – you kill the guy who comes to collect . . .'

In Zurich Norton was surprised when the line went dead. He'd never have thought March could have dreamed up such a diabolical trap as the thermite bomb.

At the Schweizerhof, after talking to Paula, Tweed was in a rush to keep his appointment with Jennie Blade. He asked Newman to phone the Zurcher Kredit to make sure Walter Amberg was still in Basle.

Newman recognized the voice of the girl who answered the phone. She was the attractive personal assistant who had shown them into the banker's office.

'Bob Newman here. I was with Mr Tweed when he called on your boss . . .'

'I remember you well, Mr Newman. How are you? How can I help?' she enquired.

'Well, I just wanted to check that Mr Amberg is still at the Basle branch, that he will be there tomorrow.'

'Oh, he will be. He'll be in Basle for several days. You can count on it. And you are the second person within the hour who has asked that question.'

'Who else did? Or shouldn't I ask?'

'Oh, that's all right, Mr Newman. He didn't leave a name. I'm new here, don't yet know all the clients. The man who called had a husky growly voice. Not very polite.'

'A lot of people aren't. I really am very much obliged to you. Thanks a lot.'

Newman wondered who 'growly voice' could be, made a mental note to tell Tweed.

Newman sat in the dimly lit bar leading off the lobby, drinking a glass of white wine. He was recalling the tough interview with Beck after the Swiss police chief had arrived at Theo Strebel's office.

'I'm not easily shocked, as you know,' he told Tweed as he viewed Strebel's corpse. 'But before he left us to set up a private investigator business – you can make more money that way – he solved a baffling murder case I couldn't crack. He was a great detective and it's a great loss.'

Beck kept his voice down. The office was swarming with the forensic and fingerprint teams. The police doctor had just left after officially pronouncing Strebel dead.

They had then hurried over to Klara's apartment. Newman had come with them and was not disappointed when Old Nosy poked her vulture-like nose out of the door.

'Is there some trouble upstairs?' she asked.

'Stay in your apartment,' Beck ordered. 'I'll want to talk to you later.'

'And who do you think you are?'

'Police.' Beck flashed his folder under the nose. 'I said stay until I get round to you . . .

'Local Eye-at-the-Keyhole,' he remarked as he strode up the stairs. 'There's one in every district . . .'

The doctor had visited Klara's apartment first and by the closed door to the ante-room stood a uniformed policeman. He saluted Beck, opened the door and they went inside.

Beck stared at the garrotted woman. He pursed his lips, turned to Tweed.

'I see now why the doctor said it was a bit nasty here. Never known him make a comment like that before and he's seen everything.'

Beck leaned against a wall. He folded his arms as he stared first at Tweed, then at Newman.

'Yesterday there was a small blood bath in Bahnhofstrasse. Have you seen the papers? No? Well they report a cripple in one of those battery-operated wheelchairs blew himself to pieces with a grenade. At about the same moment an American was shot dead – holding a machine-pistol. Now would you by chance know anything about these events?'

Tweed explained exactly what had happened – that he'd been up to his neck in trying to track down who was behind the murders. Beck nodded without comment as Tweed continued, then concluded: 'I'm sorry I didn't contact you earlier.'

'And I'm damned sorry too you didn't. I do like to know what is happening on my patch, as I think they say in Britain. And my patch is the whole of Switzerland – which includes Zurich.'

'I have apologized,' Tweed said quietly. 'How close are you to discovering what is happening, to solving the murders of this poor woman, Klara, and Theo Strebel?'

'I've only just arrived,' Beck pointed out. 'You mean you have some idea of who the murderer is?'

'The pieces of a huge international jigsaw – stretching all the way from Washington via Cornwall to here – *are* beginning to fall into place. I'm a long way from seeing the whole picture, but I'm getting there. Your further co-operation would be much appreciated.'

'Oh, you have that. Unreservedly. You're continuing your investigation in Zurich?'

'Not for much longer. Tomorrow we leave for Basle.'

'May I ask why?'

'You just did,' Tweed told him tersely. 'Walter Amberg is reported to have gone to Basle. I need to talk to him again.'

'Thank you. I think I can hear the technical teams arriving. Let's get out of here. If you could come to police headquarters I can take statements from both of you. It will take time, I fear. Oh, while we are still alone, I have had installed at Customs at Zurich, Geneva and Basle airports a special new machine. It checks the contents of cases without the arrivals knowing. A Swiss invention.'

'You mean an X-ray machine?' Newman asked.

'Much better than that. It photographs all the contents of a closed case. I want to see what any new American arrivals are bringing in to this country . . .'

Louis Sheen, from Washington, arrived at Kloten Airport. He waved his diplomatic passport and prepared to walk past Customs.

'Excuse me, sir,' the Customs officer behind the counter said. 'Please place your case on the counter.'

Sheen was tall and slim, his face long and pale, and he wore rimless glasses. He put down the case, waved the passport again, spoke in a nasal drawl.

'This is a diplomatic passport. Something wrong with your friggin' eyesight? You can't examine my bag.'

The Customs officer nodded to one of his subordinates who stood on the same side of the counter as the American. The Swiss picked up the case, placed it in a certain position on the counter, which was etched with a curious mosaic design.

'Goddamnit! You can't open that case,' Sheen shouted. 'It would be a breach of diplomatic etiquette.'

'Who said anything about opening the case, sir?' asked

245

the Customs officer. 'Could I have a closer look at that passport?'

'Your friggin' Passport guys saw it.'

'And now I would like to see it. This will only take a moment.' The officer opened the passport, walked a few steps along the counter, flipped open the pages. He handed it back, put his hand on the case as Sheen reached for it.

'Just leave it there for a moment longer. I have to check this passport number. It will only take a moment.'

'Friggin' Swiss bureaucracy,' Sheen stormed.

'It takes up a lot of our time too.'

The officer smiled, disappeared through a doorway behind him. The technician who had photographed the case through a hole in the patterned wall showed the officer the photo which was already developed. After one glance, the officer nodded to a plain-clothes policeman standing in the small room. The policeman nodded back.

When Sheen, fuming, was ushered on his way – fuming because he'd had to hold his left hand with the handcuff chain on top of the case – he was followed. Sheen was sweating as he sank into a cab.

It will take time, I fear. Beck had proved to be right. He'd had an excellent lunch brought in for Newman and Tweed at police headquarters. Each dictated a statement of considerable length and then both statements had to be typed out. By the time they had signed them the lunch had arrived. It was early afternoon. Tweed decided they might as well eat it and Beck joined them, chatting about past experiences.

It was late afternoon when a tired Tweed reached the Schweizerhof and listened in her room to Paula's account of her visit to Eve Amberg.

When she had finished, he thanked her and left for the Hummer Bar. It was dark as he walked down the side street to the direct entrance to the bar. Behind him on either side of the street Butler and Nield strolled along as though taking the night air.

Tweed pressed the bell which opened the door. He took a deep breath before walking inside to meet Jennie Blade. What would the girl he'd first met that grim afternoon outside Tresillian Manor have to tell him, he wondered.

26

Norton checked his changing appearance in the bathroom mirror before he left the apartment. After the second application of the colourant his hair was starting to look very grey. The half-moon glasses perched on his nose gave him a professorial look. He carried a large file full of business statistics which he had no interest in.

Checking his watch, he left the apartment to arrive in good time at the Baur-en-Ville before Louis Sheen turned up. The cab he flagged down swiftly transported him to Parade-platz. A short walk across Bahnhofstrasse and he was inside the Baur-en-Ville.

He entered the hotel, made certain arrangements with a messenger boy, then sat in a chair where he could see reception. The boy stood a distance away and watched Norton. It was precisely 5.30 p.m. when Louis Sheen walked in with the brown suitcase attached to his left wrist with a handcuff chain.

Norton was ice cold as he watched over the top of his file. The reception area was crowded with soberly dressed Swiss men greeting each other. Norton knew they were bankers. He had phoned the hotel earlier, pretending to ask for a room.

'I'm sorry, sir,' the girl had told him. 'We have no rooms at all available. There's a convention of bankers from all over Switzerland . . .'

Sheen went up to the reception counter, perched on it the suitcase to rest his hand. His voice was loud and overbearing when a receptionist turned to him.

'Louis Sheen, Philadelphia. I have a room reserved for several nights.'

'Certainly, sir.' The receptionist checked his records. 'Did you say Sheen, sir? I fear there is no reservation.'

Norton put down the file in his lap. It was the signal the generously tipped messenger boy had been waiting for.

Norton also noticed a man in a Swiss suit who wandered in within thirty seconds of Sheen's arrival. He stared as the man checked his watch, picked up a magazine, remained standing. It appeared he was waiting for someone – but he hadn't glanced round the reception area. Norton pursed his lips. Sheen had been followed from the airport.

'Now look here,' Sheen continued at the top of his voice, 'Louis Sheen, Philadelphia. I phoned the booking—'

He broke off as someone touched his right arm. Glancing down he saw a uniformed messenger boy.

'Mr Sheen?' the boy asked.

'Maybe. Why?'

'I have a message for him. Are you Mr Sheen?'

'I am. Give it to me . . .'

He turned away from the counter, ripped open the envelope. A white sheet of paper without a printed address at the top was inside. The message was brief.

Take a cab at once to the address given below. Walk out now and get a cab. Lincoln Memorial.

Underneath the address the message was signed with a flourishing 'N'. Sheen had been warned this was how

Norton always signed his instructions. He resisted the temptation to look around at the people assembled in the reception area.

Norton waited as Sheen left the hotel entrance leading to a side street. The man in the Swiss suit strolled after Sheen. Something would have to be done about him, Norton decided. He left by the same entrance in time to see the Swiss climb in behind the wheel of a BMW. His own limo, ordered in advance, was parked by the kerb. He climbed in the back as Sheen entered a cab.

'That cab is the target,' he ordered the driver, one of Mencken's subordinates. 'Don't lose it. Just don't make it obvious we are following it – we have company. The white BMW. It will follow our target. You follow the BMW. One more thing you will not do. Just listen. Do *not* look at me in your rear-view mirror. See me and you're dead. Now, for Chrissakes, get moving . . .'

Jennie's golden hair glowed in the subdued lighting of the Hummer Bar. She sat on a bar stool and Tweed had to admit to himself she looked stunning.

She wore a deep purple suit, the jacket open to reveal a low-cut white blouse. Round her neck was a string of pearls which disappeared in the dip between her breasts. On the stool beside her lay a folded pale lilac coat.

She swung round off her stool to greet him. Her short skirt exposed her long legs. She kissed him on the cheek and a faint waft of perfume drifted in the air.

'I hope I haven't kept you waiting,' Tweed remarked as they hoisted themselves on to the stools.

'Not for one second. I like a man who is prompt. And I arrived early. You look very fresh and eager.' Her blue eyes were animated and she was giving him her full attention.

'I don't feel all that fresh,' Tweed confessed. 'I've been on the go all day.'

249

'Time to relax then.' She squeezed his arm. 'Sorry I didn't make it last night. But from my point of view that gave me this evening to look forward to.'

She was openly flirting. Tweed decided to hit her hard when the time came with his first question. He suggested champagne. He rarely drank but he wanted her in a co-operative mood – she might tell him more that way.

'Lovely,' she said. 'My favourite tipple. You'll join me?'

Tweed ordered two glasses of champagne from the waiting barman. Glancing along to the end of the bar he saw Philip Cardon sitting on a stool, nursing a drink as he read a paperback.

Jennie gazed in the same direction as Cardon looked up from his paperback. She waved to him, then shook her golden mane as though to say, 'No good. You were pipped to the post.'

'Cheers!' said Tweed and they clinked glasses.

Jennie drank half the contents of her glass while Tweed downed his in two long gulps. Before leaving Paula he had drunk a lot of water, hoping it would keep him sober. Jennie finished off her drink.

'Another?' Tweed urged. 'You'll join me?'

'Sky's the limit.'

She grinned appreciatively at his using her own words back at her. They consumed most of the refills before Tweed threw the question without warning.

'When did you first know Julius Amberg was coming to stay at Tresillian Manor?'

'But I didn't.' She looked at him, her eyes wide open with innocence. 'Not until we were leaving for the cottage at Five Lanes an hour or so before he arrived.'

'Then why did you think you were leaving at all?'

'The Squire said he had some friends coming he rented the manor to from time to time.'

'Did you ever talk to one of his servants, a girl called Celia Yeo? She was found dead at the foot of High Tor –

which is not far from Five Lanes. Someone pushed her over the abyss.'

'How perfectly horrible.' She played with the stem of her empty glass. 'Tweed, you're some kind of investigator. You know something? I'm beginning to get the idea you're investigating me.'

'What I am investigating,' Tweed said grimly, 'is a series of murders . . .'

'You mean those poor people at Tresillian Manor?'

'Within the past twenty-four hours three more people have been murdered here in Zurich – one man and two women,' Tweed said grimly.

'You're frightening, Tweed. How does any of this concern me?'

'Where is Gaunt?' he asked.

'He's on his way to Basle . . .'

'By plane?'

'No, he's driving the hired BMW there . . .'

'Why is he going to Basle?' Tweed demanded.

'On some sort of business. How the hell would I know? I don't know anything about his affairs.'

'Don't get worked up,' he said quietly.

'Why the bloody hell shouldn't I?' Jennie blazed. 'I'm being interrogated like a suspect.'

'It's Gaunt I'm interested in, not you,' he said mildly. 'How long have you known him? Now don't jump down my throat. I am trying to find out why those poor people were brutally massacred.'

'I've known Squire Gaunt just over two weeks. Really, I think I should go.'

'Stay a little longer – help me to find out who is behind these hideous murders . . .'

Louis Sheen was startled to find after he had shown the cab driver the address on the sheet of paper that they were driving back along the route to the airport. The BMW with the Swiss driver followed them carefully, keeping one vehicle between himself and the cab. Behind him Norton's driver adopted the same tactic.

Within ten minutes the cab turned off the main road and pulled up outside a modern apartment block. Sheen paid him, climbed out carefully, manoeuvring the suitcase clamped to his wrist. Norton watched him go inside the building, then gave his driver fresh instructions.

'There's a phone box a few hundred yards beyond where we are now. I have to make a call. Drop me outside it, then wait for me. Keep your eyes staring ahead . . .'

Norton had seen the BMW park out of sight behind a big truck which stood stationary. He realized that from this point the Swiss could keep the exit to the apartment block under surveillance. As his own car stopped he jumped out, ran to the phone box, inserted coins, dialled the Baur-en-Ville, asked for Marvin Mencken.

'Yes, who is this?' Mencken's distinctive drawl asked.

'It's me. I arranged for you to check on a competitor.'

He was referring to Tweed, but was careful not to mention him by name.

'We know his exact whereabouts now,' Mencken snapped.

'And?'

'Well, it *is* all arranged,' Mencken said irritably.

'You pick him up and escort him to the meeting?'

The word escort meant *exterminate*.

'We're all set up for when he pokes his nose into the side-street. Don't worry any more about the competition. He'll co-operate. End of problem.'

'Make damned sure it is. The end . . .'

Norton slammed down the phone, went back to his car. It was all beginning to come together. Amberg had flown to Basle – so the film and the tape must have been transferred to the Zurcher Kredit Bank branch in that city.

252

He would fly that evening aboard flight SR 980, departing Zurich 7.15 p.m., arriving Basle 7.45 p.m. Sheen would find the message waiting for him in the apartment with the air ticket to board the same flight, to take a cab on arrival at Basle Airport to the Hotel Drei Könige. Norton, under a different name, would be staying at the same hotel.

Earlier he had given Mencken instructions over the phone to lead a team of men who would also fly to Basle. They would stay at the Hilton. While he waited for Sheen to emerge another cab had already drawn up outside the apartment block. Norton glanced at the parked BMW. He had no doubt the Swiss inside it would follow Sheen to Basle. There Norton himself would personally take care of the nuisance.

Yes, everything was coming together. And within the hour Tweed, who was proving to be a potential menace, would be dead. Norton felt the adrenalin surging inside him at the prospect of final action.

'Have you ever met Eve Amberg?' asked Tweed, casting about for a significant link between Cornwall and Zurich.

'I'm pretty sure I saw that woman in Padstow,' Jennie recalled as she sipped her third glass of champagne.

'I wasn't aware you knew her. If I'm right how would you recognize her?' Tweed queried.

'When Gaunt was leaving her villa the other day – not the day when you came up to me in the BMW – I saw her very clearly saying goodbye to Gaunt at the front gate.'

'But surely that was after you'd seen her in Padstow?'

'That's right. I have a photographic memory for faces.'

'So when did you see Eve Amberg in Padstow? I suppose you couldn't recall the exact day?'

'The day her husband arrived at Tresillian Manor just before the massacre. I was with Gaunt, having a quick drink at the Old Custom House early in the day. He went outside to look at his wretched boat – I followed him after finishing my drink. I saw Eve when she was hurrying away from South Quay.'

'And you're positive it was Eve Amberg?' Tweed pressed.

'I'm damned sure it was that woman. Damned sure.'

Tweed wondered why he thought she could be lying. Was it the double reference to 'that woman'? Also, if true, what she had said placed Jennie in Padstow at the time.

'I must go now,' she said. 'To a party.' She had checked her watch. 'It's been lovely talking to you. Do let's do it again . . .'

He helped her on with the lilac coat but she said she'd carry her scarf which had lain underneath the coat. As they moved towards the door Cardon was already opening it, disappearing outside. Tweed opened the door, let Jennie go out first. She dropped her scarf as he joined her and the ice-cold atmosphere of night hit them.

A cream Mercedes parked at the top of the street began to move towards them. The rear window was open. From inside the barrel of a gun projected. Cardon, standing against the wall, cannoned into Tweed. As he was falling to the ground Tweed deliberately collided against Jennie, who was still crouched low to retrieve her scarf. A hail of bullets thudded against the wall, sending chips of masonry flying in all directions.

Cardon, holding his Walther in both hands, fired three shots. More shots were fired by Butler and Nield who stood on either side of the street. The Mercedes sped off, weaving from side to side, reached an intersection, disappeared. Unhurt, Tweed helped Jennie to her feet. She was shivering and shaking, but also unhurt. She looked at Tweed.

'What happened, for God's sake?'

'Someone tried to kill me. Are you all right?'

'I'm OK.'

'Still want to go to your party?'

She was brushing grit off her coat. She opened it to check her suit, closed and re-buttoned it.

'Yes,' she decided. 'I'll recover faster at a party.'

'You're coming with us,' Cardon intervened.

He grasped her firmly by the arm. His expression was grim. Tweed spoke as he tightened his grip when she tried to free herself.

'Let her go, Philip,' he ordered. 'Here's a cab. Flag it down for Jennie . . .'

'She signalled to that car that you were coming out,' raged Cardon as the cab drove off. 'She dropped her scarf and that car started moving.'

'Possibly,' Tweed agreed. He looked at Butler and Nield who had joined them. 'Jennie may be a very skilful liar. *May* be,' he emphasized. 'Back to the Schweizerhof.'

'A brief council of war, everyone,' Tweed announced.

He had summoned Paula and Newman to his room. Cardon, Butler and Nield had come up with him. Cardon had tersely told Newman and Paula what had happened.

'Let's not dwell on it,' Tweed said briskly. 'They missed. Thanks to Philip, Harry and Pete I'm still very much alive. We are leaving for Basle first thing tomorrow. The key to everything, I'm now convinced, lies in the mysterious film and the tape Dyson left at the Zurcher Kredit. Those items are now in the vault of the Basle branch. Amberg is in Basle. I want to see him again. It's time we watched that film, listened to the tape.'

'Hadn't you better report that assassination attempt to Beck?' Paula suggested. 'He's going to get very annoyed if we don't tell him something else.'

Tweed phoned police headquarters. He was put straight through to Beck who worked all hours. Briefly Tweed explained, leaving out any reference to Jennie Blade.

255

'A patrol car has already found your cream Mercedes,' Beck informed him. 'Abandoned near the Quai-Brücke down by the lake. The bullet holes in the windscreen and windows attracted their attention. There was blood on the rear seat. Do you have to take such risks?'

'Zurich seems to be the battlefield. So perhaps you'll be relieved to hear I'm flying to Basle tomorrow.'

'There will be plain-clothes men watching you all the time. Good night. Stay in your hotel until you're leaving . . .'

Tweed put down the phone. He looked at Newman.

'Bob, I doubt if that girl at the Zurcher Kredit you seem to get on with is still there, but try. I'd like to be quite sure Amberg is still in Basle . . .'

Newman dialled the number of the Zurcher Kredit. The same girl answered immediately. The Swiss worked late.

'Bob Newman here again. Sorry to keep bothering you.'

'That's all right. I'm catching up on finding things out. I am new here, after all.'

'I wanted to double-check that Mr Amberg is still in Basle. In case I have to call him in the morning at an early hour.'

'Yes, he's definitely there. Will be for a few days. And someone else wanted to know – besides the man with the growly voice who phoned earlier. This time before I told the new caller I asked for a name and looked at the client file. He is a client of the bank. I think he wanted to see Mr Amberg urgently.'

'Could you possibly give me that name?' Newman coaxed.

'I suppose I shouldn't, but you're always so polite, unlike a lot of the clients.'

'So the name was?'

'Joel Dyson.'

27

The express train from Zurich to Basle thundered across northern Switzerland. Tweed sat in a first-class compartment with his case on the seat beside him while Paula sat opposite. Across the central aisle Newman occupied the seat next to the aisle while Cardon sat in the next two seats by himself. Cardon was in a corner, facing Tweed so he had a good view of him diagonally.

'We are not flying to Basle,' Tweed had announced in his hotel room before they left. 'Philip has been over to the Hauptbahnhof and bought return tickets for all of us to Basle.'

'Why the train?' Paula had asked.

'Because it's quicker for a start. Driving out to the airport, waiting to board a flight, taking a cab from Basle Airport, which is half an hour's journey – it all takes longer. Also, we can slip away more easily with the station just across the way.'

'But you told Beck you were flying there,' she reminded him.

'So I did.' He had smiled. 'I don't want to be hemmed in by his protectors. In any case, I have my own. I'll call him from the hotel in Basle . . .'

Paula sat looking round the sparsely populated compartment, alternately gazing out of the window. So far there were few mountains on this trip. They were travelling through industrial Switzerland, where many factories stood close to the railway line.

Out of the corner of her eye she saw someone

approaching their compartment. She glanced in the direction of the automatic door. A tall monk had entered. He wore a dark robe, his waist spanned with a rope girdle. A hood was pulled over his head and he had a pair of hornrimmed glasses perched on his nose. She slid her hand inside her shoulder bag, gripped the butt of the Browning.

The train was swaying round a bend as the monk, carrying a case in his left hand, made his slow progress towards them. Newman had seen Paula's reaction. He glanced quickly in a mirror, saw the monk coming, slipped his hand inside his jacket, rested his hand on the Smith & Wesson.

Tweed, apparently absorbed in writing names on a pad, linking them with different permutations, sensed the tension. He glanced up as the monk arrived alongside him. At that moment the express lurched again as it roared round a curve.

The monk's case hit Tweed's, toppled it over on the seat. Tweed stared at the face under the hood. Cord Dillon.

The uniformed conductor who had checked their tickets a few minutes earlier left another first-class compartment which had been empty. Not many people travelling at this time of year. It was early March.

Out of a lavatory where the door had been open a few inches a tall heavily built man stepped into the deserted corridor. At this point no other passengers were visible.

'Ticket, sir,' the conductor requested.

'Sure, buddy. Got it here somewhere . . .'

The American glanced in both directions. No other passengers in sight. The train swayed again. The conductor, accustomed to the movement, stood quite still, feet splayed.

The American, as tall as the conductor, appeared to lose his balance. He lurched against the conductor. The flick knife concealed behind him appeared, was rammed swiftly up through the open jacket and between the ribs of the conductor. As he grunted, sagged, the American grabbed him and hauled the body inside the lavatory, used an elbow to close the door. He lowered the body on to the seat, locked the door. Checking the neck pulse he felt nothing.

Swiftly he began the awkward task of removing the conductor's uniform – jacket, trousers and peaked cap. As he stripped off his own suit, folded it roughly, shoved it inside a plastic carrier, the eyes of his victim stared at him.

Tucking the carrier behind the seat, the American took out a penknife. He opened the door a few inches, saw no one. From the outside he used the penknife to move the small notice which indicated that the lavatory was occupied.

Straightening his cap, he checked his watch. Only a few minutes left before the train stopped at Baden. Mencken had a car with a driver waiting there to take him back to Zurich. He checked the Luger tucked inside his shoulder holster to make sure he could whip it out quickly from under the jacket, felt the handle of the second flick knife tucked inside his belt. The jacket, buttoned up, was a little tight across the midriff, but who notices a conductor? Holding the instrument used to clip tickets in his left hand he made his way back to the first-class compartment where Tweed was sitting. He'd be able to kill him and any guards in seconds . . .

Three things happened at once as the 'monk' toppled Tweed's suitcase. Newman rammed his revolver into Cord Dillon's back. Paula's Browning appeared in her hand. Tweed held up a hand to indicate all was well.

'My apologies,' Dillon whispered to Tweed, relieved when the gun muzzle was withdrawn from his back. 'The train lurched . . .'

259

As he spoke he dropped a card with writing on it in Tweed's lap. The message was terse, clear.

Barton Ives is aboard the train. Where can he meet you? Not on this train.

'No need to apologize,' Tweed said in a low tone. 'You can both contact me at Hotel Drei Könige – the Three Kings – in Basle. Sooner speak to you first.'

'Thank you, sir,' said Dillon.

He proceeded on through the compartment, carrying his bag. The last Tweed saw of him was when he disappeared beyond the compartment door. Paula leaned forward.

'What was all that about? I nearly shot him.'

'That was Cord Dillon. He did take a chance, but he's on the run still, obviously. On the train that outfit is a perfect disguise.' He folded the card, tucked it inside his wallet without showing it. 'He had an urgent message for me. We could take a mighty leap forward at Basle.'

'How in Heaven's name did he know you were on the train?'

'Because he's a trained observer, one of the best in the world. I can only guess – I imagine he saw us leaving the Gotthard for the Schweizerhof. He could have been up all night watching the hotel exit from the station across the Bahnhofplatz. That station never goes to sleep.'

'Tweed,' Paula persisted, speaking loud enough for Newman to hear her, 'there must be danger aboard this train. For Dillon to go to such lengths. If he saw us waiting at Zurich to board the express the opposition could also have seen us.'

'I doubt that. I didn't tell you I'd phoned Swissair and booked reservations for us on a flight to Basle. In our own names. They'll be watching the airport . . .'

He stopped speaking. Paula wasn't listening to him. In a mirror she was watching a uniformed conductor about to enter their compartment. She started fussing with her hair in the mirror to give a plausible reason for staring in that direction.

'Tickets, please . . .'

Paula shifted swiftly into the empty seat beside her so Newman could also hear her. She leaned forward.

'We've already had our tickets checked by one conductor. This is a *different* man . . .'

Paula had travelled on many Swiss trains. She knew that the conductors had remarkable memories. They would instantly spot a fresh passenger who had boarded *en route*, ask him for his ticket. But they *never* asked the same passenger twice.

The only people in the compartment were Tweed and his five companions. The conductor could see that from the moment he had entered. And yet he had said . . .

'Tickets, please . . .'

The conductor clipped Cardon's ticket a second time. He was walking slowly as he approached Tweed and Paula. His right hand slipped inside his tight jacket, which slowed down his lightning movement. The Luger was half out from behind the cloth when Newman jumped up. He grabbed the barrel of the gun, forced it to point at the ceiling of the car. The American was strong as an ox. He began to press the barrel down to aim it at Tweed.

Butler, seated at the other end of the compartment, hurtled forward. His bunched right hand hit the assassin a savage punch in the kidneys. The assassin sagged, butted Harry Butler in the chest. Butler grunted, stayed standing where he was, gasping for air.

Paula was on her feet, holding the Browning by the barrel, awaiting her chance to smash the butt against the attacker's head. Cardon came up behind him, tried to kick his legs from under him, but it was a confused struggle, everyone close together. Newman's fingernails, hard as a chisel, dug deep into the American's gun hand. He

261

loosened his grip and Paula caught the weapon in mid-air.

'Get the bastard out of the compartment,' Newman panted.

Nield was standing at the far end of the compartment where he had sat near Butler. He was watching to make sure no one was coming. An extra body flailing into the turmoil would be one too many.

In the violent struggle in the aisle the conductor's cap the assassin had worn fell off. Paula bent down, picked it up off the floor. Newman now had worked his way behind the American, had an arm round his throat. Butler bent down, grasped both legs by the ankles, crossed them and elevated. The thrashing assassin was now held between Butler and Newman who carried him out of the compartment.

The struggle became more violent outside the compartment as they carted the American towards the platform joining two coaches. The assassin twisted his head, his teeth were closing over Newman's hand. Newman let go, jumped back, hauled out his Smith & Wesson. He had no intention of firing it – even above the rumble of the swaying express's wheels it would be heard. Butler held on to the ankles and Newman cannoned against Cardon, whose back hammered into a lavatory door. Not completely locked, the door gave way and Cardon fell inside the confined space.

'It's occupied . . .' Newman started warning him.

'It bloody well is,' Cardon agreed. 'Take a look but don't move the door any more . . .'

Newman glanced round the door. A tall man in shirt and underclothes sat on the seat. A knife handle projected from the shirt, the blade was inside the body. From its position Newman realized it had penetrated the heart. The conductor . . .

In the corridor the attacker had broken free from Butler. He was on his feet faster than Newman would have believed possible. The flick knife in his hand was aimed at Butler's abdomen. As he lunged forward Newman moved. He brought down the barrel of his revolver with all his strength on the assassin's skull. The knife point was within an inch of Butler's abdomen when the barrel bounced back off the skull. For one incredible moment the assassin remained standing and Newman raised the revolver for a second blow. Then the assassin fell backwards into the lavatory.

Newman caught him round the waist. Cardon had sidled out of the lavatory to give assistance. Newman was heaving the assassin's inert body back into the lavatory when he saw Butler stooping to pick up the flick knife which had dropped from their adversary's hand.

'Don't touch that!' he shouted.

'You want this?'

Paula had appeared, holding the conductor's cap. Through the gap on the hinged side of the door she had seen what was sprawled on the seat.

'Yes. Give it to me,' Newman snapped.

He had fitted the body of the assassin into the corner facing his victim and under the washbasin. A brief check of the carotid artery told him the man was dead as his victim. He rammed the cap on to the corpse's head, kicked the knife inside the lavatory.

'Fingerprints,' he told Paula and the other two. 'It has to have his fingerprints on that knife. Now to shut this damned door . . .'

Using a handkerchief round his fingers, he closed the door. He then took a slim gold pen out of his pocket. Working with a steady hand, he eased shut the slide which indicated the lavatory was occupied. He'd made a better job of it than the assassin had earlier. Paula, delving in her shoulder bag, handed him a wad of tissues.

'Your gun,' she said. 'Blood on the barrel.'

Newman had automatically clung on to it while he had

wrestled the body inside the lavatory. He thanked her, quickly cleaned the barrel. Paula held out more tissues she had flattened out.

'Drop the messy ones here. I'll get rid of the lot in a litter bin at Basle . . .'

Nield was standing by the entrance door to the compartment, his right hand inside his jacket. Paula told Butler to wait a minute. She then refastened two buttons on Newman's shirt which had come undone in the struggle. She straightened his tie, told him to comb his hair, then gave Butler similar attention.

'What about me, Paula?' Cardon asked, looking doleful to lighten the atmosphere.

'You can look after yourself, Cry-Baby,' she told him, hoping she was keeping the tremble out of her voice.

Tweed sat very upright in his seat, staring at them as they came back. Newman sat in his old seat and Paula perched herself facing Tweed. His expression was grave as he asked the question.

'What about the real conductor?'

'He's dead,' Newman said simply. 'The assassin killed him to get his uniform.'

'I see. Was he married, do you think?'

'Don't know. No sign of it,' Newman lied.

Tweed was too quiet. Both Paula and Newman realized he was very upset because he knew he was the target the conductor had died for. And Newman had seen that the conductor *was* married. A gold band had adorned the third finger of his hand hanging down by the side of the lavatory.

'It's a bit scary,' Paula suggested. 'The way they're following us like wolves, know exactly where we are. Whoever "they" may be.'

'The mastermind behind all this,' Tweed said quietly, 'is going to pay a heavy price for the loss of life. I'll see to that personally . . .'

28

Basle – where Switzerland meets France and Germany. The moment Tweed alighted from the express he found a phone box, called Beck in Zurich. To his surprise they told him Beck was already in Basle. He phoned police head-quarters in that city.

'Beck speaking . . .'

'More bad trouble I'm afraid, Arthur. Aboard the express from Zurich . . .'

Tersely he told Beck what had happened, that the bodies were inside the lavatory of the fourth coach from the rear, that the express was scheduled to wait twenty minutes before proceeding north into Germany.

'Hold on,' Beck interjected.

He returned to the phone three minutes later. His tone was crisp, calm.

'Patrol cars and an ambulance are already on the way to the Bahnhof. I phoned the station superintendent. That express won't leave until they've done their job. Which hotel are you staying at?'

'Drei Könige. I'm speaking from the station . . .'

'Go straight to your hotel. Do not leave it under any circumstances until I get there, which may not be for some time. The killers have tracked you. Once again. Drastic action must be taken. *Stay in your hotel* . . .'

Tweed arrived at the Drei Könige with Paula and New-man. As planned, Butler, Nield and Cardon would come later one by one, as though they didn't know each other. The concierge greeted Tweed warmly.

'So good to have you back with us, Mr Tweed,' he said in his perfect English. 'We have three nice rooms for you, all overlooking the Rhine . . .'

As Tweed registered, a man wearing a Swiss business suit with half-moon glasses perched on his nose sat in the large lounge area adjoining reception. He was reading a local newspaper, his eyes hooded with disbelief as he saw Tweed enter. His grey hair was shaggy and he raised the paper a little higher to conceal his presence. Norton was recovering from the shock of seeing Tweed still alive.

Paula went along to Tweed's room. She had showered and changed into her blue suit in fifteen minutes. Tweed opened the door a few inches, then swung it open wide and ushered her inside with a sweeping gesture. He immediately relocked the door. Paula looked round the double room.

'What a super room. Mine's like this. And it has a magnificent view of the Rhine.'

She ran to the window. It was a brilliantly sunny day and very cold. The hotel was perched on the very edge of the Rhine which was about a hundred yards wide even as high upriver as Basle. On the far bank a number of ancient houses with steep pointed roofs lined the river.

'Look,' she called out, 'a barge train.'

Tweed joined her and they watched a stubby tug hauling downriver a string of huge barges. They were container craft and the German flag flew from each stern.

'I've got the same view,' she enthused. 'Oh, dear, I suppose I shouldn't feel so buoyant after the horror on the express. That poor conductor . . .'

'He was dead before we knew anything was happening.' Tweed put his arm round her. 'So we couldn't have saved him. Now we go after the people responsible for the atrocity. But first, interested in lunch?'

'Ravenous.'

To reach the lift they moved along a railed walk which surrounded a well looking down on to the floor below. Not a very high rail, Paula observed. Newman arrived from his room as they entered the lift and squeezed inside with them. Stepping out into the lobby the first person they saw was Eve Amberg.

'It's a small world, to coin a cliché,' Eve greeted them. 'My, it's cold outside.'

'I love it,' Newman said cheerfully. 'I can work and think better in this weather.'

'Bully for you.' Eve turned her attention to Tweed after nodding to Paula. 'I'm just going in to lunch.' She smiled at him warmly.

'By yourself?' Tweed enquired.

'As it happens, yes.'

'Why not join me for lunch, then?'

'How nice of you.' She glanced at Paula and Newman. 'But you have your friends.'

'Oh, that's all right,' Paula said quickly. 'Bob and I have something to work out. Do it better on our own.'

Eve was again looking as smart as paint, reminding Paula of their first meeting, as opposed to when she had caught Eve leaving the villa on a shopping trip. She wore a soft green tailored jacket, a mini skirt and a cream blouse with a high neckline. Must have cost a bomb, that outfit, Paula estimated.

As they followed Tweed and Eve towards the dining room Paula looked round the large lounge area. Out of the corner of her eye she'd seen someone sitting there when they arrived. The grey-haired man had gone.

They entered the dining room – oblong with windows to their right giving a view across a canopied platform extending over the Rhine. Tweed pointed towards it as a waiter showed them to a window table.

'That's what they call the Ry-Deck. In summer you eat

out there and it's like being aboard an ocean liner.'

'I know,' Eve agreed. 'Julius brought me here when he was visiting Basle.' She sat down. 'What a coincidence – the two of us arriving at the same time at the same hotel.'

'Not really, if you are visiting Basle. This is the most prestigious hotel, as I'm sure you know. Goes back ages and the food and service are excellent.'

Like the entrance hall and the lounge area, the walls were covered with old panelling and the comfortable atmosphere suggested somewhere which had existed for ever.

'There are buildings just along here by the river which have amazing dates of origin,' Tweed remarked as he studied the menu. 'Incidentally, why are you in Basle, if I may ask?'

'You may,' she teased him, squeezing his hand. 'I came to have a serious talk with Walter, to pin him down – about money, of course. My money. I phoned the bank and the pest has flown to France.'

'Really?' Tweed concealed his anxiety. 'Any idea where in France?'

'Oh, I can tell you exactly. Walter owns a place up in the Vosges mountains. Very remote. The Château Noir. Easiest way to get there is to take the train to Colmar, a picturesque town only half an hour from Basle Bahnhof. Then you hire a car to drive you up into the mountains. I'm going to catch him up if I have to follow him all over Europe.'

'Would you like a drink? Wine? White, then how about Sancerre?'

'Love it.'

'Would you excuse me for a few minutes?' Tweed asked when the wine had arrived. 'I have to phone London – should have done it before I came down to lunch . . .'

He left Eve sipping her wine appreciatively. Newman and Paula sat together at a table some distance away.

Seated alone at a table which gave a view of the whole room was Harry Butler. At two other tables, also by themselves, sat Pete Nield and Philip Cardon.

In his room Tweed checked the number of the Zurcher Kredit in the directory, dialled the number. A woman with a severe voice answered his call.

'Mr Amberg is away at the moment. No, I have no idea when he will return.'

'I am a client,' Tweed persisted. 'Mr Amberg was going to collect two items which belong to me from the bank vault. Do you know if he did visit the vault . . .'

'I really have no idea. If you will leave your name . . .'

Tweed put down the phone, waited a moment, dialled police headquarters, asked for Beck. He explained what he wanted. Beck said he'd contact the Zurcher Kredit and call him back. Five minutes later the phone rang and Beck was on the line again.

'I put pressure on the old dragon who took my call, told her I was investigating three murders which took place on Swiss soil. Amberg did collect something from the vault before he left . . .'

'For his château up in the Vosges behind Colmar,' Tweed interjected.

'Don't go into France,' Beck warned. 'I can try to protect you here but France could be even more dangerous. The train incident has been dealt with. I'll need some more statements.'

'You'll get them before we leave.'

'For France? *Don't do it*, for God's sake. I'm carrying out a sweep through Basle. They obviously know you're here. Take care . . .'

Tweed was leaving the room when the phone rang again. He locked the door, ran to answer it, sure it would stop just as he reached it.

'Yes?' he said.

'There's someone on the phone for you, Mr Tweed,' the

269

operator told him. 'He won't give a name but says it's very urgent.'

'Put him on.'

'Dillon here. We have to take a decision—'

'Operator!' Tweed interrupted suddenly. 'This is a bad connection. I can't hear the caller . . .'

He waited. For the hotel operator to answer. For the click which would betray the fact she had been listening in. Nothing.

'Sorry, Dillon. It's all right. Go ahead.'

'Barton is in town. But so is the opposition. Believe me. Barton won't come to see you in Basle.'

'Cord, first give me a description of him. Detailed, if you please. I need to be able to recognize him.'

There was a pause. Tweed was taking no more chances – not after the fake Barton Ives, whom he was convinced had been Norton, had turned up at the Gotthard. Dillon spoke tersely.

'Six feet tall, slim build, wiry, black hair, now has a small black moustache, a small scar over his right eye – where a scumbag caught him with a knife. Speaks very deliberately. Economical in movement. Except in a crisis. Then he moves like a rocket taking off from Cape Canaveral. That enough? It had better be.'

'Enough. Today or tomorrow latest we move to the Hotel Bristol, Colmar, in Alsace. A thirty-minute train ride. He contacts me there. And so do you. In person. I'll meet you both in Colmar – together or separately. I don't give a damn. The alternative? Forget it.'

'Look, Tweed, when you're on the run . . .'

'By now I know at least as much as you do – maybe more – about being on the run. Time to stop running, to face the swine who don't care what methods they use. Ives *must* see me in Colmar. So *must* you. I have to go now . . .'

Tweed, his mood cold as ice, put down the phone. He had meant it. No more being driven from place to place by the opposition. Time to lay a huge trap for them. Probably in the Vosges mountains.

Tweed apologized to Eve as he rejoined her. She was smoking, waved her ivory cigarette holder.

'Please, say no more. I've been enjoying myself now I'm away from Zurich. Awful thing to say, but I'll always associate that city with Julius. Does that sound too too dreadful?'

Tweed noticed she must have drunk about three glasses of the Sancerre during his absence. Some of these women had heads like rocks. She showed no sign of being even slightly inebriated. He refilled her glass.

'No, it doesn't. If he gave you a bad time. The lines to London were busy. Hence my neglecting you.'

'Nonsense. As regards Julius, all those women. Ah, here is the waiter . . .'

They both ordered grilled sole. Tweed remembered from a previous visit that sole was particularly good at the Drei Könige. When they were alone again Eve leaned towards him, her greenish eyes holding his.

'You've changed since you made that call. You're like a pulsating dynamo now. Like a man about to do battle. I can sense the change.'

Tweed became aware that he was sitting very erect in his chair, that as he spoke he'd been making vigorous gestures. It was uncanny the way Eve had hit the nail on the head. He felt rejuvenated at the prospect of meeting Barton Ives, a man he was convinced knew a great deal about why the world was exploding about them.

He chatted to Eve about Switzerland in general until the main course arrived. They ate in silence, devouring the excellent fish. He began probing again when they had ordered their dessert. But first he refilled her glass. So far he had consumed one glass of wine and a lot of mineral water.

271

'How did you get here? By car?'

'Lord, no! The traffic is terrible. I flew from Zurich. It's only a half-hour flight. For some stupid reason I got to the airport at the last minute, boarded the plane and it took off.' She toyed with her half-empty glass. 'Are you still investigating the horrible murder of that woman – what was her name? Helen Frey.'

'I have other fish to fry – pardon the unintended pun. Could there be a link with her murder and the fact that she . . . knew Julius?'

'Why on earth should there be?'

'Just a thought. When are you leaving for Colmar?'

'Haven't made up my mind.'

'Where is Squire Gaunt at this moment?'

'No idea.' She emptied her glass. 'He comes and goes. I'm not his keeper – if I can put it that way.' She played with his sleeve. 'He's just an acquaintance – if you were thinking something else.'

'Never crossed my mind,' Tweed lied.

The orange mousse with Grand Marnier they had chosen was as mouth-watering as their grilled sole. Tweed was puzzled. Eve seemed so poised and interested in him. When she had finished her mousse she carefully wiped her full lips with a tissue and swung round in her chair to face him. Her jacket was open and the movement drew attention to her well-shaped breasts protruding against the white blouse. She plucked at his sleeve again.

'Why don't we have coffee upstairs in my room? It will be quieter there. And I would like to hear how you got on with Julius. He was, after all, my husband. Please excuse me for a moment. The powder room . . .'

As she left the restaurant Tweed glanced across at the table where Paula sat with Newman. Paula was watching him with a half-smile, roguish. She beckoned to him, got up to meet him.

'Something fascinating you must see. There's a really

weird ferry which keeps crossing the Rhine.' She led him to an end window. 'It's like a gondola. Bob says it's controlled by a wire running from the ferry to a cable which spans the river. There it is . . .'

In some ways the very small ferry did resemble a gondola. The stern half was roofed over with the for'ard part open to the elements. A strong current was running as it made its slow way across from the opposite bank. The craft was swaying in a brisk breeze and inwardly Tweed winced. His mind flashed back to the ferry from Padstow to Rock, the large powerboat which had attempted to overturn them, Cardon lobbing his grenade. They watched it until it reached the side.

It carried a single passenger. A large man with his back to them. He wore a deerstalker.

'A curious contraption, that ferry,' Tweed commented.

'Your lady friend awaits,' Paula mocked him.

'I've just had a message that I have to go somewhere,' Tweed explained to Eve as they left the dining-room.

She looked at her watch, glanced at the reception clock.

'My watch is fifteen minutes slow. No wonder I nearly missed my flight at Zurich. There you go. A Swiss watch. It must have been slow for days . . .' She hesitated. Tweed thought she'd been going to say more, had changed her mind. 'Oh . . .' she said.

She was staring at the revolving entrance doors. A man in a deerstalker had just entered the lobby from outside.

'Ah! So we meet again,' a familiar voice boomed. 'What about drinks in the bar? My round . . .'

Squire Gaunt had arrived.

Marvin Mencken, his expression unpleasant – because he had failed again – hurried out of the Hilton Hotel in Basle to call Norton from a phone box in the station. He only had a number – a Basle phone number. Norton never gave him an address, the cunning bastard.

A bitter east wind blew through the large Bahnhof as he found the nearest phone. He took a deep breath, dialled.

'Who is it?' the abrasive voice at the other end demanded.

'Mencken here. The large team which flew with me from Zurich is in place. We've hired transport . . .'

'And botched up everything on the train. I saw them unloading the useless cargo. You really must get your act together this time,' Norton said in a dangerously soft tone.

'Sure thing . . .'

'There don't seem to be any sure things. Listen. Tweed is at the Drei Könige down by the river. The profile of him says he likes fresh air, taking a walk. So this time you eliminate the competition. Or your head is on the block. Shut up and listen, damn you! This is what you do . . .'

This conversation, which involved the killing of Tweed, took place while the target was finishing lunch at the Drei Könige.

'Thank you,' Tweed said to Gaunt, 'but we have an urgent appointment.' He looked round at Paula and Newman who came closer, then lowered his voice to speak to Eve. 'I appreciate your invitation to join you for coffee. But seeing the time when you looked at your watch made me realize I was behind schedule. Another time?'

'Yes, please,' Eve said in a whisper. She ran a hand through her hair slowly, her eyes half-closed as she stared at him. 'I get so lonely.'

'I do understand. There is always another time,' Tweed assured her.

Paula and Newman collected their coats from the concierge who then helped Tweed put on his heavy overcoat. As they went outside and Tweed turned right Paula asked her question.

'What appointment? Or was she moving in too close for comfort?'

'An appointment with a walk so I can think. We could be close to discovering something important – even the key to the mystery.'

As they walked uphill and along the deserted street called Blumenrain Tweed told them about his conversation with Cord Dillon. They passed a short side-street which, Newman pointed out, led to the landing point for the strange little ferry shuttling back and forth across the Rhine. Another narrow street of ancient buildings continued on parallel to the river. Totentanz. Tweed stopped briefly in the piercing wind to look at the different dates. 1215. 1195. 1175.

'One of the oldest cities in Europe,' he commented.

'It's early Middle Ages,' Paula added.

The wind dropped suddenly and it became very silent and still. Paula's mood changed to one of premonition. The narrow street was still deserted – they were the only people walking in the silence.

The ancient stone houses were tall and slim, all joined together to form an endless wall. Each house had a heavy wooden door flush with the wall and she had the feeling no one lived there. The old pavement was very narrow, so narrow they moved in single file.

Tweed, hands deep inside his coat pockets, shoulders hunched against the cold, was in front. Paula followed on his heels while Newman brought up the rear. It was like a city abandoned by the inhabitants who had fled from the plague. Creepy.

The sun had vanished. The sky was a low ceiling of grey clouds which suggested snow. It did nothing to dispel

Paula's premonition of imminent doom. Do pull yourself together, she thought. At that moment she heard the car coming ahead of them, the first vehicle they'd seen since starting out on their walk. It's the time of day, she reassured herself – mid-afternoon in March and most people inside offices at work . . .

Tweed had stopped, put out a hand to grasp her arm as he searched desperately for a protective alcove to thrust her into. Newman had no time to whip out his Smith & Wesson. Racing towards them on the opposite side of the street was a large grey Volvo. The driver wore a helmet and goggles. Newman had a glimpse of other men inside the car as it swerved across towards them, mounted their pavement, hurtled forward like a torpedo.

Nowhere to run. They were hemmed in by the wall of houses. It was going to mow them down, drive on over their bodies. Tweed grasped Paula round the waist, prepared to try and throw her out of the way across the street. He doubted whether he'd manage it. The Volvo was almost on top of them. The driver wearing the sinister goggles accelerated. They were dead.

The white Mercedes appeared out of nowhere, rocketing down the street from the same direction the Volvo had appeared. It drew alongside the Volvo. The driver swung his wheel over, his brakes screeched as he stopped just before he hit the wall.

The Volvo, unable to stop, slammed into the side of the Mercedes. Four uniformed policemen, guns in their hands, left the Mercedes as it rocked under the impact. As three of them leapt to the doors of the Volvo, guns aimed, the fourth man waved as he grinned at Tweed, waved again for him to go away.

'Back to the Drei Könige,' Tweed said, his arm round Paula, who was shaking like a leaf in the wind.

29

In a state of shock, no one spoke until the Drei Könige
came into sight. Tweed was the first to recover. He glanced
at Paula. The colour had returned to her face. They could
talk now.

'That was Beck who saved us,' he said. 'He told me he
was carrying out a sweep of the whole city.'

'But it was sheer luck that unmarked police car turned
up in the nick of time,' Newman objected.

'Organized luck. Don't stare at him,' Tweed warned,
'but see that man standing near the bridge over the Rhine?
Note he's carrying a walkie-talkie by his side, that from
where he's standing he would see us leaving the hotel. He
was standing there when we started out on our walk.
Obviously he radioed to Beck at HQ. So now the question
is – who signalled to the opposition that we were staying
here, maybe even reported when we were leaving for the
stroll?'

Pushing his way through the revolving door, he noticed
the concierge had gone off duty. A girl he had not seen
before was on duty behind the counter. He leaned on the
counter as he asked for the key, waited until she handed it
to him.

'You have an English friend of mine staying here – or
you will have. Has he arrived yet? A Mr Gregory Gaunt?'

'Oh yes, sir. Mr Gaunt checked in early this morning.
Do you want me to see if he's in his room now?'

'Don't bother him, thank you. I'm going up to have a
rest. I'll surprise him at dinner.'

'So Gaunt has been here for quite several hours,' Tweed remarked as they entered the elevator.

It was three o'clock in the afternoon in Basle when Tweed narrowly escaped with his life.

In Washington it was nine o'clock in the morning. Bradford March had a black stubble all over his jaw and upper lip. Which told Sara Maranoff that neither Ms Hamilton nor any other attractive woman would be visiting the President in the Oval Office today.

When she had bad news she always tried to tell March in the morning. He was fresher then and less inclined to react viciously. Standing by the window, March glanced at her, scratched with his thumbnail at his stubble. He had guessed from her expression that something he didn't want to hear was coming.

'Go on, spit it out, Sara,' he snapped.

'Tom Harmer, who contributed a sizeable proportion of the big bucks you sent to Europe by courier, has been on the phone.'

'So Tom wants what?' he demanded.

'The money he gave you back. Apparently a large loan he took out has been called in. Needs the money back inside fourteen days.'

'Does he now.' March hitched up his pants and smiled unpleasantly. 'You've got those photos of Tom screwing that bimbo – use one of them. Tom's wife would find them interesting souvenirs on her coming wedding anniversary.'

'You mean send one to her? Brad, that will get you no place.'

'Slept badly last night, did you? Wake up, Sara. I mean you send a copy – choose a good one yourself – to his office marked for his confidential and personal attention. Soon as it's arrived call him. Ask him how he likes his picture. Then tell him the money he gave was a contribution to party funds, can't be sent back.'

'I think he's desperate, Brad. He has to repay that loan or he's in deep trouble.'

'That's his problem. Handle it the way I told you.'

Sara, her black hair perfectly coiffured, wore a plain grey dress belted at the waist. As long as she looked neat she never bothered much about clothes. March's 'hatchet' woman from his early days of obscurity in the South, she tried to watch every angle to protect her boss. She bit on the end of her pen, decided to take the plunge.

'I hear a team of Unit One has returned from Europe, a large team. At your request to Norton, I presume.'

'So what?' March demanded impatiently.

'I didn't know they were taking over the duties of the Secret Service. You never consulted me.'

It was a tradition that the President's safety was in the sole hands of the Secret Service. They sent men ahead to any destination the President was flying to, checking out the lie of the land in advance, with full powers to override the local police. They were professionals to their fingertips.

'That's right,' March said off-handedly. 'As from today those Secret Service types are out. They seem to think they can run my life. Unit One takes over from them. And you're right again – I didn't consult you.'

'I don't like it . . .'

'Don't recall asking you to like it. That's the way it's going to be. Unit One types are tougher than the Secret Service. My own ruthless boys. I want men I can trust around me.'

'They haven't the experience of the Secret Service,' she persisted.

'They shoot on sight. They don't monkey around. I like their attitude. And I tell *them* what to do.'

'I think it's a mistake . . .'

279

'You're due for a break.' March leaned against a wall, ankles crossed, hands shoved inside his baggy trouser pockets. 'Go climb Mount Rushmore. Drop off it.'

Sara gave up, said nothing. There was a time when he'd listened to her. All of the time. The phone rang. The private line. She answered it, put her hand over the mouthpiece.

'Norton on the line.'

He raised his thick eyebrows, walked slowly towards her, grinned. He stroked her strong-boned face with his index finger. He grinned at her again.

'I know I'm an old grouch. Pals again? Don't know what I'd do without you. Let's hope Norton's cleaned up.'

He took the phone and waited until she'd left the office. Sara's head was spinning. One moment she could kill him, then he turned on the charm and she knew she'd go on being his right arm.

'President March here,' he said in a cold voice. 'You've got the two items I'm waiting for?'

'Not yet, but I'm close . . .' Norton began.

'Close to Mencken taking over from you. Norton, how many of the four targets have you hit?'

'Taking twenty men away from me back to Washington hasn't helped . . .'

'Bullshit. You still have over thirty under your control. What do you need? The friggin' Army? Norton!' March shouted. 'This is final. You have ten days to bring me those two items. In case your memory is failing, you'll recognize the film in the first few seconds when you see who is on it. You then switch it off. On the tape you will hear a hysterical girl screaming because she's seen fire. She's in no danger but as a kid she had to run out of a burning building. Soon as you hear screaming you switch off the tape. Bring them both to me. Got it now?'

'Nothing wrong with my memory, Mr President . . .'

'So maybe you lack guts. Now you listen and listen good.

You have ten days to take out that Brit Tweed, Ives, Joel Dyson and Cord Dillon. To remove them from the face of the earth. It's March 3. That ten days includes today. That's your deadline. I stress the word "dead" . . .'

March put down the phone, took out a handkerchief, mopped his brow and his thick neck. He was sweating like a bull. Within twenty-four hours of handing over to him the film and tape Norton would suffer an accident. A fatal one.

'We may well be close to the moment of decision,' Tweed said. 'Tomorrow we take the train to Colmar and go up into the Vosges. We'll have an advantage there we've lacked so far.'

He had phoned Beck, had thanked him for saving their lives. He'd had to take a gentle lecture from the Swiss about the risk of leaving the hotel. In his bedroom he was outlining his plan of action to Newman and Paula.

'What advantage?' Paula queried.

'So far it's been like street fighting – we've been in cities, not sure where the opposition would strike at us next. Out in the open we'll see them coming – in the mountains.'

'When we go up to see Amberg at the Château Noir?' Newman suggested.

Earlier, Tweed had told them of his conversation over lunch with Eve. He had recalled the information she had given him about Amberg leaving for France. Newman was dubious when Tweed confirmed that was their destination.

'Here we have Beck's protection,' he pointed out. 'The moment we cross into France we're on our own. There appears to be a huge apparatus operating against us. Have you any idea who is controlling it? If it's the film and the tape Dyson brought here, what could be on it to cause all these deaths?'

'I've no idea. That's why I'm going to see Amberg. I'm convinced he's taken the film and the tape with him.

Maybe he's been threatened – so he's using possession of the film and the tape to stay alive. That's one thing.'

'What's another?' Newman asked.

'I'm determined to watch that film, to listen to that tape. I've phoned Monica and she's been in touch with Crombie, who's supervising clearing the rubble at Park Crescent.'

'Why?' Paula queried.

'Because he's still digging for my safe – which has the copies of the film and the tape inside it. No sign of it yet.'

'I'd also like to know what Cardon has been up to,' Newman remarked. 'We hardly saw him in Zurich.'

'Then let him tell you. I'll get him along here now.'

Tweed grabbed the phone, dialled Cardon's room number, asked him to come at once. He looked at Newman when he put down the receiver.

'You want to know. Ask him yourself . . .'

Tweed stood staring out of the window while they waited. An incredibly huge oil tanker was moving upriver. Along its deck was a network of pipes and warning notices. Newman let in Cardon when he knocked on the door.

'The floor is yours,' Tweed said, moving around restlessly.

'Philip,' Newman began, 'we're interested in what you spent your time doing in Zurich.'

'Using the photocopy of Joel Dyson Paula helped to produce. Criss-crossing Zurich hour after hour. Looking for Dyson.' Cardon grinned. 'Then I found him.'

'You did!' Paula exclaimed. 'Where? Why didn't you grab him? He can probably tell us all we desperately need to know.'

'Hold your horses.' Cardon smiled at her. 'I spotted him getting into a cab in Bahnhofstrasse. Couldn't grab him when the cab was moving, could I?'

'You lost him, then?'

'I said hold your horses,' Cardon went on patiently. 'I took another cab, followed him to Kloten Airport. Lots of

282

people about – a plane had just come in. Plus security men. Again, couldn't just walk up and stick a gun in his ribs.'

'I suppose not,' Paula agreed. 'What happened next?'

'The only thing that could happen. I watched him check in. I was close behind him. He had one case. He really has a foxy-looking face.'

'He's a creep!' Newman snapped.

'Do get on with it,' Paula urged, knowing Cardon was playing with her.

'He'd worked it so he just had time to catch his flight. Without a ticket – and no time to get one – I couldn't follow him through Passport Control and Customs. Guess what his destination was.'

'The planet Mars,' Paula said in exasperation.

'Not quite as far as that. His destination was Basle. He's somewhere in this city.'

Paula looked stunned. Newman suggested a course of action immediately.

'Let's trawl Basle like we did Zurich. Philip came up trumps there eventually. We all have photocopies of the sketch of Dyson.'

'No,' said Tweed. 'Beck told us to stay in the hotel. We ignored his advice – at least, I did. The result? I came within a hair's breadth of getting us all killed. Basle, like Zurich, is a big city. Within a few hours – tomorrow morning – we leave for Colmar. I'm not risking anyone's life again in this city.'

'What about the weapons we're carrying?' Cardon queried. 'Won't Beck want them back?'

'Significantly, knowing we will be venturing into France, he hasn't mentioned them. And Arthur Beck never forgets a thing.'

'But we'll be crossing a frontier,' Paula reminded him.

'Bob, you remember when we once went to Colmar? It's

283

the most curious set-up at the station here. You walk direct from the Swiss Bahnhof into the French station. If we catch a train at eleven in the morning there should be no one manning either control point. There wasn't before.'

'Supposing the control points are manned this time? No way to guard against that,' Paula insisted.

'Yes, there is,' Tweed explained. 'I'm carrying nothing. I go through first, you lag behind. If you see me stopped, turn back. We'll think of something else.'

'I wonder where Joel Dyson is now,' Paula mused.

'What I'd like to know is who murdered Helen Frey, Klara and that detective, Theo Strebel,' Newman commented.

'I think I've worked that out – from information one of you provided me,' Tweed replied.

Bankverein, the tram-stop midway between the Rhine and the railway station, is where most of the Basle banks are situated. The Zurcher Kredit was one of them. The hippie sitting on the pavement near the bank's entrance had his legs sprawled out in front of him. He wore a shabby old Swiss hat, the brim pulled down over his forehead. His worn dark overcoat was buttoned up to the neck against the cold. His stained corduroy trousers were too long and draped over his ancient Swiss climbing boots. By his side Joel Dyson had a large canvas bag.

Dyson had rubbed dirt into his plump face and a torn scarf concealed his receding chin. Several Swiss who passed by glanced at him curiously, but Dyson knew the American watcher on the other side of the street would find nothing strange in his presence.

Dyson was waiting his opportunity to slip into the bank without the American seeing him enter. He had worked out the moment – providing a customer went inside the bank at that moment. The guard inside the bank would then escort the customer out of sight of the lobby and take him or her to whoever they were visiting.

Dyson knew it would take split-second timing, but he'd learned to move fast taking compromising photographs of celebrities. He gripped the canvas bag tightly by its wooden handle as a woman dressed in black approached. Three small green trams – toys compared with the modern blue giants of Zurich – trundled up from the direction of the Rhine close together. This could be the right moment.

The woman in black entered the bank, the guard spoke to her, escorted her out of sight. The trams masked him from the American. Dyson leapt up, pushed open the door into the empty lobby, then moved even faster.

Unbuttoning his disreputable overcoat, he tore it off, revealing a smart blue business jacket. Slipping out of his trousers, he exposed the blue suit trousers. Hauling off the boots, he opened the canvas bag, took out a pair of smart slip-ons, tucked his feet inside them. Pulling off the hat he bundled the boots and old clothes inside the canvas bag, closed it. Smoothing his hair with a comb and wiping his face with a cloth he had dampened earlier, he held a visiting card in his hand when the guard returned. He presented the card without saying a word. The guard examined it, turned it over to look at the writing on the back. He read the message in German carefully.

Please give every assistance to this gentleman. He is a most valued client.

On the front side was printed *Walter Amberg, Zurcher Kredit.* The printing was embossed. Dyson had asked Julius's brother for his card when he had deposited the film and the tape with Julius. On his recent visit to Zurich he had entered several bars before he struck up a conversation with a Swiss by buying him several drinks. He had then asked him to write this message in German on the card, saying he was playing a joke on a Swiss friend.

Dyson was an expert at bluffing his way into offices and houses where he wasn't known. The guard said something to him in German.

'Sorry,' Dyson said, 'I only speak English.'

'I think you should see Mrs Kahn,' the guard suggested in English.

'I think that was the name of the lady I was given . . .'

Mrs Kahn was a dark-haired lady of uncertain age wearing gold-rimmed glasses. She studied the card after asking him to sit down. Then she said she would be back in a minute. She closed the door to another room carefully after leaving.

Dyson grinned to himself. He knew exactly what she was doing. She was phoning Zurich to check on him. Dyson had deposited a small sum of money when he had handed over the film and the tape for safekeeping. He had realized that if you were a client – no matter how small or large the account – you had joined the club.

While he was alone he took out his handkerchief, wet it with his tongue, rubbed vigorously at his cheek. He had already cleaned off most of the dirt in the lobby but he was anxious to make a good impression. A man of substance was the phrase. A pukka member of the club. Mrs Kahn returned, sat behind her desk.

'What can I do for you, Mr Dyson?'

'I have to get in touch with Mr Amberg. He is keeping something valuable for me. He said I should ask for him when I needed to collect the valuables. The matter is rather urgent.'

'Mr Amberg is in France.'

'I know.' He smiled briefly. 'I've left the address he gave me at my London apartment. I'm a bachelor so there's no one there I can call to look it up for me.'

'He's in Alsace . . .'

'I can remember that. Foreign addresses go out of my head.'

'It is not too far. The Château Noir in the Vosges. You can take the train to Colmar.'

'I travel by car. I've driven there before. To Colmar.'

'It's difficult to find, Mr Dyson. Up in the mountains. I suggest you purchase a road map. When you get to Colmar there is a hotel outside the railway station. The Hotel Bristol. Show them the map and they will guide you.'

'I am much obliged, Mrs Kahn.'

'It is my pleasure. The guard will show you out . . .'

That was inconvenient. He had hoped to change back into his hippie clothes in the lobby before emerging from the bank. The guard appeared, escorted him to the main front door, opened it, nodded to him.

Dyson stepped out into a freezing cold afternoon. The interior of the bank had been cosily warm. He walked a few paces down the street, watching the American who still stood on the opposite side of the street. A gun barrel was rammed into his back from inside a trench coat.

'Where is Amberg, Mr Dyson? A correct answer means I may not pull the trigger.'

'At the Château Noir. France. Up in the Vosges mountains. Near Colmar.'

Dyson was scared stiff, but he was a survivor. So close now to a huge fortune. He wasn't going to risk a bullet in the back at this stage. The man with the American voice behind him might be testing him.

'So let's you and I go for walkies,' the voice continued. 'There's a short cut through an alley . . .'

He stopped speaking. Dyson had spotted a police car patrolling slowly along the street. He shoved both hands in the air, way above his head. Everything happened in a flash. The patrol car stopped, the gun was removed from his back, he heard the sound of feet running as a policeman, gun in hand, came up to him.

'He held me up with a gun, wanted my passport and money.'

Dyson glanced over his shoulder. No sign of the American.

'He didn't get anything. You arrived . . .'

The policeman had nodded, was now running with long strides towards where several streets radiated. He disappeared round a corner. Dyson sighed with relief, picked up the canvas bag he'd dropped, walked quickly away.

He'd already hired a silver Mercedes. Within the hour he'd be driving across the frontier, heading for Colmar.

Talking to the President, each time Norton started out by giving the phone number of his latest perch. The President had no idea what city the first numbers identified – Sara found that out after he'd closed the call.

Norton, his 'grey' hair now getting shaggy, was sitting in the Basle apartment he'd commandeered. It was normally occupied by a diplomat from the Berne Embassy. The Ambassador, Anderson, hadn't liked it when Norton had told him to throw out the present occupant.

He'd had no option but to agree to Norton's demand when the man with untidy grey hair and wearing half-moon glasses had waved his Presidential aide pass at him.

Anderson had also told him that he was clearing his desk, going home. A man called Gallagher was taking his post. Norton had smiled to himself – Anderson, an old-school diplomat, must have rubbed March up the wrong way. The phone rang.

'Mencken here. We've located Amberg. The Château Noir in France. Near a place called Colmar. The château is up in the Vosges mountains . . .'

'Move the whole unit to Colmar. Where will you be staying? The Hotel Bristol. Got it. It's a short drive from here. I'll be there. What about the courier with the dough?'

'Locked in a hotel room. You know which hotel. I have the key.'

'Take him with you – with the money. Whoever has what I'm after will try a fresh exchange. Get moving . . .'

Norton began packing his clothes in the single case he moved around with. Small enough to take aboard a plane. Save hanging about at the friggin' carousel. The phone rang again.

'Yes, who is it?'

'The guy who's given you ten days to clean up,' March barked. 'I know now you're in Basle. What gives? You had three different places to cover in the Zurich area to exchange the money for the film and tape.'

'It was a bust. I had them covered. No one turned up. Someone is playing smart. Using kidnappers' technique. Send you to one place – three in this case – then they don't turn up. Trying to break our nerve. You'll get a fresh call, new rendezvous. I'm just moving to the Hotel Bristol in Colmar, France. Give you the phone number when I get there. We're going to score. All four targets wiped out, plus grabbing your film and tape . . .'

'Norton, you've no idea how encouraging I find what you just said,' March replied with vicious sarcasm. 'You read me? And how are you going to play it this time – before March 13?'

'They'll be in mountain country. I'll use the mountains to get them. By ambush . . .'

For the first time Norton was the one who slammed down the phone.

PART TWO

The Terror

30

Norton was the first to arrive in Colmar. Clad in a black astrakhan coat and a fur hat, he looked like a Russian professor as he peered through his half-moon glasses at the receptionist of the Hotel Bristol.

What was it about the new arrival that made the girl behind the counter shiver inwardly? He stood motionless and the eyes behind the lenses which stared at her seemed dead, devoid of all human feeling.

'I want to book a double room for five days,' Norton told her. 'I have business elsewhere so I may not be here every night. I will pay in advance for the five days . . .'

He registered in the name of Ben Thalmann, paid in French francs, then produced the Michelin map of the Vosges area he had purchased in Basle. He had left that city within twenty minutes of speaking to President March.

'I have to visit the Château Noir, the residence of a Mr Amberg, a Swiss. Can you show me how to reach this château by driving there?'

'You'll have to hurry, sir,' she replied in her excellent English. 'It gets dark early and there is snow on the mountains. The roads will be icy . . .'

'Just show me . . .'

She stopped talking, studied the map, marked a route up the N83 to Kaysersberg and then high up into the Vosges mountains along the N415. It became complicated and she carefully drew her pen along a side road. She was repeating her warnings about the hazards when Norton interrupted her brusquely.

'Can I use that phone to make a private call?'

'Certainly, sir . . .'

Discreetly, she opened a door behind her and closed it. The truth was she was only too anxious to escape from the presence of that black figure. Norton smiled as he dialled the number of the Drei Könige. He had sensed the fear the girl had felt and it gave him a kick. He asked the hotel operator for Tweed. There was a brief pause.

'Who is speaking?' a man's voice enquired.

'Barton Ives,' Norton said through the silk handkerchief he had stuffed in the mouthpiece. 'Who is that?'

'Tweed here. Where are you, Ives . . .?'

Norton put down the phone. Tweed was still in Basle. At last he had arrived ahead of the enemy. Which would give him time to prepare the death-trap. And it was interesting that Tweed expected to meet Barton Ives. Clean up the whole lot out here in the wilds of Alsace.

Norton hurried outside and got behind the wheel of the blue Renault he'd hired in Basle. He had never stayed at the Drei Könige – he had simply had an early lunch and sat in the lobby area afterwards. In time to see Tweed and his friends arrive.

Using the same approach, he wouldn't be staying at the Hotel Bristol. He had picked up a brochure in the railway station opposite the hotel, a brochure which gave the names of several small hotels in the Old Town. One of those hotels would be his base.

He drove rapidly across the flatlands beyond Colmar. It was a cold sunny afternoon, the air fresh as wine. But this was wine territory – grids of vineyards stretched away on either side as he came close to the foothills.

He drove more slowly through the medieval town of Kaysersberg, little more than a large village. Norton did not notice its picturesqueness. He did notice a narrow stone bridge spanning a small river in the centre.

An excellent place to plant a bomb under the bridge,

detonated by remote control. Mencken, who still had to reach Colmar, was an expert with explosives. Driving from Basle to Colmar, Norton had observed a stone quarry, a shed with the warning sign in French, *Danger – Explosives*. He had marked this location on his map.

He drove on beyond Kaysersberg into the foothills. Looming above them was the long chain of the snow-bound Vosges mountains. Norton had taken the precaution of hiring a car with snow tyres. The road began to twist and climb, up, up, up . . .

There was no other traffic and dense stands of firs began to close in on both sides. The road surface was icy, treacherous, then covered with snow. The temperature nose-dived. The firs were blanketed with frozen snow, the branches pressed down under the weight. It was like Siberia.

Norton smiled to himself. This was ideal territory for what he had in mind. At numerous places the topography lent itself to lethal ambushes. He foresaw that Tweed and his minions would disappear from the face of the earth until spring came – only spring would reveal the frozen vehicles, the rotting bones of their occupants.

On the other side of the road the mountain slope fell away into a sheer abyss. Norton had a view of a deep ravine plunging into the depths. The territory was getting better and better. He had no doubt Tweed would be driving up to see Amberg at the Château Noir.

He drove on up the steep winding ascent, alert for hidden ice under the snow. By his side the map the girl at the Bristol had marked lay open. He glanced at it frequently. Soon he'd be coming to the turn-off on to the side road leading to Lac Noir.

The intense cold was penetrating his coat. He turned up the heaters full on. His breath steamed up his glasses. He took them off – they were merely a disguise. Still only rare signs of human habitation – the odd whitewashed old house with its ancient pantile roof crusted with snow. Norton could stand the cold, but this was something else again.

He passed through a small village called Orbey, which was on his route. No sign of a soul. Everyone huddled inside, he imagined. By now he had turned off the N415 and studied the map more frequently. Driving along a narrow road he suddenly arrived at Lac Noir and gasped.

Once, still with the FBI, Norton had operated in Europe for the State Department on secret missions – which under American law were forbidden and were extremely illegal. Norton was familiar with the Continent, but he had never seen anything like this.

On the far side of the lonely silent lake rose a sheer granite wall, towering above him. At its summit was perched a castle with turrets and lights in some of the windows. He was staring up at the Château Noir. On an impulse, he decided to visit the elusive Mr Amberg.

Norton drove up a steep spiralling road which, again, the girl at the Bristol had marked for him on the map. Arriving at the summit, he saw the castle's high point was a massive keep.

Most people would have been overawed by the grandeur of the edifice. To Norton it was just the type of a monster of a building they'd erected in medieval times. A high wall surrounded the château and Norton scanned it swiftly before leaving his car and approaching on foot the tall wrought-iron gates which closed a gap in the wall.

He pressed the button below a speakphone with a metal grille embedded in the left-hand pillar. He'd have to hurry this up: he wanted to be out of the mountains before dusk descended on those hideous roads. A voice said something in German.

'I don't speak German,' Norton replied, muffling his American accent.

'Then kindly identify yourself,' the precise voice said in English.

'Tweed. Tweed . . .'

'Please be so good as to enter.'

There was the sound of a buzzer. Norton pushed at both gates. The left-hand one opened. He took out a matchbook, inserted it in the lock. He suspected the gates opened and closed automatically from controls inside the château. It was a trick he'd used before. And sure enough, as he walked across the paved courtyard and glanced back, the gate was closing.

As he hurried up the wide flight of stone steps leading to a massive porch he took out the Luger from his shoulder holster, held it by his side. The great wooden door swung inwards, a small portly man with black hair brushed back from his high forehead stood inside the entrance. He wore a black business suit and surprise, then alarm, appeared in his shrewd blue eyes.

'You're not Tweed.'

He was starting to swing the door shut when Norton showed him the Luger. He lapsed into his normal voice.

'Mr Amberg? Don't lie. I've a nervous trigger finger.'

'Yes, but . . .'

'Let's talk inside. You could catch a cold. You have two items I'm in the market for. You can make a lot of money, Mr Amberg. Let's negotiate.'

While he spoke Amberg backed inside and Norton followed still holding the Luger. He had the impression of a vast hall which was dimly lit by wall sconces.

'I have no idea of what you are talking about, *Mr Tweed.*'

Norton was puzzled by the emphasis the banker put on the name. His words echoed round the enormous hall. Norton, watching Amberg closely, was vaguely aware that a wide staircase climbed out of the hall to his left, climbed a considerable height. He also thought

297

there was the silhouette of someone on the staircase.

The next moment Amberg took a handkerchief out of his pocket as though about to blow his nose. There was a click, an object landed at Norton's feet. Amberg was backing away. Grey vapour enveloped Norton and his vision swam. Swiftly holstering the Luger – Norton was no longer able to see clearly – he held his breath and grabbed for a handkerchief with his left hand. The tear-gas had reached his eyes just before he clamped the handkerchief over them. Amberg had covered his own face with his handkerchief.

Norton, able to see – but with blurred vision – turned round and headed back to the door. Removing the hand-kerchief, he turned the lock on the door and hauled the heavy slab open. Staggering out on to the porch, he grasped the round black iron handle, pulled the door shut, took in a deep breath.

Stumbling towards the gate, his vision was better with the cold air clearing his eyes. He'd only taken a small quantity of the stuff, mostly in his left eye. The match-book had prevented the gate locking. In a hurry to get away, he still paused to retrieve the matchbook – he might want to use the same trick when he returned to the Château Noir.

He stood by his car, sucking in great breaths of the mountain air, then slid behind the wheel, closed the door quietly, turned on the ignition. The girl at the Bristol had marked an alternative route back via the D417 down the Col de la Schlucht. He'd go back that way.

He turned the car round, determined to check the second route Tweed might use to visit the Château Noir. His left eye was still watering as he drove carefully, expertly negotiating the bends in the road.

Norton was livid – and furious with himself. He had broken his golden rule – never act on impulse, always check out the target in advance, then send in the soldiers.

He had given in to the temptation to do the job on his own. Never again . . .

His great regret was that he'd not had the remotest idea what the figure which had stood on the stairs looked like. Who the hell could that have been, the figure which had fired the gas pistol? One thing was for sure – he was returning to the Château Noir with Mencken's complete team. Norton had observed a lot during his brief humiliation. There was a wire – presumably electrified – spanning the top of the wall which surrounded the stone monstrosity.

Norton had also noticed a stone-flagged path leading behind the château in the direction of the towering keep. One man on top of that with a machine-pistol could command all the exits and entrances.

He had turned on to the D417 a while back, a much more main highway. He reached a point where a large building carried the legend LA SCHLUCHT 1139. He was 1139 metres high, over three thousand feet. Norton drove on and it was then he encountered a hideous and endless spiral of hairpin bends.

At one point he stopped, marked the location on his map. To his left a sheer granite cliff rose vertically from the road. To his right the world dropped into another bottomless abyss. The cliff wall was covered with steel mesh to prevent it crumbling on to the road. A first-rate ambush point.

He was still well above the snow line as he drove on down and round icy spiral bends. Despite the risk he kept his foot on the accelerator – the light was fading. Dusk was beginning to fall over the Vosges.

Norton kept moving, meeting no traffic. He dropped below the snow line and rammed his foot down further. The lights were on in Colmar as he entered the town. He stopped outside the station, went inside to ask how to get to the Old Town, saw a huge wall map of Colmar.

He soon realized that the Old Town where the small hotels were situated was called Little Venice. Amazing how many Venices there were in Europe. The next thing to do when he'd found a room was to call the Bristol, ask to speak to a Mr Tweed. He felt sure that was where he'd hit the sack. When Tweed came on the line – if he did – he'd put down the receiver. That should twitch at his nerves. Mr Tweed didn't know it, but they'd bury him in Alsace.

31

'I expect the Vosges to be an area of maximum danger,' Tweed announced to the gathering in his bedroom at the Drei Könige.

Newman and Paula shared a couch, Butler and Nield sat in armchairs and Marler adopted his usual stance, leaning against a wall and smoking a king-size cigarette.

Marler, a member of the SIS and the deadliest marksman in Europe, had been summoned to fly from London to Basle when Tweed had phoned Monica. Of medium height and light build, he had fair hair, was in his early thirties and wore a smart check sports jacket and razor-creased slacks. He spoke in an upper crust drawl and was always crossing swords with Newman.

'Is this intuition on your part?' Marler asked. 'Or have you solid data to base your warning on?'

'Does it make any difference?' Newman snapped.

These two men were hardly mutual friends. But if it came to a firefight each knew they could rely on the other to the hilt.

'Yes, it does, old man,' Marler replied patronizingly. 'Is there any solid data?' he asked Tweed.

Since his arrival Tweed had brought Marler up to date on everything that had happened. Marler, with his fresh eye, might notice something significant they had missed.

'There is some data,' Tweed told them. 'Beck phoned me and reported that a man whose description sounds very like Joel Dyson's was held up outside the Zurcher Kredit here.'

'Held up?' Paula queried.

'Yes. An American shoved a gun into Dyson's back as he left the Zurcher Kredit. Fortunately a patrol car turned up, the American with the gun fled, and if it was Dyson he'd asked a Mrs Kahn at the bank where Amberg was. Beck never overlooks a thing – he phoned the bank, spoke to Mrs Kahn. She confirmed what Eve Amberg told me – that the banker is at the Château Noir.'

'You said *if* it was Dyson,' Paula commented. 'Not like you to accept an identification without proof.'

'Which is why,' Tweed told her, 'I sent Cardon to show the photocopy of your sketch of Dyson to Mrs Kahn . . .'

There was a knock on the locked door. Newman opened it and Cardon strolled in. He winked at Paula who made a moue.

'It was Dyson who called at that bank here in Basle,' Cardon addressed Tweed. He handed back the envelope containing the photocopy. 'She recognized him at once from the sketch. Beck is helpful – he had a detective waiting there to escort me into Mrs Kahn's office. She didn't hesitate to talk to me.'

'All of which confirms my warning about danger waiting for us in the Vosges. That American who held up Dyson and then escaped probably asked him where Amberg was. We shall have company – unwelcome company – in Alsace.'

The phone rang. Paula picked it up, listened, said she

would tell him, put down the receiver and looked at Tweed with an amused smile.

'You already have company waiting for you in the lounge. More welcome company. Jennie Blade is anxious to talk to you.'

'She didn't mention Gaunt?' Tweed asked, frowning.

'Not a word.'

'When I spoke to Monica she told me she'd added to her profile on Mr Gaunt. At one time he was an officer in Military Intelligence. Intriguing . . .'

Jennie Blade sat upright in an armchair. She was dressed in ski pants tucked into smart leather ankle boots and a blue silk polo-necked sweater which hugged her figure. Folded neatly on a nearby chair was a fur-lined jacket.

When Tweed stepped out of the lift she was smoothing down her blonde mane with one hand, checking her appearance in a compact mirror with the other. The moment she saw Tweed she snapped the mirror shut, put the compact inside a Gucci handbag with a shoulder strap.

'Long time no see,' she greeted him.

She tilted her head, held up her right cheek. He bent down and kissed it, perched himself on the arm of her chair. It was an unusual place for him to sit but he sensed she was putting herself out to be seductive. Her long legs were crossed.

'Not so long since we had a drink in the Hummer Bar in Zurich. Where is Gaunt?' Tweed asked.

'Oh, the Squire? God knows. He's a pain in the prover-bial. Disappears for hours, days. He told me he'd seen you here. I have the strong impression you're a very reliable man – by which I mean a man a woman can rely on.'

'Depends on the woman, the circumstances.'

'And I thought you liked me.'

She twisted round – as she had on the stool in the Hummer Bar – clasped her strong slim hands and rested her forearms on his leg. She gazed up at him pleadingly.

'Let's say I do like you,' Tweed suggested. 'What comes next?'

'I'm frightened. I'm being followed by someone. They appear when I'm least expecting it. As I'm leaving a shop just before closing time when it's dark outside. When I'm getting my keys out to enter the apartment Gaunt has near Bankverein. It takes a lot to scare me but I admit I'm really worried about this shadow man.'

'Describe him.'

She took hold of his right hand. Holding it between both of hers she continued gazing up at him.

'I said describe him,' Tweed repeated in a hard voice.

'Wears a black wide-brimmed hat, tilted down over his face. About five foot six tall. I might be wrong about his height. He also wears a long black overcoat and a woollen scarf.'

Without showing it, Tweed was taken aback. Jennie had just given almost exactly the same description of the man seen leaving Klara's apartment in Rennweg after she had been garrotted. Her words were almost precisely those used by Old Nosy who occupied the ground-floor apartment in the Altstadt building where Klara had been murdered.

'You are talking about Basle?' he checked. 'This man is following you here in Basle?'

'Yes. The Shadow Man.' She shivered. 'It's getting on my nerves. Which is ridiculous considering the jobs I've had.'

'What jobs might those be?' he asked gently.

'I had a training as an accountant. Found it frantically boring. Then I got a big job with a huge firm in New York. They checked up on the financial stability of firms all over the world for a fabulous fee. Also on prominent individuals. I had to bluff my way into offices and private apartments to check on the lifestyle of certain individuals. That's how I saved quite a packet. I left them when one target threatened me with a gun. Felt my luck was running out. I came back to Britain, to London.'

She was interlacing her fingers with Tweed's as she spoke. He thanked Heaven that Paula wasn't there to see him. She'd pull his leg unmercifully.

'And then you met Gaunt?' he suggested.

All the time she told him the story of her life she was gazing at him, her glowing eyes almost hypnotizing him. Watch it, he warned himself.

'No, Gaunt came later,' she went on. 'Back in London I got a job with a private investigation agency. That lasted six months and was sordid work, but it led me to Gaunt.' She paused.

'Go on, I'm still listening.'

'You make a good audience. My last job at the agency was to check up on Walter Amberg.'

Again Tweed was taken aback. Again he maintained a poker-faced expression, but stared back at her to try and penetrate her character. Her voice was soft and soothing, which added to the hypnotic effect. Gaunt was mad not to grab her. For the first time since his wife had left him years ago for a Greek millionaire Tweed wondered about throwing overboard his solitary life. He pulled himself up sharply. This was a job he was working on, the most dangerous he'd ever encountered.

'Who asked the agency to check on Walter?' he enquired.

'Julius Amberg. He came to the London office once with Gaunt – which is how I met Gaunt.'

'When you were checking up on Walter Amberg what aspect were you looking for? Did you come to Switzerland?'

304

'Yes to the second question. As to what I had to check on, Julius was very precise. Had Walter an expensive apartment in another city? Now what else was there?' She played with the string of pearls looped over her sweater with her free hand. 'I remember. Was he keeping a mistress? If so, was she expensively dressed and had she her own car? Had Walter any other cars which he kept in other cities? Stuff like that. I drew a blank – except for his visits to a girl in Basle. I never reported that because I'd had enough. There was another reason. Gaunt asked me to come and live with him. I love Cornwall, the sea and the cliffs.'

'I'm going to ask you some more questions. I want you to answer them quickly. Your jobs must have made you unusually observant. First question, describe the face of the Shadow Man.'

'Can't. Never saw it.'

'How did he walk, move?'

'Body language. Can't say. He was always motionless.'

'But you saw him several times.'

'I did. Looked up, saw him, paid for what I'd bought. Then he'd gone.'

'Outside the Bankverein apartment, finding your keys?'

'He stood at a corner. When I looked again he was gone.'

'You're saying you never actually saw him move?'

'Never.'

'Ever see him in Zurich?'

'No. Always here in Basle.'

'How many times have you seen him?'

'Five. Six. No more.'

'Within what space of time?'

'Couple of days.'

'Is his surveillance on you getting more frequent?'

'Yes, it is, Tweed. What the hell am I going to do?'

305

'You're staying at the Bankverein apartment with Gaunt?'

'Yes. He's not always there. As I told you.'

'You're going back there now. I'll get a taxi for you. Stay inside until Gaunt returns. Tell him about the Shadow Man.'

'You have to be joking. He'd say it was a figment of my imagination.'

'I'll get that taxi . . .'

The concierge, who had just returned on duty, phoned and a taxi arrived in five minutes. Tweed accompanied Jennie outside into the icy cold – it seemed even more Siberian. She kissed him on the cheek before leaping inside.

'We must see each other again,' were her last words.

Tweed remained standing outside on the pavement for a short time. He wanted to be sure no one was following Jennie. He was also beginning to think she was telling the truth. Her story about the Shadow Man bothered him. He was turning to go inside when a white BMW appeared, pulled up in front of the hotel with a jerk and screeching brakes.

Gaunt jumped out. He handed the car keys to a porter who had come out through the revolving doors.

'Park my car for me. I'm staying here. Gaunt is the name.' He clapped Tweed on the shoulder. 'What a splendid welcome. You guessed I was coming! Brrr! It's cold out here. Forward march to the bar. The drinks are on me . . .

'Two double Scotches,' he told the barman when they were comfortably seated in an otherwise deserted bar. 'And hurry them up. Need some internal central heating, my good man.'

'No Scotch for me,' Tweed said firmly. 'Mineral water.'

'Can't cope with alcohol, eh? A man of your experience. Shame on you, sir.'

'You ought to take more care of Jennie,' Tweed told him bluntly. 'She's scared out of her wits – someone is following her, someone I don't like the sound of.'

He waited while Gaunt doled out money to the barman and added a meagre tip. Gaunt raised his glass.

'Here's to survival of the fittest. Down the hatch.'

'I said Jennie is being followed by an unknown man. He's tracking her, prior to something pretty unpleasant happening, I fear.'

'Stuff and nonsense! She gets these fancies. She's an attractive-looking filly. Of course men notice her, try to get to know her.'

'Gaunt!' Tweed hammered his glass down on the tabletop. 'Keep quiet and listen. In Zurich a girl called Klara was foully murdered – her head was damned near severed from her neck. Garrotted. Someone saw the murderer leaving. Their brief description fits the man following Jennie. Don't you care a fig?'

He watched Gaunt closely. His visitor had worn a camel-hair coat which now lay thrown across a chair. He was clad in a check sports jacket, a cravat with a design of horses' heads, corduroy trousers and hand-made leather shoes. His sandy hair was windblown. His grey eyes above a strong nose stared back at Tweed. His mood had suddenly become serious and his firm mouth was tightly closed. Tweed thought he glimpsed the ex-Military Intelligence officer.

'Think I read something about that murder in the paper. Before I left Zurich. Can there really be a link-up between that murder and this man who is supposed to be following Jennie?'

'Who *is* following Jennie.'

'How do you know all this?' Gaunt asked brusquely. 'Has Jennie phoned you?'

'She's been here. Was telling me about it not five minutes before you turned up. Hadn't you better get back to your apartment near Bankverein? Make sure she's all right? *Now*, I suggest,' Tweed said emphatically.

'She'll be safe.' Gaunt stared hard at Tweed. 'We leave early tomorrow morning for Colmar in Alsace. We'll be out of Basle by daybreak.'

'Why Colmar?' Tweed asked quietly.

'Because that's where Amberg's gone to. Place called the Château Noir. Up in the Vosges. I've just come from a brief visit to Mrs Kahn, his assistant at the Zurcher Kredit here in Basle. Had to put a bit of pressure on her to get that information. Thought maybe you'd like to know. Amberg must know something about his twin brother's last visit to Tresillian Manor. No one kills a guest in my house and gets away with it. I'm going now. Remember what I said. Survival of the fittest.'

Gaunt stood up, shoved his arms into his coat, walked out. Tweed sat thinking before returning to his room. Gaunt didn't strike him as a man who ladled out information without a purpose. And had there been a hint of a threat in his last remark?

32

'Norton here,' the American reported when he was connected with the President. He gave him the phone number of the Hotel Bristol. 'When you want to contact me get Sara to leave a coded message. I'll come back to you as soon as I can . . .'

'Like hell you will. I need the number I can reach you at pronto. There's been a development.'

'That's my best offer,' Norton snapped.

'OK, if that's the way it has to be,' March agreed in a deceptively amiable tone. 'Now pin your ears back. I've had a fresh message from the man with the growly voice. About the exchange. The big bucks for the film and the tape. Where are you? Basle?'

'No, Colmar, France. On the edge of the Vosges mountains.'

'Ever heard of a dump called Kaysersberg? I'll spell that to you . . .'

'No need. I was driving through it an hour ago.'

'Really? Department of Sinister Coincidence.'

'I don't get that . . . Mr President.'

'Say it was a joke. There's some crappy hotel in this Kaysersberg. L'Arbre Vert. I'll spell that. Sara says it means the Green Tree . . .'

'No need to spell it out. I noticed it, passing through.'

'You take a room there. Under the name of Tweed . . .'

'You can't mean it.'

'Growly Voice says you do. You wait for a call. You have the big bucks where you can lay your hands on them? The call may come tomorrow morning. It's up to you to get the film, the tape – and Growly Voice. In a box. Laid out nice and neat. You're running out of days. I said you had a deadline. Time is flying. I'm counting on you, Norton . . .'

'You can rely on me, Mr President . . .'

He was speaking into the air. March had gone off the line. Norton swore to himself as he left the phone cubicle in Colmar railway station. He'd deliberately given the Bristol number – where he'd never spend a night. He could call for messages. No way was he going to give the number of his small hotel at the edge of a stream in Little Venice.

309

He climbed in behind the wheel of his parked blue Renault. Switching on the ignition, he turned up the heaters. He didn't like the arrangement March had agreed one little bit. Registering as Tweed, goddamnit! Why? The blackmailer with the film and the tape had to be someone who knew Tweed, knew he was in the area.

Norton would make a list of everyone his unit had reported as having been seen with Tweed. One of those names on that list had to be Growly Voice.

When Bradford March had put down the phone he clasped his hands behind his bull neck and stared at the marble fireplace on the opposite wall without seeing it. He was in a vicious rage.

The blackmailer was playing games with him – with Norton, too. This constant switching of locations from one Swiss city to another – and now he'd moved the whole operation to France. Norton, persuaded to 'resign' from the FBI because the Director hadn't liked his tough, ruthless ways, was being led around by the nose. Growly Voice was running circles round him.

March looked up as Sara entered the Oval Office. He didn't like her expression.

'Very bad news, boss. Just heard about it.'

'Heard about what?'

'Harmer. Who gave you that large sum of money, then said he needed it back to pay off a bank loan. I guess he sure did.'

'What the hell are you talking about? Give, Sara.'

'Harmer committed suicide a few hours ago. Took a load of sleeping pills, then drank a lot of bourbon.'

'So.' March spread his hands, exposing their hairy backs. 'Problem solved.'

'If you say so.'

'Are you hinting he left a note?'

'For his wife, yes, he did.'

March leaned forward. 'C'mon. We'd better find out what he said in that note.'

'I know. I rang his wife to offer *my* sympathies. I also said you were shocked and sent *your* deepest sympathies.'

'Great. Don't have to write my own dialogue with you to do it for me. Just a moment. What did the note say?'

'The usual thing. He was so sorry, he loved her dearly, but the pressure of his responsibilities had proved too big a burden. She read it out to me over the phone before she broke down in a flood of tears.'

'Bye-bye Mr Harmer. It happens. All is well.'

'I hope so. I do hope so, Brad. For your sake.'

The Three Wise Men were assembled in Senator Wingfield's study. Again the curtains were closed, concealing the grounds of the estate. The lights were on. The banker and the elder statesman had been called urgently to the Chevy Chase mansion by Wingfield, who looked grim. He stared round the table at his guests.

'I am sorry to summon you here at such short notice, but the situation inside the Oval Office is not improving.'

'I heard about Harmer's suicide,' the banker commented. 'That's a big loss to the party. He not only contributed generously himself – more important still, he was a genius at fund-raising.'

'Let's face it,' said the elder statesman, gazing at the Senator through his horn-rimmed glasses, 'politics is a mobile situation. Harmer must have managed his affairs badly. He's replaceable.'

'I have a personal letter from Harmer,' Wingfield informed them. There was an edge to his cultured accent. 'I know the real reason why Harmer took his life. Read that . . .'

He tossed a folded sheet of high-quality notepaper on

the table. The statesman read it first before handing it on to the banker.

Dear Charles: By the time you read this I'll have gone to a better place. I hope. Bradford March asked me to loan him fifteen million dollars. Don't know what this large sum was for. I did so. When I wanted it back to repay a bank loan on demand he refused to speak to me. Sara Maranoff phoned his message. The money was no longer available. Go to hell was the real message. Maybe I'm going there. Someone has to stop the President. Only The Three Wise Men have the clout.

'What could March have wanted that money for?' queried the banker.

'We'll probably never know,' the statesman told him. 'I hold the same view. It's not enough – for impeachment.'

'That letter could be passed to the *Washington Post*,' the banker suggested.

'Definitely not,' Wingfield said quietly. 'Ned, can't you imagine how March would play it? He'd get handwriting experts to prove it was a forgery. Then he'd rave on about a conspiracy – about how the three of us were trying to be the power behind the throne. Give him his due, he's a powerful orator. He'd destroy us. It's not enough for us to make a move.'

'Then what the hell is?' burst out the banker.

'Cool it,' the elder statesman advised. 'Politics is the art of the possible. I worked on that basis when I held the position I did under a previous president.'

'There's the business about him dismissing the Secret Service,' the banker continued, his anger unquenched. 'I understand he has a bunch of his own thugs guarding him now. Unit One, or some such outfit.'

'Which is the paramilitary force I told you about at an earlier meeting,' Senator Wingfield said quietly.

'It's against all tradition,' protested the banker.

312

'Bradford March is breaking a lot of traditions, Ned,' Wingfield reminded him. 'Which is another popular move in the present mood of the American electorate. We can only wait.'

'For what?' demanded the banker.

'For something far worse, Ned. Pray to God it doesn't surface . . .'

The tall figure of Jeb Calloway created distorted shadows on the walls of his office as he paced restlessly. Sam, his closest aide and friend, watched him, undid the jacket button constraining his ample stomach.

'Heard from your mystery man in Europe yet, Jeb?' he asked.

'Not a word. I think he's on the run.'

'Which means someone is running after him. Which means someone over there knows he exists. You're playing with fire. This gets back to March and he'll smear you for good. He's an expert. Part of how he got where he is. Trampling over other people's bodies. That's politics. March is the original cobra at the game.'

'There's no way anyone can connect my informant with me. And there's a safe way he can contact me – if he's still alive.'

'I think you should forget him, Jeb,' Sam warned.

'No. I have a duty. To the American people.'

Tweed was proved right when he passed through the Swiss, then the French, frontier controls at Basle station. The counters were deserted, the shutters closed; no one was on duty.

He boarded the Strasbourg express with Paula and found an empty first-class compartment. The whole train was nearly empty close to eleven in the morning. Behind them

Newman followed, the two Walthers belonging to Nield and Butler tucked inside his belt at the back. Cardon brought up the rear. At eleven precisely the express moved off.

'That conversation you had with Jennie Blade which you told me about,' began Paula, facing Tweed in a corner window seat. 'I've given it a lot of thought.'

'And your conclusion?'

'Jennie worries me. Has anyone except her seen this mysterious Shadow Man with the wide-brimmed hat? Has Gaunt?'

'It was the one question I forgot to ask him,' Tweed admitted. 'Although he didn't seem to take it seriously. Why?'

'Because if no one else has seen this Shadow Man how can we be sure he exists?'

'You've forgotten something,' Tweed reminded her. 'Old Nosy in Zurich gave us exactly the same description of a man who'd left the building shortly after Klara was garrotted.'

'Maybe Jennie was close by in the Altstadt when we were there. Saw a man like that leaving that building.'

'You're stretching supposition to breaking point.'

'Jennie *was* in Zurich at the time. We know that.'

'True.' Tweed sounded unconvinced.

'You know something?' Paula leaned forward. 'When a woman persists with trying to persuade a man of something he can eventually come to believe her.'

'Like you're persisting now,' he told her. 'Sowing a few doubts in my mind.'

'Who do you think is behind all these brutal murders?' Paula asked, changing the subject. 'Have you any idea yet?'

'A very good idea. Go back to the beginning. Blowing up our headquarters in Park Crescent with a huge bomb. The timer for the bomb – a more sophisticated device

314

than Crombie had ever seen. The fact that there are so many Americans swarming over Switzerland – all holding diplomatic passports. The fact that when Joel Dyson arrived at Park Crescent to hand over copies of the film and the tape Monica saw inside his suitcase American clothes – which suggests he'd just arrived from the States. The fact that our PM seems to be in the palm of the American President. All that has happened suggests limitless sums of money, a huge hostile organization. All that adds up to *power* – great power. Work it out for yourself. It's frightening.'

'You don't sound frightened,' she observed.

'*I* am not. I'm indignant, determined. The garrotting of Helen Frey and Klara was bad enough – although sometimes it's a risk of their trade. But Theo Strebel was a nice chap, didn't deserve to be shot. And that's curious and significant – two women garrotted, a man shot by someone he *knew*.'

'How do you know that?'

'Think of the precautions he took when we arrived – how we had to say who we were before he'd admit us.'

'I don't see the significance,' Paula confessed.

On a seat across the aisle Newman sat listening. He'd removed the two Walther automatics from behind his back. They now rested inside the pockets of the trench coat folded beside him.

Their owners, Butler and Nield, had hired cars in Basle for future use in the Vosges. It would have been risky taking firearms by car past a frontier post. They were now racing along the A35 autoroute to Colmar where they'd wait for Tweed and his team at the Hotel Bristol.

Cardon was seated in his usual strategic position at one end of the long compartment. Armed with his Walther, he could see any stranger approaching from either direction. He appeared to be asleep but his eyes

315

never left the back of Tweed's head.

The express had stopped at St Louis, later at Mulhouse. Then it raced along to the distant stop of Colmar. Paula gazed out of the window to the west on the stretch from Mulhouse to Colmar. The Vosges were coming into view in the distance.

The sun was shining brilliantly again and the range, snowbound to midway down its slopes, showed up clearly. They'd be driving up into those mountains soon. Why did she find them sinister on this lovely morning? They swooped up and down in great saddlebacks with here and there a prominent summit. They looked so dreadfully lonely, Paula thought, so remote from the villages amid vineyards on the lower slopes.

As the express raced on north she reflected on the strangeness of this beautiful province. Its odd mix of French and German which appeared in the names of towns on a map she'd studied. Bollwiller. Ste-Croix-en-Plaine. Munster. Ribeauville.

In 1871 Bismarck's Prussia had annexed Alsace-Lorraine. At the end of the First World War France had taken Alsace-Lorraine back. She was still staring out of the window. Many of the houses had steep-pitched rooves like flat chutes, which suggested winter could be severe, with heavy snow.

She glanced at Tweed and he was humming to himself, which was a rare habit. Why was he so pleased?

'What are you thinking of?' she asked him.

'That with a bit of luck soon I shall meet the two men who, I'm convinced, hold the key to this whole horrific business.'

'And you're keeping their names to yourself?'

'Joel Dyson – who knows Amberg is at the Château Noir. Who is, I'm sure, so anxious to get back the originals of his film and tape.'

'The second man?'

316

'Probably the most important of all. Barton Ives, Special Agent of the FBI . . .'

'These are the ideal ambush points,' Norton said. 'All up in the Vosges. You should wipe out the whole of Tweed's team at one blow.'

Norton was meeting Marvin Mencken for the first time, because he had to make sure Mencken didn't make a mistake. But even at this face-to-face meeting Mencken realized Norton had been clever. Close together as they were, he couldn't see Norton's face.

They were sitting inside a small café in Little Venice, deep inside Colmar. Norton had searched the area to discover this place before phoning Mencken. The café was divided into two sections, separated by a heavy lace curtain. Tables on either side were close to each other.

One side was for customers who required food. Norton had arrived early, consumed an omelette and salad and a huge quantity of French bread. He needed plenty of food to fuel his exceptional energy. He had finished the meal before Mencken arrived, had waved away the waiter.

'Later . . .'

The windows facing the narrow street were also hung with heavy lace curtains. Mencken, as instructed, went into the bar entrance, ordered a glass of white wine and took it to the table next to Norton's beyond the curtain. As he sat down, facing the curtain, the only other customer had twisted round in his chair as though greeting a friend.

Yes, Mencken thought, Norton had been clever. The face he looked at was distorted by the lace curtain. Norton wore a French beret he'd purchased and his grey hair was tucked under it. He also wore a windcheater and a scarf which covered his chin. Perched on his nose was a pair of pebble glasses. The eyes which stared at Mencken

317

were huge, intimidating. The map was held so Mencken could see it clearly, pressed against the curtain.

'Each cross marked on this map locates the ambush points,' Norton continued. 'See this one in Kaysersberg.'

'I've studied my own map. That place is a short drive from Colmar . . .'

'Just listen. The cross marks a bridge. If they go that way into the Vosges you could mine that bridge with explosives, detonate them by remote control.'

'OK,' Mencken said impatiently. 'I visited hardware and electrical shops before I drove here from Basle. I have the equipment I can use to make a timer system; crude, but it will work.'

'There's a stone quarry I've marked here – on the way to Colmar from Basle. It has a shed with explosives inside . . .'

'OK, I don't miss much. I spotted it on my way here. It'll be like breaking into a piggy bank . . .'

'Kindly *listen*! Tweed and his team may arrive in this area at any moment – he moves very fast. So your first priority is to grab those explosives . . .'

'Which was my priority one anyway . . .'

'This cross, if you're listening, marks a cliff by the roadside. It looked pretty unstable and faces an abyss. Maybe you could create an avalanche when they . . .'

'OK. I like that . . .'

'This position – again high up above the snowline – is where you could catch them in a crossfire. You're not making notes.'

'Yes, I am.' Mencken tapped his forehead. 'Up here. I've a mind like a computer – one that works. Next?'

Norton gazed at Mencken from his side of the curtain. His view was also distorted – and the pebble glasses increased the effect. Mencken's face looked very skeletal with its hard pointed jaw line and prominent cheek-bones. A man who would not hesitate to carry out any

318

cold-blooded execution. Which suited Norton. But he still didn't trust him. In the slate-grey eyes which stared back he detected overweening ambition. You wouldn't miss a single chance to take over from me, he thought. So the answer was to be very tough with Marvin Mencken, a natural killer.

For several minutes he listed other areas in the Vosges marked by crosses. With his hands covered with silk-lined gloves, he eventually passed the map through to Mencken under the curtain. Mencken found the use of gloves interesting. It suggested Norton's fingerprints were on record in the States – maybe under a different name. Ex-CIA, FBI? Or a criminal history?

He snatched the map from under the curtain, put it in his pocket. He'd had a bellyful of Norton – explaining everything as though he was new to this type of work. Plus the fact that there was something patronizing in the other man's attitude. But Norton wasn't finished yet.

'Stay where you are. It's not just Tweed and his team we need to eliminate. I'm confident Joel Dyson will appear in this area . . .'

'Because *my* man spotted him outside the Zurcher Kredit in Basle, made him squawk . . .'

'And then let him escape alive,' rasped Norton. 'Not a great success, Mencken. Don't interrupt me again. Just concentrate on what I say. Joel Dyson must be eliminated. Equally important, that Special Agent FBI, Barton Ives, must be too. We need all of them wiped off the face of the earth.'

Mencken leaned forward. His nose was touching the curtain.

'I'll terminate the lot. It will be a blood bath.'

'Don't forget they could drive to the Château Noir by either route,' Norton reminded him.

'It will be a blood bath,' Mencken repeated.

33

Marler, typically, had told Tweed before leaving Basle that he'd hire his own car, make his own way to Colmar.

'I may not reach the Hotel Bristol until late in the evening,' he had warned.

Tweed, knowing Marler liked to operate on his own, had agreed immediately.

'See you at the Bristol then,' Marler ended jauntily.

Hiring an Audi, he had driven to Mulhouse. There, instead of continuing north along the autoroute to Colmar, he had turned west, heading for the Ballon d'Alsace in the southern region of the Vosges. He had reached the French glider airfield and had a long chat in his fluent French with the controller.

Marler, after training in Britain, was an expert in flying gliders. He had examined a machine, climbing into the confined cockpit. The controller had leaned against the side as Marler haggled over the price. He would want the glider for several days.

'Incidentally, you've seen my licence, but accidents happen. How much if I smash it up?'

'Sir, that would cost you a lot of money.'

'How much?'

The controller had told him and Marler had nodded. He knew Tweed had the funds to fork out if necessary. The deposit paid, Marler drove off, returning by the route he'd come until he joined the autoroute north near Mulhouse.

Keeping just inside the speed limit, he raced along the

autoroute, bypassing Colmar, continuing north to the great river port of Strasbourg on the Rhine. Arriving there, he was driving much more sedately. Marler knew Europe as well as Newman, and he thought the ancient city unique.

The old city is perched on an island and spanned by many bridges. Marler parked his Audi outside and walked the rest of the way, crossing one of the bridges, glancing up to admire the medieval architecture. This was history, the Free City where once Protestant refugees had fled from French Catholic oppression. Which probably explained why it housed so many craftsmen in different fields. It was one of these craftsmen Marler was visiting. A gunsmith – who provided on the quiet the greatest range of weapons of any secret armaments supplier on the Continent.

Near the immense mass of the looming cathedral, Marler turned down a narrow stone-flagged alley. Suddenly he entered a world of silence, all sounds of traffic and human bustle gone.

He mounted a flight of worn stone steps to a landing on the first floor. Facing him was a massive studded wooden door with a Judas window. The only modern item in sight was a metal-grilled speakphone with a button alongside it. No indication as to who lived there.

'Who is it?' a quiet voice asked in French.

'Marler. You know me, Grandjouan. We've done business before.'

The Judas window opened, eyes peered out at him through a pair of gold-rimmed spectacles perched on a hooked nose. Marler waited while chains were removed, bolts pulled back, locks unfastened. The place was a fortress. The door swung open.

'Marler, indeed. So long since we last met. Come and join me for a glass of wine.'

Grandjouan was a hunchback with tiny feet. Marler

321

was careful not to stare at his deformity. When his host had closed the door, chained and relocked it, they shook hands.

'I hadn't time to press the button, you old rascal,' Marler remarked. 'So how did you know someone had arrived?'

'One of my state secrets.' Grandjouan chuckled throatily. 'Now the wine . . .'

'Not for me, thank you so much. I have a long way to drive when we've completed our business.'

'Such a pity. I have the most excellent Riesling.'

'Well, just a small glass.'

Grandjouan had a clean-shaven weathered face. Impossible even to guess his age. He had a nice smile and his eyes twinkled behind the spectacles as he handed Marler the glass.

'*Santé!*'

'*Santé!*' Marler repeated. 'This is very good.'

'I told you so. Now, as always you are a man in a hurry. So down to business.'

'I want an Armalite rifle, dismantled, with plenty of ammo. Twelve hand-grenades. A tear-gas pistol with a supply of shells. A Luger, again with ammo. All without any history.'

'Of course.' Grandjouan sipped again at his wine. 'I believe you are going to start a small war?'

'It could be something like that.'

Marler had carried from the car a cricket bag which contained a bat and several balls. He had put it on a table when he accepted the glass. Grandjouan looked at it, shook his head, covered with thinning grey hair.

'You proposed to carry these items away in that? Yes? I can do better. The container will come free, my friend.' He opened a cupboard, produced a cello case. 'Much better. It will take the load, which your cricket bag will not. Also we like some camouflage, in case you are stopped by the police.'

Grandjouan wore an old leather jacket with a woollen blue shirt underneath, open at the neck. His trousers were old but clean corduroy. Marler looked round his lair as his host ferreted about.

The walls were lined with huge old wooden chests and cupboards. When Grandjouan opened one cupboard it was stacked to the gunwales. Heaven help any policeman who came to search this place. Illumination came from a large oval window in the slanting roof. Heating was provided by several oil heaters. The only reasonably modern item of furniture was the massive old fridge from which Grandjouan had taken the bottle of Riesling. The place reminded Marler of a hermit's cave.

Grandjouan returned holding a black beret in one hand, a folder of leather tucked under his other arm. He handed Marler the beret.

'You are English. Obvious – very – from the clothes you're wearing.'

Which was true. On the Continent Marler was always taken for what they imagined the typical Englishman to be, a member of the idle upper classes. His drawling way of speaking reinforced the impression. It had thrown more than one adversary off guard.

Under the British warm, which he had placed on an armchair, he wore a houndstooth sports jacket, heavy grey slacks, a blue cravat below his strong jaw. He looked at the beret.

'Why this?'

'You are posing as a musician with that cello case. The beret on an Englishman dressed as you are suggests the artistic temperament.'

'God forbid!'

'Wear it. And here in this folder are some sheets of music. Spread one or two on the car seat beside you. They will strengthen the impression that you are a musician.'

Marler glanced at the sheets. He paused at one sheet –

323

'*La Jeune Fille aux Cheveux de Lin*', 'The Girl with the Flaxen Hair'. Unconsciously he began to hum the tune to himself. Grandjouan performed a little dance of delight.

'Excellent, my friend! You have thought yourself into the part . . .'

Grandjouan himself packed the twelve grenades, the tear-gas shells in the cello case after wrapping each item in thick tissue-paper. He performed the same routine with the tear-gas pistol, the Luger and ammo. Then he took a box he had extracted from beneath one of the floorboards which was hinged invisibly. Inside was the Armalite, dismantled.

'I'll assemble that if I may,' Marler suggested.

Grandjouan watched with approval the speed at which Marler put the separate parts together. He attached the magnifying night scope, squinted through it at the skylight, pressed the trigger of the unloaded gun.

'It feels good . . .'

With equal rapidity he dismantled it and Grandjouan picked up the pieces, again wrapping them in the tissue-paper. He fitted them inside the cello case, added ammo. Then he took a large piece of black velvet, spread it over the case's contents. From another deep drawer in an ancient chest he took out a long slim object inside a silk sleeve. He pointed to the end projecting before laying it on top of the velvet.

'More camouflage. The bow for your imaginary cello – with the end showing.'

He closed the case, snapped down the latch. Grandjouan had been right – everything had fitted in snugly, filling the case. Marler picked it up, tested the weight as the hunchback beamed, spoke again. Marler was wearing the beret.

'Perfect,' enthused Grandjouan. 'I used the tissue-paper so there was no danger of any rattle.'

'Talking of danger, why did you say I might be stopped by the police? Oh, let's first settle up.'

Marler made no attempt to haggle over the price. Producing a wad of French thousand-franc notes he counted out the correct amount on a table. He was reaching for the cello case and his cricket bag when Grandjouan explained.

'Yes, you could well be stopped by the police. I have an ear to the grapevine. Paris has received a message that a team of terrorists is crossing into Alsace.'

'Where from?' Marler asked sharply.

'From Switzerland.'

'I see. I'll be careful.'

He shook hands, thanked the hunchback for his service. As Grandjouan closed the door behind him he paused to pull up the collar of his coat. Standing on the platform at the top of the stone steps he glanced down. Inset into the stone was a square piece of rubber. Of course! A pressure pad. That was how the wily old hunchback had known someone had arrived before he had pressed the bell.

Marler was very alert as he walked back inside the alley, pausing at the exit to glance out. No sign of a patrol car. It was, of course, Beck who had warned Paris – warned them about the Americans.

A little unfortunate from Tweed's point of view – that the Haut-Rhin, where Colmar was located, would be swarming with *flics* on the lookout. On the other hand the news confirmed that the Americans had followed them close on their heels. Maybe it was only just beginning.

In mid-afternoon at the Château Noir the banker, Amberg, stared at his uninvited guest, listening, saying nothing. Gaunt had arrived in his hired white BMW without phoning first to make sure it would be convenient for him to call. Now his voice boomed in the Great Hall.

'I was a close friend of your late lamented brother, Julius. I am a close friend of your sister-in-law, Eve. I feel I have a responsibility to track down whoever murdered Julius so brutally. After all, my dear chap, the tragedy did take place in my house in Cornwall, Tresillian Manor.'

'I see,' Amberg replied and was silent again.

Gaunt sat in one of the very large black leather button-backed armchairs scattered about the vast space. The chair would have dwarfed most men, but not Gaunt. His stature with his leonine head seemed to dominate the room.

Swallowed up in another armchair close to a crackling log fire, Jennie Blade warmed her hands. If you were any distance from it the place was freezing. The Great Hall merited its name. About sixty feet square, it had granite walls and miserable illumination from wall sconces. She doubted whether the bulbs inside them were more than forty watts.

The walls sheered up to a height of thirty feet or so. Scattered here and there, as though rationed, small rugs lay on the stone-flagged floor. The entrance hall was grim enough, but this so-called living-room was pure purgatory, Jennie said to herself. There was hardly any furniture except for the chairs and two large, bulbous – and repellent – sideboards standing against a wall. Gaunt was ploughing on, as though unaware of the lukewarm reception.

'The question I have to find an answer to is *why* he was murdered, Amberg. I had a chat with him when he arrived. He told me he had fled Switzerland because he was scared stiff. Apparently a Joel Dyson had deposited with him at the Zurich headquarters a film and a tape. Is that so?'

'That is correct,' Amberg replied and again lapsed into silence.

Gaunt leaned forward. Jennie had the impression that he was studying the banker carefully. His voice became a rumble, his manner like that of an interrogator.

'You saw what was on the film, you heard the tape?'

'No. Dyson handed them to Julius.'

'And did he watch the film, listen to the tape?'

'I don't know.'

'Where are they now?'

'They have gone missing.'

'What!' Gaunt exploded. 'Look, Julius told me he had first stored them in a vault at the Zurcher Kredit in Zurich. He then had them transferred to a less obvious place of safety. The bank vault in Basle.'

'I know. He told me.'

'So how the hell can they be missing?' Gaunt demanded. 'I always thought Swiss banks were like fortresses, that they kept the most meticulous records of every single transaction. Now you tell me they are missing.'

'Mr Gaunt, if you can't speak more quietly I may have to ask you to leave.'

'Plenty of room for my voice in this mausoleum. You haven't answered the question.'

Amberg, perhaps to compensate for his lack of height, sat in a low-backed hard chair perched on a dais behind an old desk Jennie thought could have come from a second-hand stall in the Portobello Road. To break the tension, to get a little more warmth, she reached into a basket, took out two logs, placed them on the fire. Amberg frowned at her.

'Those logs are very expensive.'

'Oh, pardon me.'

Stuff you, she thought. Everything here is rationed. The logs, the rugs, the words Amberg allowed to escape his lips. She stood up, straightened the jodhpurs she'd worn against the cold, thrust her hands inside her pockets

327

to ward off the chill, wandered past the dais.

At the far end of the hall, down a wide flight of stone steps, was an indoor terrace. A huge picture window gave a panoramic view across the lower slopes of the sunlit Vosges. The glare of the sun off the snow was intense. The air was so clear Jennie could see in the distance another range of mountains. The Black Forest. In Germany beyond the Rhine.

She happened to glance down and sucked in her breath. Beyond the picture window the ground fell away into a sheer precipice. At the bottom was a sinister black lake, shrouded from the sun by the Vosges. Behind her the conversation continued. Assuming 'conversation' now meant one man talking to another.

'I have no idea why they went missing,' Amberg replied. 'It was Julius who supervised the transfer.'

'I thought you were Chairman of the bank,' Gaunt threw at the Swiss.

'That is correct. Day to day business was handled by Julius.'

'Are you saying you have no idea what happened to two items given into the bank's safekeeping?'

'That is correct.'

'Put that remark on a record so you can play it,' Gaunt snapped.

As he stood up, his expression grim, Jennie decided to intervene. Amberg had also stood up, small, portly, dressed in a black business suit. He turned to her in surprise, as though he'd forgotten her presence. Jennie realized the intensity of his concentration on his duel with Gaunt.

'How on earth do you manage to run this enormous place?' she enquired. 'Surely you need servants?'

'True. They don't live in. Too much of an invasion of privacy, which I value highly. The peasants from the local villages provide all the manpower needed.' His blue eyes twinkled. 'Of course, I have to pay them more in summer, but that's understandable. They can make a living tending the vineyards. I own a vineyard myself. Next time you come and see me you can sample some of my wine. I think you will like it. But your friend appears anxious to leave.'

Jennie had been staring straight into his shrewd blue eyes for every second he spoke. The transformation in his personality astounded her. Then she thought of the probable explanation. He was a man who preferred the company of women – and Gaunt had gone at him like a bull at a gate. She glanced at the Squire. He stood like a man carved out of stone. Furious that he'd got nowhere with the banker.

Amberg escorted them into the entrance hall. As she was stepping out of the château Amberg held out his hand, shook hers warmly.

'Don't forget my invitation to taste the wine . . .'

His expression changed suddenly as he looked at Gaunt. It reminded her of the expression the Swiss had adopted during the 'conversation'. Like a slab of ice.

'Goodbye, Mr Gaunt.'

'And it hasn't been a pleasure,' Gaunt roared at the top of his voice.

34

'Trouble. Here it comes,' Marler said to himself.

He was driving along the autoroute towards Colmar in mid-afternoon and it was still light. He was in the middle of nowhere, tilled fields stretching away on both sides, when he heard the police siren, saw the patrol car racing up to him in his rear-view mirror. Slowing down, he stopped.

As he lowered his window icy air flowed inside. He was humming the tune of '*La Jeune Fille aux Cheveux de Lin*' when the patrol car parked a few yards ahead of him. Before leaving Strasbourg he had pushed back the front passenger seat to its furthest extent and perched the cello case with its base on the floor and the rest of it angled against the seat. Several sheets of music were spread on the seat itself.

A tall lean-faced uniformed policeman got out of the patrol car. Leaving his companion behind the wheel, he wandered back to Marler. The flap of his pistol holster was unbuttoned.

'Papers!' he demanded.

Marler had his passport and driving licence ready and handed them over. The *flic* perused both documents carefully, returned them to Marler. He peered inside.

'You are on holiday?' he asked in French.

'No, I'm a musician,' Marler replied in the same language. 'I'm working.'

'Where are you driving to?'

'Berne in Switzerland. To perform in a concert.'

Marler hoped there *was* a concert hall in the Swiss capital. But he doubted whether the *flic* knew either. He was saying as little as possible, using the minimum of words to answer. The police were always suspicious of voluble travellers. The *flic* stared at the cello case.

'Your concert is today?' he asked truculently.

'No, tomorrow. I'll put up somewhere for the night to get some rest. I need to be fresh for the concert.'

Marler's mind, racing, was considering every angle. It was not impossible he'd bump into this same *flic* when he reached Colmar. Walking round the front of the car, the policeman opened the door to the front passenger seat, leaned in, opened the clasp, lifted the lid of the cello case. He stared down at the long slim silk sleeve with the end of a bow projecting.

Marler said nothing. He was careful to display no sign of impatience, nervousness. No drumming of his fingers on the wheel. The *flic* peered into the back of the Audi.

'What are you carrying inside that bag?'

'It's cricket. One of our national games. Inside is what we play the game with – a bat and a ball.'

The policeman frowned, reached in, unzipped the bag, stared at its contents. He shrugged, re-zipped the bag. The English had peculiar tastes. Marler realized he'd made one of those glaring mistakes the most careful people sometimes make. Who played cricket in winter in this part of the world?

Slamming the back door shut as he had done the front, the policeman shrugged again at the strangeness of the English. Without another word he walked back to his vehicle, climbed inside. The patrol car took off like a rocket.

'And that experience is enough for one day,' Marler said to himself as he closed the lid of the cello case and resumed driving.

For Jennie the drive back from the Château Noir to Colmar was a nightmare. Gaunt was moving over snow-covered roads which might conceal ice underneath, racing round hairpin bends on the edge of precipices. Once he skidded close to an endless drop. With great skill he came out of it, proceeded down another steep slope. Jennie had her hands clasped tightly inside her gloves.

'We didn't get much out of Amberg, did we?' she remarked. 'Very Swiss. Although most Swiss I've met have been so polite and helpful.'

'Shut up! I'm driving.'

She knew Gaunt fairly well now, his volatile moods. As they swerved round another bend she studied his profile. No tension, no sign that the BMW could slide at any moment into a fatal skid. She suddenly grasped that only half his mind was on driving the car.

A superb driver, he was controlling the car automatically. Half his mind was miles away, pondering something which bothered him. What could it be that he was mentally gnawing at like a dog with a bone?

A yellow tractor was emerging from a snow-covered field a score of yards or so ahead of them. If it occupied the road ahead of them it would be difficult to overtake. Gaunt rammed his foot down on the accelerator, pressed his hand on the horn, blaring out across the mountains non-stop. God! He was going to try and get in front of it!

Jennie closed her eyes, waited for the shattering collision, couldn't bear not to see what was happening, opened them again. She gritted her teeth. Racing down the curving road, the BMW increased speed. The tractor driver seemed to take no notice. Its yellow hulk loomed over Jennie as the car sped past, almost skimming the side of the machine. She let out her breath.

'Silly devil,' Gaunt commented offhandedly. 'Should have waited. My right of way.'

'Only your right of way if the other chap gives it to you,' she reminded him.

'What was that you said?' He glanced at her briefly.

He hadn't heard a word she had spoken. Now she knew she was right – he was driving on automatic pilot. *Most* of his mind was miles away. Where?

She went over in *her* mind all that had been said while they were at the Château Noir. Was it frustration that was affecting Gaunt? Frustration at hearing that the film and the tape had gone missing?

Then it hit her. Did Gaunt *know* what was on the film, the tape? During an early stage of his verbal exchanges with Amberg she recalled one thing Gaunt had said. When Julius had arrived at Tresillian Manor Gaunt had had a chat with him. Had Julius told Gaunt then what he had seen on the film, what he had heard on the tape? It was possible, maybe even likely.

Suddenly as they approached Colmar a dense mist crept in from the fields, entering the town. Gaunt switched on his fog lights. He was crawling now as they came close to the Hotel Bristol, were passing a shopping parade. She put a hand on his arm.

'Greg, could you drop me here. There are lights on in the shops, they're still open. I want to buy something from the chemist.'

'Here do you?'

He pulled in by the kerb. She opened the door, swung out her long legs. As she turned to close the door and looked at him he seemed to be finally aware of her existence.

'Bristol's just down the way. You'll know where to find me. In the bar. Of course . . .'

The rear of the BMW was swallowed up in the mist which had now become a fog. Glancing in the mirror, Gaunt's last sight of her was a vague silhouette standing by the kerb.

At the Bristol Tweed had chosen the Brasserie for a belated lunch. After their arrival he'd spent a long time alone in his bedroom studying a map of the Vosges, checking the different routes to the Château Noir.

There was a more upmarket restaurant at the hotel, entered from the reservation lobby. The waiter who met Tweed as he led Paula and Newman wore formal black jacket and trousers. His manner, as he attempted to guide them to a table, was that he was conferring an honour on them.

333

'I'm looking for the Brasserie,' Tweed told him in English.

'Really, sir?' The waiter's tone conveyed that he'd misjudged the quality of the client. 'Through that door, then turn left and left again.'

'This is more like it,' Tweed remarked. 'More homely. That other place you could wait an hour for the first course with a lot of chichi nonsense, removing the covers from the plate and all that rubbish.'

Paula agreed the atmosphere was more welcoming. And in contrast to the restaurant, where the guests had sat like waxworks, the few customers here were locals having an aperitif, eating a main meal.

In the main dining area a waitress led them to, the panelled walls were painted a bright ochre. The cloths on the table were a cheerful pink, Paula noted with approval. The Brasserie faced the railway station across a wide road. Tweed had chosen well.

'I think I'll have a glass of wine,' Tweed announced to her surprise when they were seated. 'We're in Riesling country. A beautiful wine.'

The waitresses, bustling about, wore white blouses, black skirts and short white aprons. Tweed ordered a bottle of Riesling when the others agreed enthusiastically.

'This is when you say it's a good year,' Newman chaffed him, when a bottle of 1989 vintage arrived.

'Let's hope it is. I've no idea. Have you heard of the Château Noir?' he asked the waitress in French.

'Yes. Up in the mountains above the Black Lake. A bad place. It is fated.'

'Why do you say that?'

'Its strange history, sir. It was built by an American millionaire years ago. Built of granite from plans of a medieval fortress. It cost many millions of francs. He committed suicide.'

'Who did?' Tweed asked.

'The American millionaire. He jumped from the château into the Black Lake. No one knows why. It remained empty for years. Who would buy such a place?'

'I heard that someone did. A Swiss banker.'

'Of course. He bought it for a song. Mr Julius Amberg from Zurich. Maybe he was not superstitious. He did not think he would become dead before his time. Good luck to him. He is a nice man.'

Paula was watching Tweed, wondering whether he was going to tell her that Amberg was no longer alive. Tweed simply looked interested, asked the waitress another question.

'You said he is a nice man. You have met him?'

'Many times. When he comes to Colmar he always comes in here – to the Brasserie. For an aperitif, for a main meal.' She lowered her voice. 'He said the restaurant is for snobs, that the food here is much better and you get it quickly. I must go now . . .'

'Has Mr Amberg been here recently?' Tweed asked before she could rush off.

'No, not for some time. Yet when it was clear this afternoon just before dusk we saw lights in the château. Maybe a ghost walks there. You have decided what you would like to eat? I can come back.'

'The veal escalope *panée* for me, with sauté potatoes.'

Tweed looked at Paula. 'What do you fancy?'

'The same for me, please,' Paula said, looking at the waitress.

'Make that three,' Newman requested.

The waitress darted away. Paula, who was facing the rear of the Brasserie, stared at a huge mural painted in oils above the door leading to the kitchen. It depicted a small lake sunk in the grim heights of the Vosges. Tweed followed her gaze.

'I wonder if that's Lac Noir,' she mused. 'If so, it looks pretty forbidding. And what a strange story she told us

335

about Château Noir. Obviously Walter Amberg doesn't patronize the Brasserie.'

'Walter,' Newman commented, 'from what I've seen of him, would patronize the restaurant, silver-plate covers and all that jazz.'

'From what we've gathered,' Tweed pointed out, 'Amberg has only been at the château for two or three days. It was interesting to hear that the place *is* occupied. The lights the waitress mentioned.'

'We are going up there to beard him in his den, aren't we?' Paula enquired.

'It's one reason why we came here. Incidentally, I don't want to spoil your meal, but I think the opposition has already arrived. As we walked through the restaurant I noticed six men sitting at a quiet table in a corner. I also caught a snatch of conversation – with an American accent. They're not pleasant-looking characters.'

'But why here, for Pete's sake?' Paula asked.

'In Zurich there is a whole number of first-class hotels. In Basle there are only two, the Drei Könige and the Hilton – if you prefer that. Here the only major hotel is the Bristol. It's logical some of them would choose to stay here. They may even have detected its strategic position.'

'Strategic in what way?' Paula wanted to know.

'If their objective is also the Château Noir then we are on the right side of the town. From here we can drive straight into the outskirts across the railway and up into the Vosges. We practically bypass Colmar.'

'There's a heavy fog drifting in,' Newman remarked.

Twisting round in her seat, Paula looked at the windows fronting on the street and hung with net curtains. For customers coming in off the street there were double doors leading into the Brasserie.

Newman was right. As she watched the fog seemed to grow denser every minute. The blurred headlights of crawling cars appeared, disappeared in the milky haze.

And the temperature had dropped swiftly. A man came in through the entrance and briefly a current of ice-cold air drifted into the Brasserie.

A waiter, wearing a white shirt, black trousers and a long apron tied round his waist, went to push the door shut quickly. Outside stooped silhouettes of people hurrying home as fast as they dared passed beyond the windows.

'I like this wine,' Tweed said, finishing off his glass. 'It really is a very good Riesling.'

Out of the corner of her eye Paula saw Newman refilling his glass. She turned round, picked up a bottle of Perrier the waitress had brought, topped up Tweed's water glass.

'You'll end up floating,' she teased him.

'Riesling is my favourite wine. It helps me to think. I'm going to order another bottle.'

'Any excuse is better than none,' she teased him.

She twisted round again. The ghostly tableau of cars and people beyond the window fascinated her. Then she stiffened. A woman had hauled open the door, came inside looking frightened to death. Jennie Blade. She spotted Tweed, ran to his table. 'I've been followed again,' she burst out. 'By the man with the wide-brimmed hat.'

Her blonde hair glistened with fog vapour. Her eyes were wild. Tweed stood up, walked round the table, pulled out a chair for her which faced his. Returning to his seat he sat down, gazed at her as he spoke.

'When did this happen?'

'Just now. He damn near caught up with me. Thank God this place was so close. The same man – following me with his bloody wide-brimmed black hat, turned down so I couldn't see his face. I'm scared to death, Tweed.'

35

'I need a drink,' said Jennie as she took off her coat, draped it over the back of a nearby chair. 'Brandy.'

'No spirits at the moment,' Tweed advised. 'You are in a state of shock. Try a glass of this Riesling.'

Paula reached across to another empty table, picked up a glass, placed it in front of their guest. Tweed was glad he'd placed Jennie facing him as he poured the wine – she was not looking at Paula, whose expression was full of doubt.

'Can you tell me exactly what happened?' Tweed suggested.

Jennie drank half the contents of her glass, put it down, then almost immediately raised it again, drained it. Tweed refilled it.

'Why were you outside in this fog?' he coaxed.

'I'd been with Gaunt in the BMW. We'd just returned from the Château Noir. I asked the Squire to drop me by the shopping parade so I could go into a chemist. It was when I came out that it happened.'

'Go on, you are doing fine,' Tweed encouraged her.

'I came out of the shop and it was eerie. I hadn't realized how dense the fog had become. He was standing with his back to me, holding up something in his left hand. The same black wide-brimmed hat, turned down as I told you so I couldn't see his face. The same long black overcoat. I began to walk towards the Bristol, towards here. I heard him coming after me. I panicked, began to run. Behind me he was moving much faster.'

'How do you know that?' Paula enquired. 'Did you look back?'

'God, no! I was too scared. But there was no other sound in the fog – just the clack of his shoes catching me up. The clacking sound hit the pavement at longer intervals – so I knew he'd increased the length of his stride.'

'Very shrewd of you,' Tweed commented. He sipped at his coffee which the waitress had brought just before their frightened guest appeared. 'Especially as you were so scared.'

'Then I saw the Brasserie. I dived in here, saw you. What a relief.'

'Drink some more wine.' Tweed waited until she had swallowed half her second glass. He topped it up. 'What happened to your pursuer?'

'I've no idea. At least he didn't follow me in here. But then I'd have been all right.' She smiled wanly for the first time. 'You were here.'

'Are you feeling better?' Tweed reached across, took hold of her right hand resting on the table, squeezed it reassuringly. 'You are safe, among friends.'

Newman had remained silent, leaving it to Tweed. He noticed that in the warmth of the Brasserie the vapour drops had melted on Jennie's golden hair, giving her a somewhat bedraggled look. She was still incredibly attractive.

'Would you like something to eat?' Tweed asked her.

'Just some bread. My stomach can't face anything else.'

She took a piece of French bread, piled on it some of the butter Newman had ordered, chewed ravenously, then reached for a second hunk.

'That's better,' she announced a minute later. 'Pardon my table manners. I haven't eaten for hours.'

'You said you'd just returned from the Château Noir with Gaunt in his BMW,' Tweed began. 'Would you mind telling me what took place? You met Amberg?'

'Yes. That was an experience for Gaunt . . .'

She started to tell Tweed in detail everything that had taken place. She recalled almost every word of the conversation between the two men. Gaunt's expression, Amberg's lack of it. Then at the end the warmth of Amberg when he talked to her, the theory she had come up with that the Swiss preferred the company of women. Her descriptions were graphic.

Paula glanced at Tweed. He was leaning forward, totally absorbed by what Jennie was saying. Paula sensed that Tweed was *seeing* the scene which had been enacted in the Château Noir, so strong was his imagination. Newman was also gazing fixedly at their guest. As an ex-foreign correspondent maybe his mind was also inside the Château Noir.

'So,' Jennie concluded, 'after the hideous drive back when I thought we'd end up dead, Gaunt – at my request – dropped me outside the shops.'

There was a long silence. Tweed was still staring at her as she drank more wine, watching him over the rim of her glass. He eventually leaned back in his chair.

'You have remarkable powers of observation. So many see but do not *observe* what they see.'

'Coming from you I'm taking that as a great compliment.'

'Just a statement of fact.'

'I think I've taken up enough of your time – and I could do with a hot shower.' She stood up, looked at Paula and Newman. 'I do hope I haven't spoilt your meal – and thank you for putting up with my maunderings.' She looked at Tweed. 'If we could have a quiet talk sometime at your convenience?'

'I'm in Room 419. It has a sitting area. Come and see me any time you feel like it. So I know it's you beat a little tattoo on the door. Like this.'

He drummed his fingers briefly on the table. Jennie

340

repeated the rhythm. Newman also stood up, collected her coat.

'You don't want to go out into the fog again to find the main entrance. There's a short cut through the restaurant. I'll see you safely to your room.'

'That's very kind of you.' She gave him her warmest smile. 'I do still feel a bit shaky.'

Paula waited until they had disappeared. Then she turned to Tweed.

'I don't believe one word she said.'

Tweed sipped some more wine before replying. He put down his glass.

'That really is first-rate Riesling.'

'Translation, you don't agree. You think I'm being catty. Maybe I am.'

'Not like you, so that I don't agree with. Give me your reasons.'

'It's stretching the imagination to breaking point. In Basle she gives you the same story. The famous Shadow Man. We are quite a distance from Basle. Now the Shadow Man turns up here on the edge of the Vosges in Alsace. I don't go for it.'

'Have you forgotten?' he enquired gently. 'An impartial witness in Zurich – Old Nosy – described the Shadow Man leaving the building in the Altstadt where Klara was murdered.'

'But we thought of an explanation for that. Jennie was in the square out of sight, saw him leaving the building – which gave her the idea.'

'What motive could she have for inventing this menace? Also, how could she have known we were in this brasserie?'

'Made it up on the spur of the moment when she came in that door from the fog. No flies on our Jennie. She's got mental reflexes as quick as lightning. I will give her that.'

'Possible. Yes, you could be right. And her motive?'

'She's after the film and the tape. I'm beginning to think they must be very valuable to someone.'

Tweed nodded his agreement. Paula's theory had disturbed him. Women were so often more perceptive than men about their own sex. Paula had produced a very plausible theory.

'Then why the charade – rushing in here as though scared stiff?' he questioned.

'She'd seen you were in here – maybe we didn't see her starting to come in by the short cut. She then goes back into the fog, puts on her act? Why? To get closer to you. She thinks you'll lead her to the film and tape.'

'I can't fault your reasoning,' he admitted.

'Another thing,' Paula went on. 'When she was relating her experience at the Château Noir – and I admit I was a little jealous of how well she did it. Supposed to be my forte, that. Sorry, I'm off the track. When she relayed what happened at the château, I think something she reported as said – or happened – struck you with great force.'

'It did. I don't want to talk about it until I've had time to mull it over.'

'Bob is taking a long time.' She grinned wryly. 'Maybe he not only saw her safely to her room, but inside it. He's smitten with her.'

'You've underestimated him,' Tweed told her. 'I've seen him do this before – pretend to have fallen for some attractive girl. And all the time he's asking himself, "What's she after?"'

'Shush! Here he is. And with more feminine company . . .'

Eve Amberg was laughing at something Newman had said as they approached Tweed's table. She had one hand looped inside his arm and used the other to brush away a lock of her titian hair from her face. Paula studied her outfit.

She wore a dark green jersey suit and a low-cut cream blouse. Bet that cost a mint, thought Paula. Newman, who was clearly enjoying himself, made a pantomime of introducing her. Sweeping one arm low, he used the other hand to pull out a chair.

'Look at the jewel I found hiding upstairs,' he joked.

'Hello, Paula,' Eve greeted her, bent and kissed her on the cheek. 'And a big hello to you,' she went on, turning to Tweed, administering a lingering kiss on his left cheek. 'Bob caught me coming out of my room, thank God. I'm an abandoned woman.'

'Sounds exciting,' Tweed chimed in, continuing the game. 'You look like a glass of this excellent Riesling.'

'And he says that!' Eve addressed Paula. 'After I spent half an hour on my make-up. Isn't he just too awful?'

'We can't take him anywhere,' Paula joked back.

'Wish me success.'

Eve raised the glass Tweed had filled, tasted the wine, looked mischievously at Newman.

'At least the man knows his wine. This is delicious. I may be after more.'

'Why abandoned?' Tweed asked.

'The Squire. Again. He drives me here with his latest girl friend, Jennie Blade. Then he ups and offs with her to some unknown destination. For the whole afternoon. Seriously, Tweed, it's good to see you again.'

'Likewise.' Tweed paused. 'What success do we wish you?'

'It's Walter again. Walter Amberg, my dear disliked brother-in-law. I phoned him from here. I was going to take a taxi. The Squire can drop dead, mooning over his Jennie. So what reception do I get when I call Walter? Not this afternoon. Out of the question. Have guests.

343

Some time when he's not so busy. Guests? I didn't believe a word of it. He's avoiding me. I'll catch him off guard – drive up there without phoning first.'

'Why the reluctance on his part?' enquired Tweed.

'Same reason as I told you before. He doesn't want to hand over my money. But he will, he will, I promise you. Face to face, he's putty in my hands, the little creep.'

'And Gaunt?'

'God knows where he is.' She glanced to her left when someone entered the Brasserie. 'Speak of the devil, here he is. After a drink, of course.'

Gaunt, still clad in his sports jacket and corduroy trousers, had stormed in via the short cut from the hotel. As he arrived his voice boomed out, causing the few locals sitting at other tables to stare.

'I want a double Scotch, *garçon!*' he roared in English. '*Tout le suite.* Over at that table.' He looked at Tweed and Newman, turned back to the waiter he'd shouted at. 'No, make that three double Scotches. And get a move on, I'm parched.'

The young waiter, who had smiled every time he passed their table, glared at Gaunt. Newman called out in a loud but polite voice.

'No, waiter, please. Only one double Scotch. Thank you.'

Gaunt marched up to their table. He stood for a moment, surveying the glasses.

'Drinking local plonk? That's just for pansies. A Scotch would put some guts into you.'

Eve was furious. Her greenish eyes gleamed with a venom Paula would never have suspected she was capable of. Her full lips, treated with scarlet lipstick, tightened as Gaunt hauled up a chair, joined them.

'Greg,' she raged, 'you will apologize immediately for using that term about my friends. Or go to hell.'

'I apologize immediately,' Gaunt mimicked as he sat

down. 'No offence meant,' he said in a more reasonable tone. 'I take the word back. Unpardonable of me – but I've had a helluva drive up and down the Vosges this afternoon.'

You've also had a skinful already before you came in here, Newman thought. Whisky fumes drifted across the table. But Eve wasn't finished yet. She leaned towards Gaunt.

'And, you ignorant hulk, it's *tout de suite*. You can't even insult a waiter in correct French.'

'Sorry, sorry, sorry.' Gaunt sounded sincere this time. 'You're quite right, Eve. Again, my apologies to everyone. Had a strange experience this afternoon. Threw me off my balance. That doesn't often happen.'

His mood had changed suddenly. He had spoken the last three sentences in a sober, almost grim tone. Tweed frowned, then spoke to him.

'Care to tell us about it? Get it out of your system?'

'Do you mind if I don't for the moment? Sorry, but I need to mull it over.'

Paula stared at Gaunt in astonishment. He had used almost precisely the same words Tweed had spoken earlier. Moreover, it sounded as though, like Tweed, he was referring to the Château Noir.

Gaunt looked up as the waiter placed his drink before him. He had his wallet out in a flash, added a generous tip as he stared at the waiter.

'Thank you very much. Your service is really excellent.' He looked round the table. 'Jennie disappeared. I can't find her anywhere.'

'She was sitting at this table a while ago,' Tweed informed him. 'You dropped her off in the fog, apparently.'

'At her own request,' Gaunt barked back defensively.

'She then left us to go to her room to take a shower,' Tweed continued, ignoring Gaunt's rudeness.

345

'But I hammered on her door before I came in here. There was no reply. Her door was locked. I pressed my ear to it, couldn't hear a shower running. In any case, she'd have wrapped something round her and come to see who it was. Like most women' – he glanced at Paula and Eve – 'present company excepted. Like many women she's always curious. I'd stake my reputation she's not in her room.'

'What reputation is that?' Eve snapped at him.

Tweed rose from the table. Newman and Paula stood up almost at the same time. They'd had enough of Gaunt. Tweed nodded to Eve and Gaunt, led the way out by the short cut and through the restaurant. Paula noticed there were several groups of Americans at different tables, none of whom she liked the look of. Tweed was hurrying into the reception area which had a minute sitting area off to one side. Philip Cardon sat reading a paperback. No one was present behind the reception counter.

'I had an early lunch,' Cardon explained. 'Since then I've sat here keeping an eye open. No less than fifteen Americans have arrived, booked in. Most are stuffing their stomachs in that restaurant.'

'Have you seen Jennie Blade?'

'No.'

So Gaunt was right, Tweed thought grimly. Jennie had disappeared.

36

Tweed stood quite still in the lobby. The only people in the place besides himself were Paula, Newman and Cardon. They all kept quiet – they knew Tweed was thinking furiously. He turned round once to gaze at the deserted reception area, the closed door behind it. He turned back to Cardon.

'Philip,' he said in a low voice, 'you counted fifteen Americans arriving. Did they see you?'

'Of course not.' Cardon was incredulous at the idea. He raised his book to above eye level, completely concealing his face. 'Can you see me?'

'No. Where are Butler and Nield?'

'Here.' Cardon handed Tweed a piece of paper with the names of the two men, their room numbers. 'Like me they had an early meal. They're up in their rooms now.' He checked his watch. 'Harry is due down to relieve me in five minutes. We worked out a roster to keep an eye on who comes and goes out of this place.'

'I see. They're both on the first floor? Good. Now, I want you to think hard. Did some of the Americans arrive here recently?'

'Yes, they did. They turned up in batches.'

'So at times there was a lot of movement here in this lobby. You were concentrating on concealing yourself – at the same time as you checked people arriving. You might have seen a woman with long blonde hair without really registering the fact.' Tweed gave a brief description of how Jennie had been dressed. 'Think hard. Did a woman like that walk *out* of the hotel?'

'Half a mo! – now I come to think of it a woman like that came out of the dining-room exit just as you did. Fifteen minutes ago – roughly. She entered the lift. That was the last I saw of her.'

'Did all the Americans go straight into the restaurant? All fifteen of them?'

'Yes, to start with. Come to think of it two of them, ugly-looking types, came out of the restaurant almost on the heels of Jennie Blade. They must have taken the lift immediately after she'd gone up.'

'Thank you. Stay here.' Tweed turned to Newman and Paula. 'We must hurry, but first I need to collect something.'

He lifted the flap at the end of the reception counter, slipped behind it, grabbed hold of the master key hanging from a hook apart from the other room keys. He ran across to the lift, went inside as soon as the doors opened and pressed the button for the first floor as soon as Paula and Newman were inside.

'What are you up to?' Paula asked.

'First we get hold of Butler and Nield, with their hand-guns. You may need yours. No shooting unless it's the only way . . .'

Paula was still puzzled until Tweed had collected Nield and Butler, had explained the situation.

'We'll check this floor first . . .'

Tweed began to walk up to each room door, pressing his ear close to the wooden panel. He had acute hearing and soon moved on to the next door. It was outside the third door he tried that he froze, ear pressed hard against the panel. Voices inside. One with an American accent.

'Look, do you smoke? You don't? Well, honey, you're going to when I press this lighted cigarette into your face, then lower down. What man will ever look at you again . . .'

348

'No, you bastards—'

The woman's voice was cut off with a scream. Tweed inserted the master key quietly, turned it noiselessly, took hold of the handle, glanced at Butler who stood with a Walther in his hand. Tweed nodded, turned the handle. Standing aside, he threw the door wide open.

Butler, Walther gripped in both hands, charged into the room in a crouch, prepared to drop to the floor, gun swinging in an arc. Behind him Newman followed with Nield. Tweed removed the key, stepped in after them, inserted the key back into the lock and turned it to the locked position.

Jennie was sprawled back in an armchair, ankles bound with rope, her wrists pinioned behind her. The blouse was pulled down, exposing her breasts. A cloth gag had slipped from her mouth. One tall lanky American was standing behind her, holding her head back with a hand round her throat. A shorter stocky American stood stooped over her, holding a lighted cigarette close to her cheek.

Butler was on his feet in a flash. He brought the muzzle of his Walther down hard on the stocky American's nose. His target screamed with pain, dropped the cigarette. Tweed picked it up off the carpet.

At the same moment Newman reached the lanky American who reacted more quickly. He'd let go of Jennie, his hand had slid inside his jacket. Newman's left arm coiled round his neck from behind, squeezed his Adam's apple. The hard nails of his right hand dug into the back of the American's. There was a grunt of agony, a Luger dropped to the floor. Nield kicked the American's feet from under him and he sagged, gasping for breath.

Tweed had picked up the Luger as the stocky man had one hand over his damaged nose while his other hand fumbled inside his jacket. Tweed rammed the muzzle of the Luger into his abdomen, shook his head. The fumbling hand emerged empty. Tweed used his left hand

349

to explore under the thug's armpit, gripped the butt of a weapon in a shoulder holster, withdrew it. Another Luger.

Everything had happened in a matter of seconds. The stocky man began to swear, using filthy words. Paula hit him across the mouth with her Browning, breaking teeth. He spat out blood.

'Mind your language,' she told him. 'There are ladies present. Any more of that and you know something? *All* your teeth will go.'

The stocky man glared at her with hatred as he took out a handkerchief, emptied two teeth and blood into it. He saw the expression in her eyes and looked away hastily.

By now Butler and Nield had the lanky American sprawled on the floor, face down. Butler checked him for weapons, found nothing more. As Newman administered the same treatment to the stocky man Tweed and Paula tended to Jennie. Butler handed Paula his clasp knife. She used it to remove the ropes round the victim's ankles and wrists while Tweed untied the gag. He could see no signs of burns on her.

'I'm going to ask you a silly question,' Tweed said and smiled. 'How are you feeling?'

'OK.' Jennie rubbed each wrist in turn. 'The fat one is Eddie, the tall one Hank.' She stood up and Paula stood close, ready to grab her, but she seemed quite steady. 'Do me a favour,' she requested. 'Get Eddie on his feet, two of you hold his arms tight.'

Puzzled, Butler went over to help Newman when Tweed had nodded to them. They hauled Eddie upright, held him tight by each arm. Paula had pulled up Jennie's blouse so she was decent. Her feet were clad in walking shoes. She walked forward slowly until she was within a few feet of the stocky man.

'Eddie is the sadist. Eddie enjoys his work.'

She picked up the burning cigarette Tweed had perched

in the lip of a clean ashtray. Flicking off the end of the ash, she faced the stocky man.

'Eddie likes giving people a bad time, *revels* in it.'

'Look, lady . . .' Eddie began.

Jennie stabbed the burning cigarette towards his face and he flinched. Tweed frowned, came close to her and whispered.

'Don't burn him. It would take you down to his level. And I won't permit it.'

She shook her head to indicate that wasn't what she had in mind. Her eyes were blazing at the stocky man, who was sweating profusely.

'Spread your feet, Eddie,' Jennie ordered. 'Or you get this cigarette smeared down your face.'

Eddie, mystified and frightened at the same time, stretched out his feet. Jennie moved. Her right leg arched up with all her strength. Paula was startled by the muscular power she displayed, then recalled she was a horse rider. She kicked her target in the groin. He groaned, gulped, gasped, bent over. Released by Newman and Butler, Eddie crouched on the floor, hands clasped to where her foot had contacted him.

'I like to settle my accounts,' Jennie said. 'Can we get out of here?' she asked Tweed.

'Of course. Now . . .'

As soon as she was inside his room she sank into a chair and broke down, sobbing endlessly.

'I've got a message for you to take back to your boss,' Newman told Hank and Eddie. 'You never come back here again. If I ever see either of your faces one more time you'll never leave Alsace alive. Get out . . .'

Newman was controlling a pent-up fury. Butler opened the door of the room and Hank walked out, one hand nursing his injured Adam's apple. Eddie had trouble making his exit. Stooped over, he duck-waddled into the corridor. Butler closed the door and with Nield they began a quick search of the room. The most valuable treasure they found was an Uzi sub-machine-gun with plenty of ammo. They took these items with them.

Paula had accompanied Tweed and Jennie to his room. It had plenty of space, was like a small suite with the sitting area just inside the door and sleeping quarters beyond. After consulting Jennie, Paula had nipped down to the Brasserie and asked for a mug of milky coffee with plenty of sugar.

There was no sign of Eve or Gaunt. He was pretty bloody hopeless at looking after a woman, Paula thought as she carried the mug to the room. She'd tell him so when she next met him.

'Hold the mug in both hands,' she coaxed Jennie.

It was a wise precaution. Jennie's hands were shaking but with a little help from Paula she drank some of the liquid. She looked up gratefully.

'Thank you so much. I felt so damned cold.'

'That's shock,' said Tweed quietly. He was standing as he watched her. 'It will wear off. Drink it all if you can.'

'The *bastards*!' Jennie burst out after she had emptied the mug.

Tweed knew then she was recovering rapidly. He had the impression she had not only considerable physical powers but also great mental resilience. He waited while Paula sat beside her on a chair she'd pulled close.

'I'm feeling much better,' Jennie announced suddenly. 'Thanks to both of you. I suppose I shouldn't have done what I did to that punk, Eddie.'

'I'd have scratched his eyes out,' Paula assured her.

'Feel up to my asking a few questions?' Tweed enquired.

'Fire away!'

352

'What information were they trying to extract from you?'

'They wanted to know about a film and a tape. Seemed to think I knew where they were after my visit to the Château Noir. I told them I didn't know what the hell they were talking about, that kidnapping was a capital offence in France if anything happened to the victim. I made that last bit up – but as they were Americans I didn't think they'd know much about Europe. When I kept that up – which is true – that I didn't know what they were talking about, they turned very nasty. I was so lucky you got there just in time.'

'Did they know you'd driven with Gaunt to the château?' Tweed asked gently.

'Oh, they knew all right. I didn't tell them.'

'Did they mention Amberg?'

'Not a word. Just kept on about their flaming film and tape.'

'I see . . .'

Tweed saw more than she realized. To know of Gaunt's visit to Amberg the opposition had to have the Château Noir under close surveillance. It was valuable information, but disturbing. It meant the American apparatus had had no trouble tracking Amberg from Zurich to Basle and then to the Vosges.

'Any more questions?' Jennie asked. 'Anything I could help you with?'

'I don't think so,' Tweed replied. 'But you have been very helpful.'

'You're the ones who've been helpful. I'm more grateful than I can tell you. And now, I'm feeling a bit tired. I think a lie-down for a while would help.'

'Flop on the left-hand bed,' Tweed suggested. 'I'll see there's always someone in this room to guard you. If you could take over for a start, Paula? Thank you. The bathroom is through that door.'

'Do you think they'll try something else?' whispered

Paula as she accompanied him to the door into the corridor.

'Bound to,' he whispered back. 'And next time it's likely to be something pretty diabolical – worse than what they were going to do to Jennie. These aren't just barbaric thugs. They're top professionals.'

'So you two made a real balls-up,' Mencken commented.

It was a deliberately cruel remark in view of the fact that Eddie sat on a bed in Mencken's room, still nursing the injured part of his anatomy. He glared at Mencken, then looked quickly away. Mencken's eyes had all the soul of a python's.

Hank stretched his lanky frame, standing against a wall. He didn't like the remark, he didn't like Mencken. Who did?

'We'd have got it out of her if Tweed's troops hadn't burst in on us,' he protested.

'Troops?' Mencken sneered. 'I could strangle Tweed with two fingers. What else had you to deal with? Newman, a tabloid gossip gone to seed. Some broad. And another amateur.' He took out a cigar, lit it slowly, blew smoke in Hank's face. 'You two are straight out of Mickey Mouse. My old mom could have done a better job.'

'Didn't know you ever had one,' blazed Hank.

He regretted the insult the moment the words had left his mouth. Mencken had leapt out of his chair as though propelled by a spring. His skeletal head was inches from Hank's as he held the burning cigar end so close Hank could feel its heat on his face. Mencken projected two long talon-like fingers into Hank's painful Adam's apple.

'You said what?' Mencken asked.

'Sorry, boss.' Hank gulped. 'Sure we made a balls-up. Sure we did. Next time we'll do better,' he croaked.

'If there *is* a next time.' Mencken removed his hand,

puffed at his cigar as he stood back a couple of feet, the smoke getting into Hank's eyes. The lanky American licked his lips.

'Something we never got time to tell you, boss. There was a third man came into that room. Thought you should know.'

'So now I know.' Mencken continued staring at him, puffing the cigar. 'For Chrissakes, you mishandled it from the start. One of you should have been enough to deal with the twist . . .' Which was his flattering reference to Jennie Blade. 'If the other had stood guard with the Uzi you could have cut down the lot – including Tweed. Then taken the twist to your car, driven into the foothills, screwed the information out of her, then phoned me. That is how I'd have handled it.'

'The noise that sub-machine-gun would have made—' Hank began.

'Would have woken up the hotel,' Mencken interrupted. 'So you moved straight out of the hotel as I suggested. You blow a lot of smoke, Hank. You and Eddie never sat with us in the diner. We'd have been OK. No more crap.'

Mencken had decided Eddie and Hank were expendable. They were known now to Tweed and his team. He'd terminate that problem once they got up into the mountains. The phone rang. Mencken walked towards it with a slow deliberate pace, picked up the receiver. It was Norton.

The shaggy grey-haired man with half-moon glasses perched on his nose had to use the phone from his room. He had registered at the small hotel, L'Arbre Vert – the Green Tree – in Kaysersberg, as Harvey Cheney. There were no public phone boxes in this village.

'Norton here. Time you gave me a progress report. Watch any confidential information about our competitors – we're on open lines.'

'I visited that place you noticed where the product is stored, obtained sufficient samples. Get me?' Mencken rasped.

Norton got him – he had broken into the explosives shed near the stone quarry, had walked off with an ample supply. Mencken had moved fast, but Norton had no intention of congratulating him.

'What about the construction of the bridge? Have you surveyed it?'

For 'construction' Mencken understood 'destruction' of the hump-backed bridge in the centre of Kaysersberg.

'A team has examined it. Some blasting operation will be necessary. Long-distance work. Everything is prepared. Goddamnit! I know my job.'

Norton ignored the irritable outburst. Explosives had been placed under the bridge, waiting for Tweed's team to drive over it. The explosion would be detonated by someone who needed a good view of the target.

'Since it's a remote-control operation we need to have an observer at a distance but close enough to see the result.'

Mencken sighed audibly. 'That also has been worked out. All that we planned is arranged. OK? OK?'

Norton sensed resentment about his authority. That had to be stamped on immediately. Mencken must be in no doubt as to who was running the show.

'Then,' Norton went on remorselessly, 'there's the section of rock which has to be cleared. Have you attended to *that*?'

'Jesus! Why don't you come and hold my hand,' snarled Mencken. 'Yes, the rock is ready to come down. Now, if that's everything . . .'

There was silence at the other end of the line. Mencken had just confirmed that the rock above the cliff looming over the road had been drilled, explosives inserted. He had sent up two men per team on a roster basis.

He had hired plenty of transport in Basle, had drawn

356

up a roster of men, giving them their objectives as soon as he had returned from the café in Little Venice after talking with Norton through the lace curtain.

'You'll have to do something about your manners,' Norton said eventually, very abrasive. 'Talk to me like that just once more and you're on the first plane back to the States. I'll take over the operation myself. Imagine what will be waiting for you when you leave the aircraft. I trust, Marvin,' the voice continued softly, 'you do have some imagination?'

Mencken froze. Fury gave way to fear. Yes, he knew what would be waiting for him. A limo with an open window and the muzzle of a gun aimed point blank.

'I'm trying to do my best for you. No one is going to let you down. Maybe I was a little bitchy. Everything is under control. It will be a breeze . . .'

'No, it won't, sonny boy. Get that into your thick skull. Our competitor, Tweed, is a barracuda. Don't you ever forget that. Sonny boy . . .'

The phone went dead. Mencken kept his face to the wall so his men couldn't see his expression, a mixture of fright and rage. He was careful not to slam down the phone. Glancing down at his cigar, he saw that a length of ash had dropped on to the floor. He ground it savagely into the new carpet. When Tweed was blown into a thousand pieces he'd be top gun. And when Joel Dyson and Special Agent Barton Ives raised their heads above the parapet he'd personally put the bullets into both of them. Then he'd take out Cord Dillon.

Norton wandered out of the small hotel into the dark and paused. Snow had begun to fall. He adjusted his fur hat, pulled up the collar of his astrakhan coat. It was bitingly cold, well below zero, he reckoned. He began to stroll back into Kaysersberg – the Green Tree was located on

357

the northern outskirts. No one else was in sight.

Norton had no eye for the beauty and character of the medieval village with its cobbled streets and leaning houses. Disneyland, he thought contemptuously.

A few minutes later he saw the bridge. He paused and studied it. Glancing up to his left he saw an ancient castle looming over the village – the perfect vantage point for the watcher who would control the detonation of the explosive under the bridge. Norton had a strong feeling this was the route Tweed would choose. He'd never even see the Château Noir. He turned back to the hotel. He was expecting a call from Bradford March. He had already informed Sara of his new phone number.

37

'We must prepare a battle plan for our expedition into the Vosges,' Tweed announced. 'Especially after what Philip has reported, which is alarming.'

He was standing in the sitting area of his bedroom. It was nearly midnight. When he had slipped down several hours before to put back the master key the hotel had been deserted.

Jennie had woken earlier, and said she wanted to go back to her own room for a shower. Nield had been selected to go with her to sit in the room on guard. Jennie had been secretly pleased with the choice. She rather liked the look of the slim Pete Nield with his trim moustache. He could be fun.

Paula sat on one of the beds, hands rested on the coverlet on either side, her legs crossed. Newman, Butler,

Cardon and Marler listened. The latter, adopting his usual stance, leaned against a wall, smoking a king-size. The others occupied various chairs.

Marler had arrived back recently, carrying his cello case, cricket bag and a suitcase. He had carefully placed his wares in a corner.

'You'd like some sustenance?' Tweed had asked him. 'We got the Brasserie to prepare sandwiches and coffee in a Thermos.'

'Thank you. Might indulge later. I stopped for a snack on the way back from Strasbourg,' Marler had replied.

'What alarming news did Philip bring?' Paula asked. 'I was in the bathroom when he came in.'

'Philip,' Tweed told them, 'was observing comings and goings from a discreet position off the lobby. He told me he'd seen at least six pairs of Americans leaving the hotel at intervals. He heard cars starting up and all of them were a long time before they returned, again at intervals. I find those movements ominous.'

'Why?' pressed Paula.

'Butler,' Tweed continued, 'took over from Philip. He also reported pairs of Americans returning late in the evening. They had snow on their boots.'

'Why ominous?' Paula persisted.

'First, because I'm convinced that Norton – the man who impersonated Ives, I'm sure, at the Gotthard – is the evil genius behind the huge apparatus brought over here from the States.'

'Evil genius?' drawled Marler. 'A bit strong that, isn't it?'

'Is it?' Tweed looked grim. 'I told you how convincingly he bluffed us when he turned up at the Gotthard. Then when he ran for it he left behind a present for me. Prussic acid in my mouthwash. And that trap he had organized in Bahnhofstrasse. The fake cripple with the grenade – backed up by a second man with a machine-pistol. Norton

359

is a top pro. I'm not making the mistake of underestimating him.'

'And the second point?' Cardon enquired.

'Those Americans who have been away from the hotel this evening for hours. Some returning with snow on their boots. I think they've studied the routes up into the Vosges to the Château Noir.'

'I think so, too,' Newman agreed. 'And God knows what booby traps they've prepared for us – whichever of the routes we use.'

'So we must outmanoeuvre them,' Tweed went on. 'First we should list our resources. Yes, Harry,' he said, addressing Butler.

'Pete Nield and I brought in some useful transport. First, a Renault Espace V6, a spacious vehicle. I drove that and carried a couple of high-powered motorbikes inside it. Pete Nield hired a station wagon. We crossed the frontier into France without trouble. No one tried to search us. We could have taped our handguns under the chassis.'

'Anyone like to see my contribution?' enquired Marler.

Unfastening the cello case he had placed on the bed next to Paula, he raised the lid, removed the bow and then the black velvet cloth. Paula glanced at the contents, dropped off the bed, walked to the other bed and perched on it.

'If you don't mind,' she snapped at Marler. 'That little collection looks lethal.'

'Oh, very!' Marler assured her and grinned.

The men all gathered round the cello case. Cardon gave a yelp of delight.

'Grenades! Could I borrow six of those?'

'Which means I don't get them back,' Marler commented in mock annoyance. 'Help yourself.'

'I'll relieve you of the Luger,' Butler suggested. 'It makes a good back-up for a Walther.'

'Go ahead,' Marler told him. 'The Armalite is mine, of course. And I'm hanging on to the tear-gas pistol.'

'Like to see my contribution to the arsenal?' Newman suggested.

Fetching a canvas hold-all he'd dumped in a corner he unzipped it. When he produced the Uzi sub-machine-gun Paula stared.

'Are we thinking of starting a small war?' she asked.

'Which is just what the chap who supplied me with my toys said,' Marler recalled.

'We're well equipped,' Tweed decided. 'Put it all away. Now we must decide how we move into the mountains when the time comes. Which may be tomorrow. I have to talk to Amberg urgently – while he's still alive.'

'I could ride ahead of the cars on one of those motorbikes,' Cardon suggested. 'I can sniff danger a mile away.'

'Agreed,' said Tweed. 'Next suggestion . . .'

They spent less than half an hour working out the details of a convoy which would make its way up to the Château Noir. Cardon would be the advance scout on his motorcycle. He would travel ahead of the large Espace which Newman would drive, with Tweed and Paula as passengers.

Butler would ride the second motorcycle, was given a 'roving' duty to travel back and forth along the well-spaced-out convoy – well spaced to make a smaller target.

Nield would drive the station wagon, sometimes behind the Espace, sometimes ahead of it. A tactic which should confuse the opposition, if they were waiting for them.

That left Marler, who insisted on driving his red Mercedes. Tweed was doubtful of the wisdom of this, pointed out its colour could be spotted a long distance up in the mountains.

'I realize that,' Marler commented. 'But it moves like a bird. That's what I'll be driving.'

'Then we've worked out an action plan,' Tweed concluded. 'Time you all went to bed, got some sleep. Harry, do you mind relieving Pete Nield, who's watching over Jennie? Fix up with Bob when he'll take over guard duty from you . . .'

'All this sounds like an assault force attacking the Château Noir,' Paula said to Tweed as everyone except Marler left the room.

'It may be just that,' Tweed warned her. 'If Norton has already taken over the place before we arrive.'

'I won't be coming with you,' Marler told Tweed when Paula was the only other person still in the room.

Tweed listened as Marler told him about his visit to the glider airfield at the Ballon d'Alsace. Paula was appalled, thought that Marler's plan sounded like a suicide trip, said so.

'I'm touched that you should worry about my welfare.' He grinned. 'Don't worry. I had a Met forecast over the radio on my way back from Strasbourg. Wind direction is perfect. A southerly – blow me north. Tweed, you'll have a spy in the sky above the château. Cost you a bomb if I crash the bird landing.'

'We'll find the money, I suppose.'

'And the glider will act rather like a flying bomb – if Norton's thugs are crawling round in the area.'

'We go into the mountains tomorrow, then?' Paula asked.

'Yes,' Tweed replied. 'I've decided not to delay. Amberg may be in great danger. We'll go via Kaysersberg.'

'Jolly good.' Marler gave Paula a little salute. 'Get to bed now. I'll be up at crack of dawn. For *Der Tag*.'

*   *   *

362

Norton had returned to the Green Tree, satisfied that the bridge was a perfect ambush location – if Tweed chose the Kaysersberg route. He took off his fur hat and astrakhan coat in the entrance hall, shook off the snow, went up the staircase to his room.

As he inserted his key he heard the phone ringing inside. Once in the room, he slammed the door shut, locked it and hurried to the phone. He had no doubt it was the President calling yet again.

'A call for you,' the hotel operator informed him and he heard the click as she went off the line.

'Norton here.'

'Good evening to you, Mr Norton,' a hoarse growly voice said. 'You will know who has given me your number. Now please be so good as to listen carefully to my instructions. If you really want the film and the tape.'

'Who is this?' grated Norton.

'Are you deaf? I told you to listen. One more comment and I go off the line. Have you got that?'

'Yes,' Norton replied with great reluctance. He was used to giving orders, not receiving them.

'You will drive to Lac Noir in the Vosges tomorrow, arriving there at sixteen hundred hours. Since you are American that is four o'clock in the afternoon . . .'

'I damn well know that . . .'

'One more interruption and this call ceases. Someone in Washington would not be pleased with you. The *patron* of the Green Tree, where you are staying, will show you on a map how to reach Lac Noir. Tell him you want to arrive at four and he will tell you when you must start. Have you understood me so far?'

The growly voice purred with menace. Even Norton, who thought he had experienced everything, was disturbed. He was careful with his reply.

'Yes, I have understood you.'

'Lac Noir – the Black Lake – is a lonely place. It is also

easy to observe from many points. You will bring the money and you will come alone. I said *alone*. If you bring anyone else we will never meet. I will show you the film, play the first section of the tape. You will give me the money. The exchange will be completed.'

Norton instantly saw his chance to manipulate the arrangement to suit his own purpose. His tone was dominant and grim.

'OK so far. But hell, you think I have that kind of dough in my back pocket? Because I haven't. It's in a safe place under heavy guard. I might be able to bring it up to you by six in the evening. No earlier. In any case, I want proof you have the items I need. So now you'll listen to me – if you want that dough. Or, to use your own words, we'll never meet. Six o'clock,' he repeated emphatically.

'Washington isn't going to like this at all . . .'

At this point Norton knew he had Growly Voice on the defensive for the first time. He hadn't broken off the call. He hadn't refused the later time of six o'clock Norton had laid down. Keep up the pressure, Norton told himself, and barked into the phone: 'Screw Washington. You can tell them I said that. I am the guy in charge of this operation. I am on the spot. I know where the money is. You're dealing with me? Get it? Just me. I'll be at the Black Lake at six o'clock in the evening tomorrow. All on my ownsome. And since presumably you're a European, six o'clock is eighteen hundred hours. Good night . . .'

Norton slammed down the phone before the voice at the other end could respond. He lit a cigar, dwelling with satisfaction on how he'd turned the tables on Growly Voice. Four in the afternoon it was still daylight, but by six it was black as pitch. The blackmailer was going to get a very nasty surprise tomorrow. And the timing fitted in with eliminating Tweed and his team if they went up into the mountains – they were bound to choose daylight hours. The big bucks were safe, too. Maybe he could

364

clean up the whole operation by this time tomorrow evening. He took another puff at his cigar, a choice Havana. Banned in the States – just because it came from Cuba.

Twenty million dollars is a lot of money to have suspended from a chain attached to your right-hand wrist. Louis Sheen still had the chain linking his wrist with the brown suitcase containing the fortune in US banknotes. From his room in the Basle Hilton he had been transported by car across the frontier to the Hôtel Bristol in Colmar.

His room, on the first floor, was probably the most heavily guarded area in Alsace-Lorraine. At all times three armed men occupied the room with him. Sheen was beginning to get fed up with room service. He peered at Mencken who had just been let into the room, glared at him through his rimless glasses.

'Look, Marvin, there are too many scumbags infesting this room. If I have to stay here a night longer I want them cleared out. You think I enjoy trying to sleep with this case as a bedmate? Because I don't.'

Mencken stroked a finger down the side of his long pointed jaw. Through half-closed eyes he studied Sheen with an expression which hardly radiated liking or sympathy. He spoke throatily as he made his casual suggestion.

'You've got the keys to unlock those steel cuffs hidden somewhere. Must have for when the time comes to hand over the billion dollars. So why not unlock the cuff on your wrist? No one can fool with trying to open the case. You're the only one who knows the code for those combination locks. Anyone who did try fooling around would end up igniting the thermite bomb inside – burning the money to a crisp, probably themselves, too.'

'I have my instructions,' Sheen snapped. 'And they

365

come from a far higher source than you'll ever meet, let alone reach.'

Sheen, wearing a grey Brooks Brothers suit, was an accountant by training. He felt himself superior in intellect and class to these people. It was just unfortunate he had to spend time in such bad company. This attitude was not lost on Mencken. He leaned his face close to Sheen, who sat on the bed, propped against pillows, the case next to him.

'I'm Marvin to a few good friends,' he informed Sheen. 'But you don't come into that category. So, in future it's Mr Mencken. I'm the boss. OK?'

'Makes no difference to me,' Sheen retorted in a bored tone. 'And the boss is Norton. He's the only one who can tell me to release what's inside this case.'

'You listen to me.' Mencken's expression had become ugly. 'These men are here to protect your worthless hide. They heard you call them scumbags – so if that door burst open and the Marines arrived, just how much enthusiasm do you think they'd have protecting you?'

'*You* were ordered to protect me. You must have a good idea how high up that order came from. And the amount in this case is not a billion. You know that. Now, go away and put these men outside in the corridor.'

Sheen's eyes gazed contemptuously at Mencken from behind the rimless glasses. Mencken shoved the fingers of both hands inside his belt. At last Sheen had given him an opening to hit back at the creep.

'Listen, buddy boy, you know this is a hotel, that we're keeping you under cover. So what the hell do you think it would look like if I put the three scumbags – wasn't that the word you used? – outside your door in the hotel corridor? I've got news for you, Sheen. You look after the dough, I'll look after everything else. Sleep well, buddy boy . . .'

Mencken left the room which was immediately locked

366

again from the inside. The secret order from Norton gave him a big kick. When the case had eventually been opened, the thermite bomb removed, at the first opportunity Mencken had personally to shoot Louis Sheen in the head and dispose of the body. He couldn't wait for that happy moment.

Prior to going to bed, Newman had gone into the Brasserie to buy a large bottle of mineral water. He often woke up in the middle of the night feeling parched. They were cleaning up in the Brasserie as he entered, sweeping floors, wiping the counter, polishing glasses. Newman was surprised to see Eve Amberg nursing a glass of champagne at a table. She raised her glass to him.

'What's the celebration in aid of?' he enquired, accepting her invitation to join her.

'Victory! I've pinned down Walter Amberg. He's agreed on the phone to see me at the Château Noir tomorrow morning. This time I won't leave till I get all the money which is mine. Hence the champers. Come on, Bob. Join me in my celebration.' She summoned a waiter, ordered a glass before Newman could protest. Worried, when the waiter had brought his glass, he tried to think of how to get her to delay her visit.

'Cheers, Bob!' Eve clinked his glass. 'Wish me luck up at the château.'

Even at this hour she was full of energy and the enthusiasm he found so infectious. She leaned her head on his shoulder, her long titian mane draped over his jacket, face turned sideways so her greenish eyes could study him. I could fall for this woman if I don't watch it, Newman told himself.

He was worried that if Eve went up into the mountains tomorrow she could easily drive into an area where the guns were firing. Because the guns *would* be firing –

Newman was convinced of this. Norton would exploit all the advantages of the mountain terrain to annihilate Tweed and his team. He'd already tried to wipe them out on a smaller scale in Zurich's Bahnhofstrasse, plus the memory of how he himself had just been saved by Beck's police car from being run down in Basle. Eve was stroking his hand when he spoke.

'Amberg has been very difficult with you recently – he's deliberately avoided you. Now he's agreed graciously to receive you into the presence, shouldn't you play hard to get? Throw him off balance – phone him tomorrow morning and say you'll be driving up to see him the following day.'

'You don't know Walter like I do. I appreciate what you suggested. With many men it would work. Not with Walter. He's more stubborn than a mule. Now I've pressured him into seeing me I must grab my chance. He may have decided to pay me off to get rid of me. You only get one chance with Walter—' She broke off and, her head still resting on Newman's shoulder, stared at the newcomer who had entered the Brasserie by the short cut. It was Tweed.

'We're celebrating!' Eve greeted Tweed buoyantly. 'Champers for you. Drink to my successful trip tomorrow.'

The waiter had already arrived with a fresh glass of champagne. Tweed waved it aside, asked for a glass of Riesling.

'Helps me to sleep,' he explained amiably to Eve. 'It's the only wine I really like – so being in Alsace I'm making the most of it. Thank you,' he said to the waiter, raised his glass, stared at Eve who was eyeing him sideways. 'So what are we celebrating at this late hour?'

Newman explained Eve's plans, emphasizing that he'd

tried to persuade her to wait for twenty-four hours. Tweed grasped at once Newman's motive in attempting to delay her visit. While listening to the explanation Eve stared fixedly at Tweed, her full lips moving slightly. It was a situation not unfamiliar to Tweed – an attractive woman who liked to flirt, who pretended to be interested in one man while she took aim at her real target. In this case, he suspected, himself.

To Newman's surprise Tweed made no attempt to back up his failed argument to stop Eve driving to the Château Noir tomorrow – almost today now. Sipping his Riesling, Tweed held Eve's inviting gaze and then took a view which infuriated Newman.

'I think you're right to keep the appointment with Amberg. It's taken long enough to track him down. What time are you to meet him?'

'Eleven in the morning. He even said he might provide lunch since there wasn't anywhere else to eat near the château. I accepted.'

'You were surprised when he suggested lunch?' enquired Tweed.

'Very. I've never taken to Walter and assumed it was a mutual feeling. I'm beginning to think maybe it could be pure shyness where women are concerned. Perhaps I'm due for a pleasant shock tomorrow.'

'Don't bank on it,' Newman told her sharply.

'What a pessimist Bob is.' Eve raised her head from his shoulder. Smoothing down her hair, she leaned over the table to where Tweed faced her, grasped his hand. 'Do you object to my driving up to see Walter in the morning?'

'Why should I? Because of the ice and snow the roads are very dangerous, I gather. And very low temperatures during the night won't help. But you must make up your own mind.'

'Then I shall be going, so I suppose I'd better get up to bed.'

Tweed noted she moved very steadily as she came round the end of the table, bent down, kissed him on the cheek. Her hair brushed the side of his face, giving him a tingling sensation.

'Thank you, Tweed. For your moral support.' She turned her gaze on Newman. 'As for you, Mr Pessimist, have a nice day – as the pathetic Americans are always saying.' She gave him a little wave, a wry smile and disappeared into the hotel.

'What the devil are you up to?' Newman burst out when they were alone. 'All hell is liable to break loose on those mountain slopes tomorrow . . .'

'I agree,' Tweed interjected amiably, then finished off his wine.

'Every conceivable weapon could be used against us,' Newman raved on, keeping his voice down. 'So why send Eve into a battlefield?'

'You'd managed to persuade her not to go then?'

'Well, not exactly . . .'

'Be frank. Didn't she refuse point blank to take any notice of your attempt to get her to change her mind?'

'Yes, she did,' Newman admitted.

'I sensed this as soon as I arrived. Eve is a woman of great character, of exceptional willpower. By agreeing with her, I made her sympathetic to me. There is a faint chance – no more – that when she recalls what I said about the dangerous roads she'll change her mind.'

'So why do I get the feeling you're conducting some very devious manoeuvre?' Newman demanded. 'And what time do you plan we reach the Château Noir?'

'Not long after eleven in the morning – when Eve Amberg has arrived there, if she makes the trip.'

38

Paula tapped on Tweed's door at seven the following morning. He called out for her to come in and she found him in the bathroom, shirt collar open as he stood before a mirror shaving.

'Should I come back later?' she suggested. 'You ought to be able to get ready in peace.'

'You've seen a man shaving before today. Sit down while I talk. I need a sounding-board about this whole business – going right back to the massacre at Tresillian Manor.'

'Fire away.' She perched on the edge of the unused bed. 'I'm listening with all my ears, as the French say, and we are in France.'

'So far I have assumed that the same people who blew up our Park Crescent HQ also perpetrated the hideous massacre at Gaunt's manor. You were always sceptical.'

'Yes, I know. Maybe I underestimated the enormous power of the apparatus we're up against.'

'I'm wondering now if *I* gave them a little too much credit for almost superhuman organization – synchronizing the two events.' He wiped soap off his face, cleaned his brush and razor. 'It *would* require truly superhuman planning – to blow up our HQ in London and then commit the massacre all within a few hours.' Tweed's tone sharpened as he put on his tie. 'I honestly don't now believe such timing was possible, that it happened that way. They wouldn't have the information in time – that Amberg was at the manor and that Joel Dyson had deposited copies of the film and the tape with us. Not enough time to organize both the massive car bomb and the massacre way down in Cornwall.'

Paula frowned as she snapped her compact shut after checking her appearance behind Tweed's back. She stared at him as he put on his jacket.

'What you are suggesting contradicts all our theories.'

'*My* wrong theories.' Tweed folded his arms on the back of an upholstered chair and stared down at her. 'It came to me in the middle of the night when I couldn't sleep. I've assumed I was trying to assemble the pieces of a single complex jigsaw. Now I'm sure that there are *two* jigsaws.'

'Help!' said Paula in mock confusion. 'I don't think I could cope with that. Two *separate* jigsaws?'

'No, it's far more diabolical than that. These two jigsaws interlock. To put it simply, one couldn't exist without the other.'

'Simply? If you say so.'

'Paula, it all started with Joel Dyson flying in from the States with a film and a tape. Whatever is recorded on those two items is so earth-shattering that an army of top professionals flies in after Dyson. Those pieces of the jigsaw fit. One jigsaw so far.'

'And these cold-blooded professionals – killers – are all American,' she pointed out.

'True. Ponder that and you might get a glimmer as to who is behind the apparatus controlled by Norton. I admit the idea is world-shaking. Want to guess who?'

'No idea. Go on.'

'Maybe we should have breakfast . . .' Tweed began.

'Let it wait a bit. I want to hear more,' Paula urged him on. 'I sense you've had a mental breakthrough.'

'Let's call the American apparatus Goliath. They track Dyson to Park Crescent, assume – correctly – that he's left the film and tape with us, although they don't know they're copies. Goliath organizes the massive car bomb to destroy the film and tape. Still with Jigsaw One.'

'What about Jigsaw Two?'

'I'm now convinced the massacre at Tresillian Manor was carried out by someone else. Let's borrow Jennie Blade's Shadow Man. He knows Dyson flew on to Zurich with the copies of the film and the tape—'

'Assumption,' Paula objected. 'How do you know that?'

'It's the only sequence of events which explains the new theory I've developed, which I'm sure is the right one. Do let me finish. Shadow Man has to be someone who knows the Ambergs – and therefore knew what Dyson had left with them. He has to be someone who knows the Ambergs,' he repeated, 'because he knew Amberg would be at Tresillian Manor on the day of the massacre. Those two items are worth a fortune – proved by the tremendous efforts the Americans are making to get them back, to eliminate anyone who might know about their existence. Am I going too fast?'

'No. I'm beginning to get ahead of you. Shadow Man wants to lay his hands on film and tape, wants the fortune they could bring him.'

'So, logically, he plans and carries out the massacre at Tresillian Manor. His real target was, of course, Amberg.'

'Why?' Paula enquired.

'Because he knows he can handle the more passive twin – Walter. He also knows he'd never get Julius to release them to him. Solution? Murder Julius. Which leaves the weak Walter to obtain the film and tape from. Hence the two interlocking jigsaws – and the fact that one couldn't exist without the other.'

'I do see what you mean now. Whatever happened in America created a chain reaction among a lot of people.'

'Which is why I insist the two jigsaws are linked like

identical twins.' Tweed gazed into the distance out of the window. The sun shone on steeply slanting rooftops. 'What we need to do is to get hold of that film, see what is on it, and listen to the tape. Which is what I'm going to demand from Amberg when we reach the Château Noir today. He must have hidden them somewhere, may even be carrying them around with him. Now, breakfast.'

'Just before we go down, we have a problem,' Paula warned. 'It's called Jennie Blade. Somehow she's found out we're going up into the Vosges this morning. She insists on coming with us. I argued but got nowhere. She's scared stiff of the Shadow Man.'

'Let Gaunt take care of her,' Tweed said, grasping the door handle. 'She's his girl friend.'

'Gaunt has driven off early this morning in his BMW. He had Eve with him. She didn't look too happy with him. I saw Gaunt heading off towards the Vosges and Eve had her chin up, staring fixedly away from him.'

'I can guess what that was about,' Tweed remarked and smiled wrily. 'Eve wanted to go up to see Amberg at the Château Noir on her own and Gaunt – dominating as ever – bullied her into going with him. He may have made a mistake. Eve can handle even Gaunt if push comes to shove. And we can't be lumbered on this trip with Jennie.'

'Better tell Jennie yourself. Oh, I waved off Marler when he drove away at dawn on his way to the Ballon d'Alsace.'

'Why were you up at that hour?'

Tweed had paused, still holding the door handle. He had not yet unlocked the door while he waited for her reply.

'Couldn't sleep,' Paula told him. 'Something someone said was important and I can't recall it. Got up in the middle of the night, had a shower, got dressed, went downstairs. Which is how I saw Marler before he left for that gliding school. I had an early breakfast, then saw Eve leaving with Gaunt. But I'll join you for more coffee. This is going to be a rough ride up into the Vosges, isn't it? I found all the Americans had checked out early.'

'Yes, it will be a very rough ride up to the heights of the Château Noir,' Tweed warned her.

Tweed and Paula did not breakfast alone in the Brasserie. They had hardly sat down and ordered continental breakfast when Jennie Blade appeared. Clad in ski pants tucked into ankle boots, a white woollen polo-necked sweater which emphasized her figure, and carrying a sheepskin, she sat down at their table, facing Tweed.

'May I join you?'

She gave him a ravishing smile and nodded to Paula who stared back at her without comment.

'You just did,' Tweed pointed out.

'I hope I'm not interrupting an intimate tête-à-tête,' she went on, glancing again at Paula.

'Hardly, at breakfast time,' Tweed replied drily.

'I hear you're driving up into the mountains today. You know' – she gave him her most beguiling smile – 'I couldn't sleep a wink last night – I couldn't get out of my mind my experience with that Shadow Man in the fog. So, please, please, take me with you. You could come back and find me dead.'

'Anything is possible,' Tweed agreed neutrally.

'Then that's settled, you'll take me up there with you – and with you by my side I'll feel perfectly safe, Tweed.'

'Paula is likely to be by my side.' He drank the coffee a waiter had appeared with as though by magic, which Paula had then poured. 'Space will be at a premium,' he said.

'What is the premium you would like me to pay?' Jennie shook her golden mane off her shoulder, gazing at

Tweed with an expression which made Paula grit her teeth. 'I will pay in any currency you specify,' she went on suggestively.

'How about Hungarian forints?' Paula snapped.

'I am asking Mr Tweed,' Jennie said politely, not looking in Paula's direction. 'Seriously, it was a horrible experience last night. And the Met forecast is for more fog this evening. That's when he appears – the Shadow Man. I won't be any trouble. I'll do exactly what you tell me to do – or not to do.' Her voice trembled. 'Please. Oh, please, Tweed. Let me come with you.'

'If I let you,' Tweed said grimly, 'you will obey orders from the word go.' He held up a hand. 'No more protestations. I've laid down the conditions. No more to say.'

Inwardly Paula swore as she savagely piled butter on her croissant. You wily, conniving little devil, she said to herself. What surprised her most was that Tweed had fallen for Jennie's feminine tactics. Or had he? She glanced at Tweed and he looked back without any expression.

Brilliant sunshine reflected off the snow which had descended on Colmar overnight. Tweed screwed up his eyes against the glare of the strong light as he walked alone outside the main entrance to the Bristol. He was waiting for Newman to drive the Espace from where it had been parked overnight.

Locals were hurrying to work. A girl slipped on a patch of invisible ice beneath the snow and Tweed saved her, grabbing her arm. She peered at him gratefully from beneath her hood. '*Merci!*' With her hair concealed under the hood, a scarf pulled up over her chin and drainpipe trousers protruding from under a long padded wind-cheater Tweed had briefly mistaken her for a man.

As he stood near the kerb a large man wearing a hood

with earmuffs and a long heavy trench coat brushed against him. Tweed stiffened as a strong hand gripped his arm.

'Now don't get alarmed, old chum. I've waited for ever for you to come out. Important development . . .'

The American twang was distinctive. Cord Dillon's voice. Tweed stood quite still, clapping his gloved hands together as though feeling the cold. He spoke without looking at the American, his lips hardly moving.

'From now on we must keep in close contact. You can phone me at the hotel after nine in the evening. What is the important development?'

'Special Agent Barton Ives is near by. Wants to talk with you. The recognition signal will be a Union Jack, your national flag.'

'Describe him to me again, briefly . . .'

'About my height. Much slimmer build. Thick black hair. Now clean-shaven. Aged thirty-seven. Strong Anglo-Saxon features. Ice-blue eyes. He'll find you when it's OK. This place is crawling with watchers – hostile.'

'Ives will be taking a chance unless he's careful,' Tweed warned.

'He's careful. He's FBI. Was. Be in touch . . .'

Tweed was still clapping his gloves together in a slow rhythm as Newman arrived with the Espace, punctuating his thoughts. Was one of the two key men in this crisis – Barton Ives and Joel Dyson – really going to contact him? If so how? He wished he'd told Dillon they were on their way into the mountains. Paula walked briskly out of the hotel. It was no surprise that close on her heels Jennie Blade, clad in sheepskin, hurried up to the vehicle.

Tweed wondered if Jennie would have been so eager to join them if she'd known what was facing them during the long climb into the even more heavily snowbound mountains.

39

'We're being followed already,' Newman commented as he drove the grey Espace along the snow-covered road across the plain below the foothills rising in the near distance.

'The big cream Citroën, you mean?' Tweed suggested.

'That's the bastard.' Newman glanced over his shoulder to where Jennie sat. 'Excuse my French but if you had any idea this would be a holiday outing you're in for a very big surprise.'

The Renault Espace V6 was a spacious vehicle which could easily seat six people in three rows. Its large curved snout reminded Paula, seated next to Tweed, of a shark. Tweed occupied the middle seat with Newman on his left. In the row behind them Jennie, huddled in her sheepskin, was curled up like a cat on her seat.

Butler, clad in leathers with a large helmet, had passed them riding a Harley-Davidson and was leading the convoy as it drew closer to Kaysersberg. A distance behind them Nield drove the station wagon with his Walther tucked under a cushion on the front passenger seat.

Philip Cardon, astride his own motorcycle, roared past them, then slowed as his eyes kept swivelling from side to side. The Citroën shadowing them had so far kept well back from Nield's station wagon.

'Why should anyone follow us?' called out Jennie.

'Presumably to see where we're going,' Paula snapped without bothering to turn her head.

'Why would they want to do that?' Jennie persisted.

'So when we skid they can see in time the dangerous stretches of the road,' Paula snapped again. 'Could we possibly have a little quiet so the driver can concentrate? Also I'm checking a map. We're coming into Kaysersberg very shortly,' she warned Newman. 'I can see the old buildings on the outskirts.'

'I'm not worried at all about us skidding,' Jennie went on. 'Bob is a marvellous driver. You should have more confidence in him.'

Paula's eyes blazed as she checked the map again. So far as she was concerned Jennie Blade was spare luggage which could be dumped by the roadside at any time. Tweed, seeing her expression, was secretly amused. He was also suspicious.

Jennie's air of naïvety was just a little too innocent and he was certain she was baiting Paula. Cardon returned on his motorcycle, made a gesture for them to slow down. Newman responded immediately, saw Cardon perform a highly skilled U-turn in the snow, then come racing back, speeding up as he overtook them.

'We shall soon be inside Kaysersberg,' Paula warned again. 'Which probably means we'll have to crawl.'

'Presenting a slow-moving target,' Newman commented.

The ancient buildings of the medieval gem closed round them on both sides as Newman reduced speed to little more than walking pace. Paula stared with admiration at the antique buildings, many with wooden cross-beams buried in the plaster walls and slanting at crazy angles.

'This is wonderful,' she enthused. 'It reeks of character, of the Middle Ages. And look at that hump-backed bridge . . .'

Standing by himself in an alley-way midway inside Kaysersberg, the man wearing a fur hat and an astrakhan

379

coat held a mobile phone to his ear. The aerial was extended as he peered at the bridge through his half-moon glasses and listened to the report from another mobile phone inside the cream Citroën.

'Our main competitor is aboard the grey Espace,' the driver reported. 'Plus a man and two women.'

'Maintain your present position,' Norton ordered. 'Keep well back. I'm talking about survival . . .'

He slid the aerial back inside the phone. Once the Espace started to cross that bridge it was the end of Tweed. One mission accomplished. Château Noir next.

'Brake!' Tweed ordered. 'Stop this vehicle at once.'

Newman obeyed immediately, sat behind the wheel with the engine ticking over. Cardon was approaching on his motorcycle. Newman was mystified by Tweed's sudden command.

'What is this in aid of? The pause?' he enquired.

'Something about that bridge I don't like. If I were planning an ambush – and ruthlessly, didn't care tuppence about innocent civilian casualties – that bridge would be the death-trap.'

'I think we may have a problem,' Cardon said, speaking through the open window, straddled on his machine. 'I suggest you don't proceed any further until Butler and I have spied out the lie of the land. OK?'

'What triggered off this mood of caution?' Tweed asked.

'There's an old castle perched up just behind these old houses. Anyone located on top has a perfect view of the bridge and any vehicle crossing it. Harry and I saw at least one man at the summit of the keep – with what looked like a rifle in his hands. I'm going to check under the bridge, Harry takes the castle. Sit tight.'

'Look! A lovely cat . . .'

Before Tweed could stop her Paula had opened the door, jumped out and was walking briskly behind Cardon who was approaching the bridge on foot, leaving his motorbike leaning against the Espace. There was a large fat cat on the parapet of the bridge and Tweed knew she was fond of cats. But he also noticed she had undone the flap of her shoulder-bag next to her hip. Inside was an easily accessible pocket which had been specially designed to take her .32 Browning.

Tweed watched as Paula, clad in a padded windcheater and ski pants tucked into leather boots with rubber soles, strode confidently on to the bridge. Any watcher was unlikely to suspect her of being anything but a ski-season tourist.

She picked up the heavily furred cat which was coffee-coloured with white 'stockings' and a white chest. She glanced around as it purred at her attentions and saw the swiftly moving figure of Harry Butler disappearing below the looming castle. Cardon had referred to a 'keep' and this was a great round tower rearing up above the rest of the edifice. She nipped one of the ears of the cat which protested, prepared to leap out of her arms. She aimed it over the edge of the parapet on to the snow-covered bank at the edge of the frozen stream.

Cardon, seeing the opportunity she'd provided, lowered himself over the stone wall as though in pursuit of the animal. Agilely, Paula dropped over the wall, followed him under the bridge. The cat perched on a snowbound rock at the far end of the arch, glaring at them. Cardon raised a warning hand.

Paula followed the direction of his pointing finger. An explosives expert, Cardon recognized lethal hardware. Attached by ropes to ancient iron rings in the centre of the arch was suspended a large metal plate supporting a large number of what appeared to Paula to be Roman-candle type fireworks.

'Dynamite sticks,' Cardon commented. 'That collection adds up to one big bomb, powerful enough to blast the stone bridge and any vehicle on it sky-high.'

'It can hardly work by pressure of a vehicle crossing the bridge,' Paula mused. She was scared stiff and kept talking to conceal her reaction. 'Otherwise a farm wagon could have set it off at any time.'

'Correct,' Cardon agreed. 'A bit diabolical this one. See that grey cable running from the bomb to the other end of the arch near where the cat is? Butler, who has a nasty mind, scraped away snow from the base of one of the old buildings near the climb to the castle. He found more of that cable. The snow kept people indoors last night, now it's concealing the cable this morning.'

'Where does the cable end? Can we cut it?'

'My guess is that if we did it would blow us sky-high. It runs to the top of the castle keep – where someone watching can press the button at the right moment.'

Butler took long careful strides through the snow as he reached the heavy wooden door leading into the castle rearing up above him. The snow was a giveaway – other footprints had preceded his to this same doorway.

He turned the iron ring-handle slowly, making not a sound as he pushed the door inwards inch by inch. For a sturdily built man Butler could move with deadly silence. He held the Luger in his right hand as he padded inside, closed the door with the same care behind him.

Waiting while he listened, while his eyes accustomed themselves to the dim light, he heard nothing. Ahead of him a stone staircase climbed alongside the outer wall of the castle. He used a large handkerchief to clean snow off the soles of his shoes. If it came to a showdown he did not want his feet slipping from under him. He began to mount the staircase, following a trail of snow patches which he guessed the man above him had left behind off his own soles when he'd made the same ascent.

Butler came to a point where an archway led off the main staircase to another narrower staircase which curved up constantly. He guessed that this led up round the sides of the looming turret to the high roof where he'd glimpsed a man with a weapon. Again Butler knew he was heading in the right direction – a fresh tell-tale trail of snow patches smeared the well-worn stone steps, steps smoothed down by footfalls over the centuries.

A draught of even colder fresh air warned him he was near the exit at the summit. It was freezing cold on the spiral staircase and the snow patches had frozen solid. He took a firmer grip on the Luger as he edged round a corner and saw an archway framing the clear blue sky beyond. He had to get there in time – he knew Cardon would be investigating what the opposition had planted underneath the bridge.

'You really should get the hell out of here, Paula,' Cardon warned. 'I make one false move deactivating this bomb and we both end up playing harps in the sky.'

'You mean two and a quarter of us,' Paula joked to hide her fear. 'Don't forget Puss. He would take a fancy to me at this moment.'

The cat had come running back to her, had reached up with its forepaws on her right leg. She'd picked it up and tickled it under its ear while Cardon made his preliminary examination with a pencil torch. Philip, she thought, always seemed to carry a complete tool-kit with him.

'Can't I help you in some way?' she pressed.

'Well . . .'

He was reluctant to agree, but he knew it would be safer if he had an extra pair of hands. No, he decided, scare her well away from this potential tomb before he

383

started experimenting. He gestured with the secateurs he'd taken from a small cloth hold-all.

'Look, Paula, this is the score. I count six sticks of dynamite – probably stolen from a stone quarry. Plenty of them with explosives stores in the Vosges. Now – to neutralize, make them inert sticks of nothing – I have to cut six cables attached to six detonators. It's a crude but effectively improvised bomb. So I cut each of the green cables . . .'

'Not the red ones?' The cat was still purring as she tickled it under the ear. 'I always thought red was for danger.'

'That is the crude trick they played.' Cardon turned his pink healthy face towards Paula and grinned. 'I've checked this thingumajig carefully. To render it harmless I've got to snip through six *green* cables. That was their idea of a boobytrap. Assuming, of course, I know what I'm doing. You know what an explosives expert will tell you? That you can never rely on explosives reacting as they're supposed to. Still want to risk hanging about here?'

'What can I do to help?'

'It's your funeral – mine too. See this canvas bag I brought from the bike? As I snip a cable I'll take hold of a stick of dynamite and hand it to you. Then you lay it carefully in the bottom of the bag. Put the next jigger alongside it.'

'What are we waiting for?' Paula enquired as she placed the cat in the snow.

'I don't like it,' Tweed said from his seat in the Espace. 'Philip has found something under that bridge – and Paula is down there with him. I'm going to see what's going on.'

Newman grasped him by the arm, forced him down back into his seat.

'You're going nowhere at all. What's the matter with you? Lost your capacity for waiting? You've always been hot on that aspect of our work. How many times have you told members of your team who were getting impatient that they must learn to wait?'

'I suppose you're right.'

'I know I am,' Newman said firmly. 'We may be under observation. Two people under the bridge is enough. Just hope there's no big bang.'

Butler stood three steps below the archway leading out on to the flat roof. He held the Luger gripped in both hands, aimed at the Norman arch. He was waiting to hear something that would tell him where the man – or men – who had climbed the tower before him were located.

The waiting was getting on his nerves. He couldn't forget the cable he'd found by scraping his foot along the base of the stone wall of a house near the castle. He couldn't forget that Cardon was probably now beneath the bridge, fooling around with God knew what devilish device.

The pressure was almost unbearable, the urge to dash out on to the roof, but he resisted the overwhelming temptation. Then, without warning, the back of a heavily built man clad in a windcheater and jeans appeared as he stood close to the edge of the low parapet. Butler realized he was staring at something through binoculars. He spoke to some unseen person. The twang was American.

'Gary, that friggin' Espace is still stuck a distance from the bridge. Looks like they could be staying there all day. Would the bomb reach them? Debris from the bridge? Great hunks of rock. Shall we give it a try?'

'Norton said to wait till it was on the bridge.'

'Gary, Norton is the friggin' Invisible Man. We can see the situation. And that girl who was fooling with that cat has gone to earth under the bridge. What say we give it a try? Hell, Norton is probably filling his belly in some upmarket restaurant in Strasbourg while we freeze.'

'If you say so, Mick. But it was you who . . .'

Butler jumped on to the platform. Mick, by the parapet, reacted with the speed of a pro, hauled out an automatic from inside his windcheater. He never had a chance to take aim as two bullets from Butler's 9-mm. Luger slammed into his chest. The force of the bullets toppled the thug over the edge. Butler never saw his arms and legs splay in his final fall into eternity. He had swung the Luger's muzzle to where Gary was crouched over a square box with a handle protruding a foot from the top. Gary's clawed hands descended, ready to grasp the handle, to depress the plunger.

Butler shot him twice in the left armpit. Gary jerked upright, blood streaming over his windcheater, staggering above the deadly box. Butler walked forward, used the muzzle of his weapon to shove the reeling American to the brink. He fell backwards and this time Butler saw what looked like a matchstick man plunging into the depths, both arms stretched out like a swimmer. He struck a projecting rock, was thrown off it by his own momentum and vanished into a tangle of deep undergrowth. No sign of Mick. He must have vanished into the same wilderness.

Butler slid the Luger back inside his hip holster, bent over the detonating mechanism. Cardon had trained him in explosives and Butler realized this was a crude improvised effort, reminiscent of photographs he'd seen of similar devices used in the First World War.

He took hold of the handle gently, twisted it slowly. It unscrewed anti-clockwise. He lifted the handle clear of the box, went to the edge of the parapet and threw the handle into the undergrowth which now concealed two bodies.

*   *   *

Paula had taken five of the six sticks of dynamite from Cardon and placed them carefully in the open canvas bag. The danger came from a most unexpected direction.

'Here you are. That's the last one. All OK,' Cardon said as he handed Paula the sixth stick of dynamite.

She had reached out her right hand, had grasped the stick, when the fat cat appeared out of nowhere, leapt up on to her left arm. It must have weighed almost nine pounds and threw her off balance.

She performed several reflex actions at once. Moving her right foot out, ramming it deep into the snow, she stood straddled in a desperate attempt to maintain her balance. Still gripping the dynamite stick in her right hand, she clutched at the great ball of fur and muscle with her left hand, hugging it to her breast. The cat dug its forepaws into the shoulder of her padded jacket, which at least relieved her of some of the weight. For Paula, the last straw was when it began to purr with pleasure.

'I could kill you,' she said in a deliberately affectionate tone which wouldn't disturb it.

'Stay just as you are,' Cardon said. 'I'm going to take the stick out of your hand. I'll tell you when to let go. Easy does it . . . Now, I've got it . . .'

Crouching down, he slid the last stick alongside the others, used a collection of chamois cloths he kept inside the bag to separate one stick from another. When he'd zipped the bag closed he looked up.

'I could throw this hunk into that frozen stream,' Paula told him.

The cat, still purring, had closed its eyes. It was going to sleep – unlike Norton who was standing in the main street of Kaysersberg, waiting expectantly.

Norton had been standing patiently outside the entrance to a small bar for over half an hour. He excelled in patience. He had pushed up his fur hat so that it was clear of his ears. His eyes showed no warmth, no particular expression as he waited for the sound of the explosion. He had stepped back from viewing the bridge. It was a sizeable bomb his men had placed under it during the ice-cold night when the streets were deserted.

He stiffened as he heard a vehicle approaching, moved back further out of sight into the entrance. The station wagon, driven by Nield, crawled past him, bumping over the cobbles. The Harley-Davidson, with Butler on the saddle, appeared, overtook Nield, headed west out of the village for the Vosges. Almost at once a grey Espace crawled past, also bumping over the old cobbles. It was moving so slowly Norton had a clear view of Tweed in one of the front passenger seats.

A second motorcycle ridden by Philip Cardon brought up the rear of the convoy. Norton waited until the sound of its engine had died away and the heavy silence of the snowbound morning descended again. Taking out his mobile phone, Norton contacted Mencken who was located high up in the mountains.

'Norton here. Our competitors are leaving Kaysersberg. Their director is a passenger in a grey Espace which is driven by a man and also is carrying two women. Two motorcycles and a station wagon are escorting them. So activate Phase Two. Immediately. Understood?'

'OK. Understood. So OK!' Mencken's rasping voice acknowledged.

Norton slid back the aerial inside his instrument, walked down to a side street where his hired blue Renault was parked. The next stage was to drive towards the Château Noir. Long before he reached it Tweed would be eliminated. Norton didn't waste a moment's thought as to why the bomb had not exploded. A faulty detonator? It didn't matter. Mencken was waiting for his target. Norton was indeed a man who excelled in patience.

40

'There will be fresh attempts to ambush us,' Tweed warned as they left Kaysersberg behind and the road spiralled up.

'What made you really suspect that bridge?' Newman asked.

'Sixth sense. Reverse thinking, if you like.'

'What's that?' Paula asked.

'Knowing the route between Colmar and the Château Noir the average man would assume the real danger would lie high up in the remote regions of the Vosges . . .'

'But you're not the average man,' Jennie remarked, leaning her arms on the back of Tweed's seat. 'Do go on.'

That's right, dear, Paula was thinking cynically, lay on the flattery with a trowel.

'Reverse thinking,' Tweed explained, ignoring the interruption, 'is like looking through the wrong end of a telescope. Turn everything round, and learn from any precedent where you can. We have one – demonstrating Norton's callousness when it comes to loss of innocent human life. The attack on us in the Bahnhofstrasse – where the second killer had a machine-pistol and was about to use it until Bob shot him. Spraying a weapon like that in a crowded city street could easily have caused fatal casualties to bystanders. So blowing up a bridge in Kaysersberg which could have killed several locals bothered Norton not one jot.'

'This is going to be a dangerous journey, then,' Jennie suggested.

'Well, you were warned before you joined us,' rapped out Paula.

'Oh, I'm not frightened. That man on top of that rock was watching us through something,' she went on. 'I saw the sun flashing off glass, maybe binoculars.'

'Are you sure it wasn't imagination?' queried Paula.

'Check it,' Tweed ordered Newman. 'Jennie may well have seen something . . .'

Despite its snow tyres, the Espace was rocking as it passed over hardened ruts. Newman slowed to a stop on a steep incline, lowered his window. Arctic-like air flowed into the vehicle. Paula could now see the massive bluffs and high knife-edge ridges of the Vosges very clearly in the glaring sunlight. Cardon appeared at Newman's window, paused astride his machine.

'Something suspicious ahead of us,' Newman began.

'On the top of that ridge,' Jennie said, leaning forward, aiming her extended arm and index finger like a gun. 'I *know* I saw at least one man.'

'Keep the Espace parked here,' Cardon said as Butler returned and pulled up astride his own machine. 'We'll investigate.' He looked at Paula. 'Those dynamite sticks we collected may come in useful. I've got them in my panniers.' He pointed to the containers slung from either side of his machine. 'See you . . .'

'He's got grenades,' Tweed commented.

'Saving them for a rainy day,' Paula suggested.

After a brief conversation between Cardon and Butler the two men sped off up the curving ascent, bouncing

390

over the ruts. Newman took out a pair of binoculars and scanned the ridge Jennie had pointed at. No sign of anyone, so maybe Paula had been right in suggesting it was Jennie's imagination.

Carrying out the plan they had improvised, Butler and Cardon each played a separate role. Butler continued riding at reduced speed up the road, acting as bait. Behind him Cardon had turned his machine off the road and sped under the lee of the ridge which made him invisible to any watcher on the heights. Before leaving the Espace he had tucked one stick of dynamite, folded inside his scarf, behind his belt. The ground was rough, treacherous, the snow concealing rocks and dips, and he prayed the vibration would not disturb the dynamite. Should have used a grenade instead. Too late to worry about that now.

Cardon was aiming to mount the ridge at its northern extremity where he was likely to have a sweeping view over the entire terrain. He just hoped he'd reach that position before Butler rode up the section of the spiral road which passed under the ridge. He gritted his teeth as the machine bucked like a wild bronco, kept his balance, saw he was close to the end of the ridge. Then up, up, up!

Newman sat very erect in his seat, binoculars screwed close to his eyes. Butler was now approaching the point where he'd be most vulnerable – *if* Jennie had seen someone up on the ridge.

Cardon had vanished from sight. Newman guessed he was driving his machine to the limit over very rough terrain. He wished to Heaven he was with them, helping out.

Tweed had steeled himself to remain calm, passive. Every instinct made him want to snatch the binoculars from Newman. *To see for himself!* Beside him he felt

Paula shift her position and guessed the tension was mounting for everyone inside the Espace. Then he felt Jennie's gloved knuckles pressing into his shoulder. His tone of voice was off-hand when he spoke.

'Not much going on up there, Bob?'

'I'm not sure. I thought I saw something.'

'Tell us what you think your something was,' Tweed requested, his manner still deliberately low-key.

'Movement on the ridge,' Newman said tersely.

'Can you be a little more specific?'

'Thought I saw two men, but it was only a quick glimpse.'

'Keep looking. Let us know if there are any fresh developments, please.'

Newman had closed his window earlier and now the heaters were beginning to build up a more bearable atmosphere inside the Espace. The two men and the two women sat like waxwork figures, not moving as they stared up the ascent to the ridge which reminded Tweed of the back of some prehistoric beast. But the growing warmth did nothing to reduce the rising tension inside the vehicle.

'Harry Butler is nearly at the real danger point,' Paula observed quietly.

She was right, Tweed thought grimly. Butler was approaching a location where to his left the road stood at the edge of a sheer abyss. Worse still, to his right the eastern tip of the ridge was a gradual and shallow slope from the summit to the road – exposing him fully to any firepower which might be aimed at him from above.

'Oh, God!' Paula exclaimed. 'No . . .!'

'Two men, both armed with machine-pistols, point-blank range,' Newman reported in a dull tone.

Butler must have sensed danger. Through his glasses Newman saw him bring his machine to a sudden halt. He was staring up to the summit of the slope as both men took aim with their weapons. Cardon appeared out of nowhere from behind the ridge, stopped his machine so suddenly the back wheel jumped off the ground. He was about thirty feet from the American killers. Distracted for a moment, they turned round as Cardon hoisted his arm like a cricket bowler about to throw the ball. A missile sped through the air, landed almost at the feet of the two potential assassins.

The dynamite exploded with a thumping roar they heard inside the closed Espace. A fountain of rock hurtled skywards, mingled with the blood-stained remnants of his targets. The mangled debris moved in an arc, fell straight down on to the road a few yards in front of where Butler had paused. The upper half of one American, severed at the trunk, littered the road. Butler walked his machine forward, used the wheel to nose the relic over the edge into the abyss.

On the ridge Cardon had ridden his machine the short distance to where he could look down on the road. Butler gazed at him, gave the thumbs-up sign, which Cardon returned. Perched on the summit Cardon couldn't resist the gesture. Staring towards where the Espace waited, he beckoned them on with a grand wave. *Advance!*

'Let's get moving,' Tweed said in a businesslike manner. 'I want to be at the Château Noir as close to eleven as we can. And Pete Nield behind us is champing at the bit in his station wagon. I *must* talk to Amberg.'

Higher up amid the snows of the Vosges there was another more distant watcher who had observed everything. Seated in a green Renault – the colour merging well with surrounding evergreens – Mencken had positioned himself on a platform which provided an almost uninterrupted view of route N415. He now had the undesirable obligation to report to Norton.

'Don't apologize to the creep,' he told himself.

He dialled Norton on his mobile phone, watching the progress of the convoy towards him far below. They were well organized – he'd give them that, the bloody Brits.

'Norton here,' the familiar voice answered after a lot of atmospherics.

'Mencken. Phase Two of the experiment was a complete bust. I do mean complete,' he continued, piling it on. 'There are two more players out of the game.'

'Plenty more from where they came from,' Norton responded with his usual considerate regard for human life. 'I am now sure our competitors, who are coming up via Route Two, will return via Route One. There the possibilities for the neutralization of the opposition are more promising. You will now assemble the team for the château.'

'Understood,' confirmed Mencken.

'And I hope you also understand that our competitors must never reach Colmar again. That would disturb me. More to the point, you would find it disturbing . . .'

Mencken swore as he realized Norton was no longer in touch on the phone. His language was an attempt to ignore the fear he felt from Norton's last words. They had implied a lethal threat to Mencken in the event of failure.

Seated behind the wheel of his Renault, Norton drove on up into the mountains after giving his orders to Mencken. He was beginning to have his first doubts as to whether Marvin Mencken was the man for the job. He'd decide about that later.

Norton's next priority was the coming assault on the Château Noir. It was just possible that Amberg had the film and the tape with him in his castle. That would solve the whole problem.

But Norton was not banking on this. He had his six in

394

the evening rendezvous with Growly Voice at Lac Noir. Here he had a problem. He'd been instructed to come alone – and to continue to conceal his appearance he would have to go to this isolated spot by himself. It was not a prospect he relished – meeting someone whose identity was as secret as his own. He hoped it was a rendezvous he'd never have to keep.

Finally, Norton thought, ticking off priorities, Tweed and his team would be eliminated before nightfall. Phoning Mencken in Colmar, he had coded the way into the Vosges via Kaysersberg as Route Two – N415. The more southerly way into the mountains – D417 – had been coded as Route One. Which was where Tweed would perish.

41

Paula gazed in wonderment at the Ice Age world they had entered at this high altitude. Massive snow-covered bluffs loomed far above them as Newman guided the Espace higher and higher up a diabolical spiral. Suspended from overhanging crags were immense spears of ice like stalactites. They were now near enough to the summit to have lost the sun, driving in cold menacing shadow on the side road Newman had turned along.

She shivered inwardly as she peered up at the immensity of snow and ice hovering above them. She had the feeling it might all topple on them at any moment, burying them under a sea of snow and ice for ever.

'Don't think the sun ever reaches here,' Tweed commented.

'I think it's getting creepy,' Jennie replied.

'You ain't seen nothing yet,' Newman joked. 'Look what is coming up. Ladies and gentlemen, our guided tour of the Vosges has just reached Lac Noir. The infamous Black Lake.'

'Time we stretched our legs, limbered up,' Tweed suggested. 'We're close to the château and want to arrive fresh.'

'Oh, my God! What a horror,' Paula burst out as she stepped out after Tweed.

Newman had switched off the engine and a terrible silence descended on them. The Espace had been stopped close to a low stone wall. Beyond it the waters of Lac Noir stretched away – waters black as pitch and still as a pit of tar, which Paula thought it resembled. Worse still, the small lake ended at the base of a black granite cliff facing them – a cliff which rose vertical and sheer in the bleak shadows. Paula looked slowly up the wall of the cliff and felt dizzy when she saw the iron-hard line of the summit, the hideous medieval-like castle which stood perched way above them on the high brink. It was the intense stillness as much as the Siberian cold which paralysed her mind as she gazed at the monstrous edifice, the fantasy brought into existence by some crazy American millionaire Heaven knew how long ago. There were lights in the château windows – there would have to be on this grim shadowed side.

'A bit bleak round here,' Tweed commented.

'Bloody terrifying,' replied Jennie who had climbed out after the others.

'That's a bit of an exaggeration,' Tweed said, aware the atmosphere was affecting morale. 'Bob, I want to get up to the château at the earliest possible moment – to see Amberg . . .'

The drive up the narrow precipitous road overhanging the southern end of the lake was a nightmare. Newman had his headlights on as he drove up and round hairpin bends with fearsome drops into the black water now far below.

'Some Grand Tour of the Vosges,' Paula said bitingly.

'At least it's a unique experience,' Jennie responded as she peered out of the window down the endless drop.

'One way of looking at it,' Paula snapped.

'One positive way of looking at it,' Jennie corrected her.

'Are you trying to pick a verbal fight with me?' Paula demanded, twisting round in her seat to glare at the other woman.

'Why should I want to do that?' Jennie flashed back, her eyes blazing. 'And I do have my uses – in case it has slipped what passes for your mind, I spotted those men on the ridge. Butler could be dead by now if I had not warned Tweed.'

'All right. You were a help, a big help. You saw something I missed and should have seen.'

Paula was startled. Jennie could be a hellcat, had looked at Paula as though she could have strangled her. Tweed wasn't prepared to be distracted by a female dispute as the moment approached when he would confront Amberg.

'If both of you would keep quiet maybe I could think. So not another word. Bob, we must be close now.'

'We'll reach the summit within five minutes,' reported Paula, who despite her altercation with Jennie had kept a close eye on the map. 'From there it appears to be no distance at all to the château.'

Tweed looked ahead at a moment when the snake of a road was inclined at an angle of forty-five degrees. Butler, who was still preceding them on his motorcycle, paused briefly, waved Newman on, continued the ascent on his machine.

Glancing back over his shoulder the view made Tweed

feel dizzy. Inclined at this precipitous angle he was staring down direct on to the deathly stillness of Black Lake – so far below now he almost suffered an attack of vertigo.

'Don't look back,' he warned Paula and Jennie. 'That's an order.'

Behind the Espace Nield was driving the station wagon up the ascent with Cardon bringing up the rear on his motorcycle. The system of the two outriders racing back and forth past the vehicles which had been employed earlier was now impossible. Any attempt by Cardon to overtake the station wagon and then the Espace would undoubtedly have ended with his machine falling over the brink and plunging hundreds of feet into the still waters of Black Lake.

'I think we've reached the top,' Paula called out, unable to suppress the relief she felt.

Butler had again paused, twisting round in his saddle to give the 'V' for victory sign. The road levelled out, Paula risked a quick glimpse back, saw only a projecting rock bluff which masked any view of the lake or the panorama beyond. She swung her head to face front.

'We're home and dry! There's the Château Noir. A grim-looking brute, but it's heaven to be back on the level. Home and dry,' she repeated.

'Not my idea of home,' Tweed commented. 'Just look at the place.'

Paula gazed at the high granite wall surrounding the great castle, at the huge square stone keep rising up even higher than any other part of the grim structure. Newman had stopped the Espace close under the lee of the wall, close to but out of sight of the tall wrought-iron gates which barred the entrance.

Nield parked his station wagon behind the Espace, got out to speak to Tweed, and was joined by Butler and

Cardon. Tweed had jumped out of the Espace and stood stretching the stiffness out of his arms and legs. It had been a somewhat tense journey, he reflected.

'How do we handle it?' asked Newman as Paula and Jennie followed him out into the bitter air.

'Tactfully – until we get inside,' Tweed replied.

Paula gazed round, relieved also to be able to exercise her limbs which had become tense with fear and anxiety. At least on this side of the château they were in the full blaze of the sun shining down out of a clear blue sky. But still there was the brooding silence of the high Vosges and she stamped her boots in the iron-hard snow to stop herself shivering. Cardon pointed to a wire elevated above the top of the wall which ran out of sight.

'Electrified,' he commented. 'I hope Amberg doesn't rely on that for security – I could neutralize it inside five minutes.'

Tweed addressed Nield, Butler and Cardon after checking his watch.

'I'm going to insist that Amberg allows you inside with your transport. As soon as you're parked check the layout of the whole set-up from the outside. Look for weak points where an attack might be launched. Plan a defence of the whole castle.'

'You're expecting an assault?' Newman queried.

'Norton's objective right from the beginning has been to get hold of the mysterious film and tape. He'll think – as I do – that Amberg has them in his safekeeping. So yes, an assault is possible – even probable. Now let's hope Amberg is at home . . .'

Tweed left the others hidden behind the wall. Marching up to the closed gates, he operated the speakphone he'd seen embedded in the left-hand gate pillar, pressing the button below the metal grille. He had to press it again before a disembodied voice he recognized spoke.

'Who are you?' the voice demanded in German.

399

'This is Tweed outside,' he said, speaking in English. 'I must talk to you urgently.'

'Someone else called here yesterday, said he was Tweed. He was an imposter, an American. How do I know you are the genuine Tweed?'

Paula, who was watching Tweed closely, saw a very strange expression cross his face. If she hadn't known him so well she'd have sworn it was bewilderment, but Tweed was never bewildered.

'All right,' Tweed continued, 'you want proof of my identity. You had an identical twin brother, Julius. He was murdered in a wholesale massacre at Tresillian Manor in Cornwall. Just before he left Swizterland on that fatal trip he was separated from his wife, Eve, who is English. I visited her at her villa on the heights above the Limmat in Zurich. I met you, Walter, a few days ago before you left Zurich for Basle. Bob Newman was with me. Look, surely that's enough, for God's sake!' he ended with deliberate exasperation.

'I am sorry, Tweed. I do hope you realize I have to take precautions. Actually, you have said more than enough for me to recognize your distinctive voice. When the buzzer sounds the gates will open . . .'

'One more point,' Tweed interjected. 'I have Newman and Paula Grey with me. I also have three guards – members of my organization. I want them to enter the courtyard I can see through the gates as protection.'

'I agree. Listen for the buzzer.'

Paula had again been watching Tweed closely. He had bent his ear close to the metal grille while Amberg spoke and when he straightened up he was frowning. He looked at Paula and his expression became blank. Raising his hand he gestured for them all to move into the stone-flagged courtyard as the automatically operated gates swung inwards. Paula joined him as they walked swiftly towards the large stone porch which appeared to be the main entrance.

'Has something disturbed you?' she asked.

He pointed towards the right-hand corner of the huge stone façade which reared above them. Parked almost out of sight was a white BMW.

'Looks very much like Gaunt's,' Paula commented.

'I think we'll find it is Gaunt's . . .'

Amberg himself, again neatly dressed in a black business suit, opened the heavy door to let Tweed, Paula and Newman inside. Paula blinked at the vastness of the entrance hall, at the poor illumination provided by the sconces on the walls. Amberg stroked a hand across his well-brushed hair after closing and locking the door.

'Will you please excuse me for a few minutes? I can hear the phone going and I'm expecting an important call. Eve has come for a business discussion. Gaunt, who brought her, will take you to her. A little pleasant company in my absence . . .'

Gaunt, who greeted them as though their arrival was the most natural event, led them through a series of stone passages and up and down flights of ancient stone steps. As he led the way he called back to them as though he owned the place.

'Remarkable place, this château. Of course the Yankee who had it built on the basis of old plans was mad as a hatter. But he was Yankee to the core. Show you some of the bathrooms later. Now, ladies and gentlemen, we are about to enter the largest bathroom of all,' he boomed.

His voice echoed back along the labyrinth of passages they had walked through. Paula was dying to tell him to cut down on the decibels. Gaunt had paused before a pair of large double doors shaped like a Norman arch. With a grandiloquent gesture, he opened both of them, gestured for them to enter. Tweed nodded to Paula to go ahead in front of him. She did so and stopped abruptly, suppressing a gasp of astonishment.

She was gazing at a vast swimming pool, entirely constructed of marble. Enclosed under an arched roof, the marble covered all the surrounding surfaces. A figure was swimming in the pool, racing up and down the full length with powerful breast-strokes.

Eve Amberg had tucked her titian hair inside a black cap and was clad in a one-piece black bathing costume. She waved to Paula as she reached one end, paused at the foot of a ladder, called out to her.

'Welcome to Valhalla! Be with you in a minute. I have to complete thirty lengths. Make yourselves comfortable in those chairs . . .'

Then she was off again. As Tweed and Newman walked over to comfortable chairs round a table, Paula watched Eve. The Englishwoman was an incredibly strong swimmer. Her long limbs glided through the greenish water, her slim arms moved like pistons. Thirty lengths! I couldn't do that, Paula thought, and I'm a few years younger than she is. As she wandered towards the table Eve reached the ladder, paused, shinned up it, stood on the edge of the pool, reached for a large towel. Drying her shoulders, she stripped off her cap and her mane cascaded down her back.

'You look stunning,' Paula commented as she sat down at the table.

'Thank you, Paula. After that, I do feel good.'

Eve had a flair for clothes, Paula mused. With her titian hair the black one-piece costume was a perfect choice. Gaunt, who had stood by the side of the pool, watching her with his arms folded, joined the others at the table. There was a whole array of glasses, bottles and one decanter.

'I'm mine host,' Gaunt announced. 'Amberg was involved with yet another phone call when we arrived, showed us the way to this palace of pleasures. Talking of pleasure, who's for a double Scotch to get things going?'

'I'll have a glass of Riesling,' Eve called out. 'Tweed, maybe you'd pour me a glass – providing you pour one for yourself. It's good Riesling.'

'Certainly,' Tweed replied. 'You brought a swimming costume with you?' he suggested conversationally as he poured two glasses.

'I did. This pool is heated. I used to swim here when poor Julius brought me here from time to time. Hate the rest of the place. Like a blasted mausoleum. But the pool is terrific.'

She had towelled herself all over, brought another dry towel to sit on. She stood very erect while she answered Tweed's question.

'I'll go change into something decent in a few minutes, but if you don't mind me like this I'm gasping for some wine.'

'I don't mind you like that at all,' Newman told her and smiled. 'Feel free to join us.'

'I suppose you're both here on a social visit,' Tweed suggested after raising his glass to Eve.

'You know jolly well I'm not,' she rebuked him, following it up with a winning smile. 'Business is business.'

'And you, Gaunt?' Tweed enquired, turning in his seat to the large figure occupying the seat next to him.

'I'm here to find out who used my manor as a blood bath . . .' Gaunt had lowered his tone so only Tweed could hear. 'I'm not leaving until Amberg has put on his picture show, with talkies.'

'He's admitted he has those items here?' Tweed queried in a whisper.

Newman, sensing the two men wanted to talk in

403

secrecy, was joking in a loud voice, causing Paula and Eve to become near-hysterical.

'Not exactly,' Gaunt confessed in the same grim tone. 'He can be very evasive, very Swiss in the least complimentary sense.'

'Then I'll have to talk to him. By myself. Now would be a good moment if I knew where to find him.'

'Show you the way.' Gaunt stood up, bent down as he added the remark, 'Suspect you and I are on the same side in this one.'

I wonder, Tweed thought, but he smiled agreement as he stood up. Gaunt explained to the others that they had a bit of business to discuss with Amberg, hoped they'd excuse their absence.

'Take all day as far as I'm concerned,' Newman assured him breezily. 'I'm more than happy chatting with two interesting women . . .'

Gaunt left Tweed in the strange quarters Amberg used as his office, the vast room with the raised dais and behind it the huge picture window with a panoramic view down over the Vosges, across the flat plain to the distant hump which was the Black Forest in Germany.

Still standing, Tweed studied the small, portly Swiss with his black hair slicked back over his high forehead – no parting – and the thick brows above the shrewd blue eyes. Did he always wear this depressing black suit? Tweed asked himself.

'Please sit down,' Amberg invited, indicating the low chair placed beneath the dais.

'Thank you. I'm sure you won't mind if I join you,' Tweed said at his most amiable.

Picking up the chair, he stepped up on to the dais, walked round the large desk, planted the chair next to Amberg's and sat down, facing him.

404

'What is the problem?' Amberg asked in a peevish tone. 'I haven't a lot of time.'

'You have all the time in the world,' Tweed assured him, 'but first I want to view the film, listen to the tape – the two items Joel Dyson left with you for safekeeping.'

'I don't understand what you're talking about,' snapped the Swiss, and he pursed his thin lips.

'I'm talking about murder on a grand scale. Mass murder at Tresillian Manor in Cornwall.' Tweed's manner was no longer amiable. 'I'm talking about the murders of Helen Frey, her friend Klara and the private investigator, Theo Strebel. All of which took place on your home patch – in Zurich.' He paused. Amberg stared back at him with a blank expression, but Tweed thought he detected a hint of alarm in those blank eyes. 'Theo Strebel was an ex-member of the Zurich Homicide force, a close friend of Arthur Beck who, as you know, is Chief of the Swiss Federal Police at the Taubenhalde in Berne. Beck also happens to be a close friend of mine. So produce the film and the tape or Beck will be waiting for you the moment you return to Zurich. Which is it to be?'

Unusually, Tweed had fired all his guns in one massive verbal barrage. The effect was electrifying.

'It is a question of ethics,' Amberg began in a feeble tone. 'Joel Dyson gave us those items to keep for him.'

'Forget the ethics. Didn't you know? Dyson may be dead. He hasn't been seen alive since he visited your bank in Talstrasse. Another fact which will interest Beck.'

'I do have a small cinema at a lower level,' Amberg said.

'And the film and the tape?'

'They are in a safe here. I'll get them now. Also we have a recorder to play the tape on.'

'Good. I want to synchronize the film with the sounds on the tape. And Gaunt also would like to be present. At long last we are getting somewhere.'

42

Like a general planning a major battle, Mencken stood up in the front of the Land-Rover he had driven up into the Vosges. He had hired the vehicle before leaving Basle, anticipating driving over some rough country.

From where he'd parked the four-wheel drive – on the edge of a small copse of evergreens – he could look down on the Château Noir, scanning the interior courtyard with binoculars. In the back two of his men sat carrying machine-pistols.

'We launch the attack precisely at noon. So synchronize your watches,' Mencken ordered. 'It is now exactly fifteen minutes to noon. Repeat the instructions I gave you. Word for word or I'll break your necks.'

'At noon,' Eddie began, reciting by rote, 'I blow open those gates to let the cars burst into that yard with the troops they'll be carrying.'

'Hank?' Mencken prodded.

Eddie and Hank were the two men who had been on the verge of torturing Jennie Blade when Tweed and his men had stormed into her bedroom at the Hôtel Bristol. Both men were still on Mencken's list for liquidation, but maybe someone else would do the job for him in the coming assault.

'At one minute to noon,' reported the tall lean Hank, 'I neutralize that electric wire running atop the outer wall. The telescopic ladders are in position—'

'OK,' Mencken interrupted him. He elevated the aerial on his walkie-talkie. 'Calling Blue, Green, Yellow,

Orange, Brown. Are you in position? Check back in the sequence I called you . . .'

'So that's it,' Mencken commented when the last team leader had confirmed. 'Everything really depends on Johnny,' he remarked, speaking half to himself. 'He's an expert at scaling heights. With a rope and grappling iron he'll get to the top of that tower – I guess they call it the keep. Armed with machine-pistols he'll dominate all entrances and exits to the château. He'll be way above everyone. And if Newman and his amateurs get in your way, kill 'em. OK.'

Mencken twisted round, stared down at his henchmen. 'So what are you waiting for? Take up your positions – this is going to be an easy run. Who can stop us? I'll be inside roughing up Amberg by a quarter after noon.' He glanced up at the clear blue sky as Eddie and Hank hastily jumped out of the Land-Rover. 'What a perfect day for a slaughter . . .'

Earlier, Marler had arrived at the Ballon d'Alsace high up in the southern Vosges. The controller of the gliding school, Masson, a large genial Frenchman, was apologetic.

'My own team has been laid low with this accursed flu. I felt I could not let you down – especially after the large deposit you paid me.'

'So you didn't let me down? What is the problem?' Marler enquired genially in French.

'Problem solved. I contacted a Swiss friend who also runs a gliding outfit. He has sent a Swiss pilot with his own machine to take you into the heavens.'

Marler had wondered why a Piper Tomahawk, a single-propeller plane with Swiss markings, was waiting on the runway. Behind it, attached to the Tomahawk's fuselage, stretched along the runway was the tow-rope linking it

407

with the glider which Marler would be flying a long way north.

'I got the Met report on my bedroom radio,' Marler told Masson. 'But although it sounded good the data you get is what counts.'

'For a flight to the north? To the Col de la Schlucht, sir? The wind direction is perfect. At the moment, I must emphasize. The weather' – Masson shrugged – 'it can change its mind faster than the most temperamental woman. But this I am sure you know. It is quite a trip you plan to make. Now, the Swiss pilot is waiting . . .'

Marler chose a moment when he was alone with the Swiss to give him instructions which differed from those he had suggested to Masson the previous day. He wanted the pilot to tow him considerably further north – closer to the Col du Bonhomme, and closer to the Château Noir, an objective he did not mention.

It was cold as Marler settled himself inside the cockpit of the glider, adjusted his helmet and goggles. Alone – for Masson had returned to the single-storey admin. cabin – Marler unzipped his canvas hold-all, swiftly assembled and loaded the Armalite. Then he loaded the tear-gas pistol and tucked both weapons by his side in the confined space of his little world. Round his neck he had slung a pair of field-glasses.

He tested with his feet the pedals controlling the glider, especially the rudder which guided the plane once it was turned loose. Satisfied he had done all he could, he raised a hand, dropped it, signalling to the Swiss pilot of the Tomahawk that he was ready.

The pilot already had his engine tuned up. The revs increased, Marler saw the Tomahawk begin its take-off down the runway, the tow-rope linking him to the mother plane stiffened, elevated above the runway. The glider moved forward after a brief jerk.

Less than a minute later the Tomahawk was airborne

and so was the glider. Marler glanced at his watch. If he had timed it properly he would arrive over the Château Noir just before noon.

While Tweed had been talking to Amberg in his strange working quarters, pressurizing the Swiss banker, Newman had stayed by the indoor pool with Paula and Eve. From the beginning, Jennie, who had accompanied them inside the château, had sat in a chair near the entrance, well away from the pool.

Seated with her legs crossed, an elbow perched on them, she had supported her chin with her right hand while she appeared to be observing Eve closely as she completed her lengths in the pool, and later when she sat with Newman, Paula and Gaunt. Newman had called out for Jennie to join them but she had smiled and shaken her head. He offered her a drink.

'Orange juice, no ice, would suit me very well, thank you.'

'Jennie seems a bit stand-offish,' Paula remarked to Newman in a low tone, standing up and joining him as though stretching her legs. He paused, the drink he was carrying to Jennie in his hand, replied also in a whisper.

'My impression is something important struck her and she's mulling it over. Let her be.'

'Struck her?' Paula persisted. 'What do you mean?'

'At some point since we arrived at the château and Amberg let us in. Let it rest. I'll make sure Jennie's not feeling out of it when I give her this drink.'

'Remember to come back sometime,' Paula chaffed him. 'She is very attractive.'

'Paula!' Gaunt roared at the top of his voice. 'Paula, I need your company. I always work on the principle that a man should have two devastatingly sensual women so he can play one off against the other. Eve is seducing me with her gorgeous eyes.'

And not just with her eyes, Paula thought when she saw how Eve had arranged her legs as she sat in full view of Gaunt. It was shortly after this that Tweed appeared briefly and spoke to Gaunt.

'Amberg has something to show you in the cinema. Can you find it? At a lower level, Amberg said.'

'Enjoy the picture show. I suppose it's pornographic as we're not invited. Let's time you.' Eve looked at her waterproof Blancpain. 'In ten minutes from now it will be noon. Tell Walter I shall want lunch . . .'

Tweed was not surprised to be shown with Gaunt into a large luxurious cinema by Amberg. There was row upon row of comfortable seats and the floor slanted downwards towards a large screen.

'I have set up the tape on a recorder,' Amberg informed them in his fussy manner. 'I will operate the projector to show the film. Make yourselves comfortable. It is air-conditioned, of course.'

'Of course!' Gaunt whispered to Tweed as they walked together towards a middle row. 'That Yankee millionaire who built this horror wasn't short of a dollar. Damned place reminds me of pictures I've seen in magazines of a pre-Second World War Odeon.'

'I'll take an aisle seat,' Tweed said, glancing back to where Amberg had retreated to a large projector mounted on a high dais.

'At least we didn't have to buy a ticket,' Gaunt continued as he settled in a seat next to Tweed. 'Which is a surprise – considering Amberg's love of money.'

'This should be what we have come all this way to see.'

'What happened to Newman?' Gaunt enquired. 'He disappeared on our way down here.'

'Probably gone to the loo.'

Tweed was lying. Newman had taken Tweed aside and told him he was going outside.

'I think I'd better see how Butler, Nield and Cardon are getting on with checking the defences.'

Tweed had nodded agreement. He'd also noticed Newman was carrying the hold-all he had kept close to himself ever since they had arrived inside the château. The hold-all contained the Uzi sub-machine-gun Newman had taken off the two American thugs who had kidnapped Jennie at the Bristol.

'Time, gentlemen, for the big picture,' Amberg called out with unaccustomed humour.

The lights were switched down. Tweed and Gaunt sat in near darkness. Taking off his glasses, Tweed cleaned them on his handkerchief, put them on again, looked back once more to where the vague silhouette of Amberg was crouched over his projector.

'How on earth does he keep this place clean without any servants?' Tweed mused.

'He brings in peasants off the lower slopes,' Gaunt told him. 'Pays them a pittance but in cash. This is France. The tax man never sees a franc of their earnings, which makes it all worthwhile – for the peasants and for Amberg.'

A glaring light flashed on to the screen, white with odd streaks of black. Tweed leaned forward intently. In the heavy silence he could hear the tape recorder revolving, spewing out atmospherics. No voices yet.

The light continued to blaze at them. No picture yet. Tweed checked the running time by the illuminated hands of his watch. Almost noon.

The light continued glaring non-stop. The tape recorder went on spewing out atmospherics. Tweed stirred restlessly. It was about time they saw something in the way of images. He suspected Gaunt was equally irked. Gaunt took out a cigar, lit it, blew the smoke away from Tweed, who now had a grim expression.

411

The strong light vibrated for a while longer, accompanied by the recorder's atmospherics. Without warning the light was turned off. Gaunt blinked, but Tweed had earlier taken the precaution of staring at the floor to keep his vision. The screen went blank. Tweed jumped up, made his way along the aisle to where Amberg stood.

'It's blank,' the banker said in a bewildered tone of voice. 'There's nothing on the film, nothing on the tape . . .'

'That's because you've substituted an unused film for the real one,' Tweed said in a ferocious hiss. 'Same with the tape. Where have you hidden the real ones?'

Then he heard the distant rattle of a machine-pistol and froze. None of his team possessed one. Newman had the Uzi sub-machine-gun, but Tweed could hear the difference. The Château Noir was under attack by Norton's murderous professionals.

When Newman had left the château by a rear exit, armed with the Uzi and his Smith & Wesson, his objective had been to take the high ground – to get inside the keep and reach its flat roof.

Close to the keep's wall, which sheered above him, he had reached a closed door inside an alcove when he saw Butler waving frantically to him. With the Luger in his right hand, Butler was crouched inside and close to the open doors of the old building used as a garage. He appeared to be warning Newman for God's sake to keep under cover.

Newman then spotted Nield and Cardon pressed against the side wall of the building. What the devil was going on? He suddenly saw a strong rope, knotted at intervals, hanging down the side of the tower. A climber's rope.

He glanced upwards in the nick of time. Way above

him on the roof a man was peering down, aiming a machine-pistol at him. Newman jumped back inside the alcove as a fusillade of bullets hammered down on the cobbles only feet from where he had been standing. They were trapped.

43

Marler's glider had been released from its tow-line some time before by the Swiss pilot, who had waved and flown away towards the Ballon d'Alsace. It was a beautiful sunny day and below him Marler saw the savage summits and snowbound ravines of the Vosges drifting past.

He had crossed route D417 and the formidable endless hairpin bends of the Col de la Schlucht. He was approaching the Château Noir. On the lower slopes of the map-like landscape spread out beneath him he saw the tiny figure of a man guiding a snowplough. The driver waved to the pilot of the glider. Marler briefly waved back.

He was concentrating on operating the controls. Since he was deliberately losing altitude he was wary of down-draughts, sudden gusts of air which could suck him down without warning. Then he saw it. The massive pile of the pseudo-medieval castle which was the Château Noir. As he removed his goggles he was surprised by its vast size.

He checked the time by his watch. Noon. As the glider continued to lose height he raised his binoculars, pressed them to his eyes. He frowned as he detected a Land-Rover half-hidden inside a copse of evergreens. Only one man – behind the wheel – but the vehicle probably was positioned to give the driver a clear view down inside the château wall. Not one of ours, he thought.

Marler continued to swivel his binoculars, focusing them now on the château which was coming closer every second. He stiffened as he saw Butler crouched, as though hiding, inside the entrance to a building. Then he saw Newman at the base of the keep, saw a burly figure in a sheepskin on the flat roof of the tower, peering over as he aimed a machine-pistol. Newman jumped back out of sight as the heavy silence of the Vosges was fractured by the rattle of a hail of bullets.

'You really shouldn't have done that, old man,' Marler said to himself, addressing the man on the roof of the keep. He pressed the foot pedals gently. 'Time for a really smooth glide. This will only take seconds . . .'

He heard a muffled explosion. Out of the corner of his eye he saw the wrought-iron gates guarding the entrance collapse. He did not allow his attention to be diverted from the task in hand as he reached for the Armalite.

On the roof of the keep the burly man in a sheepskin was peering over the edge, his machine-pistol reloaded, ready for a fresh burst, when his target reappeared. Confined inside the garage, Butler had fired three shots from his Luger but the range from where he crouched to the summit of the tower was too great.

Praying that the glider would continue on its level course for a few more seconds, Marler took careful aim. With his eye glued to the sniperscope attached to his rifle, he saw the cross-hairs covering the upper back of the burly thug on top of the keep. Holding his breath, Marler pressed the trigger.

His target jerked upright in a convulsive movement. The machine-pistol left his hands, dropped to the cobbles far below. He staggered, then fell forward, following his lost weapon, screaming in terror as he plunged down the

414

side of the keep. His body hit the cobbles with a bone-breaking thud close to the alcove where Newman sheltered. The corpse lay inert.

Up to this dramatic incident the odds had been heavily in favour of Mencken's assault force. From this moment they swung decisively the other way.

Newman noticed that the heavy studded wooden door leading inside the keep was not completely closed. It was simply stuck. He hammered his shoulder against the obstacle. It seemed to give a little. He took a deep breath and thrust against it with all his strength. It burst open, flying inwards so suddenly he nearly lost his balance.

Diving inside, gripping the Uzi in both hands, he saw a flight of stone steps, worn down in their centres, leading upwards, curving out of sight round a corner. He began to run up them non-stop, unaware of what was happening at the front of the château.

At the first rattle of machine-pistol fire Tweed had reacted instantly. Grabbing Amberg by the arm, he forced him to the cinema exit, up the flight of stairs leading into the main hall. Gaunt, hauling a .455 Colt automatic from the shoulder holster under his thick sports jacket, took giant strides, close on their heels.

Entering the hall, Tweed saw Paula, Jennie and Eve – now wearing winter clothes – appear from the direction of the swimming pool. With his free arm he waved them back, a commanding gesture.

'Return to the pool at once. Don't argue. Do as I tell you. There is great danger.'

Eve and Jennie rushed back into the labyrinth of passages but Paula stayed her ground. From the special pocket inside her shoulder bag she had whipped out her .32 Browning.

'I'm staying here with you,' she snapped at Tweed. 'You are not armed.'

'I am,' Gaunt assured her aggressively.

'We may need someone who can shoot straight,' she told him.

'What the hell—' Gaunt began.

He never completed his sentence. Tweed, still dragging a reluctant Amberg, had headed for the main door. Outside he could hear the sound of some large machine approaching. Reaching the door he peered through the tall Norman window with leaded lights at one side of the door. The view was not reassuring. Norton – or his henchman – who had organized the attack knew what he was doing.

The clanking grinding machine proceeding across the cobbled courtyard towards the door was a huge orange bulldozer, its massive grab elevated several feet – ready to batter down the heavy door and open the way for the final assault. Tweed compelled Amberg to glance through the window. The Swiss shuddered, tried to get away, but Tweed had a firm grip on his arm.

'I must go to the swimming pool as well,' Amberg protested. 'There is a rear exit. I am a banker . . .'

'Surely you want to witness the defence of your own home,' Tweed said grimly, determined to break his nerve. 'You will stay with us in any case.'

'I might be able to shoot the driver,' suggested Gaunt who had also peered through the window.

'Not a chance, not yet,' Tweed snapped. 'And behind his cab the driver has several armed men clinging on aboard the bulldozer. We must wait until it appears in the gap after it has smashed down the double doors. Then shoot. We might jam the machine in the doorway, although I don't issue any guarantees. So, we stand back and wait . . .'

The one thing which irked Tweed was that he had no

idea what his team outside the château were doing –
assuming they were still alive.

Having disposed of the gunman who had pinned down all
Tweed's men, Marler immediately turned his attention to
what was going on at the entrance. His glider was still
airborne but he knew he must soon land or crash – maybe
both. What was happening was taking place in seconds.

He had fired the Armalite from a distance, but now the
glider was cruising very close to the château, would be
above the courtyard at any moment. Afterwards, if he
survived, Marler hoped to land on the summit of the ridge
close to where the Land-Rover had been parked.

Then he saw the orange bulldozer advancing, the clutch
of armed men hanging on behind the driver's cabin. The
machine was a deadly menace. Marler took a dangerous
chance, lost more height, and was now gripping the tear-
gas pistol with a spare shell in his other hand. The wings
seemed to almost skim the roof of the keep, although the
machine was higher. Marler looked down.

The bulldozer had covered two-thirds of the distance
between the ruined gates and the porch entrance to the
château. His arm rested firmly on the edge of the fuselage
of the glider as he pressed the trigger. The tear-gas shell
was aimed for the glass window in front of the driver's
cabin, smashed it to pieces, exploded inside the cabin.
Marler had reloaded, fired again at the rear of the
machine where the armed men were hanging on.

The outcome was devastating. Overcome with the
fumes the driver lost all control. The bulldozer swung
through an arc of a hundred and eighty degrees. In his
panic the driver pressed his foot on the wrong pedal. The
machine rocketed over the cobbles at speed, spilling its
passengers, who were disabled by the second tear-gas
shell. The bulldozer thundered towards the outer wall,

hurtled into it with tremendous impact, crushing the cabin and the driver inside it.

At that moment a Citroën drove in through the gateway, crammed with armed men. Cardon, Nield and Butler had emerged from under cover. The Citroën driver, startled by the disaster to the bulldozer, skidded to a fatal halt. Cardon carefully lobbed a grenade. It landed under the petrol tank of the Citroën. Before any of its passengers could get out the petrol tank exploded. There was a fountain of flame and Newman saw its occupants incinerated in the ferocious heat.

He had reached the top of the keep and was crouched behind the low wall. As several of the men who had dropped off the bulldozer produced weapons, rubbing their eyes, he fired a long burst from the Uzi. A 9-mm. weapon, it fired at the rate of six hundred rounds a minute. He rammed in a fresh magazine, continued firing.

Butler saw a man perched on the top of the wall, guessed he had cut the electrified wire. He aimed his Luger, fired twice. His target shot out both arms as though about to swim, dived head first down on to the cobbled courtyard.

Marler's glider continued on course, away from the château, heading for the ridge as he struggled to maintain a few more feet of height. He braced himself for a crash landing. The ridge rushed towards him, the nose of the glider lifted briefly of its own accord. It was this accident of luck which saved Marler from the machine upending. It scraped along the rocky ground, came to a stop.

No more than thirty feet away Marler saw that the Land-Rover was still stationed at the edge of the copse with its driver behind the wheel. He snatched up the Armalite as the vehicle began to move, fired at random. Mencken, who had witnessed the débâcle, shuddered as his windscreen was shattered, all the glass blown away from the frame, but the bullet had missed him. He drove

418

off at speed, heading for the vital ambush area on route
D417.

Half a mile away, well clear of the action, Norton sat in
his Renault at a road intersection. He lowered his field-
glasses. This time he was not feeling too philosophical
about the next stage of the struggle. What could he tell
President Bradford March? At that moment he had no
idea – and he had lost a lot of trained men.

44

'That is what we have saved you from . . .'

Tweed almost thundered the words as he stood in the
snow, still gripping Amberg's arm. They had walked out
of the front door and beyond the porch to survey a scene
of carnage.

Blood disfigured the white of the snow, the bodies of
Mencken's assault group lay in grotesque attitudes. Paula
stood on his other side, the Browning still in her hand,
ready for use. Gaunt had brought up the rear.

As they stood in the bitter cold Butler, who had medical training, completed checking each body to see if anyone was still alive. He stood up from the last corpse and
shook his head. A station wagon full of Mencken's troops
had followed the Citroën into the yard. The occupants, all
armed, had been despatched by Newman with his Uzi as
they had emerged.

Butler, Cardon and Nield, with Newman's help, were
now carrying the bodies and laying them inside the station
wagon. Amberg was shivering with fear. Tweed gripped
his arm more tightly.

419

'All this havoc has been caused by the accursed film and the tape. I've lost track of how many have died – many of them innocent of any crime. My patience is exhausted, Amberg. You will produce the real film and tape or I will contact Beck, Chief of the Federal Police at the Taubenhalde in Berne. You will be charged as an accessory to mass murder, so make up your mind now. I repeat,' he continued in the same grim tone, 'I've run out of patience with you.'

'As a banker I felt I should keep my word to Joel Dyson who deposited . . .'

'Forget Dyson. Your own life is in great danger. Can you at long last grasp that? Look at those corpses – those men came to kill you. For the last time, where have you hidden the film, the tape?'

'At my bank in Ouchy on the shores of Lake Geneva,' Amberg gulped, using his free hand to wipe beads of sweat off his high forehead. 'It belonged to Julius but it was registered in a different name. It was the only place no one could connect with us.'

'So they are still in Switzerland,' Tweed commented more quietly.

'Yes. After this terrible experience perhaps we should return at once to my country. To Ouchy, I mean,' he added quickly.

'You will travel with us.' Tweed made no attempt to reassure the Swiss. 'I must warn you we shall face other attacks on our way back to Colmar. Whether we arrive there alive is in the lap of the gods.'

He looked at Paula. 'Where are Jennie and Eve? They are safe, I assume?'

'Safe as houses – safer than this castle was,' Paula replied. 'When you first came out here I nipped back to the swimming pool. They were both sitting down at the table, drinking hot coffee from a percolator.'

'To steady their nerves?'

'In the case of Jennie, yes. Eve is made of sterner stuff. She had an automatic rifle across her lap – she'd brought it from somewhere. She made the remark that if any thugs arrived at the pool she'd take some of them with her. Tough as old hickory,' Paula ended in an admiring tone.

'She is a very strong-minded woman,' Amberg agreed in a regretful tone. 'I expect she will want to come with us. A little business matter which can only be settled in Ouchy.'

'Why?' Tweed demanded. 'Have you transferred all the assets to the shores of Lake Geneva?'

He was suspicious. Ouchy faced the shore of France and there was a regular boat service from there to Evian.

'Merely a matter of banking policy,' Amberg replied. 'Is there a safe way down to Colmar?'

'No,' Tweed informed him. 'It will be a journey of pure terror . . .'

Norton had recovered swiftly from the shock of the fiasco of the assault on the château. Sitting in his Renault, he used his mobile phone to contact Mencken. It took him several minutes to establish a link free of atmospherics.

'I'm on route D417,' Mencken said, talking quickly before he could be questioned. 'I'm sure they will come this way heading back to Colmar. After what they faced on their journey up by the other route. All the roads west are blocked by snow.'

'You'd goddamn better be right,' Norton rasped. 'What happened at the château? You only sent in two cars and you had five.'

'I kept Yellow, Orange and Brown in reserve. They'll be needed to finish the job on route D417 . . .'

'You could have overwhelmed them if you'd kept to your original instructions.'

'I don't think so,' Mencken rapped back in a burst of

421

fury. 'It was that friggin' glider which took us by surprise . . .'

'Crap!' Norton shouted down the phone. 'It should have been shot down . . .'

'That's what I like,' Mencken snapped. 'Armchair strategists who stay a safe distance from the action. I'm closing this conversation. The new ambushes have to be checked . . .'

'Mencken! You talk to me like that just once more . . .'

Norton swore foully when he realized no one was listening at the other end. He sucked in a deep breath of cold air to calm down. There was an important job waiting for him – at six in the evening he was due to meet Growly Voice at the Lac Noir rendezvous. It could be that inside a few hours he'd have both the film and the tape. He'd then drive to Strasbourg, catch an Air Inter flight to Paris where he would board Concorde for Washington.

'Here is Marler, the man who saved the day,' announced Newman. 'I sent Nield out to find him.'

Tweed was waiting impatiently inside a huge living-room which led to Amberg's bedroom. Newman had earlier briefed Tweed on the arrival of the glider. Paula ran forward and hugged the new arrival.

'Thank you,' Tweed said simply. 'You saved our bacon – and our skins.'

'Really, it was dead easy,' Marler drawled. He lit a king-size. 'Pure luck I floated in when I did. What's next on the agenda? I see they've tidied up the courtyard.'

'The station wagon with the bodies is parked inside the garage building at the back as you suggested,' Newman confirmed. 'What about the French authorities?'

'We'll wait until we get to Basle,' Tweed decided. 'I'll call my old friend Chief Inspector René Lasalle in Paris.

Otherwise we could be delayed in France for ages with red tape, statements, all that hogwash—'

He broke off as he heard Eve's voice calling out to Amberg in the bedroom. She was helping him to pack.

'Two clean shirts here, Walter. They'll see you through until we reach Ouchy.'

'Shouldn't I have more?' Amberg's voice asked querulously.

'Two are enough,' Eve responded firmly. 'We have to get a move on. Now, these documents . . .'

'Put them in the zip-up folder.' Amberg's tone was decisive. 'Don't alter the sequence. They're important.'

Paula had winked at Tweed when she heard Eve again running the show as she had done a few minutes earlier. Tweed, who had glanced at his watch a moment before, frowned and stared at Paula without seeing her.

Marler had amused himself by asking Jennie to show him the indoor swimming pool. He returned with her, stubbed out his cigarette in a crystal glass ashtray. Jennie was gazing at him with more than normal interest as she played with the string of pearls round her neck. Marler reached out to touch them.

'Those are quite beautiful . . .'

'*Don't touch!*' She coloured as Marler withdrew his hand, raised an eyebrow. 'Sorry I snapped at you. It's just that I'm superstitious about anyone else handling them.'

Paula noticed that Tweed, despite his impatience to be on their way, wasn't missing even the most trivial incident. He frowned again briefly, glancing at the pearls and then at her expression. Eve strode out of the bedroom at that moment, carrying a large Louis Vuitton case. Behind her ambled the banker, looking unhappy.

'I'm not sure I've packed enough.'

'You haven't packed anything. I have,' Eve reminded him. She slapped her hand against the case she'd perched on a table. 'Enough in there to get you to Cape Town. We

423

are only going to Ouchy. And I can see Tweed is in a hurry. In case you've forgotten it, Walter, from now on Tweed is your protector. He may even get us to Colmar and points south alive.'

'Don't joke about things like that,' Amberg protested. 'It's bad luck.'

'Someone else is superstitious,' Jennie remarked. 'I'm not the only crackpot round here. Am I riding in the same chariot I was transported up here aboard? Hope so. Bob and Tweed got me here in one piece. Oh dear. You are shaking your head, Tweed.'

'One thing I forgot to tell you, Tweed,' Marler broke in. 'The glider is a complete write-off. I warned you. Cost you a bomb.'

'Don't worry about that. Jennie has raised the question of transport. I've discussed that with Newman and we've made some changes in the sequence of the convoy. Object, to confuse the opposition.'

'I insist I'm driving back down those mountains in the BMW,' Gaunt barked out. 'Feel comfortable behind the wheel of that car. Eve, are you joining me? If not . . .' He turned to Jennie. 'You'll be most welcome as a passenger. And I'm a good chap as escort – with my trusty Colt.'

Gaunt appeared to be adopting a jovial manner to lighten the atmosphere. Watching him, Paula couldn't decide whether he was just a show-off, full of his own importance, or a formidable personality.

'I'd like to ride back with Tweed,' Eve said, gazing at him. 'If that's all right with you.'

'Newman will head the convoy, driving the station wagon this time,' Tweed explained. 'He has the advantage of being armed with the Uzi, a deadly weapon. Marler will travel next to him. He has the advantage of carrying his Armalite and the tear-gas pistol. The station wagon becomes the spearhead of the convoy.'

'What about the Espace?' Paula asked.

424

'That will follow behind the station wagon and I will be driving it with you alongside me. Cardon, armed with grenades, will travel in the row behind us. That leaves Butler and Nield, who will ride the motorcycles. But this time the convoy will maintain its sequence come hell or high water – with Butler as outrider in front of the station wagon all the time and Nield bringing up the rear. Eve sits next to Cardon in the Espace.'

'Hold on!' Gaunt boomed out, raising a hand. 'I'm with this party in case you've forgotten.'

'Which I hadn't,' Tweed shot back. 'You're car number three, following my Espace, with Nield behind you. And Philip,' he said, addressing Cardon, 'I know that inside your hold-all you have a collection of walkie-talkies. Give one to Marler, one to Paula, who has sharp eyes, one to Butler, one to Nield, and one to Jennie, who proved on the way up she also has sharp eyes.'

Cardon unfastened his hold-all and had distributed the walkie-talkies in less than a minute, including a clear instruction to Jennie as to how to operate it. Holding the instrument, Jennie looked at Eve with a mocking expression. She spoke to her in a whisper.

'You're lucky, darling. Nothing to do except make up to Tweed. They call it spare luggage.'

'Not too spare, dear.' Eve reached behind a couch, came up holding an automatic rifle in both hands, the muzzle pointed at the ceiling, Tweed noted with approval. 'And I'm a crack shot,' Eve went on, also in a whisper.

'Modesty really has become an old-fashioned virtue,' Jennie flashed back. 'I'll look after Greg for you.'

Tweed's acute hearing had picked up the catty exchange. He put his hands round the shoulders of both women.

'I am relying on both of you to back up the team when it comes to a crisis. Both of you have my full confidence.'

'What about me?' asked Amberg, who had remained silent and still while he listened to the arrangement of the convoy. 'I do have a Mercedes in the garage . . .'

'Leave it there,' Tweed told him. He'd purposely not mentioned the banker earlier, exerting a little more psychological pressure. 'You will be sitting in the Espace, in the second row of seats between Eve and Cardon.'

'Will you be carrying that rifle?' Amberg demanded, staring at the weapon Eve was holding.

'Bet your life I will,' she told him cheerfully. 'So when we're attacked, keep your head down. Now, what are we waiting for, everybody?'

'I'm waiting for you all to get a move on,' Tweed said brusquely.

'Amberg,' Newman snapped, 'you'd better hurry out to the garage and lock it up. Has anyone else a key to this place?'

'Yes. The woman who acts as housekeeper in my absence and lets in the other servants.'

'Wouldn't want them poking around in that garage, considering what it contains besides your car.'

'No, of course not . . .'

The convoy was drawn up in the deep snow in the courtyard and everyone was aboard their allotted vehicles when an ashen-faced Amberg, huddled in a fur coat, returned. Only Newman stood outside the Espace. He gestured for the Swiss to get aboard.

'I saw that car – and what was inside,' Amberg remarked. 'The garage is like a charnel house.'

'And may I remind you,' Newman said brutally, 'that all those men came here to kill us? Get in your seat and shut up.'

'This could be a memorable journey,' commented Eve as the banker climbed in beside her, the rifle across her lap. 'Who knows? We might even survive it . . .'

45

'Ives, whichever route Tweed and his team use to come back down off the mountains they have to pass this point,' said Cord Dillon. Seated inside his car, his window open, Dillon had the hood of his coat pulled well down over his head.

He was speaking to a man astride a motorcycle parked next to the open window. At the front of his machine a Union Jack fluttered in the icy breeze, attached to the top of the extended radio aerial.

Barton Ives, Special Agent of the FBI, was even more muffled up. Wearing a helmet and goggles, the lower part of his face was masked with a thick woollen scarf. He had lifted it above his firm mouth to converse with Dillon.

'Tweed knows the Union Jack is partial proof of your identity,' Dillon went on. 'But he'll need more than that . . .'

'I have my papers . . .'

'He'll need more than those,' Dillon warned. 'So he has your description. When you contact him show him your face and hair immediately. He has a tough bunch with him who don't hesitate to shoot any suspect character.'

'I'll tell him my story as soon as I get the guy on his own. Trouble is,' Ives went on, 'he'll never believe it. Too goddamn earth-shaking.'

'It's all of that,' Dillon agreed. 'Didn't believe it myself when you first told me. It's quiet here but we'd better not be seen together any longer.'

'That gas station over there,' Ives commented. 'It has a

coffee shop. I'll buy myself a drink, sit at a window table. I'll have a good view of the road from there.'

'OK,' Dillon agreed, reaching for the brake. 'But make contact before Tweed and his team hit the heavy traffic. I saw him go up in a Renault Espace, with a Renault station wagon and two motorcycle outriders as escort. The Espace is a grey colour. On your own now, Ives. So stay lucky . . .'

The convoy's journey down through the Vosges had been uneventful so far. That is discounting the fact that an icy breeze combined with a fall in temperature had made the twisting road like an endless skating rink. Inside the Espace, even with the heaters turned up full blast, Paula felt the chill penetrating her gloves, her clothes.

Several times Tweed, behind the wheel of the Espace, had felt the insidious slide of a skid. On one occasion he had a cliff wall to his left, a bottomless abyss to his right. He had driven with the skid, which had taken the front right-hand wheel within centimetres of the drop.

'Oh, my God!' Amberg cried out, jerking upright.

'Shut up, like Newman told you to,' snapped Paula.

She glanced at Eve, saw her hands had tightened on the rifle. Paula's own hands had stiffened inside her gloves. Eve turned on Amberg.

'Walter,' she said in a cold voice, 'I'm beginning to suspect you are the real target. After all, whoever those people were, they attacked the Château Noir. So you could be the one who is putting our lives at risk. That being so, kindly shut your face. I hope you are understanding my message, Walter.'

Cardon turned slowly sideways and nudged the banker before he spoke.

'Do keep quiet, old chap. The driver needs all his concentration. Ready for the next skid.'

Tweed heard all this with a corner of his mind as he stared ahead at the next bend, trying to detect whether there was more ice under the treacherous covering of snow on the steep downward spiral.

Ahead of them, Newman, behind the wheel of the station wagon with Marler next to him, had negotiated two skids and had been driving slowly. Now he reduced his speed to a crawl. It was only a few minutes later that the road levelled out, widened on a small plateau. He signalled that he was stopping.

Tweed pulled up behind him after signalling to Gaunt who was following them in the BMW with Jennie huddled in a sheepskin next to him. Newman had alighted and Tweed, his arms aching with tension, was glad to join him in the snow as Paula and Cardon followed him. Marler then stepped out, the Armalite gripped in his right hand. Newman pointed to a large sign in front of a large single-storey wooden building which appeared deserted. Paula read it.

LA SCHLUCHT 1139.

'I don't believe it,' she said. 'We're still over three thousand feet up in the Vosges. I assume that height is in metres.'

'You assume correctly,' Tweed responded, banging his gloves together to get the circulation back into both his hands. 'In summer I imagine that place is open for refreshments. This is what is called a panoramic viewing point on maps – something like that.'

'A panorama it is,' Paula agreed.

To the north and south stretched the Ice Age world of the peaks and crevasses of the Vosges, the white summits reminding Paula of shark-like teeth. They had emerged from the zone of shadow and everywhere the sunlit snow sparkled like a million diamonds.

The cold was intense and Paula, like Eve and Jennie,

429

who had run down from the BMW, began stamping her booted feet, which felt like blocks of ice. Gaunt came striding up as Tweed conferred with Newman, Marler and Cardon.

'I don't like it,' Tweed warned. 'So far there has been no sign of the opposition, no attempt to stop us. Yet! Something pretty nasty has to be waiting for us beyond here.'

'Oh, I don't know about that,' said Gaunt, who had taken no part in the defence of the château. 'My bet is they shot their bolt, back up there, whoever they were. Let's press on, regardless. Get back to Colmar and the Brasserie before dark. I can feel a drink comin' on.'

Paula stared at him blankly. Jennie raised her eyebrows to heaven. Tweed ignored him, hauled out his walkie-talkie, called Butler.

The two outriders, Butler and Nield, posted at the front and rear, had stopped their machines without coming to join the conference.

'Butler,' Tweed said, 'keep your eyes skinned for anything unusual. I don't like the peace we have enjoyed so far.'

'Agreed. Neither do I,' Butler responded.

Nield also agreed when Tweed contacted him, made a similar reply to Butler's.

'Let's get moving,' Tweed ordered. 'Proceed with extreme caution . . .'

Beyond the Col de la Schlucht the road descended at a precipitous angle round a series of hellish hairpin bends. During their brief stop Paula had been struck by the sinister silence which had fallen over the Vosges. A heavy silence which you could almost hear. She sat upright, staring ahead.

The mountain began to rise up sheer to their left. To

the right the abyss became a white chasm with no sign of where it reached bottom. Beside Newman, in the station wagon, Marler had laid his tear-gas pistol in his lap, was craning his neck to check the heights. It was Butler who issued the early warning.

'Everyone slow to a crawl. Be prepared to stop the moment I tell you. Two men on top of the big cliff ahead.'

'Message received,' Tweed replied, holding the wheel with one hand briefly along a short straight stretch.

He had finished speaking when, thirty seconds later, he heard Nield calling him. An urgent note in his tone.

'We're being followed. Bloody great truck. Nestlé. A half-mile behind me and coming like the clappers.'

In the distance, just short of yet another bend, Butler had propped his machine against the rock wall, had begun to climb up a ravine. Marler told Newman to stop, jumped out, Armalite in his left hand, tear-gas pistol in his right. Keeping close to the rock wall, he ran down the icy road like a marathon entrant, reached the ravine and shinned up it close behind Butler.

Paula had focused her binoculars on the rock wall near the bend. She pursed her lips before she spoke.

'That's a huge granite cliff sheering up vertically from the road by the bend. Obviously unstable. I'm sure it's covered with a curtain of steel mesh.'

Tweed nodded as he stopped the Espace. Paula's news was disturbing. They had something possibly very danger-ous ahead of them – and coming up fast behind them was this huge Nestlé truck Nield had spotted. Tweed didn't think the two incidents were a coincidence. They were caught in a pincer movement of potential destruction. It all had the signature of Norton written across it.

'I'd better go and give them back-up,' Paula suggested.

Tweed swung round in his seat, grasped her arm. He shook his head.

'Stay here. Marler and Butler will be more than a

431

match for two thugs. I just hope they clear the way before that truck coming up behind us arrives. It's going to try and push us all off the road into eternity.'

'If I run back now past the BMW I could probably shoot that truck driver,' Eve suggested.

'Stay put. No one moves,' Tweed ordered.

'Are we just going to sit here?' Amberg demanded.

'We are going to do just that.'

'Surely someone can do something,' Amberg persisted.

'Two men are doing something,' Tweed replied in the same flat tone. 'You can do something – keep quiet.'

Tweed had experienced similar reactions before. In a crisis people couldn't just wait. To soothe their nerves they needed action – anything which involved movement. So often it was safest to wait – once counter-measures had been taken. And they had been.

Butler and Marler, using their gloved hands, had hauled themselves up to the top of the ravine. Butler peered over the rim of a rock. Then he crouched down again and looked at Marler below him over his shoulder.

'Tricky,' he reported. 'Two thugs about thirty feet away. Top of the cliff is flat. Boulders scattered in groups across it.'

'I could take them with the Armalite.'

'Not that simple,' Butler objected. 'They have set up explosives to bring down the cliff on the road . . .'

'How do you know?' Marler whispered impatiently.

'Because I can see another of those old-fashioned plunger devices like the one on top of the tower at Kaysersberg. Hang on, you weren't there. They're both near the handle that only needs pressing to bring down that cliff. I'm sure of it. And on the road they've got the Nestlé truck coming after them . . .' Butler had heard Nield's message just before switching off his walkie-talkie and knew they were desperately short of time before the truck arrived.

'We have to lure those thugs away from that plunger handle,' he told Marler. 'Question is, how the hell do we do that?'

The stocky American driving the truck was grinning wolfishly to himself. He had caught a glimpse of the stalled convoy and was closing the gap rapidly. He wore a woollen cap pulled down over his low forehead and talked to himself for company.

'Won't be long now. I'll ram the lot of you over the edge down into that abyss. You'll end up dead meat. Maybe spring before what's left of you is found. Old bones . . .'

With two accomplices he had earlier hijacked the big vehicle as the original driver crossed the Vosges. They had cut his throat and thrown the body into one of the crevasses in the ice. But not before the American now driving had pulled off the victim's woollen cap. He felt the cold.

The truck was loaded to the roof with supplies, adding to the enormous weight of the juggernaut. The weight was now helping the driver to keep going, holding the surface of the snow-covered road well.

'Another five minutes,' he said to himself. 'Then it will be all over for you poor schmucks . . .'

Marler had eased himself up the ravine alongside Butler. He peered over the rim of the boulder, looked at the side of the ravine where they had pressed away snow during their ascent. With his gloved hand he began digging and clawing at a small piece of protruding rock while Butler held his tear-gas pistol. The rock came loose, Marler tested its weight in his hand and nodded.

'Give me back the pistol,' he said. 'With luck this will get

433

them well clear of the explosive box. You take the one with the sheepskin, I'll sort out the thug with the windcheater, if it works.'

'It has to,' Butler said, glancing at his watch.

Marler hoisted himself higher up, being careful to hide himself behind the boulder. Sheepskin was standing with binoculars pressed to his eyes, obviously wondering why the convoy had stopped moving. Windcheater hovered dangerously close to the plunger handle.

About thirty feet away from where the thugs waited, well inland from the brink of the cliff, was a scatter of very large boulders massed close together. Marler raised his arm, aimed for the centre of the scatter, threw the rock.

'Hey, Don, what the friggin' hell was that?' called out Sheepskin, dropping his binoculars looped round his neck with a strap.

'Came from over there, Jess,' Windcheater replied. He pointed to the scatter of boulders. 'We'd better take a look. They could've sent up someone. Get ready to take him out . . .'

Gripping machine-pistols, both Americans advanced alongside each other, their gaze fixed on the boulders. Marler smiled to himself as he half-crouched, half-stood behind the boulder. He used it to rest both arms to steady his aim. Very stupid to walk next to each other. He pressed the trigger.

The shell struck a boulder just in front of the two thugs, burst, flooded the air with tear-gas. Earlier Marler had noted the icy breeze at la Schlucht was no longer blowing. Marler and Butler moved like greyhounds as the Americans coughed, spluttered, staggered, held a hand to their eyes, still clutching the machine-pistols.

Despite the pain of the tear-gas both thugs were staggering at surprising speed back towards the plunger. Marler realized that a lot of the deadly vapour had exploded away from the targets. They were nerve-wrackingly close to the plunger when Marler reached Don, whose vision was obscured. He saw only silhouettes.

Marler had dropped his pistol, was holding his Armalite with the barrel across his chest, gripped at both ends. He drove it with a ferocious thrust against Don, forcing him backwards, preventing him from making any use of his own weapon. At the last moment Don realized he was on the edge of the brink.

'No! For Chrissakes . . .'

Marler, careful where he placed his own feet, gave one final savage shove. The American fell back into space. In a bizarre gesture he hurled his weapon away from himself. Marler caught it with one hand in mid-air. With a high-pitched yell of pure terror the American plunged down. At this point the lip of the cliff protruded well over the road below. The piercing yell continued echoing round the Vosges as the somersaulting body, arms flailing, missed the road and plunged on down, down, down into the abyss.

At almost the same moment Butler hammered the barrel of his Luger down on to the hand of Jess, forcing him to drop the weapon. He then struck his adversary across the face, left, right, left. The onslaught drove Jess back and back. He was close to the edge when Butler brought the barrel down on his skull with all his force. Jess collapsed out of sight, following his fellow American into the chasm.

Marler and Butler had worked as a perfect team, keeping to the original plan, each tackling the thug closest to him. Butler was breathing heavily as Marler ran back to retrieve his tear-gas pistol. When he returned Butler had recovered his breath, was operating his walkie-talkie.

'Tweed. Cliff laced with explosives. Later we can get down the shallow slope south of the cliff, join you on the road. Get Cardon to grab my machine if he can. Pete can

435

be bait for the truck. We'll take it from there . . .'

'Agreed,' Tweed's voice answered tersely.

There was very little time left. He gave Nield brief instructions. Nield acknowledged. Tweed signalled to Newman to move on, told Cardon the plan, started the Espace moving, warned Gaunt via Jennie over her walkie-talkie to get moving, keep close . . .

At the summit Butler pointed out to Marler several places where holes had been drilled in the unstable cliff, explosives inserted. Dynamite, he thought. Marler took up a position at the brink, looked down. It was lucky he had never suffered from vertigo. The drop beyond the road was dizzying. From this point he could see the movement of the convoy and – more important still – the position further back where Pete Nield sat astride his motorcycle, calmly waiting for the arrival of the juggernaut. Live bait. He'd have to time it to a fraction of a second.

The driver of the Nestlé truck was chewing gum. Whatever he was doing – driving, talking, waiting to kill a target – he was always chewing gum. The truck swayed a little despite its great weight as the front wheels passed over ice, but the vehicle held on to the surface as though glued to it.

He had had the heaters turned up full blast for quite a while, the windows of the cab firmly closed, and the atmosphere inside was a nauseating mixture of sweat, oil and heat. The driver was unaware of this. He was about to open the window briefly to spit out gum, prior to inserting a fresh stick in his thin-lipped mouth, when he rounded a corner and saw Nield seated on his machine, a stream of exhaust like steam ejecting from the pipe.

The driver grinned wolfishly again, rammed his foot down on the accelerator. Nield took off like a bird, keeping close to the wall of rock as he appeared to fly across the snow. Chewing Gum was startled, annoyed at the lightning take-off. He rammed his foot down further.

'You're the salad, pal,' he said to himself. 'Then we can get on with the main course.'

He was particularly looking forward to tipping the Espace over the edge. That was going to give him a real kick. He burned rubber as Nield disappeared round the corner of the massive cliff overhanging the road. This was fun, Chewing Gum thought.

The corner was sharper than he'd anticipated. He braked to take it. That was when he heard a rumbling sound. He frowned, glanced up, then stared in horror. Above him as he leaned forward, gazing up through the windscreen, he saw a vast black curtain descending on him. Huge boulders crashed on to the road ahead of him and bounced off the edge.

He was no longer chewing gum. His teeth were clamped together in sheer fright. Something hit the top of his cab, denting the roof. A small boulder rolled off and down into the white hell below. The windscreen was suddenly blotted out as shale fell, piled up on the hood. He was driving blind.

'Jesus! No . . . o . . .!'

He screamed. The wheel no longer responded to the frantic turn of his clawed hands. A sound like thunder roared out as thousands of tons of granite fell on the juggernaut like a giant sledgehammer. He felt the truck tipping over towards the brink. Through the side window he saw the chasm coming up to meet him. The juggernaut was pushed off the road, began turning like an immense cartwheel as it dropped into the depths. Chewing Gum's head, his mind, was spinning out of control. The truck gathered speed, plunged on down into the three-hundred-foot ravine. It hit ice-covered rocks, burst into flames which sizzled as the snow quenched them and the juggernaut died.

46

On the summit of the cliff Marler and Butler had operated again as a skilled team. Butler had waited by the plunger while Marler ran further along the brink away from the convoy. He had stopped at a point where he could look down on the winding road and see it clearly.

Holding his right arm upright, Marler watched the roof of Newman's station wagon pass below him, followed by the grey Espace and Gaunt's BMW. He had waited until he saw Nield on his motorcycle, speeding past. The moment Nield was well clear of the cliff he had dropped his hand and run like hell away from the brink to the centre of the plateau. That was the moment when Butler pressed down on the plunger with all his strength.

His job accomplished, he began running back to join Marler. Butler felt the ground trembling under his feet and wondered whether he was going to make it. Reaching the scatter of boulders where Marler waited he looked back and sucked in his breath.

The two Americans had misjudged placing the plunger mechanism. Butler stared in awe as a fissure zig-zagged across the plateau, as half the plateau crumbled away, taking the mechanism with it. The roar was deafening. Clouds of rock dust appeared from under the snow. Choking, both men ran for the shallow slope, Marler gripping his Armalite and tear-gas pistol.

The crash and rumble of the avalanche continued as they ran, slithered down the long slope to where the convoy was stationary, waiting for them. Cardon greeted them as they arrived on the road, calling out to Butler.

'We manhandled your machine into the back of the Espace. Paula helped me. We had only seconds.'

'I'll get it out, then,' Butler decided. 'Take up my old position at the head of the convoy.'

'Congratulations, both of you,' Tweed said tersely when he had jumped down to meet them. 'Marler, get back into the station wagon. Tell Newman to get moving. I want us out of the mountains before dark. And again, everyone keep a sharp lookout for more welcomes from the enemy.'

'I'll go ahead of Newman as before,' repeated Butler.

With Cardon's help he had been hauling his machine out of the back of the Espace. Amberg was twisted round in his seat, staring fixedly. Butler gave him a brief wave, whispered to Cardon.

'The Swiss looks stiff as a poker. Obviously not used to these day trips . . .'

Mounted on his machine, he started it and sped off as Gaunt came striding down from his BMW.

'What the devil was all that about?' he barked.

'Avalanche,' Tweed told him. 'You get them in this part of the world in winter. Get back to your car. We're on our way . . .'

Soon the convoy was driving down an even more murderous series of spiral twists and turns which went on and on. Dusk was descending and great stands of fir trees closed in on either side, immense branches weighed down with thick coatings of frozen snow. Paula shivered at the sight of them – it reminded her of films of Siberia she had seen.

The forest moved in to the edges of the road, creating tunnels which she found claustrophobic. Inside the Espace the temperature was dropping despite the fact that Tweed had the heaters turned full on.

They emerged from the tunnels as they reached lower levels and lights inside houses appeared as they passed hamlets tucked into bends and located inside ravines. Their headlights swept over small houses with red-tiled rooves showing in patches close to chimneys: heat from a stove inside had temporarily melted a little snow. First-floor balconies looked as though they'd soon sag under the accumulated snow they supported.

They passed through the small town of Munster, bumping over cobbled streets, slowing down as they approached the outskirts of Colmar. They had just passed a petrol station with a small café attached when a motorcyclist drew alongside the Espace out of nowhere. Eve, who had remained calm and quiet during the drama of the falling cliff, raised her rifle. Paula was already aiming her Browning as Tweed slowed down, saw them.

'Put down those weapons, for God's sake, both of you!' he shouted.

He stopped the Espace as the motorcyclist, a Union Jack whipping from its aerial, pulled up. Tweed left the engine running and looked over his shoulder before he opened the door.

'Paula, keep him covered with your gun, but don't fire unless he produces a weapon.'

He opened the door and the tall motorcyclist stood in the road, the machine leant against him, both hands raised above his head.

'You're Tweed. I've been waiting here hours for you. I'm Barton Ives, Special Agent FBI . . .'

'How did you know I would be coming this way?' demanded Tweed.

'Cord Dillon said you had to pass this spot when you came down from the mountains. That was in the afternoon. I have papers . . .'

'Be very careful what you take out of your pocket,' warned Paula as the stranger reached inside his leather jacket.

He slowly produced a folder, handed it up to Tweed, who examined it by the courtesy light. With the front door open the temperature inside the Espace dropped even further.

Newman appeared behind the stranger. He pressed the tip of his Smith & Wesson into his back.

'This is a gun,' he warned.

'Yeah. I guessed it was. You guys are wise to take all precautions. But aren't we exposed, standing out here?'

'Not really,' Newman told him.

Marler had left the station wagon, was now positioned at the side of the café next to the petrol station. He had loosened the belt round his fur-lined windcheater so he could thrust the tear-gas belt inside it. He was holding the Armalite, his eyes scanning the whole area. Butler, who had returned on his motorcycle, had taken up a position on the opposite side of the road.

Tweed had examined the folder, which seemed genuine, had compared the photograph with Ives' appearance. The American had removed his helmet, had pulled down the scarf from his face. What convinced Tweed of the man's identity was that he fitted the descriptions Dillon had given him. At long last he was meeting the real Barton Ives.

'Get in,' Tweed ordered, 'sit next to me, keep your hands in your lap. There are people behind you with guns and itching trigger fingers. Bob, put his machine in the back of the Espace . . .'

Tweed's careful check had taken no more than a minute. He signalled to Marler and Butler that they were moving on. He waited until Newman had returned to the station wagon and Ives whispered to him.

'I need to be alone with you. I've one helluva story to

441

tell you. My guess is you've no idea what you're up against. Doubt if you'll believe a word I say. It's all incredible, but true.'

'Not now,' Tweed replied. 'We're in a hurry to leave France to cross the border into Switzerland – travelling non-stop this evening. Norton hasn't given up yet – of that I'm sure.'

'You can bet on it,' agreed Ives.

Paula was impressed with the FBI agent's appearance and manner. In his late thirties, she estimated, he was tall, had thick dark hair, his strong-featured face with a firm jaw was clean-shaven. Despite his long ordeal of staying under cover, moving constantly from place to place in fear of his life, he showed no signs of strain. His voice was quiet, controlled, almost matter-of-fact.

'We're going to have to hurry to do that,' Ives observed. 'To reach Switzerland tonight.'

'It's just a matter of organization,' Tweed commented as he continued to drive the Espace close to the station wagon.

The rendezvous point where they had picked up Barton Ives had been well chosen. An oasis of quiet, there had been no one else about. Now, only minutes later, they were caught up in Colmar's rush-hour traffic. The convoy had closed up and Gaunt's BMW was on Tweed's tail, a little too close for his liking, but that was Gaunt.

'How shall we manage it?' Paula called out.

'I'll go out the way we came in. By train to Basle. I want you to come with me, and you too, Eve. Philip,' he called over his shoulder to Cardon, 'you'll also be with us as bodyguard, together with Butler and Nield. Ives, you come with us aboard the train.'

Tweed had no intention of letting the elusive American out of his sight after waiting so long to contact him.

'Anything you say,' Ives agreed cheerfully.

'What about the Espace, the station wagon and the

weapons?' asked Paula, her mind racing ahead to the next problem.

'I'm changing tactics from the way we came in,' Tweed said with a surge of vigour in his voice which made Paula feel tired. He glanced briefly back at her at a red traffic light and his eyes gleamed with purpose and drive. This, Paula thought, is where we really take off.

They were nosing their way closer to the Bristol as Tweed explained further.

'I'm assuming our friend, the Swiss police chief, Beck, will be on the alert at the frontier. The French frontier control will still be on the look-out for terrorists *entering* France – not the other way round. If Newman and Marler meet trouble Bob will immediately ask to be put in contact with Beck.'

'What about the Uzi Bob is carrying?' Paula pressed.

'All the weapons will be hidden, attached under the chassis of the station wagon and the Espace – including the Uzi. That is the sort of trouble Newman may run into. We shall need those weapons for a final showdown, I'm convinced of that.'

'And we stay in Basle overnight?' Paula asked.

'No! We keep on moving. We arrange to meet Newman and Marler with their transport at Basle Bahnhof. From there we drive on non-stop south-west into French-speaking Switzerland. From Basle to Neuchatel, on past the lake to Yverdon, then due south to Ouchy on the shores of Lake Geneva. Amberg, you did say that is where you have hidden the items I want to see and hear?'

'I did,' the banker replied tersely. 'But we have to stop at my branch in Basle for a few minutes – so I can collect a safe deposit key.'

'Make sure it is only a few minutes. Two of my men will accompany you into the bank. Paula, when we reach the main station in Basle phone up two hotels in Ouchy – the Hôtel d'Angleterre to book rooms for Butler and Nield,

443

then the Hôtel Château d'Ouchy to book rooms for the rest of us, including Amberg.'

'I prefer to stay at—' Amberg began.

'Your preferences went out of the window when we watched a blank screen at the Château Noir,' Tweed snapped. 'You stay with us – all the way.'

'So,' Paula mused, 'we'll be ahead of the opposition for once, may never see them again.'

'That,' commented Eve, stretching her arms above her head, 'will be a dream.'

'And if you believe that,' Tweed warned, 'considering the huge organization we're up against, you are dreaming . . .'

On the heights of the Vosges Norton, just managing to stop himself from freezing into a block of ice by keeping the engine running, the heaters turned full up, had earlier received a static-ridden report on progress from Mencken.

Progress! Norton would probably have strangled Mencken had his subordinate been close enough. Bleakly and bluntly Mencken had told his chief about the failure of the major ambush planned on D417.

'You say the Nestlé truck was crushed, sent over when the cliff came down?' Norton asked incredulously.

'It was lousy luck . . .' Mencken began, glad that he was miles away from Norton and close to Munster.

'Luck? *Crap!*' Norton shouted. 'Don't give me no smoke. What happened to Phase Two?'

'The huge log pile we were going to roll down on them was frozen solid. So was the earth-moving machine we'd planned to use . . .'

'And Tweed's convoy is where now?' Norton rarely lost his iron self-control and now had a tight grip on himself as he planned the next move. 'Also where are the cars

Yellow, Orange and Brown – the vital reserve? I am assuming you know,' he added sarcastically.

'Cars Orange and Brown got frozen up. I had to call back Yellow to jump-start them. It all took time. I sent the three of them back down route N415 and through Kaysersberg. I hoped to intercept Tweed, but my guess is they were too late. They couldn't go back down the other route – we'd have been caught by the cliff fall.'

'We were,' Norton reminded him. 'Stay where you are until I contact you again. I've got a job to do – since I want it done OK, I'm handling it myself. Keep the reserve in Colmar until I get back to you . . .'

Norton, due to arrive at Lac Noir at 6 p.m. to keep the appointment with Growly Voice, deliberately reached the rendezvous early at 5.45 p.m. Switching off his headlights, he left the engine running to avoid freezing to death.

Night had fallen and the temperature had fallen with it – to below zero. He lowered the window a few inches, his right hand gripping an HP35 Browning automatic in his lap. His headlights had illuminated a low stone wall with the black waters of the silent lake beyond it.

Very little rattled Norton's nerve but the total lack of sound, the incredible silence and tomb-like atmosphere was unsettling. Where the hell was Growly Voice?

There was no sign of another vehicle, of any human habitation, of any human being. Using his left hand he switched on a powerful torch beam, used it to slowly scan the top of the wall. It was then he saw the wooden box perched on the parapet.

He slid out of the car fast, closing the door quickly so he wasn't illuminated by the courtesy light. For a long minute he stood listening. The icy cold seeped through his astrakhan coat. He approached the box slowly. About a foot long and a foot deep, it was old and the lid was

445

closed. He had an unpleasant suspicion this was a booby-trap. No, that didn't make sense. Growly Voice wanted the big bucks.

The huge sum of money was still under guard in the care of Louis Sheen at a room inside the Hotel Bristol. Earlier Norton had been amused at the thought of Sheen staying tied with handcuffs to the suitcase. The only time he released himself from his burden was when he went to the bathroom or took a shower. Even then he took the suitcase with him.

Norton studied the old box. He was still suspicious. No sign of wires in the torch-light beam. Using the tip of his Browning, he gently lifted the lid until he could see inside. It appeared to be empty. Sucking in a deep breath of icy air, he raised the lid wide open, stared, swore in Marine Corps language.

A sheet of paper was lying at the bottom. Words had been crudely written on it by someone using a felt-tip pen. The infuriating message was clear enough.

Mr Norton. Welcome. If you really want the two items you are interested in bring the money. Proceed now to Ouchy, Switzerland, Lake Geneva. A room has been reserved for you at the Château d'Ouchy. Occupy it this evening. You will hear from me. Do not delay a minute. This time, do bring the money. This is your last chance.

Norton hurled the box into the still black waters of the lake. By the light of his torch beam he watched it sink. He returned to his car, closed the door, the window, and pulled out from the glove compartment a collection of maps until he found one of Switzerland.

It took him a while to trace his finger along the shore of Lake Geneva until he located Ouchy. He picked up his mobile phone. By some miracle Mencken answered at once and the connection was loud and clear.

'Ouchy, Switzerland . . .' Norton spelt the name of the

port. 'Move the entire reserve to this goddamned hick place tonight. Spread them out among as many little hotels as you can find. Call me at eleven tonight but don't come near the Château d'Ouchy. OK? What the hell do I care how you make it? Get on it, street bum . . .'

For the moment Norton was no longer concerned with Tweed. His mind was concentrated on getting hold of the film and the tape – and that meant reaching Ouchy fast. Disinclined to linger by the sinister lake – he had glanced up once and in the moonlight had seen the fateful château perched like a menace above him.

He drove on as fast as he dared until he reached the N415 which would take him back to Kaysersberg. There he'd make a brief call at the Green Tree, collect his few things, pay the bill. At a lonely spot he pulled in off the road on to a snow-covered verge, kept the engine running.

Taking out his collection of maps, he studied them and decided to take the autoroute to Basle. From there he'd drive on through the night until he reached Ouchy. As he put away the maps he decided he'd better later call in at the Hotel Bristol to check that all his remaining team had left. A careful man with detail, Norton was a fanatic for checking out everything.

Marvin Mencken had taken a few decisions of his own. After receiving orders from Norton, he used his mobile phone to contact car Yellow and arranged to meet the men in that car in Munster.

The leader of this team was Jason, a professional gunman from New Jersey. With a face like a bulldog and the determination of the animal, he was probably the most ruthless American below the ranks of Norton and Mencken.

Unlike Norton, Mencken was still very much concerned with the fact that Tweed still survived. It was an insult to his

447

professional integrity. Reaching Munster, he parked his car close to Yellow, got out into the bitter night and walked to give special orders to this reserve team. Cars Orange and Brown were already on their way south to Switzerland. Mencken had warned them over his mobile phone first to collect their bags from the Bristol, to pay their bills. In his own cunning way Mencken rivalled Norton in attention to detail.

'Jason,' he began without ceremony, talking through the open window, 'later you grease your butts and move like the wind to this dump, Ouchy. I've marked it on this spare map. OK? It had better be. Put your men up in a small hotel. Avoid the Château d'Ouchy – I've written that name down on the edge of the map.'

'You said later. We've got a job to do first?'

Jason spoke in a hoarse tone – he was a three-pack a day smoker. His large head and face were faintly illuminated by a nearby street lamp. With his piggy eyes, his pug nose and his lower teeth protruding slightly above his bottom lip, even Mencken thought he looked horrific.

'You've got three other men,' Mencken continued. 'I want you to drive straight to the Bristol. Make yourselves inconspicuous – and keep a lookout for Tweed and his mob.'

'We lose that guy for ever – and the rest of his team?' Jason suggested hopefully.

'You do just that. I'll be following you, get there later. Do a nice quiet job. Afterwards maybe you can prop them up in their beds in their rooms. Give the night maid a nice surprise,' Mencken suggested with his macabre sense of humour.

47

'To the Brasserie!' Tweed called out as they approached closer to the Hôtel Bristol. 'And a glass of Riesling!'

It was an attempt to cheer up his passengers. He sensed that reaction was setting in after the events of the day.

'Anyone would think you hadn't eaten or drunk a thing since leaving Colmar,' Paula chided him.

In fact they had taken refreshment 'on the hoof'. Before leaving the Bristol in the morning Paula had collected a large quantity of *sandwich au jambon* – ham inside French bread. She had also had six Thermoses, purchased in Basle, filled with coffee and another one with cold milk. In addition she had brought twelve litre-bottles of mineral water.

They had eaten and slaked their thirst during the first stage of their descent from the château, and later after the cataclysmic collapse of the cliff. At the same time, Paula reflected, they had had no more than snacks and she too was feeling peckish.

'Are we safe now?' Amberg suddenly demanded in a commanding voice.

'No,' Tweed told him. 'We are only safe when we have our hands on the film and the tape. So really,' he went on in an offhand manner, 'it's entirely up to you, Amberg.'

'They won't know we're going to Ouchy,' the banker suggested.

'Don't count on that either,' Tweed replied, determined to keep the Swiss rattled.

'Do stop fussing, Walter,' Eve broke in with one of her

rare interventions. Her manner was calm, her voice fresh. Paula admired her stamina. 'Walter,' Eve continued, 'if you're nervous don't eat or drink anything at dinner. You might get indigestion. You wouldn't like that, Walter,' she ended, her voice dripping with sarcasm.

Amberg relapsed into silence after casting her a venomous look which Paula noticed. The traffic was now very heavy and, following Newman, Tweed was inching the Espace next to the kerb along the wide pavement outside the shops facing the railway station.

He braked as Newman stopped the station wagon ahead. It occurred to Tweed that it was along this same pavement at a later hour that Jennie Blade had encountered the Shadow Man. What had been her description of the sinister figure? A man wearing a long black overcoat and a wide-brimmed hat which completely concealed his face. Had she been telling the truth? he wondered. Newman appeared at his open window.

'I suggest you all get out here and walk straight into the Brasserie where there are other people. Marler is parking the station wagon a short distance away. I'll take over the wheel of the Espace. Paula, could you run back to the BMW which is pulled up a few yards behind? I want you to escort Jennie into the Brasserie. But first tell Gaunt to follow me in the Espace. And *tell* Gaunt – I don't want any argument.'

'Butler and Nield?' Tweed queried.

'Told over my walkie-talkie to follow the convoy. Now, I want to get behind that wheel fast . . .'

Tweed dropped into the road and hurried to the pavement followed by Paula, Eve, Amberg and Cardon, who had a firm hand on the arm of the Swiss. Newman, Tweed ruminated, was now capable of taking control of the whole operation if anything happened to him.

Eve caught up with him, linked her arm inside his, her rifle concealed under her long trench coat. Paula ran back

450

to where Gaunt had begun to honk his horn non-stop, just when they didn't want to be noticed. Jennie lowered her window when she saw Paula coming. Paula stopped, her tone icy as she addressed Gaunt.

'Stop making that noise at once. Jennie, get out and I will take you inside the Brasserie.'

As Jennie opened the door, moving quickly, Gaunt leaned forward. He glared at Paula.

'Just who do you think you're addressing?' he demanded in a lofty tone.

'You, you stupid arrogant bastard!' she blazed. 'You're putting people's lives in danger. To hell with your own, but get that tin can moving pronto.'

Gaunt was so taken aback, he obeyed. As Paula slammed the door shut he nodded to her, began moving forward, following Newman who was disappearing round the corner in the Espace. Paula took Jennie by the arm, glanced at the mob of people pushing and shoving up against each other while they hurried across to the station. Gaunt had just beaten the lights before they turned red.

Rush hour with a vengeance. Everyone looked sick of doing a day's boring work, sick of trudging through the slush, sick of the penetrating cold. Paula found the normality of all this strangely reassuring after their nightmare trip into the Vosges.

A wave of warmth met them as they pushed open the doors into the well-heated Brasserie. Tweed was already seated at a table in the dining area closest to the hotel with Eve beside him. Cardon sat at the end of the long table where he could survey the whole restaurant.

'A glass of Riesling for everyone who likes the idea,' Tweed announced. 'I think we need a stimulant before we go to our rooms and freshen up before dinner.'

Well, at least we're safe in here, Paula was thinking as she sat next to Cardon and Jennie chose the chair next to

451

hers. Paula agreed enthusiastically to some Riesling and glanced round the restaurant. A handful of locals having a drink on their way home. Then she frowned.

At a table by himself, not ten feet away, sat one of the most repulsive men she'd ever seen, a man who looked just like a bulldog.

Norton drove very slowly when he reached Kaysersberg. The snow was piled up in the ancient narrow streets. This was some country. Hadn't they ever heard of snow-ploughs? He parked the Renault in a side-street some distance from the Green Tree. The less the proprietor of the small hotel knew about him the better.

He met no one as he trudged back through the snow. The old buildings, lit by wrought-iron lamps, had oak beams sunk into the plaster walls. The plaster had a different colour for each building – bright scarlet, deep ochre, flaming orange. Kaysersberg was beautiful, but Norton noticed none of it. Whole lot ought to be pulled down, replaced by modern buildings with plenty of plate-glass.

He walked into the entrance hall of the Green Tree, ignoring the iron scraper outside, littering the carpet with snow. The woman behind the desk called out to him.

'A phone call for you. The same person each time, I think. Called six times. Left a message.'

Norton nodded, took the folded piece of paper. He waited until he'd taken off his fur hat and coat in his small room, then read the message.

Call urgently. Repeat, urgently. Sara.

'Hell. Go jump off a building. A high one,' Norton said out loud.

He checked his watch. It would be 2 p.m. in Washington. He'd half a mind to ignore the message. Sitting on

452

the bed, he decided he'd better make the call. Probably he'd get such a lousy connection it would be pointless.

In a grim mood, he started the laborious business of trying to get through to Washington. The connection wasn't lousy, it was perfect, goddamnit. Sara answered.

'He's pretty anxious to talk with you. I'd go easy if I were you . . .'

'You're not me,' Norton snapped.

'Please yourself.' Sara's tone was calm, indifferent. 'I am putting you on the line. Don't ever say I didn't warn you . . .'

Norton, who had exceptional stamina, was in an ugly mood. It had been a tough day. All attempts to exterminate Tweed had failed. And he hadn't laid his hands on the film or the tape. He wasn't going to bow and scrape.

'Norton?' President Bradford March's tone was aggressive. 'What crap are you feedin' me this time? Give.'

'I know now where what you want is. I'm leaving for some dump called Ouchy in Switzerland. That's where they are. I'll give you my new number after I've got there. Later this evening, European time. We're almost there.'

'I don't give two shits for "almost",' March shouted. 'I should have sent a bell-boy to do this job. Someone is playing you like a fish on a line.'

Which was true, Norton had realized. Growly Voice *had* adopted the technique used by kidnappers. Always sending him on to a new destination to wear him down. The aptness of the President's comment did not improve his temper.

'Just you listen to me for once,' he rapped back. 'I'm the guy on the spot. I know the angles now. Get off my back. Hear me? You listenin' in that snazzy office?'

March had not reached the Oval Office by losing self-control in a crisis. His explosions of abuse were always calculated. Leaning back in his chair, March perched his feet on his desk, crossed his ankles while he thought.

453

'You still there?' Norton demanded abrasively.

'Sure I am,' March replied quietly. 'Is Mencken still around?' he asked casually.

It was Norton's turn to pause. The one possibility which bothered him was that he might be replaced by that scumbag, Mencken. He decided to hold back nothing. March mimicked in a controlled voice Norton's earlier question.

'You still there?'

'Yeah. Let's hope the line holds. You'd better realize we've taken heavy casualties . . .'

'So this Tweed is smarter than we thought?' commented the President in the same quiet tone.

'He just got lucky.' Norton was leading March away from the subject of Marvin Mencken. 'We've taken some heavy casualties,' he repeated.

'So you can't make the omelette without breakin' a few eggs,' March responded in a bored tone.

'I was going to say we could do with more manpower.'

'Would Mencken need more manpower? You didn't tell me – is Mencken still around?'

'Yes.'

'I can't spare more manpower. I need what I have left here in Washington. Certain guys have to be clamped down on. You said earlier Tweed got lucky,' March recalled, building up to bait Norton some more. 'I'd say he got smart as he's still around.' A pause. 'I don't hear no denial of that. I gave you a time limit, Norton. Time's almost up. I want the film, the tape. I want Tweed, Joel Dyson, Cord Dillon and Barton Ives dumped. For ever. Get on it . . .'

The connection to Washington had gone. Norton slowly put down the receiver and didn't even bother to swear. Ouchy was going to be a blood bath.

*   *   *

Inside his study at his Chevy Chase house Senator Wingfield looked round at his two guests seated at the round table with a cold expression. His guests, the banker and the elder statesman, watched him closely, realizing there had been a very serious development.

The Senator had summoned them to attend a meeting of the Three Wise Men urgently at short notice. It was not this factor which caused them to sense the atmosphere of tension inside the comfortable room. Wingfield normally had the appearance of a benevolent father figure. He rarely showed any emotion and it was the grimness of his aristocratic features which held their attention.

'Gentlemen,' Wingfield began, 'I have just received this highly confidential communication from the Vice President. Jeb Calloway has received the report I have inside this folder by special delivery from Europe. It makes incredible reading – I just hope its author is insane.'

'But do you think he is? Insane?' the statesman enquired.

'If he isn't – and I have a horrible idea he's as sane as any man round this table – our country faces the most serious crisis of this century.'

'You know who the report is from?' asked the banker.

'Yes. A special agent of the FBI. A man called Barton Ives.' He extracted the typed sheets from the folder, handed them to the banker. 'Judge for yourselves.'

'These documents allege this Barton Ives knows who is responsible for a number of particularly beastly serial murders in several Southern states,' the banker, who was a fast reader, commented in a shaky voice after a few minutes. 'Each involves the murder of a woman by cutting her throat – after rape had been committed, according to the medical examiner's report in the state concerned. All the murders have remained unsolved, even though they took place several years ago. It's beyond belief.'

'What is?' demanded the statesman as the banker handed him the documents.

'The man he names as the perpetrator of these vile crimes. Not only was the throat of each victim cut with a serrated knife – a kitchen knife is suggested – but similar sadistic mutilations were found on each corpse.'

'Who is this Barton Ives?' the statesman persisted before examining the documents. 'I seem to have heard the name.'

'A very senior agent of the FBI,' Wingfield said reluctantly. 'I made discreet enquiries before I called you. Ives was in charge of the investigation linking all six murders. He was about to prepare a comprehensive report when his superior at the Memphis office was posted to Seattle. The new man ordered Ives to discontinue the investigation and destroy the files. He was sent to Memphis on direct orders from Washington. Ives alleges he had to flee to Europe to save his life. My enquiries back up this strange sequence of events.'

There was a heavy silence as the statesman skimmed through the reports. He held each page at the edges between his fingertips, leaving no prints of his own. Dropping the last sheet back inside the folder, he used his elbow to push the folder back to Wingfield across the polished table.

'There is mention of a thumbprint being found on the side of a Lincoln Continental belonging to the sixth raped and murdered woman,' he pointed out. 'Barton Ives says he has that thumbprint and it still exists on the car. So where the hell is the car?'

'I enquired about that,' Wingfield told him. 'Before he left Memphis on his flight to Europe Ives hid the car somewhere. Difficult to achieve – considering the size of the car – but Ives has a wealth of experience. You see, he says he is the only one who knows its location.'

'Well,' said the statesman, 'we've had every kind of corrupt president, quite apart from Watergate. Presidents with mistresses – common enough. Some with illegitimate children. Others who've walked into the Oval Office with little more than the clothes they stood up in. By the time they stepped down from the presidency they were million-aires. So, I suppose one day – in this age of exceptional violence – we should have expected something like this.'

'*If* it's true, he can't stay untouched in the Oval Office,' the Senator said with great force.

'But you haven't enough evidence there to do anything,' the statesman objected.

'So I need this Barton Ives in this room so we can grill him. I think I'll have a word with the Veep.'

'Is Barton Ives Jeb Calloway's man?' enquired the banker.

'I didn't say that, did I?' Wingfield replied cautiously.

'And how would you handle it if all this grim business concerning six serial murders proved true?' demanded the statesman in his direct way. 'Impeachment?'

'We can't have the nation's name dragged through the mud. That's the only certainty I know now,' the Senator replied. 'As to how we'd handle it – I suggest we adjourn this meeting, tell no one of our suspicions, and await events . . .'

Bradford March was drinking beer out of an upended bottle when Sara answered his summons. She waited while he wiped the back of a hairy hand across his mouth.

'I hear strong rumours that the Holy Trinity are meeting more frequently,' he remarked. 'Don't like it.'

This was the President's irreverent way of referring to the Three Wise Men. He pouched his lips, stared at Sara. She realized he expected a reaction.

457

'So we do something about it? Is that what you're saying? If so, how do we hack it? We could be dealing with a load of dynamite. Those three may be old dinosaurs but they sure as hell carry plenty of clout. Back off, Brad.'

'Sometimes, Sara, your advice is good, very good.' March leaned back in his chair, nursing the beer bottle. 'And sometimes it's lousy, real lousy. This is one of those times.'

'It's your' – she had been going to say 'funeral' but hastily changed the word – 'decision. Just tell me.'

'I want three guys from Unit One – each in his own car – to follow the senator, the statesman and the banker night and day. Draw up a duty roster so they get relieved, stay fresh, on the job. I want daily reports of every person the Holy Trinity bums contact.' His head tilted up, he stared at her hard. 'Why not get started now?'

Sara moved fast on her new mission. Inside an hour the three chosen watchers from Unit One were stationed near Senator Wingfield's house in Chevy Chase. Sara had just heard rumours of a meeting taking place there.

The watchers arrived exactly thirty minutes too late. The two limousines had already called at the house, had picked up and driven away their illustrious passengers.

48

Seated by himself at a table in the Brasserie, Jason, the American with a head and a face like a bulldog, wore his padded windcheater despite the warmth of the restaurant. He had to – in the shoulder holster under his left armpit nestled a Luger.

As he sat drinking beer and piling omelette into his wide mouth he congratulated himself on his luck. His main target – selected by Mencken himself – was sitting facing him with a couple of good-looking chicks and a harmless young guy who couldn't be a day over thirty.

Between shovelling mouthfuls of omelette into his maw he took another look at Paula and Jennie. The target – Tweed – was a pushover, he'd decided. At that moment his eyes met Tweed's. The Englishman gazed back at him with a penetrating stare and Jason hastily glanced away. The eyes worried him – but no one shot with their eyes.

Jason glanced towards the exit leading to the street and decided he'd make the distance in seconds. After putting a couple of bullets into Tweed – which would guarantee his next destination would be the local cemetery.

Accompanied by Newman, Barton Ives walked in from the hotel. Tweed's admiration of the FBI man increased as he looked at his appearance. Ives was wearing one of those deep medical collars of foam material used to support the head and restrict its movements. With his jaw tilted up and a dark beret concealing his trim black hair his appearance was transformed. He sat next to Tweed and spoke in an urgent whisper.

'The sooner we can talk with each other alone the better. What I've got to tell you concerns the present occupant of the White House . . .'

'Later,' Tweed whispered back. 'Arrangements are being changed. I've had second thoughts. You'll travel with me by train to Switzerland and Newman will come with us. Don't look at that rough character facing me at a table opposite . . .'

At that moment Butler and Nield walked into the Brasserie by the short cut from the hotel. Tweed watched the two men as they suddenly paused.

'Don't much like the look of that chap sitting by himself and facing Tweed,' Nield commented.

'Reminds me of a pit-bull terrier,' replied Butler, who didn't know much about dogs.

'He must be roasting in that heavy windcheater. Funny he hasn't taken it off.'

'Maybe that bulge under his left armpit is the reason. I could swear he's carrying a gun,' Butler remarked. 'And he's a Yank – the sort Norton would employ. Look at the way he shovels food into his mouth with a fork. No table manners. I think he's trouble.'

'I wouldn't dispute that,' agreed Nield. 'I think maybe we ought to keep a close eye on Brother Pit-Bull. Let's outflank him. Rattle him. With a bit of luck he'll push off outside and we can follow him . . .'

As Tweed watched, the two men separated. Jason had already noticed their arrival, the pause while they stared in his direction. He began to feel less confident.

Nield made a lot of noise as he pulled out a wooden chair from a table behind Jason, scraping it across the tiled floor. Butler chose a more distant table, at a diagonal angle to the American's thick neck. To see either of the new arrivals Jason had to twist round in his seat in two different directions – making it obvious what he was doing.

Tweed had surreptitiously watched the manoeuvre of Butler and Nield with a mixed feeling of amusement and relief. The arrival of Barton Ives, despite his effective disguise, worried him. It was a very public place. Ives spoke to him from behind the menu he was studying.

'I had spotted him. A professional gunman. A Norton recruit would be my guess. Cold as ice. Except he's now hot and bothered, as I believe you Brits say. Literally – sweat is running off his forehead. Those two guys who came in are yours? Thought so. I like their tactics . . .'

Jason had decided – rightly so – that it would be suicide to draw his Luger. He called for the bill, paid the waiter, left half his beer in the glass, stood up and walked casually to the exit leading to the street. Outside rush hour had vanished like water down a plug-hole and the pavement was deserted now night had fallen.

'After you, sir . . .'

Jason paused at the open door, a door held open by Nield who had reached it first the moment Jason began to move. The American suffered a rare moment of indecision. If he said he'd changed his mind and started back into the restaurant, where would that get him? The only alternative was to proceed on into the deserted street – a course of action Jason felt uneasy about.

'OK, buddy . . .'

He stared at Nield who was smiling pleasantly while holding the door open with his left hand. Jason walked out.

Nield followed him immediately, moving as silently as a cat close up behind his quarry. Jason felt something hard and cylindrical pushed hard against his spine. He froze.

'This is a Walther 7.65-mm. automatic and the magazine holds eight rounds,' Nield informed him in a conversational tone. 'I'm prepared to pull the trigger until the mag is emptied. Turn slowly to your right, walk twelve paces, again slowly, then stop. Start counting now.'

'This a friggin' hold-up?' Jason blustered.

'Don't ask questions. Just do what I told you to . . .'

As Jason began counting paces Butler appeared alongside him, keeping in step. The American glanced sideways and didn't like the expression on Butler's face. After twelve paces he stopped. Nield pressed the Walther harder into his spine to remind him of its presence. There was no one else about as Butler stood in front of Jason, reached inside his windcheater with his gloved hand, hauled out a Luger.

'You said something about a hold-up,' Butler remarked. 'Is that the trade you practise?'

'I need protection . . .' Jason began.

'Shut up!' snapped Nield.

Near where they stood two chairs were propped against a wall. In more clement weather tables and chairs were spread out on the pavement for customers to sit at while they enjoyed a drink. Shoving the Luger behind his belt inside his jacket, Butler moved swiftly. He arranged the chairs together so they could be sat on. He went back to where Jason stood with a puzzled expression.

'Turn round and face my partner,' Butler ordered.

As the American turned away from him Butler brought down the barrel of the Luger on Jason's skull. The American was sagging when both Butler and Nield grabbed hold of his inert body, dragged him to the chairs, sat him down, arranged him so he leaned against the back of them.

Nield produced a half bottle of wine he'd brought from the Brasserie. Uncorking it, he spilt a liberal amount down Jason's chin and over his windcheater. Butler had checked his neck pulse, which beat steadily, before they walked back inside the Brasserie. He had also shoved the Luger back inside the shoulder holster.

The one thing both men omitted to notice was a Renault parked in the shadows, apparently empty.

Marvin Mencken, his seat pushed as far back as it would go, had concealed himself when he saw the three men emerging from the Brasserie. In a state of shock, he instinctively hid himself. Once again an apparently foolproof plan had gone wrong. Mencken had told Jason he'd wait outside to pick him up, drive the hell out of Colmar once he'd killed Tweed.

His expression was malevolent and evil as he climbed out of the Renault he had commandeered from one of his surviving teams. In return, he had given them the Land-Rover with a shattered windscreen. Listening, he heard only silence. At this hour even the streets were clear of traffic.

Bending over Jason, he checked the carotid artery, felt its steady beat. His expression became matter-of-fact as he pulled on a pair of gloves. Like Butler, he reached inside Jason's windcheater, hauled out the Luger. Unlike Butler, who had used only enough force to render Jason unconscious for some time, Mencken checked again to make sure he was alone.

He then raised the barrel of the Luger high above his shoulder, brought it down on Jason's skull with such vicious force it rebounded off the skull. Again Mencken checked the carotid artery. Nothing. Jason was dead meat. He'd failed in his task – and there was the added chance the police would find the corpse. Thrusting the Luger back inside the holster, Mencken was about to topple the sagging corpse on to the pavement when he heard a car approaching. He dived back inside the Renault, dipped his head out of sight. The car moved on into the night. Mencken straightened up, adjusted his seat, started the engine and drove off. Bound for this Ouchy dump on the shores of Lake Geneva.

'Do let me in on the secret,' Gaunt's voice boomed out as he joined Tweed's table unasked. 'What's our next port of call on this Cook's tour? Ouchy and points south? Eve is dying of curiosity.'

'Eve is doing nothing of the sort,' Eve Amberg rapped back at Gaunt, obviously well tanked up on alcohol. 'You're the one devoured with curiosity.' She looked at Tweed. 'Then he pretends I'm the one after all sorts of strange and weird information.'

Paula pricked up her ears. Eve sounded convincing. Why would Gaunt adopt this devious ploy?

'I've ordered the largest omelette in the world,' Gaunt

463

went on as his bulk sagged into a chair at the table. 'I trust, Eve, you'll be keeping me company in the BMW. Can't travel without some feminine companionship.'

'Your trust is misplaced,' she shot back at him. 'I'm travelling back by train with Tweed.'

'I suppose you'd accept me as a substitute companion?' Jennie suggested.

'Damn right I will,' boomed Gaunt. 'Jennie and I are on the same waveband.'

Paula glanced at Jennie and then at Gaunt. She had the impression Gaunt had known Eve would refuse, had known Jennie would offer to come with him. Paula had begun to sense that Gaunt and Jennie were working hand in glove without making it obvious.

Gaunt's relationship with the two women intrigued her. At first she'd thought it was Eve who was close to the Squire. Now it appeared Gaunt had used that as a cover for his closeness to Jennie and Eve had consistently distanced herself from him. Why?

Eve had joined Tweed for dinner soon after the incident of the man with a face like a dog. They were finishing the meal, drinking coffee and Tweed was draining his glass of Riesling while Gaunt wolfed down his huge omelette. At that moment Butler, who had strolled out of the exit on to the street for the second time, came hurrying back. He laid a hand on his chief's shoulder.

'Excuse me,' Tweed said, standing up. 'Arrangements to make!' He looked at Newman. 'Take care of the bill for me, Bob.' He guessed that some kind of emergency had just arisen from Butler's action.

Tweed was leaving the Brasserie by the short cut into the hotel when Butler, close behind him, gave a little jerk of his head to Nield who was lingering over coffee at a table by himself.

Having paid the bill earlier, Nield left the table and strolled casually after them. At Tweed's table Gaunt was holding everyone's attention with some outrageous story – except for Newman, who saw Nield leaving.

Passing through the main restaurant – now empty – Tweed led the way into the reception hall and into a small sitting area in a large alcove. There was no one behind the reception counter as the others joined him.

'A crisis?' Tweed enquired in a mild tone.

'A major one,' Butler reported, keeping his voice down as Nield sat in a third chair. 'That gunman we dealt with outside the Brasserie is dead.'

'So what happened?'

'Pete and I sorted him out. I knocked him unconscious with his own Luger, left the gun with him after we'd parked him on a couple of chairs.'

'I poured wine down his jaw and over his windcheater,' Nield added. 'No one wants anything to do with a drunk sleeping it off.'

'You definitely left him unconscious?' Tweed probed.

'Fact one,' Butler began, 'I checked his neck pulse. It was normal. Fact two, there was no blood from the blow I gave him. Now there's blood all down the side of his face – and a second blow has split his skull. Dead as a doornail.'

'Then we leave here fast.' Tweed took out a notebook, checked train times Paula had obtained earlier. 'An express for Basle leaves here in thirty minutes. I'll be aboard – with Paula, Eve, Amberg, Barton Ives, Newman and Philip Cardon. You both know what to do, where to meet us.'

'I drive the Espace to Basle, Pete drives the station wagon,' Butler replied. 'We park near Basle Bahnhof and wait for you to arrive in the station's first-class restaurant.'

'I have phoned Beck,' Tweed told them. 'He has the registration numbers of both vehicles and has given orders to the Swiss border guards to let you through. So you can tape the weapons underneath the chassis of both cars without worry. Now, speed is the order of the day.'

He had stood up, checked his watch. They had to get out of France before the corpse outside was discovered. In the Brasserie there were locals who had nothing better to do than to notice what was going on. He hurried back into the Brasserie to collect the others. It would be a race against time – to cross the frontier before a *flic* decided to check the body.

They boarded the express with two minutes to spare. At that hour and time of year they found an empty first-class coach. Tweed sat with Barton Ives. Cardon, who had left the table in the Brasserie to guard Amberg before the meal started – the banker had been locked in Tweed's room – sat next to the Swiss further along the coach.

Newman occupied a seat on his own, which gave him a good view of both entrances to the coach. Paula sat chatting with Eve in seats out of hearing of any conversation between Tweed and Ives. Earlier, Tweed had given instructions that he wanted to travel alone with Ives.

Much earlier still, Marler had left Colmar, driving his red Mercedes down the autoroute. His instructions from Tweed had been clear and decisive.

'We are approaching a major crisis – a climax to this whole business might be a better phrase. I'm assuming that in some way Norton will have discovered that Ouchy is our destination. He's discovered everything else we planned to do.'

'I'll drive like the wind – strictly within speed limits, of course,' Marler drawled. 'And when I reach Ouchy?'

'In your own individual way – you can pass for a Frenchman and Ouchy is in French-speaking Switzerland – you check all the hotels which are open at this time of the year. You're looking for recently arrived Americans.

When I say "recently", I mean today. When I arrive you should know the location of the opposition, if they have arrived. We are going over on to the offensive.'

'It's Switzerland,' Marler said thoughtfully, 'so gunshots are liable to bring the local police running. If a shop is still open when I reach Basle I'll buy some Swiss Army knives. Useful little tools, Swiss Army knives – for silent kills.'

'In this situation you have a free hand. Come to think of it, you usually have one anyway.'

'You did use the word offensive,' Marler reminded Tweed.

The express took about forty minutes to reach Basle from Colmar. During the journey Barton Ives began talking, hoping to Heaven that Tweed would believe him.

'Several years ago, Mr Tweed, I was stationed at FBI headquarters in Memphis, Tennessee. I'd been promoted to senior agent, responsible only to Humphries, the local director. There was a hideous murder in that state soon after I'd settled there. An attractive woman driving a Cadillac across lonely country was somehow persuaded to stop her car after dark. I'd gotten to know the local medical examiner – what you call a pathologist. He told me the details of the autopsy. Got a strong stomach, Mr Tweed?'

'Reasonably so. Try me.'

'The woman – from a wealthy family – had been savagely raped. Then her throat had been cut. The instrument used was a knife with a serrated blade. Most probably a kitchen knife, the ME said. She had then been sadistically mutilated in a way which suggested the murderer was a psychopath. Quite horrendous. After viewing the body I can tell you I didn't eat much that evening. The mutilation puzzled the ME. He told me it was exactly how he'd commence an autopsy.'

'Someone with medical knowledge?' Tweed queried.

467

'The ME didn't think so. But he thought the sadist who'd inflicted the wounds may once have witnessed an autopsy being performed. That was the first case.'

'You were investigating it?' Tweed asked, puzzled.

'No. The local police handled the case, never even came up with a suspect. As I think you've realized, the FBI only enters the scene when a criminal crosses a state line. I came into the picture when the second rape and murder occurred six months later.'

'Why were you able to do so then?'

'The second victim – again a wealthy woman driving home in the dark – was attacked in another Southern state. I heard about it, checked the details – the same gory procedure had been carried out as in the first case. That strongly suggested the same rapist and killer was in business again – and he'd crossed a state line. Which brought in the FBI and I was given the investigation.'

'Was any evidence left behind in either case?' Tweed enquired.

Tweed was recalling cases he had solved years before – in the days when he had held a high rank while working for the Murder Squad at Scotland Yard. So often chance had fingered the guilty party.

'Not yet.' Ives sighed. 'It was a frustrating time. Then after six months I heard the details of the third case. This time in a different Southern state. By now we were thinking in terms of a serial killer. So the data from case three was fed to me almost at once. After the autopsy. Again the victim was a wealthy woman driving home in the dark by herself in an expensive car across a lonely area. After viewing the corpse – like the others, she had been physically attractive – I began to think, to ask questions of myself.'

'What sort of person would these women stop for in the middle of nowhere in the dark?' Tweed suggested quietly.

'Yes.' Ives sounded surprised. 'That was my main

question. I saw you once at a security conference in Washington and friends who knew you said you were good. Very good . . .'

Tweed said nothing. He noticed that Paula was gazing into the night and he looked in the same direction. In the moonlight the snowbound summits and saddlebacks of the Vosges showed up clearly. There were pinpoints of light in remote villages. From her expression he guessed that Paula was contrasting the beauty of the scene with the terror they had experienced among the spiralling roads, the Siberian cold and icy ravines. Ives was talking again as the express began to lose speed.

'Then there were three more similar cases – so similar it was uncanny. In three more different Southern states. He never struck in Tennessee again. Always a wealthy woman by herself and driving across a lonely area in the dark. And he used the same hideous technique in every case. He was a serial killer – six cases.'

'And never a clue?' Tweed probed. 'Remarkable. They usually slip up once.'

'He did. In the last case. He left a clear thumbprint under the handle of the car which stopped, a Lincoln Continental. I'd heard rumours that Humphries, my old chief, was going to be recalled, replaced by someone new from Washington. Some sixth sense made me hide the Lincoln Continental in an old barn in the wilderness. It's still there, I'm sure. And I've got a replica of that thumbprint . . .'

Newman had stood up, was leaning against the end of his seat, his windcheater unzipped so he could swiftly grab hold of his Smith & Wesson. The express was approaching Basle Bahnhof. If anyone was going to make an attempt on Tweed it would be soon – as soon as they could jump out of the train at the station after they'd pulled the trigger. Tweed knew exactly what he was doing. He stood up to put on his coat as he spoke to Ives.

469

'Have to continue this conversation a little later,' he suggested. 'Cardon is strolling towards us. He'll be guarding you. And maybe you'd watch over Amberg.'

'We should be OK now we've returned to Switzerland.'

'Just how OK were you when you were dodging from one hotel to another in Zurich?' Tweed reminded him.

Tweed and Newman left the express together, walking side by side. Close behind them Paula followed with Eve Amberg. Cardon brought up the rear, a step behind Barton Ives, who escorted the Swiss banker.

French Customs and Passport Control were deserted. As they passed through the Swiss checkpoints Tweed's fears were doubly confirmed. Standing in civilian clothes behind uniformed Passport officers he saw Arthur Beck. The Swiss police chief took no notice of him. As they walked on, heading for the first-class restaurant, Harry Butler appeared. He fell into step on the other side of Tweed.

'I'm amazed you made it here so quickly,' Tweed commented. 'Mind you, the express did stop a while for no reason soon after we left Colmar.'

'We put our feet down,' Butler said tersely. 'Autoroutes help. Do you really want to go into the first-class dining-room? Pete Nield is waiting there – he's watching a member of the opposition who followed us. Head like a skull. Saw him giving orders back at the Bristol . . .'

49

Leaving Colmar on his way to Basle in the Renault, Marvin Mencken had been lucky. Butler and Nield, however, had been unlucky.

After killing his subordinate – who had failed in his mission to liquidate Tweed – Mencken had headed for the autoroute. He had only moved a short distance from the Bristol when he saw a gas station. At that same moment his engine coughed and spluttered.

Pulling into the petrol station, Mencken asked a mechanic to check his ignition when his tank was refilled. He was about to drive on when he saw two familiar vehicles pass – a grey Espace and a station wagon. Mencken grinned, followed them.

'You know we have a tail,' Nield warned Butler over his walkie-talkie as they proceeded along the autoroute.

'The Renault,' Butler replied. 'Can't do a damn thing about it. We've been told to get into Switzerland at the earliest possible moment. Just keep driving. Leave the problem until later . . .'

Reaching Basle Bahnhof, they parked their cars, walked into the first-class restaurant as two separate individuals, sat at different tables, ordered coffee. A skeletal-faced character in a trench coat walked in after them, chose a table by the wall some distance away, ordered a drink.

'I could score one off Norton,' Mencken said to himself. 'They could be waiting for the rest of their gang . . .'

He wasn't in the least worried that he was delaying his

arrival in Ouchy. Plenty of his men were on their way to the Swiss resort. Mencken had, with his usual efficiency, arranged for Louis Sheen, the courier with the suitcase containing a huge fortune, to be driven under guard to Ouchy. That, apparently, was where the vital exchange would take place. He frowned when, some time later, Butler stood up and wandered out of the place.

Pete Nield had remained sitting at his own table. Mencken glanced at the slim man with the trim moustache who was, apparently, watching a blonde girl at a distant table.

Mencken decided his opponents had made a mistake. He'd wait until he could get Moustache on his own in a less public place. Mencken had no doubt he could make Moustache spill his guts.

'When you saw this American giving orders,' Tweed said to Butler as he continued walking slowly towards the restaurant, 'did you get the impression he carried a lot of authority?'

'One of Norton's top brass, would be my guess. I saw where he's parked his Renault just outside,' Butler added.

'First, point him out to me from the entrance. Second, you then take Ives, Paula, Eve, Amberg and Cardon to the Espace. Third, you fix our American friend's Renault.'

'What are you going to do?' asked Butler, alarmed.

'It's time Bob and I had a word with the opposition face to face . . .'

Tweed had decided it was time to stop running. He'd said in Colmar they were going on to the offensive. This seemed like a good moment to start. Butler indicated Mencken to Tweed from the door, although Tweed now recognized him instantly – the same man had walked into the bar at the Baur-en-Ville in Zurich, had stared up at Paula and himself before retreating back into the hotel. At that moment the American was watching Nield.

Hands deep inside his trench coat pockets, Tweed headed straight for Mencken's table with Newman beside him. He took out one hand, pulled back a chair at the table for four, sat facing the skeletal-faced man, who stiffened. Newman sat alongside Mencken, used his left hand to stop the American pushing his chair back from the table. His right hand was slipped inside his windcheater, gripping his Smith & Wesson.

'Relax,' Newman advised him. 'Take it easy, as you never stop saying in New York.'

'What's New York got to do with anything?' Mencken sneered.

He reached inside his own trench coat. Newman's right hand closed over his wrist.

'Be careful what you take out,' he advised again.

'Your nerves all shot to hell?' Mencken sneered again.

He withdrew his hand slowly. It was holding a pack of Marlboro and a lighter. Lighting a cigarette, he blew the smoke in Tweed's direction. Tweed waved it away before he spoke.

'Maybe my friend should have said Washington,' he remarked.

'Don't give *me* no smoke,' Mencken snapped, his manner nervy at the reference to Washington.

'I hope you don't mind our joining you,' Tweed went on, 'but you've been keeping us company for a long time. Maybe you would tell me why?'

'What the shit does that mean?'

'Manners,' Newman interjected. 'You ought to wash out your mouth more often. It means you've been stumbling over us all the way from Zurich. My friend would like to know why. He just asked you.'

'I don't have to talk to you guys, whoever you are . . .'

473

'I wouldn't think about leaving.' The suggestion had come from Nield who was now sitting at the next table, his chair twisted round so he faced the American. 'Ever felt the walls closing in on you?' he enquired.

'This is a free country. We're in Switzerland.'

Mencken's aggressive manner was fading. Minutes ago he had been confident he would get Nield on his own. Now he was the one on his own. He cursed the fact that he'd sent all his men rushing down to Ouchy. He suddenly realized that the blonde girl had left the restaurant, that it was empty except for himself and his interrogators. Even the staff seemed to have vanished. The time of the year – March – and the time of day.

'Is America such a free country these days?' Tweed asked him. 'Considering the people in power? Talking about power, how is my old acquaintance, Mr Norton?'

'Look . . .' Mencken was talking fast as though making a desperate attempt to convince Tweed he didn't know what he was talking about. 'Look, I'm an executive of a company selling machine tools. Business is lousy . . .'

'You sell a lot of machine tools in the Vosges mountains?' Newman demanded.

'If you guys don't get off my back I'm going to want some police . . .'

The strain was showing in Mencken's shifting eyes, in the way he smoked his cigarette, being very careful to keep smoke away from Tweed, in the way his shoulders kept jerking under his trench coat. Marvin Mencken was coming apart at the seams.

'You can have the police,' Newman assured him. 'Right out of the top drawer. The Chief of Federal Police happens to be here in this station. Want me to go and fetch him? Just say the word.'

'Look, you guys, I didn't expect this. I've had a long day. Nothing but pressure.' He turned to Newman. 'You know? That's what gets to you when you're away from

474

home. Pressure. What's all this stuff about, anyway?'

'Maybe we could start with your name?' Tweed suggested.

'Sure. Why not? I'm Marvin Mencken . . .'

'What company do you work for?' Tweed pressed on.

'An outfit based in the Middle West. I guess you mixed me with someone else. Right?'

'Not right.' Tweed shook his head, his attitude still cool, almost offhand. 'You could spend Lord knows how many years in a Swiss gaol. Not comfortable places, Swiss gaols. Over here they believe in punishment for criminal offences.'

'What criminal offence?' Mencken stubbed out his cigarette, immediately lit a fresh one. 'Like I said, you're all mixed up . . .'

'The bomb thrown in Bahnhofstrasse by the pseudo-cripple,' Tweed went on remorselessly. 'The Chief of Police, Beck, is handling that case himself. A hard man.'

'Don't know nothin' about a bomb,' Mencken protested.

He was sweating. Beads of moisture had formed on his low forehead. Newman passed him a handkerchief.

'Use this. Clean yourself up.'

Mencken took the handkerchief. Afraid to show fear, to take out his own handkerchief, he mopped himself dry, returned the handkerchief.

'See the state you guys have got me into? What is this? The third degree? I don't have to take this . . .'

'Then there was the mass murder down in Cornwall, England. Eight people just shot down in cold blood by a masked gunman.'

'Mass murder? In England?' Mencken had jerked himself upright. 'You guys *are* crazy. Cornwall, you said? So where's that? I ain't never been to the place. This is screwy. You *have* got the wrong guy.'

Tweed had been watching the American closely,

listening to him intently. For the first time there was vehemence in his tone, the vehemence of a man telling the truth.

Nield had been keeping one eye on the entrance to the restaurant. Now he saw Butler appear briefly, giving a thumbs-up signal. He had dealt with Mencken's Renault. Nield nodded twice to Tweed as Butler disappeared. Tweed sighed, checked his watch, pushed back his chair, stood up, both hands in his pockets as he addressed Mencken.

'I advise you to catch a flight from the airport here in the morning to Zurich. From there you can board a non-stop flight to Washington. You might just get clear of Norton.'

'Washington? I told you – I'm from the Middle West. Why this Washington thing? And Norton, Norton, Norton. Who the hell is he?'

Mencken was talking to himself. Tweed had walked away, leaving the restaurant. Newman followed, leaving Nield behind to watch the American. When they had disappeared Nield also stood up, leaned down, patted Mencken on the shoulder.

'I wouldn't leave for ten minutes. If you do there are police outside who'll arrest you. They'll take a great interest in that gun you're packing under your armpit. Do yourself a big favour. Start counting now . . .'

'I think I achieved my aim,' Tweed said to Newman as they walked towards the station exit.

'Which was?'

'To shake Master Mencken to the core – to rattle his cage. Above all, to persuade him to underestimate me. He'll report the encounter to Norton sooner or later. I want them off guard for the final confrontation . . .'

Butler escorted them to the Espace. Barton Ives had

476

done exactly what Tweed had quietly suggested to him as they earlier conversed briefly before leaving the train. He'd escorted Amberg to the Espace, parked just outside the station. The two men were sitting near the rear while Ives, alert as ever, watched Tweed and his companions approaching.

Paula, assuming that Tweed would again be driving, sat by herself in the front passenger seat. In a row further back Eve sat on the other side of Amberg, flanking the banker with Ives. Was she also suspecting that the Swiss was going to try and run off if he got the opportunity?

Tweed climbed in behind the wheel while Newman boarded the Espace at the rear. Closing the door, Tweed suddenly stood up, made his way swiftly to where Amberg sat in grim silence. He tapped the banker on the knee.

'You said the key to the security box in Ouchy is kept at your branch in Bankverein. I'm driving there now. You will, accompanied by Newman, open the bank, go in, collect the key, come straight back to the Espace. You understand me clearly?'

'At this time of night there are alarms . . .' the banker began.

'Which you know how to deactivate so they won't wake up half Basle. Don't play games with me, Amberg. I'm no longer in the mood for them.' He looked at Newman. 'Where is Philip Cardon?'

'Just about to come aboard. He insisted on maintaining a watch hidden in the entrance to that hotel over there. He told me he'd wait outside just before we entered the restaurant. Cardon is smart . . .'

As Tweed settled himself behind the wheel again, started the engine, he glanced all round. In the depths of winter no one lingered outside the station. A tram, ochre-coloured and smaller than its Zurich counterpart, trundled in to a nearby stop. No one aboard except the

477

driver. No passengers waiting to board it. The empty tram seemed to Paula to symbolize the deserted desolate atmosphere of Basle in March after dark. She had purposely said nothing to Tweed, sensing his concentration on his secret thoughts. He saw Butler and Nield hurrying towards the parked station wagon, waited until they were inside the vehicle and moved off. To the Zurcher Kredit Bank.

Tweed followed the tramline along a deserted street which curved and sloped steadily downwards – towards the distant Rhine and the Drei Könige where they had stayed. Was it a million years ago? There was no other traffic and Paula found the street, hemmed in on both sides by tall, solid stone buildings, eerie and unsettling. In his wing-mirror Tweed saw the station wagon transporting Butler and Nield following him.

'Should be round the next corner if I remember rightly,' Tweed commented, sensing Paula's unease.

'They go to bed early in Basle,' she remarked.

'Not a lot to stay up for, is there?' Tweed replied.

'Stop the car! There are lights in my bank. Someone has broken in . . .'

Amberg's voice, calling out in surprisingly commanding and vigorous tone. Tweed signalled, pulled in to the kerb. Unfastening his belt, he twisted round in his seat, staring at the banker and Eve, who had laid a restraining hand on his arm.

'There is a woman who works for you at the bank . . .' Tweed began.

'It can't be her, I tell you,' Amberg rapped back with an air of authority. 'Karin would have gone home hours ago. Always at the same time to her apartment near by.'

'And always by the same route?' Tweed suggested.

'Yes. It's the quickest way for her to get home. Even when she's going shopping she goes home first to collect her basket . . .'

478

'Always at the same time and by the same route?' Tweed repeated.

'Yes. I've already told you that . . .'

So even Swiss security can be fallible, Tweed thought grimly. The deadly scenario was so obvious. Someone had followed Karin home after checking her routine. They had probably forced her at gunpoint to return after dark with the keys to the bank. They'd been clever enough to foresee the alarm system, to force her to deactivate it. Now they were inside and doubtless she knew about the key to the vital safe deposit. Tweed thought he now knew why Mencken had lingered in the restaurant at the station – waiting for his thugs to do this job.

'I'd better go inside, see what's happening.'

Newman had left the Espace, was now outside Tweed's open window. His right hand by his side held the Smith & Wesson.

'Take Butler and Nield with you,' Tweed ordered. 'They may have a number of armed men inside.'

'So I'll go with them too,' said Cardon, who had materialized beside Newman.

'I'm coming,' said Paula, her Browning already in her hand.

'You're staying to guard me,' Tweed told her.

Paula bit her lip, opened her mouth, closed it without saying anything. Tweed had cleverly checkmated her. Newman had to hold on to Amberg's arm to compel him to accompany the team.

'I wonder what hell is going to break loose inside that building,' Paula remarked aloud.

'I'll take the lead,' Newman told the others. 'I don't like the look of this. They've forgotten to close the door properly . . .'

All the lights were on the first floor. The entrance hall

479

was a cavern of darkness. Newman paused, held the others back with his left hand while his eyes became accustomed to the dark. He'd have liked to use his pencil flash, but they might have left a lookout at the top of the wide curving staircase. It had a wrought-iron rail and the hall floor was solid marble. Some Swiss banks liked to show clients they had come to the right place.

'Can't hear a thing,' Cardon whispered in his ear. 'It is too quiet. Maybe they've come and gone . . .'

'Assume an army is waiting up there,' Newman whispered back.

Holding on to the rail to help guide himself, he began to mount the steps. His rubber-soled shoes made no sound as he continued higher and higher – the first-floor landing was a surprising distance above the ground floor. Then he heard a voice.

'Come on, my dear, we haven't got all night. Before I spoil your face for ever open the bloody safe . . .'

The voice had spoken English with an upper-crust accent. Blurred by distance, Newman thought of Gaunt, who, when he had caught up with Butler at Basle Station, had said he was driving straight on to Ouchy. A brief remark of Butler's which hadn't really registered. Until now . . .

'No! Don't! Please! I'll do it . . .'

A woman's voice also talking English, a woman's voice expressing the last extremes of panic. Newman moved, ran up the last few steps with Cardon at his heels and the others close behind. He ran across the landing to an open doorway framing light, rushed in, crouching low, gun in front of him, then stopped in sheer surprise.

A man was holding a knife close to a woman's throat as she bent in front of a large safe, operating a combination lock. A small slim man with a plump face and pouched lips. In his thirties, he had a receding chin and a sneering smile as he watched the terrified woman opening the safe.

There was a click and she heaved the massive door open.

'Drop the knife,' Newman ordered. 'There are four of us.'

'Stand back or I'll cut her throat,' the slim man screeched.

Newman smiled, walked forward, placed the muzzle of his Smith & Wesson carefully against the side of the man's head. He pressed the metal close to the skull.

'You won't cut anything,' Newman said in a quiet voice. 'Because if you did in the next second half your head would be plastered over that wall. So stop playing silly games. *Drop it!*' he roared. 'Or you're dead.'

The knife clattered to the floor. Cardon noticed that the hand which had held the knife was trembling like a leaf in the wind. The woman's assailant stared at Newman as though seeing a ghost.

'Who the heck is this creep?' Cardon asked impatiently.

'Meet Mr Joel Dyson, notorious member of the paparazzi mob. Someone outside wants to meet you badly, Joel.'

PART THREE

The Power

50

In Washington it was late afternoon, the lights were on, blurred in a steady snowfall. President Bradford March was pacing the Oval Office restlessly when Sara came in.

'What is it now?' he snapped. 'More trouble? And when do I get a report on the treachery of the Holy Trinity?'

'It may be good news,' she replied in a soothing tone. 'Norton is on the line.'

'Leave me while I talk to the bastard . . .'

March took a deep breath as he sank into his chair and picked up the phone. He was in a foul mood.

'Norton here. I've reached Neuchâtel . . .'

'Have you? Great. Where is the friggin' place?'

'In Switzerland. French-speaking Switzerland . . .'

'Cohabiting with the Frogs now, are we? You haven't got a woman with you, have you? Because if you have I'll hear about it from Mencken and . . .'

'I'm alone and in a hurry. Are you going to listen for a change or shall I put down the receiver?'

'Norton . . .' March's tone became dangerously soft. 'If you ever threaten me again Mencken takes over instanter. Get to it.'

'I'm close to Ouchy – where the exchange will take place. The money for the two items you need. The place is ringed with my troops. I may clean up the whole job before the night is out . . .'

'You'd better. You're running out of time. Remember? I gave you a deadline. Of course, if you obtain what I'm after without paying over the big bucks there'd be a nice fat bonus waiting for you.'

'Any point in asking how much?' Norton enquired.

'Thought you were in a hurry to get to this Owchy. OK. You asked. Fifty big ones,' March said, clutching a figure out of the air.

'I'll be in touch. My new number at the Hôtel Château d'Ouchy is . . .'

'Got it. Get on your horse . . .'

In the Neuchâtel hotel where he'd paid for a room for the night so he could use the phone, Norton put down the receiver. At least this time he'd beaten March to the punch in contacting him and giving him his new phone number.

He went downstairs, pulling on his coat, told the receptionist he'd be back for dinner later, went out into the arctic night to drive on to Ouchy.

In Washington March was pulling at his stubby nose with his thumb and forefinger. A bonus? The only bonus Norton would get when he returned would be a bullet in the back of the neck.

March never took a chance he didn't have to. He was working on the assumption that – despite orders – Norton would take a peek at the film, would listen to the tape when he laid his hands on them. That risk could only be eliminated by eliminating Norton. Maybe things were now looking good. He opened a bottle of beer, drank from it and wondered about the Holy Trinity.

Senator Wingfield was alone in his study with the curtains closed against the night. He was also drinking but his beverage was Brazilian coffee from a Royal Doulton service arranged on a silver tray. He was studying a typed message which had come special delivery from Europe. No indication on the sheet of paper of the whereabouts of the sender – except the stamps were Swiss.

'That's right, Calloway,' he said to himself, referring to the Vice President. 'When the bullets start to fly keep your head down.'

The experienced Senator was cynically amused that this communication had come direct to him. He could imagine the brief phone conversation Jeb Calloway had had with his FBI contact.

'Barton, from now on I guess it would be best if any further communication was sent direct to Wingfield . . .'

The message was very direct – and highly dangerous if it got into the wrong hands. The Oval Office, for example. Events appeared to be moving to a climax and the Senator knew he was going to have to devote thought as to how to handle a potentially explosive situation. The ball was now in his court.

Have positive evidence as to identity of six-serial murderer in the South. Expect soon to have conclusive data. Will then communicate with you again – in person if at all possible. Barton Ives.

'Meet Joel Dyson,' Newman said, introducing his captive to Tweed, who had climbed down from the Espace. 'At long last,' he added.

Cardon, who always seemed equipped with everything, had produced a pair of handcuffs inside the Zurcher Kredit Bank. Dyson's hands were now pinioned behind his back and Butler, who was holding him by one arm, had shown him his Walther. The slim little man, his hair dishevelled, stared at Tweed.

'I'm going to complain to the British consul. I'm still a British citizen.'

'I have a better idea,' Tweed suggested. 'We can hand you over to the American Embassy in Berne. I'm sure there's a man very high up in Washington who would be happy to meet you.'

'Blimey, guv, for Gawd's sake don't do that. Like handing a Christian to the lions,' he pleaded in his best cockney mimickry.

'Some Christian,' Newman commented. His voice hardened. 'Don't play silly games with my chief. He means what he says.'

'God, no! I'm begging you . . .'

Dyson's nerve had broken suddenly. Tweed looked down at the man who had sunk to his knees, his body shaking with terror. He pursed his lips with distaste, nodded to Butler.

'Take him to the station wagon. Keep him quiet while we drive to Ouchy. I'll question him later.'

Dyson opened his mouth to scream. Newman clamped a gloved hand over the mouth before it could utter a sound. Nield twisted his handkerchief into a gag, inserted it inside Dyson's mouth, tied it at the back of his neck. Butler and Nield carried him away to the station wagon. Tweed and Paula listened as Newman gave a brief account of what had happened inside the bank.

'Karin, Amberg's kidnapped assistant, is in better shape than you'd expect,' Newman reported. 'She insisted on staying back to make coffee for herself and the guard Dyson coshed when he first arrived with Karin. You're looking impatient,' he ended.

'I think we ought to get out of Basle like bats out of hell,' Tweed ordered. 'The sooner we reach Ouchy the happier I'll be.'

'Who was that funny little man your people carted away?'

The voice called out from the back of the Espace – Eve Amberg's.

'A minor member of the opposition,' Tweed called back quickly.

488

'Eve does like to know what's going on,' Paula commented. 'Unlike Amberg, who seems to have thrown in his hand.'

A door slammed. Newman and Cardon were aboard. Cardon took up his old position next to the Swiss banker while Newman sat behind Paula. Tweed replied as he started the Espace moving, heading out of Basle, 'Amberg is sitting there with a grim expression. Typical that he hasn't enquired if Karin is all right. But he always was the cold fish of the two brothers as I recall. Let me concentrate on driving,' Tweed said brusquely.

Paula glanced at him. What he really meant was – let me concentrate on thinking this thing out.

They were well south of the city, driving with the Jura mountains rearing up to their right, when Tweed began talking to Paula in a voice which wouldn't carry to his passengers in the rear.

'I was right in my theory about two different jigsaws interlocking, that one wouldn't exist without the other. Two quite different styles of murder have been committed, which suggests two different groups are involved.'

'Two different styles of murder? That's a graphic phrase,' she remarked. 'Explanation, please.'

'The blowing up of our headquarters at Park Crescent, the bomb thrown at me in Zurich, the planned demolition by explosives of the Kaysersberg bridge, the second use of demolition by explosives of that cliff up in the Vosges. All those are what I'd call organization acts, requiring the services of a large and powerful apparatus. In short, Norton and the Americans. That is one distinctive style of attempted murder.'

Tweed accelerated a little more. There was no other traffic on the road below the mountains. He was anxious to reach Ouchy, to question Joel Dyson, to compel

Amberg to produce the film and the tape, and to hear the rest of Barton Ives' story. Paula glanced back and saw Ives, seated next to Newman, staring out into the night with a far-away look.

'You said *two* different styles of murder,' she reminded Tweed. 'What about the second style?'

'Highly individual. One person, disguised as the postman, arrived at the manor, knifed the butler, walked into the kitchen, sprayed the staff with tear-gas, then marched into the dining-room with a machine-gun and mowed down the seven people sitting there. Cold-blooded, audacious.'

'Not Norton, you mean?'

'A different style from Norton. Then take the hideous garrotting of the call girl Helen Frey and her friend Klara. I think the killer had a wire garrotte disguised as a string of pearls – hence the single blood-stained pearl found in Frey's apartment.'

'How do you think it was managed with such horrific skill?'

'Oh, not difficult. You offer to loop the pearls round Frey's neck so she can see how she looks in them. What woman could resist such an offer? Same technique with Klara.'

'A man,' Paula said thoughtfully. 'Maybe he even offered to give them the pearls. That *would* be irresistible.'

'Again an individual murder – as opposed to Norton's mass killing attempts.'

'But what about that nice detective, Theo Strebel? He was shot,' she reminded him.

'You'd hardly play the murderous trick with the pearl garrotte on a man, would you? But I'm sure he was shot by someone he knew, who put him off his guard. Again an individual murder. Don't forget the Shadow Man with the wide-brimmed hat who stalked Jennie Blade.'

'Butter wouldn't melt in Jennie's mouth. That type of woman always makes me suspicious.'

'It couldn't be simply that you dislike her?' Tweed probed.

'Men can be very naïve about attractive women,' Paula persisted. 'Especially when a woman like her gazes at a man adoringly. And much earlier Jennie remarked she'd seen Eve in Padstow about the time of the massacre. I think she was lying, but it could be a significant lie.'

'In what way?' Tweed enquired.

'It suggests that *Jennie* herself could have been in Padstow at the time of the massacre.'

'You could be right, I suppose.'

'And,' Paula went on, in full flood, 'I only caught a glimpse of the fake postman who killed all those people, riding along the drive up to the mansion.'

'Which suggests something to you? Remember Jennie has a mane of golden hair.'

'There again men don't know enough about women. Jennie could have piled up her hair on top of her head. That fake postman wore a uniform cap which could conceal the hair. It was a cold day so I didn't think it odd that the figure on the cycle wore a cap – it was a *very* cold day.'

'I still find it difficult to believe,' Tweed commented.

'And now she's gone off with Gaunt, who, according to Butler, was in the devil of a hurry to get to Ouchy in his BMW.'

'If you add Gaunt to the equation you do make out a very strong case,' Tweed admitted. 'I have an idea we'll break this mystery open in two bites. First the film and the tape will tell us the Washington angle – solving Norton's frantic efforts to stop us. Later we may have to return to Padstow to pin down who was responsible for the massacre. To say nothing of the murders of Frey, Klara and Theo Strebel.'

491

'You think you know who is guilty of those murders, don't you?' Paula challenged him.

'I've known for some time. The key is Jennie Blade's references to the so-called Shadow Man appearing in Colmar.'

When Marvin Mencken left the restaurant in Basle Bahnhof – he had carefully waited for fifteen minutes to be on the safe side – he hurried to where his Renault was parked. He was about to climb behind the wheel when he noticed his front right tyre was flat.

He swore aloud, then began the time-wasting task of changing it for his spare tyre. He had no way of knowing it was sabotage. While Tweed was confronting him inside the restaurant Butler had used a simple method of disabling the car.

Crouching down by the front tyre as though lacing up his trainer, he had taken out a ballpoint pen, unscrewed the cap, inserted the end of his pen and pressed down the valve, holding it there until all the air had escaped. He had then replaced the cap.

Mencken worked frantically in the vain hope of arriving in Ouchy before Norton. Sweating with the effort, despite the bitter cold, he eventually got behind the wheel and started the car. The delay meant that when Norton reached his destination there was no one to tell him where his troops were located in different hotels.

The Hôtel Château d'Ouchy was one of the weirdest, most intriguing hotels Paula had ever seen. Tweed had driven the Espace down a steep hill, had turned on to a level road and as the moon came out from behind a cloud Paula had her first view of Lake Geneva, the largest of all the Swiss lakes. The water was calm, without a ripple, stretching away towards distant France on the southern shore.

Butler overtook them in the station wagon as Tweed paused, crawling ahead to sniff out any sign of danger. As Tweed waited Paula peered up at the Château d'Ouchy. Illuminated by external arc lights, it was built of fawn-coloured stone and its steep, red-tiled roofs were decorated with a black, almost sinister zigzag design. At the corners steepled turrets reared up and it looked very old.

'Looks as ancient as history,' she commented.

'Used to be a castle in the twelfth century,' Tweed told her, 'before ages later it was rebuilt and converted into a hotel. At least it's quiet down here.'

Paula thought that was an understatement, recalling the furious hustle and fast tempo of Zurich. Across the road from the hotel was an oyster-shaped harbour encircled with eerie green street lamps, their light reflected in the harbour water. Boats cocooned for winter in blue plastic covers were moored to buoys.

But it was the stillness which most struck her – the waterfront was deserted, there was no other traffic, no one else in sight. To their left beyond the road they had driven along was a line of small hotels and cafés, all apparently closed. Tweed had lowered his window and refreshing air drifted inside – so different from the ice-cold of the Vosges. Marler appeared from nowhere alongside the window.

'OK to come ashore,' he drawled. He handed a sheet of paper to Tweed. 'That lists the hotels round here where Norton's men are stationed. The Château d'Ouchy, so far as I can tell, is clean . . .'

Tweed had parked the Espace in a courtyard alongside the hotel and next to Marler's red Mercedes. He entered reception with Paula, who spoke to the girl behind the

493

counter, reminding her of the phoned reservations.

'And you said we could have dinner even if we arrived at a late hour.'

'The dining-room is at your service, but only when you are ready.'

'I think we'd like to go up to our rooms to freshen up first,' Tweed told her.

He had seen Ives coming in, accompanied by Amberg and Cardon. Behind them followed Butler and Nield flanking a defeated-looking Joel Dyson. He ordered Butler to take turns with Nield in guarding Dyson in his room, that the photographer was only to be given sandwiches and mineral water, then he asked Paula and Newman to accompany him with Ives to his room after registering. There was no time to waste. Lord knew what the morning would bring.

'What sort of person would those six wealthy women who were then brutally raped and murdered stop for – driving in the middle of nowhere in the dark?'

Tweed deliberately repeated the key question he had put to Barton Ives aboard the train from Colmar to Basle. He had previously recalled, for the sake of Paula and Newman, in abbreviated form the story Ives had told him. The FBI man sat up straight on the couch he occupied with Paula, facing Tweed and Newman who were sitting in chairs.

'Yes, that *was* the question I asked myself over and over again. Then, in the last two cases, there was someone else driving late on the fatal nights. They overtook the cars of the victims – and saw a brown Cadillac parked in a nearby field. I had a hunch, a sudden flash of inspiration, luck – call it what you will. I began checking the movements of a certain man to see whether by chance he was in the state concerned on any of the six fatal nights.'

494

Ives paused, lit a rare cigarette. Paula glanced round at the suite she had booked for Tweed. It had its own sitting area, spacious and comfortable, and beyond a row of arches, the bedroom. She concentrated again on Ives as he continued.

'The checking on this point wasn't too difficult. What was difficult was carrying out my enquiries without anyone knowing what I was doing. If I was right I knew my life could be in danger. Power carries a lot of clout.'

'So you were investigating a powerful man?' Paula suggested.

'Powerful and ruthless,' Ives agreed. 'To get where he had, to get where he is now. As I checked I began to get more excited – I was hitting more pay dirt than I'd ever really believed I would. The person I was after had made a political speech early in the evening in the same state in the first three cases. And the city where he'd made the speech wasn't all that far, in driving distance, from where a woman was raped and murdered later that same evening.'

'Circumstantial. But not conclusive,' Tweed commented.

'Wait!' Ives held up a hand, stubbed out the cigarette. 'I went on checking the last three cases. Certain that the same circumstances wouldn't apply. But, by God, they did. Senator X – as he then was – had again spoken in public in all three states hours before the last three women victims were attacked and died. A lot of speeches in six states, but then he was running for the highest—' Ives broke off briefly. 'I'll get to that in a minute.'

'What about this Senator's movements after he'd made his speeches?' Tweed asked. 'Were you able to check them?'

'That was my next task. Even more difficult to conceal. And he has a very shrewd hatchet woman who runs a whole network of informants. But over a period of time I did manage to do just that – to check his movements after he left the place where he'd made his speech, lifted his audience out of their seats – a real rabble rouser. He was known for wanting to be on his own after bringing the roof down. Always says he needs to recharge his batteries, go some place on his own, drink one bottle of beer. He did exactly that after all six speeches – on the nights when later within driving distance, I checked the times – a woman was raped, murdered.'

'So at least he has no alibi,' Tweed remarked.

'But he does have a brown Caddy he likes driving. And this I haven't ever told anyone so far. I explored round the area of the sixth victim, combed the grass for hours. I was about to call it zilch when I found this empty beer bottle, with a complete set of fingerprints. Some beer that the guy I was checking on likes. That bottle – inside a plastic bag – is in the boot of the Lincoln Continental I have hidden away in an old barn.'

'Again the evidence is circumstantial,' Tweed pointed out. 'No offence, but the trouble is a court would only have your word for where you found that bottle. Unless you can get the fingerprints of the man you were tracking. Of course, if they match . . .'

'Not so easy.' Ives lit a fresh cigarette. 'Not so easy,' he repeated. 'Not to obtain the fingerprints of ex-Senator Bradford March, now President of the United States.'

51

In Switzerland it was not difficult the following morning for Marler to obtain a film projector, a screen and the other equipment he needed on Tweed's instructions. He arrived back at the hotel at 8.30 a.m. to find Tweed having breakfast with Paula and Newman.

'I lay awake half the night,' Paula was saying. 'I still can't believe the President of the United States is guilty of such horrific crimes.'

'Read the history of previous occupants of the Oval Office,' suggested Barton Ives who had overheard her remark as he joined them. 'Under our crazy electoral system a really depraved guy was bound to get there one day. He has.'

'What do we do next?' Paula asked.

'You've got everything?' Tweed checked with Marler as he sat down.

'Everything.'

'Then our next trip is to take Amberg to his branch here, force him to produce the film and tape Dyson gave them in Zurich for safekeeping. Then we view the film inside the bank . . .'

Amberg was still under guard in his room with Cardon keeping him company. Their breakfast came up from room service. Joel Dyson was also trapped in his room with an extremely unsympathetic Butler acting as his guard.

'You know we were followed here all the way from Basle?' Newman warned his chief.

'Not to worry – it was an unmarked car but they would be Beck's men. After seeing us pass through the control at Basle Station when we arrived from Colmar he's not a man to let us out of his sight. Talk of the devil . . .'

Arthur Beck, wearing a smart grey suit, walked into the dining-room, which overlooked a small garden. He refused an offer of coffee, bent down to whisper to Tweed.

'I have brought a small army of men into Ouchy. We saw the Americans returning. So-called diplomats waiting for their postings. This is too much. I'm organizing a dragnet to check all the hotels.'

'I can save you time.' Tweed produced the list Marler had drawn up the previous evening. 'This lists where they all are. They will be armed.'

'So are my men.' Beck smiled wryly. 'Thank you for doing my job for me. May I ask how you tracked them down?'

'Marler, tell our friend about your researches.'

'Not difficult,' drawled Marler. 'I'd call at a hotel, tell the night clerk some American friends of mine had arrived, that I wanted to pay them some money I owed to them. Also I needed a room for the night and how much would it be? I had a handful of Swiss coins – which can be of reasonable value – and pushed them over the far edge of the counter. While he was scrabbling for them I checked his box of registration slips, memorized all names where the nationality was American. I then told the clerk I'd left my passport in my car, that I'd be back for the room I'd paid for. Then on to the next hotel. Quite easy.'

'And very skilled – to pull it off with Swiss hotel staff.' Beck glanced at the list. 'I should have this lot within the hour – for immediate deportation via Geneva Airport. Spoil their breakfasts . . .'

He had just disappeared when Gaunt trooped in with Jennie clinging to his arm. Marching straight up to

Tweed's large table, he sat down uninvited.

'Top of the morning to you,' he greeted them breezily. 'Lovely day. Sun shining on the mountains of the Haute-Savoie across the lake. A large English breakfast for two,' he commanded the waiter.

'I just want croissants,' Jennie said, her eyes glowing with annoyance. 'And I do like to be asked.'

'Nonsense! You must stoke up. Busy day ahead of us, eh, Tweed? Saw a bunch of American thugs filing into the Hôtel d'Angleterre just opposite last night. Have to keep a sharp lookout for spoilers.'

'We have an appointment,' Tweed wiped his mouth with his napkin. 'May see you later.'

He had hardly spoken when Eve Amberg appeared, asked if she could sit with them. Tweed gestured to an empty chair and Paula caught Jennie glaring at the new arrival. What was it between these two women? Eve wore a form-hugging purple sweater and black ski-pants tucked into knee-length leather boots. A striking outfit, Paula admitted to herself.

'Where is Walter?' Eve enquired as she selected a roll. 'Coffee for me,' she told the waiter. 'So where is Walter?' she repeated.

'He's exhausted,' Tweed lied. 'Sleeping in until about ten before he surfaces.'

'A poor fish,' Gaunt boomed. 'No energy . . .'

He was talking to a smaller audience. Tweed, followed by Paula and Newman, was leaving the restaurant. Walking briskly, he went up to Amberg's room, rapped on the door with the agreed signal, walked in with the others when Cardon opened it. Tweed was in his most aggressive mood when he addressed the banker, who was again neatly clad in his sombre black suit.

'Had your breakfast? Good. Time to get moving. To your bank. I want the film and the tape out of the vault five minutes after we arrive. We'll accompany you everywhere.

In case you feel like staging a protest, Beck, the Chief of Police, as you know, is here in Ouchy. He'd be very interested to talk to you about those murders in Zurich.'

'I had nothing to do . . .' Amberg began.

'Policemen never believe a word you say. We'll get moving now. By the back way into the car park. Avoid the dining-room that way. Three tough-looking American types are having breakfast. Don't want to meet them either, do you, Amberg?'

Marvin Mencken, who was staying at the d'Angleterre, had risen early and had a quick breakfast at another hotel. He liked to be up before any of his subordinates and he made a habit of not following a routine. He never ate where he was staying.

Returning from a brisk walk alongside the lake he saw two Audis pull up in front of the d'Angleterre. Men in plain clothes stepped out, walked towards the entrance with almost military precision, disappeared inside the hotel. Seconds later more cars pulled up outside two other hotels where his men were staying and uniformed police, holding automatic weapons, climbed out swiftly and moved inside.

'Jesus Christ!' Mencken said to himself.

Without hurrying, he crossed the road, reached his car parked behind a stretch of grass and trees. He got in behind the wheel, pulled out of his trench coat pocket a Swiss hat he'd bought in Basle, rammed it on his head and slid down out of sight as he started the engine.

Mencken waited until he saw the police bringing out his men, wrists handcuffed behind their backs. More cars with only a driver had arrived. His captured men were bundled inside the vehicles. Mencken had no worry that he would be betrayed – he'd been careful to ensure that none of these men knew he was driving a Renault.

As the convoys drove off he cruised slowly round the park towards the Château d'Ouchy. Norton had given him explicit instructions he was not to be contacted, not that Mencken had any idea what he looked like. But he had been told Norton would be using the name Dr Glen Fleming. He'd have to phone him, warn him quickly.

The Zurcher Kredit Bank was open for business when Tweed arrived in the Espace with Amberg alongside him. Paula, Newman, Ives and Butler were travelling with him. In the rear of the vehicle Marler sat with the projector and the rest of his equipment.

In the station wagon following close behind were Cardon, guarding Joel Dyson, and Pete Nield who was driving. Before leaving the Château d'Ouchy for the short drive to the bank Tweed had spoken to Dyson, making no bones about the position he was in.

'Cardon has a gun, won't hesitate to use it if you make one wrong move. But more likely, we'd put you aboard an aircraft for Washington at Cointrin Airport, Geneva.'

Watching the little man closely, Tweed had seen a flicker of triumph in Dyson's shifting eyes. Joel Dyson clearly knew Europe well, knew the lines of communication by air travel. There was no better way of subduing a man than by raising his hopes and then dashing them.

'Of course,' Tweed went on, 'there are no direct flights to Washington from Geneva. So Cardon would escort you aboard a flight from Cointrin to Zurich. Then you'd be put aboard the first non-stop flight for Washington. A phone call would be made so certain people would wait at Dulles Airport for you to disembark. Something wrong, Dyson? You've gone pale as a ghost . . .'

Amberg nodded to the guard at the entrance to the bank. As Marler came inside carrying his equipment the guard stopped him to examine what he was carrying.

'Do not worry, Jules,' Amberg called out over his shoulder. 'That gentleman is with me, as are the people behind him.'

Obeying Tweed's instructions, Amberg took everyone first to his private office, telling his secretary he must on no account be disturbed. Leaving the others inside the spacious room, Tweed accompanied Amberg with Newman and Paula to the vault where the Swiss opened his private box. Inside were two familiar-looking canisters. Was this really the end of their long journey, Tweed wondered as they returned to the private office.

In their absence Marler had drawn the curtains over the windows. After turning on the lights he had assembled the projector, had erected the viewing screen, had placed on the same desk the American tape recorder so he could synchronize viewing and listening.

He had removed a number of chairs from a boardroom table, arranging them in short rows like a makeshift cinema. He took the canisters from Amberg while Tweed personally made sure the door was securely locked.

Paula sat in the front row with Tweed next to her. Beyond Tweed sat Amberg with Barton Ives on his other side. In the row behind them sat a nervous Joel Dyson flanked by Newman and Cardon. The third row was occupied in the centre by Pete Nield, his Walther in his hand, and Butler. While Marler was fiddling with his machines Nield tapped Dyson on the shoulder with the muzzle of his Walther.

'Just to remind you you're never alone,' he informed the photographer genially.

'Ready to go,' Marler called out in a neutral tone as he switched out the lights.

A harsh white light appeared on the blank screen. Tweed could hear the tape reel whirring. Then, sharp as crystal, the images began to appear . . .

*   *   *

502

A one-storey log cabin in a forest clearing. A short, powerfully built man in a windcheater, open at the top, exposing his thick neck, struggling with a girl with long blonde hair. One hand gripped her hair, the other shoved her in the small of the back. She was screaming at the top of her voice and Paula gritted her teeth.

The man pushed her inside the log cabin, both faces were very visible before they disappeared into the cabin. The hard crack of the door being slammed shut. But they could still hear her screaming even with the shutters closed over the windows. Her screams stopped suddenly. Silence.

Now Paula could only hear the whirring of the machines behind her. Why did the silence seem even more awful than what they had seen so far? She was startled when the stocky man emerged by himself, closed the door, locked it, tossed the key on the roof. Why?

'Oh, my God, no!' she whispered to herself.

The answer to her question was horrifically clear. Smoke was drifting out from behind a shuttered window. Almost at once it burst into flames. The camera zoomed in for a close-up of the killer. A look of sadistic satisfaction. Sweat streamed off his face.

The camera now showed the man full length. He appeared to be staring straight at the lens. Snatching a gun from his belt, he moved closer. Paula flinched back in her seat. Her hand clenched as the whole cabin seared into a flaming inferno. The girl left inside would be incinerated.

The loud crackle and roar of the huge fire made the man pause, look briefly at the dying cabin. Gun in hand, the man turned again towards the camera, began advancing towards it, his famous face again so clear, identifiable . . .

The screen went blank, the white glare returned, vanished as Marler switched off the machines. The audience sat as though frozen. The only sound was the click of Marler switching on lights. Paula blinked, glanced at Tweed, at Ives. It was difficult to decide which man looked grimmer.

It was Tweed who broke the silence. He leaned forward to speak to Ives across Amberg.

'Now you have your evidence. That was Bradford March, President of the United States.' He turned round, looked at Joel Dyson whose pouched lips were quivering.

'You took those pictures. Don't argue with me. I just want a simple answer. Who was the girl – the victim?'

'His secret girl friend. Cathy Willard, daughter of the San Francisco newspaper magnate.'

'So, well-heeled,' Ives commented.

'Oh, a very wealthy family. I heard later it was called an accident. She got herself shut in the cabin. The weather was cold, so she had a log fire' – Dyson was reverting to his normal loquacious self, Newman thought, as the story continued – 'a spark jumps out, sets fire to the rug and *whoosh!* the whole place goes up. Windows shuttered so she can't get out that way.'

'Sounds as though you wrote that version yourself,' Newman said cynically.

'No! But that's the way I heard they told it . . .'

'You have your evidence, Ives,' Tweed repeated, interrupting Dyson. 'It follows a similar pattern, doesn't it?'

'It does indeed. You see, March was a hick from the boondocks. It flattered his ego to make it with well-educated and wealthy women. Now you have your answer to the weird question – who would a wealthy woman driving in the dark across lonely country stop for? A man standing in the headlights of his brown Cadillac, a well-known Senator running for the White House, his mug plastered on billboards along every state highway. Maybe

504

he pretended his car had broken down. They'd feel so safe with Senator Bradford March. It hit me suddenly that I'd found my serial killer – six women slaughtered. I have to take this film, this tape back to Washington.'

'They'll kill you thirty minutes after you leave the plane,' Newman warned.

'I have a powerful friend. He'll meet me at Dulles Airport with a large entourage, smuggle me into his house. Then it's up to him.'

'I think we'd better come with you,' Tweed said.

'I'm not coming,' Dyson protested.

'You'll be held in cold storage in Britain. After you've made a statement describing what you saw when you made the film.' Tweed's manner was harsh. 'A sworn statement made before a Swiss lawyer. That or come with us to Washington.'

'I'm not sure ethically I can release these items,' Amberg asserted.

'Ethically?' Tweed stared at the banker. 'You have to be joking. If you'd handed these over to me earlier think of how many lives would have been saved. Why did you hang on to them? You'd watched this film on your own much earlier, hadn't you?'

'Yes. When I saw what was on it I realized my own life was in danger . . .'

'So, ethically,' Tweed rasped, 'you kept quiet. If those are ethics I'll do without them. Amberg, from now on you had better shut up – if you want to stay alive. . . .'

52

The man with long shaggy grey hair peered over his half-moon glasses at the entrance to the Zurcher Kredit Bank. Norton was too smart to sit in the car he'd used to follow the Tweed group from the Château d'Ouchy. The rush-hour traffic had helped to mask his presence behind Nield's station wagon following the familiar Espace. He was standing in front of a book-shop, pretending to study a volume he had bought at random.

Norton, staying at the Château d'Ouchy, had watched Tweed having breakfast from his corner table, seated by himself. He was confident that the transformation in his appearance would save him from recognition – and so it had turned out.

Called to the phone, Norton had left his breakfast to take the call in his room.

'Mencken here,' the urgent voice had begun.

'I told you not to call except in case of a major crisis.'

'Which is what I'm dropping in your lap. All our troops have been rounded up, taken away in cars. Official . . .'

Which was Mencken's cautious way of saying 'police' over the phone.

'I'm glad everything is going so well. Thank you so much for calling . . .'

For Norton it was a panic situation, but Norton, ex-FBI, never panicked. He had created the core of Unit One when Senator Bradford March had offered him a large salary as his personal chief of security. It was Norton who had organized the attempts to kill Barton Ives before

Ives had fled to Europe. Norton had proceeded methodically.

He paid his hotel bill, put his bag in the hired Renault and returned to the dining-room. Five minutes later he watched Tweed and his companions leaving. Later he was ready to follow them in his Renault to the Zurcher Kredit Bank. Now he waited patiently, then saw Marler coming out with the same equipment he'd taken inside earlier – a long cylinder which could contain a viewing screen, a tape recorder, a canvas hold-all which was more tightly packed.

Pressed against the canvas was a circular shape about the size of a film canister. Turning over a page of his book, Norton shrewdly summed up the situation.

'If only I still had the troops . . .'

But he hadn't any troops left. They had all been taken by the police. Standing with the book in his hands Norton took a major decision. He couldn't report to March that he had failed – that would be committing suicide. Time to change sides again, to survive.

'That film March was raving to get his hands on must contain some deadly material. Otherwise why send such a large body of Unit One to Europe?' March was losing a battle – Norton's sixth sense, developed during his years as a top FBI agent, told him this.

He recalled a certain powerful senator he had once done a favour for, suppressing certain incriminating documents which would have ruined his career on the hill. Yes, it was time to contact Senator Wingfield, to offer him his services again. For a substantial fee . . .

Norton followed the Espace and the station wagon and was not surprised when the two vehicles entered the car park at the Château d'Ouchy. Parking his car near where the boats left for Evian in France, he walked back to

507

the hotel. He strolled into reception just in time to hear Tweed giving instructions to the girl behind the counter.

'We shall be leaving today. Could you please make up the bill for myself and Miss Grey. No hurry. We'll be here for lunch . . .'

Which gave Norton time to clear up a loose end. Mencken. Norton was very careful about clearing up loose ends. He was not going to risk Mencken reaching Washington first – maybe even telling March how all the failures had been Norton's fault.

Returning to his car, he crammed a Swiss hat on his head, pulled it well down over his forehead. On the seat beside him, next to the mobile phone, rested a walking stick he had also purchased. Picking up the mobile phone he dialled Mencken's mobile phone number, hoping he was within range.

'Yes, who is it?' Mencken's voice demanded after a long wait.

'Norton. Where are you? We have to meet, urgently. To make future plans.'

'I'm halfway between Ouchy and Vevey. Away from the activity.'

'Very wise. Everything is quiet here now. But you are right – it would be wise to keep away from the town. As you drive along the lakeside road towards Vevey there is a point where the road turns away from the lake. By the edge of the lake there is a small wood near the path continuing along the lakeside. You noticed this? Good. I will meet you there in three-quarters of an hour. Best to make sure your car is hidden just off the path. And I did say it was urgent.'

'Understood,' Mencken replied tersely.

In his room at the Château d'Ouchy Tweed was giving his own urgent instructions to his whole team. Barton Ives listened as he spoke briskly. Action this day, thought Paula.

'All of us – except Philip Cardon, who is guarding Joel Dyson in his room – are driving direct to Cointrin Airport, Geneva. From there we catch a flight to London. Which puts us on the spot to catch the afternoon Concorde flight to Washington non-stop.' Tweed looked at Ives. 'I do know Senator Wingfield, met him while attending a security conference in Washington, but are you certain you can trust him?'

'Wingfield,' Ives assured him, 'was born and raised a patriot. Not many of them about. That doesn't mean to say he has the track record of a saint – how else would he get to the position of great power he occupies?'

'You mean he can be ruthless?' Paula suggested.

'Maybe that's exactly what I do mean. But this horrific situation kinda suggests ruthless measures. I have phoned him,' he told Tweed. 'He's expecting me, with the evidence, but I omitted to tell him you'd be along too.'

'Thank God for that,' Newman said vehemently. 'Before we land at Dulles I want to radio ahead, hire several cars. I strongly urge that along with Butler, Nield and Marler, I go aboard Concorde as though I've nothing to do with you.'

'What danger could there be to you guys?' queried Ives.

'We have all seen that diabolical film which could wreck the entire government of the United States. I foresee that very strong measures will be taken to see that does not happen.' Newman looked at Tweed. 'This trip is going to take some organization . . .'

'All dealt with,' Paula interjected. 'Tweed told me some time ago to prepare for this contingency. Flights are booked, tickets waiting to be collected at airports. I'm wearing my skates, Bob.' She turned to Tweed. 'We take the film and the tape with us, then?'

'We do – to show Wingfield. Marler brings his equip-

509

ment with him to save time. I want a quick in-and-out trip.'

'Preferably coming out alive,' Newman warned.

'What about Joel Dyson?' Paula interjected again. 'I've booked tickets on a separate flight from Geneva to London for Cardon and Dyson.'

'Where, after arriving, he will escort Dyson to a safe house. Where Howard is,' Tweed added.

'And what do I do with this?' enquired Marler, lifting up a second hold-all. 'With the weapons you've taken off us it's jolly heavy.'

As though on cue, there was a knock on the door. Newman jumped up, unlocked and opened it cautiously. He said, 'Wait a minute,' closed and relocked the door before he handed an envelope to Tweed.

'A Swiss in a business suit,' he reported.

Tweed opened the envelope, scanned the letter, nodded.

'It's from Arthur Beck. Among the men picked up was one with a suitcase containing twenty million dollars. He had experts open it and they defused a thermite bomb inside. That detective outside is to collect the weapons. We can hardly try to board an aircraft carrying them . . .'

'What about Gaunt, Eve and Jennie?' Newman asked when he had handed the hold-all to the Swiss and closed the door.

'I had a word with Gaunt before we came up,' Tweed went on. 'He's changed his mind about trying to identify who assassinated Amberg in Cornwall. Maintains it's now a hopeless task – at least that's what he said. He's driving back to Basle with Eve and Jennie. Remember, he berthed his yacht, cabin cruiser – call it what you will – the *Mayflower III* on the Rhine at Basle. He's sailing back to Padstow.'

'With Eve as well as Jennie?' Paula queried.

'So he said.'

'I find that curious, very strange,' she commented.

'So do I. But as soon as we get back from Washington that's where we're off to. Padstow. We still have to track down who committed mass murder at Tresillian Manor and why. To say nothing of who pushed that poor servant girl, Celia Yeo, off the top of High Tor . . .'

Marvin Mencken was excited as he sat behind the wheel of his Renault with the window open. As instructed, he had parked the car off the road inside a copse. Invisible to traffic passing along the road, it was close to the footpath running by the lakeside.

Mencken was excited because for the first time he was going to meet the mysterious Norton face to face. He had never liked taking orders from someone he'd not even recognize if he sat next to him in a diner.

Despite the sunshine it was a raw cold day. Mencken kept the engine ticking over so he could turn up the heaters full blast. When it became stuffy he had lowered the automatic window. He also took precautions – protruding from under a cushion on the passenger seat was the butt of a 9-mm. Luger.

He stiffened as he heard the click-clack of heels approaching, then relaxed when he realized it had to be a girl. He caught a glimpse of her as she passed along the footpath towards Vevey. A tall good-looking blonde. Mencken sighed. He had been so busy he hadn't had time to indulge in his favourite form of relaxation with a girl.

The elderly Swiss man with one of their funny hats trudged slowly along the promenade towards him. From under the hat a lot of untidy shaggy grey hair protruded. Perched on his nose was a pair of those weird glasses looking like a couple of half-moons.

The old character walked leaning on a stick, staring out at the lake. Probably came this same walk every day if the weather was OK. Bored as hell with life. Mencken promised himself a lot of fun before he ever got into that state. He put a cigarette in his mouth as the old man was turning on to the footpath. In the next second Norton rammed the muzzle of an HP35 Browning automatic against Mencken's chest through the open window, pulled the trigger. The sound of the shot was muffled by the thick scarf round Mencken's neck which fell over his chest. His head dropped forward.

Norton's gloved hand reached in through the window. He extracted the portion of the unlit cigarette Mencken's teeth had bitten through, dropped it into undergrowth. Opening the door, a wave of foetid heat swept into his face. He quickly shoved the body over sideways on to the floor, grabbed hold of the Luger, pressed the button to shut the automatic window, closed the door.

There was no one about, no traffic in sight when he first hurled the Luger way out into the lake and followed it by throwing the Browning in the same direction. A glance at the car before he left showed him that the windows were already steaming up, masking the view of the corpse even if someone peered in. He had already phoned Senator Wingfield and, with luck, he'd be aboard a flight for Washington before Mencken's body was even discovered. Yes, you must tie up loose ends.

53

Senator Wingfield had operated the projector screening the film himself. When he'd seen who starred in the horror of the burning log cabin he was glad he'd taken this precaution. His audience in the Chevy Chase study – the banker and the elder statesman – had sat in stunned silence through the viewing, listening to the girl's agonized screaming.

Wingfield switched on the lights, quickly packed film and tape away in the canisters. The banker reacted first in a hoarse voice.

'My God! I need a drink. Bourbon . . .'

Wingfield, a rare drinker, joined his companions with a stiff bourbon, seated again at the table. The statesman cleared his throat, spoke in a controlled tone.

'Well, now we know the worst. And if I had to dream up a nightmare scenario I couldn't have come up with anything to touch this.'

'And he's still adding to the deficit,' the banker reminded them, for something to say.

'He's also not taking any action to counter the threat from the East,' the statesman commented.

'Kids' stuff,' Wingfield snapped. 'Compared with what we have seen. I ran it through before you arrived. This is a national crisis. March can't be allowed to sit in the Oval Office any longer. I've taken the most difficult decision of my whole life.'

'Which is?' enquired the statesman.

'An ex-FBI man called Norton has arrived in

Washington. I knew him years ago. March has announced he's flying down South tomorrow. I've given Norton certain orders. A serial murderer in the White House – calls for drastic action.'

'How did you get hold of that terrible film?' asked the banker.

'Sent here by the very cautious special FBI agent Barton Ives. A messenger delivered it – together with a highly detailed report on the six serial murders never solved in certain Southern states. Damning evidence against Bradford March.'

'Why very cautious?' enquired the statesman with a quizzical expression since he'd guessed the answer.

'Because Ives is somewhere in Washington hiding. I doubt I'll ever track him down. And in his letter he says Tweed, a top security officer from Britain, will be calling on me. I remember Tweed – the kind of man you don't forget. He is the one who eventually obtained the film and tape.'

'What the hell are we going to do?' the banker asked in a desperate tone.

'I can't imagine you doing anything. Someone has to take the responsibility for initiating drastic action. Guess I'm elected. I'm using Norton. I met him secretly early this morning. He has his instructions. The President is due to fly south today from Andrews Air Force Base.'

'What does that mean?' the banker asked, showing a great degree of nervousness.

'Sure you want to know?' Wingfield fired back.

'The Senator is more than capable of handling the problem,' the statesman said emphatically. 'Remember how the John F. Kennedy situation was solved when his domestic policies were going wildly wrong.'

'I don't think I want to know any more about this,' said the banker, draining his glass. 'Time I got back to my desk . . .'

'What about this Norton?' the statesman queried when he was alone with Wingfield. 'He could know too much for your health.'

'I've thought about that too. We don't have to worry about Mr Norton. He's a top pro, bought and paid for to do the job. But I don't delude myself I've bought a tight mouth. Arrangements have been made. Just wait for this afternoon . . .'

In the Oval Office President Bradford March was checking his shave in a mirror – got to be smart when you're making speeches to the people. Sara came in without knocking. March grinned as he turned towards her.

'Tell me I look OK for the trip.'

'You look OK, but I think you ought to cancel this trip.' She was talking at machine-gun rate. 'I've heard plenty of rumours someone high up is gunning for you. Dallas all over again is the word . . .'

'Crap! Now I have Unit One pros guarding me. I've even got a Unit One crew to fly Air Force One from Andrews. Time I talked to the folks, whipped up the support with some of the most rabble-rousing stuff of my career.'

'Don't let anyone hear you call them rabble,' Sara warned.

'That's what they are.' He gave his famous grin. 'Look, I should know, that's where I came from. I know the crap that gets them throwing their hats in the air.'

'Listen to me.' Sara felt she had to make one more effort. 'Our watchers reported there was a meeting of the Three Wise Men an hour ago. At Wingfield's place again . . .'

'That old political hack . . .'

'This time both his guests arrived with an FBI guard –

515

who surrounded each man as he dashed from his limo into the house.'

'So they're running scared. Is *my* limo ready to take me to Andrews?'

Norton left the President's plane carrying a case which was supposed to contain explosive-detection equipment. As he descended the staircase he blinked in the strong sunlight. Dressed in an orange boiler suit zipped up to the neck – it carried a badge U1, Unit One – he made himself resist the temptation to hurry away from Air Force One.

He was the last maintenance man to leave the aircraft and a motorcade was approaching. The TV crews were already penned up by guards who were careful to let the technicians have a clear view of the aircraft's staircase March would walk up. The President was very publicity-conscious.

Underneath his boiler suit Norton wore a grey business suit. Earlier, arriving at the checkpoint, he had passed through without trouble – simply showing his Unit One card issued before he'd left for Europe weeks ago.

He had prowled the maintenance shed looking for a mechanic close to his build and height wearing one of the distinctive orange suits. Approaching him from behind, Norton had put him out of action by using a tyre iron on the back of his skull.

'Sleep well, baby,' he had whispered after taking off the boiler suit and stuffing the man inside a large waste bin.

In this way, and by again flourishing his Unit One card, he had boarded the plane, choosing a moment when most of the maintenance crew had left. Now, out of sight of the crowds, which were already roaring with delight, he stripped off the boiler suit, stuffed it into the waste bin on top of its unconscious owner, smoothed out the creases of his grey suit and hurried out of the main entrance, again showing his card.

He had no hesitation in hurrying, wearing only a suit and no coat in the bitter raw cold which gripped Washington despite the sun. Again he heard the crowd roar, this time more prolonged. As he walked towards where he had parked his car Norton could picture the scene.

Bradford March climbing the steps of the mobile staircase slowly, pausing at the top. Then swinging round suddenly and hoisting both arms with clenched fists high in the air. Another louder roar from the crowd. Norton smiled to himself grimly as he climbed behind the wheel of his car and drove off. He parked his car a good half-mile away from the air base, positioning it so he could look towards Andrews.

Air Force One suddenly appeared, climbing steeply as it flew away from the parked car. Norton was peering out of the open window as he heard the scream of its jets, saw the diminishing silver dart ascend to five thousand feet.

He was wearing wrapround tinted glasses so he wasn't blinded by the sudden brilliant flash. There was a rolling boom as the plane disintegrated and tiny fragments of the fuselage spun out of a cloud of black smoke which had disfigured the duck-egg blue of the sky. Norton, who had kept his engine running, eased the car out of the side road and drove on to his house in Georgetown. While serving with the FBI he had been attached to the Explosives Division.

'Well, you haven't lost your touch,' he said aloud.

He used his remote-control device to open the door of the garage located under his house. Having parked the car, he came out, closed the door, mounted the steps to his front door. In the house opposite a woman looked out of her first-floor window, saw him climbing the steps. She was not surprised – her neighbour, security officer for some large international bank, often spent long periods away from home. She left the window to go downstairs.

Norton held his front door key in his hand when he got to the stoop. He inserted the key in the lock, frowned when it seemed difficult to turn. For once Norton's nose for danger deserted him – his mind was on what he had achieved out at Andrews. He turned the key and shards of the fragmenting front door pierced his body. The force of the explosion was so great it hurled his mangled body straight across the road. Peering down out of her shattered window, the woman opposite saw Norton's crumpled form lying on her own stoop.

54

Tweed never did keep his appointment to meet Senator Wingfield. He heard the news of the President's plane blowing up soon after take-off from a bell-boy in his hotel, saw it on television with Newman, Paula and Barton Ives in his hotel room.

'Time to leave America while we're still alive,' he said, using remote control to switch off the TV. 'You'd best come with us, Ives.'

'Reckon I had,' Ives agreed. 'They play rough over here – and I told you Wingfield was a patriot, a *ruthless* patriot. But can we make it? They could be coming for us now . . .'

'So we put into operation Plan Omega,' Tweed told

him. 'Worked out in advance for just this situation by Bob Newman and Paula – although we never anticipated a resort to assassination. Ives, you just stick with us and remember from now on your name is Chuck Kingsley when you check in at the airport.'

'Dulles?'

'No, not Dulles. That's a key part of Omega. I have to call Marler's room, let him know we're leaving within thirty minutes. No time to explain any more . . .'

They were driving by a devious route which could have taken them to Dulles Airport. Newman was at the wheel of the rented Lincoln, Tweed was beside him while Paula sat in the back next to Ives. They hadn't hit rush hour but there was traffic. Paula kept glancing back through the rear window.

'Those two black sedans which started tailing us as soon as we left the hotel are still there. With a lot of men inside I don't like the look of.'

'Can you see the three Chevrolets?' Tweed asked Newman.

'Yes, they're coming up behind us now, appeared out of side streets. Marler in the green Chevy, Butler in the white, Nield in the brown Chevy. Marler checked the map of the city with care, decided where they'd make their play. Any moment now those characters in their black sedans are in for a shock . . .'

The leading black sedan was driven by an ugly bald-headed thug, surprisingly nicknamed Baldy. He had three armed men as passengers and the twin sedan behind him carried four more armed men. As they arrived close to a complex intersection Baldy saw Newman suddenly turn right. He was about to follow when a green Chevrolet swung in front of him, stopped as its engine stalled. Baldy swore and braked so abruptly the sedan behind rammed him.

'Get off the friggin' road,' Baldy yelled as Marler got out of his car, strolled back to him.

'I say, old chap,' Marler drawled. 'Awfully sorry and all that. The old engine stalled, couldn't help stopping. These Yank chariots aren't much cop.'

'I said get off . . .'

Baldy broke off as a white Chevrolet stopped alongside and Butler got out, shaking his fist, shouting at the top of his voice.

'You want to learn to drive, buddy. Now we've missed the goddam lights . . .'

In his rear-view mirror Baldy saw a brown Chevrolet stopped behind the second sedan so his back-up couldn't move. What the hell was going on? Marler strolled back to his car while Butler continued shouting. After two attempts Marler let the engine start, waved his hand over his shoulder, drove on. Baldy rammed his foot down to catch the green lights, turned right, saw no sign of Newman's Lincoln.

'We'll catch the bastards at Dulles,' he informed his passengers. 'We know they booked aboard the London flight . . .'

Still working to the Omega Plan, Newman drove to a Hertz office near a cab rank. He was handing in the Lincoln when Marler, Butler and Nield arrived to hand in their rented cars. Two cabs took them to the railway station where they caught the Metroliner to New York.

'How did you work that one?' Ives asked Tweed as the train sped through the afternoon. 'We were dead ducks.'

'A small precaution. Paula has booked us in our own names on two flights out of Dulles Airport from Washington to London. Also in our own names she's booked us on two more flights from New York to London – in case they check. In fact, we'll be aboard a British Airways flight leaving Kennedy at 7 p.m. Seats all booked in assumed names. We use our false passports made in the Engine Room – so that's why you're Chuck Kingsley.'

'What made you foresee we might be targets?'

'We know about the six serial murders. Above all, Wingfield knows we've seen the film which could destroy America's reputation. So all witnesses have to be eliminated. I realized that as soon as I heard Bradford March's plane had been blown up. It gave me the measure of Wingfield's ruthlessness – something I couldn't be sure of beforehand.'

'And those three different-coloured Chevies?'

'Newman sent a radio message renting them, plus the Lincoln. He specified the colours to make it easy for him to spot the cars if an emergency arose. It did.'

'What are you going to do?' Paula asked Ives.

'Stay in Europe, I guess. To stay alive. Rather like my new monicker, Chuck Kingsley. Think I'll keep it. And the way things are developing in the world I guess I'll build up a security agency. I'm sure you folks will be glad to get home, have a long rest.'

'We're going straight off the plane to a place called Padstow,' Tweed said. 'There was a mass murder down in Cornwall, Paula nearly got killed, and I know who committed that cold-blooded crime.'

55

A wild gale was raging as they walked slowly, leaning into the wind, along the road in Padstow leading from the Hotel Metropole to the centre of Padstow town. Paula clung to Newman's arm while ahead of them Tweed marched with a brisk step.

'Look, the Old Custom House,' Paula shouted to make herself heard. 'Where we used to have a drink. How marvellous to see it again, to be back in England.'

'I think that's where Tweed is heading for,' Newman replied. 'No, what's he up to now?'

Tweed had paused, gestured towards the inner harbour, entered the phone box he'd used on their previous visit. From inside he pointed towards the Old Custom House, mimicked a man drinking.

Huge waves were crashing against the outer wall, hitting the stone with a tremendous crash, hurling water and spray high into the air. Paula tugged at Newman's arm to make him stop at the point where Tweed had paused. Moored to a wall inside the inner harbour the *Mayflower III* rocked up and down, but was safe from the fury beyond the closed gate of the dam.

'Gaunt must have arrived back,' Paula shouted. 'Let's get inside out of this tumult. I wonder who Tweed is phoning . . .?'

Inside the box Tweed had dialled the number of police HQ in Launceston on the far side of the moor – a distance beyond it, in fact. Responding to his request, he was at once put through to Chief Inspector Roy Buchanan.

'Have you arranged what I asked you to at Tresillian Manor?' Tweed asked.

'Since you called me from London Airport I've been run off my feet organizing your mad – not to say macabre – idea.'

'You want the criminal who committed that hideous crime? It needs shock tactics to smoke this murderer out. Go to the manor at once. Keep out of sight and hide your cars. I'll be there with the suspects as soon as I've rounded them up.'

'I don't know why I've agreed to this insanity . . .'

522

'Because you've got nowhere solving the mass murder yourself . . .'

Hurrying with Newman into the shelter of the warm bar Paula stopped abruptly. The scene was pure *déjà-vu*.

Gaunt sat in one of the large leather armchairs on the elevated level facing the long bar. He was holding court, waving a large hand at his audience. Beside him sat Eve Amberg, wearing a white polo-necked sweater which did nothing to conceal her rounded breasts. She also wore a grey pleated skirt and grey pumps. A suede riding jacket was folded on the arm of her chair as she sipped her drink.

Facing her at a three-quarter angle to Paula was Jennie, listening while she fingered her pearls. A string of pearls? Why did they disturb Paula? The fourth member of the group, seated next to Jennie, was a surprise for Paula. Amberg sat very erect in his black business suit, his slick black hair gleaming. Didn't he ever wear anything else but black – and what was he doing in Padstow, Paula wondered.

'We had a whale of a trip down the Rhine in the *Mayflower*, Amberg,' Gaunt boomed. 'Kept going through the night. Advantage of being able to get by on four hours' sleep – I can. Eve took over the wheel when I needed a bit of kip. Make a good team, you and I, don't we, Eve?'

'Well, we got here in one piece,' she said unenthusiastically. 'Rounding Land's End in this gale wasn't frankly my idea of a whale of a time.'

'Nonsense! You revelled in every second of the voyage. Put a sparkle in your lovely eyes . . .'

'Isn't it illegal to sail on the Rhine at night?' asked Amberg.

Paula had the impression it was the first time the banker had spoken. He sat with his drink in front of him untouched.

'Oh, bureaucratic regulations,' Gaunt snorted contemptuously. 'Never get anywhere if you don't display initiative. Not in this world run by those fat-cat commissioners in Brussels.' He looked at the door. 'I say! Look who's turned up. Your favourite boy friend, Eve.'

'Why don't you shut your trap?' she snapped.

Newman waved briefly, took Paula to the bar, ordered Scotch for himself, a glass of white wine for Paula. He perched on a stool, whispered to her as she sat next to him.

'I've no idea what Tweed is up to. Best to wait until he arrives.'

'I can't fathom the relationship of those three,' she said quietly. 'I mean Gaunt, Eve and Jennie. Something very odd is going on . . .'

Tweed walked in when they were sipping their drinks. He ordered mineral water, stood by the bar. He gave them the order as he picked up his drink.

'Let's join them over there. A few questions I'd like to ask. Paula, you did park the Land-Rover by the harbour earlier?'

'Out of sight, round the corner. As you suggested.'

'So, we're all back where we started from,' Tweed greeted Gaunt's group amiably. He sat perched on the arm of Eve's armchair, staring diagonally across at the banker. 'Except for you, Amberg. What brings you to this remote part of the world?'

'I have come to see where Julius died. I felt it was the least I could do. Then I wish to collect his body so it can be returned to Switzerland for decent burial.'

'You did say Julius?'

There was a sound of breaking glass. Jennie had knocked over her wine. She glanced across at the banker, who was ashen-faced, then spoke in a strangely remote voice to the bartender who had rushed across with a cloth to mop up the spilt liquid.

'I'm so sorry. That really was frightfully careless of me. Do be careful not to hurt yourself – there are pieces of broken glass you can hardly see.'

'Which is why I brought over this wash-leather. If you would just sit back and relax. Bring you another glass on the house . . .'

Paula was studying Tweed, expecting him to show sympathy to Jennie who was embarrassed by the accident. Instead, he sat very still, looking at each person seated round the table, as though assessing them one by one. Paula was conscious of a sudden change in the hitherto peaceful atmosphere. Now she sensed it was fraught with tension. If only she could identify the source. Tweed waited until the waiter had finished cleaning up, had brought a fresh glass and placed it in front of Jennie.

'I think I know why everyone's here,' he began, his manner and his tone authoritative. 'It's understandable that no one is anxious to go back to Tresillian Manor, considering the tragedy. That being so, the sooner we all do go there the better. It's called laying ghosts.'

'Bloody sauce!' Gaunt protested. 'In case you've forgotten, I happen to own the place.'

'But last night after you'd landed here in the harbour you took Eve and Jennie to the Metropole where you stayed the night. Bracing yourself for going back today. I can understand it,' he repeated.

'How on earth do you know all this?' asked Gaunt in a very subdued tone.

'I checked the hotel register, then had a word with the Harbour Master. Because it's your house you're the one most likely to be affected. No more protests. Drink up and let's get the show on the road.'

Paula glanced swiftly round the assembled company. She saw Jennie fingering her pearls, twisting her mouth, then, aware of Paula's scrutiny, she gave a cold smile. Eve sat calmly. Amberg had an expression which could have been bewilderment or controlled fury. Gaunt sat back in his chair, staring into the distance and she couldn't read his expression.

525

One thing she did know. By sheer force of personality Tweed had dominated them, persuaded them to do his bidding. He said one more thing before he beckoned to Newman and Paula and marched out of the bar.

'I insist that our Land-Rover leads the way. No attempt to overtake me, Gaunt. Let's get moving . . .'

The gale had reached a new pitch of frenzy on Bodmin Moor. Hunched over the wheel, with Paula by his side and Newman in a rear seat, Tweed drove the Land-Rover at high speed but within the limit, then slowed to turn off along the side road leading to Tresillian Manor.

Paula slid her hand inside her shoulder bag, gripped the .32 Browning in the special pocket. She had phoned Monica from Washington, and when they passed through Customs at London Airport Monica handed her the small cloth bag containing her gun.

'The gate's open,' she commented.

'That's Buchanan. I asked him to open it so we could not waste any time . . .'

He parked the Land-Rover at the foot of the long stone terrace in front of the house. They waited on the terrace for Gaunt to arrive in his BMW, Tweed met the car, held out his hand for the front door key.

'This is my house . . .' Gaunt began.

'The key. We're going in first.' Tweed looked at Jennie as she slowly stepped out of the car. 'You do want to know who killed them, don't you?'

'Why look at me?' she snapped back at him.

'Wait, everyone.' It was Eve, snug in her riding jacket, walking towards the stables at the side of the manor. She looked back at Gaunt. 'You said you'd look after Rusty, my beautiful mare.'

'Ned, a reliable chap, has come in every day, cleaned out her quarters, fed her, given her a trot over the moor.'

'I'll give you two minutes,' Tweed told her. 'We'll wait here on the terrace . . .'

Eve was as good as her word, returned in two minutes with a glowing smile for Gaunt.

'She's in beautiful condition, and so glad to see me.'

'We'll now all go inside,' Tweed announced.

Opening the heavy front door with the key, he strode inside the hall with the woodblock floor. With a firm tread he walked over to the closed dining-room door and looked back before he grasped the handle. Eve stood behind him, Jennie, looking grim, was close to her. Amberg came next, prodded forward by Newman.

Tweed flung open the door, strode quickly inside. The others followed and stopped dead in their tracks. A grotesque scene met their stunned gaze. Seven figures dressed in black men's suits were sprawled round the long table. Two were still seated, slumped across the table in pools of dark red blood. Four more, toppled out of their chairs, lay in more pools of blood on the floor. The ultimate macabre horror was at the head of the table – where Amberg had sat. This figure was bent over a broken-backed chair, its face eaten away by acid, skeletal bones like steel rods exposed, revealing the skull beneath the skin.

Epilogue

'The monster responsible for this obscene crime is in this room,' Tweed announced. 'She was seen in Padstow on the day of the mass murder – even though she was supposed to be in Zurich. Eight people – including the butler

– died. Add Helen Frey, Klara and Theo Strebel and she has coldly ended the lives of eleven human beings. Add Celia Yeo and the real postman . . .'

Jennie stifled a scream. Eve sucked in a deep breath and whipped a 6.35-mm. Beretta out of her jacket pocket. She aimed it point-blank at Tweed as Paula produced her Browning, pointed it at the widest target – Eve's chest.

'Pull that trigger,' Eve warned, 'and Tweed is dead. Very dead. Drop the bloody thing, you bitch.'

Her voice had changed, was a harsh growl, her eyes stared with a near-insane expression. Paula stood her ground as she snapped out a reply.

'Not that easy, Eve.' She lowered her aim. 'Shoot Tweed and you get bullets in your abdomen. It will take days for you to die in terrible agony.'

'Then we play it different, dear.' Eve's face seemed to be carved out of marble. 'I'm leaving this room. If anyone tries to stop me, Tweed is dead. If you all stay sensible – still – Tweed survives. Everyone except Tweed and Paula move away from the door . . .'

Newman grabbed Amberg, who seemed frozen with fear, by the arm and forced him further into the room. Gaunt and Jennie obeyed the order. Backing towards the open door, Eve kept her weapon, gripped in both hands, aimed at Tweed. Paula's Browning swivelled slowly, constantly aimed at its target.

Reaching the open door, Eve held the Beretta in one hand. With the other she slammed it shut as she stepped into the hall. As the door was closing she yelled out: 'First one who follows me is dead as a doornail . . .'

Paula was the first to react. She saw Eve dart past the windows of the dining-room, crouching low, heading for the stables. Running to the casement window, she flung it open and climbed outside. Instead of heading for the stables she ran to the Land-Rover, jumped into the seat behind the wheel. Tweed had left the key in the ignition. Men could be so careless.

She heard the clatter of hooves a second before switching on the engine. Newman was running towards her.

'Wait for me!'

'No time . . .!'

Paula shoved her Browning under the seat cushion beside her with one hand, driving in a semicircle with the other, driving towards the passage between manor and stables. She saw Eve on her horse, fleeing behind the manor, followed her. Beyond the stretch of rough grass extending away behind the manor Eve rode her horse through the gap in the firs on to the moor. Paula pressed her foot down, bracing her back against the seat, careering through the same gap . . .

Only a four-wheel-drive vehicle could have negotiated the rough rocky terrain of the ascending moor. Her target rode like the devil, titian hair streaming behind her in the fury of the gale. Grimly, Paula maintained her pursuit. This was personal: Eve had threatened to kill Tweed.

As Paula narrowed the gap between herself and the horsewoman, Eve turned several times in her saddle, fired the Beretta. Paula counted the rounds and knew when Eve's gun was empty. Not a single bullet had come close, not even penetrating her windscreen. Firing from a racing horse, Eve's self-control had finally cracked.

Paula suddenly realized Eve was heading for Five Lanes. She had a cottage there. High Tor loomed up ahead. As the cluster of whitewashed cottages came closer Paula saw a cream Jaguar parked outside one – Eve's hope of escape. She accelerated, came so close to the flying horse that Eve gave up all hope of using the Jaguar. Eve changed direction, plunged up a steep slope, heading for the summit of High Tor.

Paula drove up after her, had almost caught up with the flying horse when her right-hand front wheel mounted a boulder. She braked automatically as the vehicle tilted violently and she was hurled out to the left. She rolled like a parachutist landing, stopped, saw to her horror she was at the edge of the sheer abyss where the servant girl, Celia Yeo, had been hurled over.

Half-stunned by her fall, she saw the Land-Rover had righted itself, was standing four-square on its wheels. Then she saw Eve riding towards her, face twisted into an evil grimace of triumph. She was going to use the horse to kill Paula, its hooves hammering into her skull. On the verge of reining in her mare, the horse reacted with terror as it saw the drop. It reared up without warning. Paula stared as Eve left the saddle, was catapulted over the brink. She heard her long scream, saw her somersaulting body plunging down beyond the abyss, saw her head smash into a massive boulder, her arms jerk out sideways, then she was still, a broken corpse similar to that of Celia Yeo whom she had pushed over the same drop.

'The tableau in the dining-room was constructed of dummies with wigs,' Chief Inspector Buchanan explained as Paula drank sweetened tea. 'The blood was red oil-paint – nice and sticky. I enlisted the aid of a friend who worked at Madame Tussaud's Waxwork Museum before he retired. Most effective job.'

'But Amberg's face – or the dummy used to fake him. The face was also destroyed with acid.'

She looked round at all the people in the living-room at Tresillian Manor. Tweed, sitting close, with Newman near by. Amberg in a chair next to Newman, looking dazed. Jennie, gazing at the banker as though she couldn't believe what she saw.

'Yes, we used acid,' Buchanan went on. 'It exposed the metal struts inside so we painted them with red oil-paint.'

'It needed a powerful shock to crack Julius Amberg and

Eve,' Tweed explained, taking over. 'The tableau worked the oracle.'

'Julius Amberg? You mean Walter,' she said. 'Julius was killed in the massacre.'

'No, Walter was. That man sitting over there is Julius.'

'Identical twins,' Tweed went on. 'Julius has admitted the whole conspiracy while you were pursuing Eve. He viewed the film, listened to the tape Joel Dyson handed him for safe-keeping. He was frightened, but Eve, the driving force behind the whole thing, saw an opportunity to make a fortune – to blackmail Bradford March for twenty million dollars. Julius had been playing with the bank's money gambling in foreign currencies. He lost ten million. The other ten million was to keep them in luxury for the rest of their lives.'

'But where did Walter come in?' Paula asked.

'I said Julius was frightened – taking on the US President was a frightening thing. Eve came up with the solution. Walter, who knew nothing about the film, was persuaded to travel here, to impersonate Julius. They told him I was a specialist in securities, that I could tell Walter how to make a lot of money. But they also explained I only trusted Julius, who pretended to be ill. Walter was the scapegoat – they counted on the news of the fake Julius's death being broadcast as part of a sensational mass murder case. The guards who travelled with Walter were to ensure the secrecy of the meeting. With the news of Julius's death reaching President March they thought they'd be safe – that Joel Dyson would be the target.'

'What first made you suspicious?' she asked.

'Have some more tea,' Newman urged, refilling her cup.

After her grim experience on High Tor Paula had driven the Land-Rover back along the main road. Halfway to the manor she'd been met by police cars Buchanan had sent out to find her, but she'd insisted on driving the rest of the way.

'Suspicious that the so-called Walter was Julius?' Tweed continued. 'First the acid – why destroy his face? To make true identification of the victim impossible. Then Eve kept going everywhere with Amberg. Her excuse – to get money out of him. A lawyer could have done the job. Also it would take strength to garrotte the two call-girls in Zurich – to the extent of nearly severing the head from the neck. At the swimming pool up at the Château Noir I noticed how fit and strong she was . . .'

'So she killed Helen Frey and Klara in that horrible way?'

'Yes. Eve was suspicious Julius had been seeking pleasure with other women. Hence her employing Theo Strebel, the detective, who tracked them down. Eve never took chances. She realized call-girls would know Julius better than any of his staff, might recognize him in Zurich.'

'I'd thought using the pearl garrotte meant a man,' Paula remarked.

'Eve visited each girl, offered her money not to see Julius again. Then showed them the pearls, said they were real and would they take them instead? She stepped behind them to fit the string round their throats, then pulled the wire supporting them with all her strength.'

'But what about Theo Strebel? He was shot.'

'She could hardly use the pearls on him. The significant factor was he knew Eve, so let her into his office without any inkling of danger. I also noticed that Eve had frequently used the name Walter – a little too often – to emphasize that it *was* Walter. An accumulation of small pointers made me focus on her.'

'And she was going to kill me,' Jennie said and shivered. 'She knew I had seen her in Padstow early on the morning of the massacre. She was the Shadow Man.'

532

'How do we know that?' Paula asked.

'Because,' Buchanan intervened, 'at Tweed's suggestion I came armed with a warrant to search her luggage at the Metropole. A phone call while you were chasing Eve – that *was* foolhardy – from my men in Padstow confirmed they'd found a large man's hat with a wide brim – and a cloak.'

'Hence the varying descriptions we got from different witnesses,' Tweed explained. 'Sometimes the Shadow Man was slim, sometimes well built. She used the cloak to change her appearance.'

'We also found the string of pearls in a secret compartment,' Buchanan added. 'There appears to be dried blood on the strong wire the pearls are looped on. Forensic will confirm, I'm sure.'

'So there *were* two interlocking jigsaws,' Paula commented.

'Yes, you've caught on,' said Tweed. 'The first was Joel Dyson taking that damning film of Bradford March killing his mistress then fleeing to Europe, handing one copy of film and tape to Monica, then flying on to Zurich to deposit the others with Julius. I've no doubt it was Dyson who intended to blackmail the President in due course, but Eve jumped in first. Without Dyson's actions there would have been no incriminating material. They triggered off the biggest man-hunt by March's thugs ever launched. The second jigsaw was Eve and Amberg taking over the role of blackmailers. One led to the other.'

'How do we know all this?'

Paula glanced round at the audience. Her gaze rested on Gaunt.

'Because,' Buchanan intervened again, 'after due warning that anything he said might be taken down and used as evidence, et cetera, Amberg admitted everything.'

533

'I shall be returning to Switzerland,' Julius said in his normal commanding tone.

'I don't think so,' Buchanan assured him. 'After the statement you made you will be charged as an accomplice to ten murders – all of which took place here. You ran the devil of a risk – taking on the President of the United States.'

'I was desperate. I was short of ten million of the bank's money. Maybe British prisons are less austere than Swiss.'

'I expect you're going to have a long opportunity to find that out,' Buchanan said unsympathetically.

'The tide's gone out. It's just a solid sandbank in the estuary,' said Paula.

'I hope you're packed,' said Tweed as they stood with Newman in Tweed's room at the Metropole. 'Incidentally, Cord Dillon is safely back behind his own desk in Langley – he's officially returned from a long leave. No one connects him with what happened. And I phoned Howard – while they rebuild our HQ we move into the communications centre further along Park Crescent. They say it will take eight months to rebuild – which means a year. The PM is talking to Howard each day, feels he got it all wrong.'

'He did,' Paula snapped.

'Better news from Washington,' Newman remarked. 'The newspapers report Jeb Calloway was sworn in as President the day we flew from New York. He's sending fresh troops to Europe to reinforce NATO. That should checkmate the crisis in the East. Middle East terrorists are rumoured to have put the bomb on March's plane.'

'That's Wingfield's propaganda machine gearing up,' Tweed commented cynically. 'There'll be conspiracy theories invented for ages just as there were after Kennedy's assassination. Let's get out of here as fast as we can.'

'Why the great hurry?' Paula enquired.

'The Squire – Gaunt – wanted us to have dinner with him at the Old Custom House. He feels a bit of an idiot the way Eve fooled him, used him as camouflage to distract attention from Walter, who was really Julius. And the PM has asked me to dinner at Downing Street, according to Howard.'

'You'll go, of course,' Paula teased him.

'Another bit of news Howard gave me. Commander Crombie's men, digging in the remains of the Park Crescent rubble, found my safe. It was moved along the Crescent to our communications centre. Monica said it was intact, opened it up, found the film and the tape in perfect condition. Oh, Bob, Dyson tricked you – said they were copies. What he delivered to you were the originals.'

'Well, I'll be damned!' Paula burst out. 'Everything we've gone through was unnecessary.'

'Was it?' Tweed queried. 'We've got rid of a psychopath who sat in the Oval Office. Would the PM have permitted that film and that tape to be sent to Washington? Never. March would have remained President. As it is, the film and the tape will remain classified material for the next thirty years. It was a classic case of Lord Acton's maxim. *Power tends to corrupt, and absolute power corrupts absolutely.*'